BOOK YOUR PLACE ON OUR WEBSITE AND MAKE THE READING CONNECTION!

We've created a customized website just for our very special readers, where you can get the inside scoop on everything that's going on with Zebra, Pinnacle and Kensington books.

When you come online, you'll have the exciting opportunity to:

- View covers of upcoming books
- Read sample chapters
- Learn about our future publishing schedule (listed by publication month *and author*)
- Find out when your favorite authors will be visiting a city near you
- Search for and order backlist books from our online catalog
- Check out author bios and background information
- Send e-mail to your favorite authors
- Meet the Kensington staff online
- Join us in weekly chats with authors, readers and other guests
- Get writing guidelines
- AND MUCH MORE!

Visit our website at
http://www.zebrabooks.com

MERLIN'S LEGACY: DAUGHTER OF CAMELOT

QUINN TAYLOR EVANS

Zebra Books
Kensington Publishing Corp.

http://www.zebrabooks.com

ZEBRA BOOKS are published by

Kensington Publishing Corp.
850 Third Avenue
New York, NY 10022

First Printing: July, 1999
10 9 8 7 6 5 4 3 2 1

Printed in the United States of America

For Braedon
The heart does go on. . . .

PROLOGUE

Camelot

In spite of her blindness the healer made her way unerringly through the hallways of King Arthur's castle.

She had no need of the sunlight that spilled off pale sandstone walls by day or the brightly lit oil lamps by night to guide the way. Instead she was guided by an inner sight that served her far better, an awareness of everything about her that mortals could not see.

Those same mortals often treated her as an invalid and made the mistake of pitying her. It was when they finally sought her out with a wound that had not healed or some lingering malady that they realized she was not hindered at all by her blindness, but in fact *saw* far more than they with a simple touch of her hand upon theirs.

It was said by those who had been with Arthur since the conquest of Maelgwyn and Aethelbert near a full score years earlier that her eyes had once been deep, brilliant blue, the color of rare gemstones—the same unusual color as Merlin's. But she had been blinded in an encounter that forever robbed her of sight. It was also said that she shared far more with the counselor than the mere color of their eyes, that Meg, wife to Lord Connor of Monmouth, also shared those same gifts of power that the counselor possessed.

Sorceress, some dared to whisper about her. But her gentle spirit and healing touch belied the rumors. And if those same gossipmongers also wondered about the gnomelike creature who constantly followed her about like a shadow, none spoke of it, either out of respect, or perhaps caution, just in case the rumors were true.

Children had no fear of Grendel. Whenever he was at Camelot he was often found among them. Because he was no bigger than they, they accepted him as one of their own, a manchild with the ability to conjure magic tricks that delighted and entertained them for hours. It was others, grown men, who were wary and uneasy around the little man.

"Slow down!" he complained, out of breath from running on too-short legs and forced to take three steps for every one his mistress took.

"What is it that is so urgent that we must rise at this ungodly hour?"

Meg only marginally checked her pace. Her thoughts were elsewhere, for she had been troubled by unsettling dreams during the night and had not slept well.

It had only been four days since they'd left Monmouth. She made the journey often, yet somehow this time seemed longer, the time apart from Connor more unbearable, the need to return pressing, as though it had been weeks since they'd parted instead of only days.

They had been parted in the past, often for months at a time, when Connor and his men rode with Arthur. That had been in the early days, when Arthur fought to unite the kingdom, and through the years that followed when pockets of unrest and rebellion arose in provinces near Camelot.

She had endured the separations because she must but also because she knew with that unusual gift of insight she possessed that he was safe and protected. While he was away she kept his home and his lands safe and protected.

In recent years, with the kingdom secure and prosperity throughout it, they had found a measure of constancy and peace in their lives that they both welcomed. But if the times apart were less frequent and shorter, the reunions were no less sweet.

They shared a passion that had not dimmed through the years but had only become richer, like the fine wine that, once tasted, lingered in the senses long after they'd made love, brought a shared smile to their lips across the long table at the evening meal, and the need to touch—the simple brush of her fingers against the sleeve of his tunic, or his hand against her cheek.

This was what Arthur had envied and longed for on those occasions in the past when he visited Monmouth, where he could slip off the mantle of majesty for a few days and share in the camaraderie of fellow warriors as they once had when the kingdom was new and the times dangerous. The one thing that still eluded Arthur and would have made that hard-won peace and prosperity complete—a queen to rule beside him.

All those long years ago, Arthur had seen the future spread before him as clearly as Merlin. His first goal had been to unite the kingdom; then he brought harmony, peace, and prosperity to Britain once more. Now the one thing that remained was to secure the future of his kingdom by producing an heir.

As a simple warrior he had been free to follow his heart. As king he was not. There were many considerations to be weighed when it came to the future of the kingdom and the son whom it was hoped would follow. But with each passing year it seemed that one thing that would make the peace at Camelot complete and set the course for the future was farther from his grasp.

While Arthur took his pleasures discreetly with a number of

mistresses, he found no lasting pleasure or happiness with any of them, or any of the young noblewomen of the kingdom who were the most likely candidates for queen.

It was even said by Arthur himself—one of the handful who knew that Merlin was her brother and much to Meg's amusement—that were she not wed to Connor of Monmouth, his closest friend and ally, he would have pressed his suit with her. For it would have been a most fortuitous alliance to wed someone who possessed the powers of his counselor but with far more charm and beauty.

In time, when Arthur did not press suit, the noblewomen of the kingdom made alliances elsewhere, and in spite of the prosperity and peace it seemed the future of Camelot was even more uncertain. Until the past year, when Arthur made the acquaintance of Lady Guinevere of Lyonesse.

In truth he had met her several years before. Her father had made an alliance with Arthur when Maelgwyn threatened the southern region. That alliance provided the means to hold Maelgwyn back and buy precious time for Arthur to raise an army against Aethelbert, who had claimed the throne during a bloody period in time when it seemed Britain might be lost forever.

Guinevere had been born late in the life of the old Duke of Lyonesse and his wife, the Lady Berengaria. The birth had greatly weakened Berengaria, who never recovered completely.

She understood the tenuous position of a marriageable young noblewoman in a world ruthlessly ruled by men. Knowing this and knowing as well that she would not live to see her daughter well married, she extracted a deathbed promise from the duke that Guinevere was to be well educated, afforded all the rights of a son, including the right to make her own marriage bond, and the hereditary right to govern all of Lyonesse.

It was a bold and unusual move which the Duke of Lyonesse saw the wisdom of and agreed to. Upon his death three winters past, Guinevere had become Lady Guinevere of Lyonesse at the young age of ten and seven. Now at a full score of years and with the guidance of trusted advisers, including Merlin, she was a well-educated young woman, self-possessed, and with a keen understanding of politics, the world, and her unique position in it. She had also grown into a striking beauty.

In the natural course of perpetuating the strong alliance he had shared with her father, Arthur had extended a formal invitation to Lady Guinevere to visit Camelot.

She and her counselors and advisers wintered at Camelot that first year after her father's death. She brought a liveliness and warmth to Arthur's court that had been missing. Arthur felt it as well, and when Lady Guinevere departed for Lyonesse, he had journeyed to Monmouth and stayed a fortnight.

While at Monmouth he spoke constantly of Guinevere's intelligence, her wit and charm, her skill at riding and the longbow, the musical sound of her laughter, and the radiance of her smile, to the point that Meg and Connor rolled their eyes in silent agony.

Connor finally lost all patience, and no matter that Arthur was king, he had exploded with frustration. "Good God, man! Cease! Either make her your mistress or make her your wife, but bed the woman and be done with it!"

Arthur had stared at Connor with stunned surprise. Then he slammed his goblet of wine down onto the table.

"By God, I will! But Guinevere will not be my mistress. She will be my queen!"

"If *she* will have you," Meg had calmly interjected, which caused both her king and her husband to look at her as if she had just said something profoundly amusing.

She promptly dispelled their humor when she reminded them both, "Lady Guinevere is high-born. She has hereditary title to Lyonesse, and no need of any man, king or pauper. She may marry whomever she chooses. Or not at all."

Arthur's mood altered drastically. With the usual male certainty of their power over such things, he had thought the matter settled merely because he had decided it would be so. He had not considered that Guinevere might refuse.

"What am I to do, then?" he had demanded. "Court her like any common fool?"

"That is usually how it is done, milord," Meg answered, then bid both her husband and the king good eventide and left them stewing in a brew of their own making. Connor had not been pleased with her when he finally made his way to their bed many hours later.

Even now the memory of it brought a smile to her lips. Arthur had kept him up most of the night trying to determine just how to go about courting Lady Guinevere, something most unusual for Arthur of Camelot who had only to crook his finger at any young maid and have her willingly tumble into his bed.

"You see, milord," Meg informed Connor as they lay naked together, and his anger cooled while his body heated beneath hers, " 'tis much sweeter to court a lady." And he had *courted* her thoroughly until the first light of dawn broke over the window ledge.

When Arthur had left Monmouth several days later he said nothing of his plans to court Guinevere. He had previously promised to send an ambassador to Lyonesse who might also act as council in political matters that affected both Camelot and Lyonesse. He sent Merlin as his ambassador to act in that capacity, and to determine just where the lady's interests lay.

Merlin stayed the spring and summer at Lyonesse. He sent regular dispatches back to Arthur. It was learned that Guinevere had several suitors, but none to whom she showed favor. It was also learned that Guinevere of Lyonesse was as intelligent as she was beautiful, as politically skillful as she was charming, as good with a sword as she was with a bow.

Merlin had also sent letters to Monmouth and as Connor read them to her, Meg sensed far more in what had been left unwritten. She sensed it in the turn of a word, and far more that was left unsaid. She sensed that her brother admired Guinevere deeply.

He had returned to Camelot late the previous summer. She and Connor were at Camelot as well. It was then, at evening banquet, that Arthur made his intentions toward Guinevere known to his counselor.

Though there was no outward reaction, Meg sensed the intensity of Merlin's response to Arthur's news. It had left her stunned and deeply shaken, for she realized then that her brother had fallen in love with Guinevere. It was a dilemma for which there was no easy or happy solution.

Merlin had dutifully returned to Lyonesse carrying with him a formal proposal of marriage from Arthur. She and her brother were bound to each other by forces far beyond the mortal world. The powers and knowledge she possessed were a mirror image of his. They were connected to each other in ways beyond life and death, beyond what she shared with Connor. She understood his every thought before it formed, just as he understood hers. But for all they shared, this part of him—what mortals called the human heart, with all its complex emotions—was closed to her.

Merlin still had not returned. Only days ago, a messenger had arrived from Lyonesse, and carried with him Guinevere's acceptance of the marriage proposal. But there had been no word from Merlin, and with his silence she experienced a profound sense of uneasiness and disquietude, as if some course had been set by invisible hands on an uncertain and perhaps dangerous road.

And then there were the dreams that haunted her sleepless nights since leaving Monmouth, dreams of blood and death in clouds of swirling mist. She had tried to see through those clouds to what lay beyond, but always the images eluded her, leaving her only with that growing sense of urgency, that awareness that the way beyond those clouds of mist was shrouded in darkness and evil.

"If we leave early enough we will make Monmouth by eventide," she said, more to herself than Grendel, and found some measure of comfort that in only a few hours she would be home with Connor.

Grendel stopped dead in his tracks. "Home before eventide?" Just the thought conjured up memories of the journey days earlier to Camelot. To say that he was not an experienced horseman was a woeful understatement. He had barely survived and the very thought of riding atop a horse again any time soon made his backside ache.

Before it was spoken, almost before the thought had formed, Meg sensed his protest. "There is nothing to discuss. We leave this day."

Grendel shuddered. "I'd sooner attempt to ride a hedgehog than climb atop a horse again."

He hated horses, foul-tempered, foul-smelling beasts that they were. He'd never gotten used to them and he was prepared to argue to his last breath as he puffed up like a rooster ready to do battle.

" 'Tis a half day's ride over the worst roads in all of Britain! We have been here but four days; my backside is still black and blue. I won't do it. I won't, and you can't make me."

They both knew his protests were futile, but it was not in his nature to go willingly or without an argument.

"And have you forgotten? There is a celebration tonight in honor of the king's betrothal to the Lady Guinevere. We cannot leave, it would be unseemly. . . ."

But Meg was not listening to him. She heard something else that whispered through her blood and closed an icy hand around her heart—something she had not heard or felt in so long that she might have forgotten. Had tried to forget. Except that once experienced it was never forgotten.

She stopped in midstride and whirled around.

"Do you hear it?" she asked.

In the heat of protest, Grendel barely saved himself from running headlong into her.

"What?" he demanded in a low, foul humor. "The rattle and clatter of a chamber pot? The crowing of a rooster? I hear nothing, for no one else is up at this ungodly time of day."

Her sightless gaze angled toward the length of wall at one side of the hallway. Her mortal senses felt the warm glow of the sun that spilled over the wall of the adjacent courtyard and flooded the hallway with light, as it did every day during the spring and summer months. But her mortal senses felt something else, a shadow of coldness that stalked the sunlight, unseen by the mortal eye, not felt by mortal flesh, seen with inner knowledge and awareness, felt as it had been felt and experienced that long ago day amid the ring of standing stones in a confrontation with evil incarnate.

Morgana—a name not even Arthur had mentioned all these years since, when his half sister had tried to destroy him and seize the throne of Britain for herself in an unholy alliance with the powers of darkness.

Was it only an illusion? What was it that should make her think of Morgana now, when she had not thought of her all the years since, not even in some moment of mortal weakness to mourn the loss of her sight that long-ago day.

That was what Morgana had taken from her. But Morgana was dead and her powers of darkness had been destroyed. Still, the memory of it would not be willed away. She had sensed a foreboding of evil in those dreams and the coldness that moved through her blood just as it had on that long-ago day.

"We've been away from Monmouth too long," she whispered, unable to *see* with her gift of inner sight the shadows that she sensed were there. And said with a finality that would not be argued or challenged, "I wish to return home."

"Find Tristan. Tell him we leave as soon as I am finished in the infirmary."

Tristan and several knights from the guard at Monmouth had

accompanied her to Camelot. He was like a son to her and Connor, orphaned when his own family was slaughtered by Maelgwyn's warriors all those years ago. Afterward, when Arthur was made king, he had gone to live with her and Connor at Monmouth. He had filled the painful void when she lost her own babes. He was a son to be proud of.

She had seen little of him since their arrival at Camelot but had no doubt where he could be found, for the daughter of one of the nobles had caught his eye on a previous visit and he was eager to make a conquest. Neither had she any doubt that the young lady in question had yielded all to him, for no one had ever been able to resist that lethal combination of handsomeness, soulful intensity, and boyish humor that could charm the gown off any young maid, high born or low.

In spite of the early hour she found young Cynwin in the infirmary just as she knew she would, already tending the first of several injuries.

Merlin had begun Cynwin's instruction in the healing arts, but he had been gone these long months past to Lyonesse. So Meg had continued her instruction, spending several days each month instructing the young woman in the art of herbal medicants made into poultices, draughts, and healing potions to treat various ailments and complaints.

Meg was pleased with the girl. She was intelligent, quick to learn, and not faint of heart at the sight of a gruesome wound or putrefied flesh.

"This is the worst of it," Cynwin informed her as she peeled a soiled linen bandage from a young boy's foot. "His father did not think the injury serious. His mother brought him this morning when the flesh began to discolor."

Meg recognized the lad as one of the stableboys. She stepped beside Cynwin as easily as though sighted and with a gentle probing of the swollen foot sensed the broken bones, as well as torn tendons and ligaments.

Already the flesh putrefied with poisons from the dirt and

filth common in any stable. If untreated he would most likely lose the foot and never walk again, and there were limited opportunities for crippled stableboys.

"Does this hurt?" Meg asked as she gently probed to sense the extent of the damage.

"Nay, mistress," he replied, but she sensed the tensing of every muscle within his young body as he held himself against the pain, and she sensed the poison that moved through his blood. Soon there would be fever. He might even die if left unattended.

"It's bad, isn't it?" his voice quivered with fear.

"Aye, bad enough," she agreed. She had not the ability to lie, but she tried to ease his fear with a gentle smile and a calming touch.

"You should not have argued with the horse," she admonished and sensed the quiver of a smile. "They're bigger than you."

"Aye, big enough." Then he anxiously asked, "Will I lose the foot?"

In the simple connection of her touch upon his crushed foot, she eased the pain and the fear.

"Are you of so little faith in my skills?" she gently admonished, then assured him, "You'll not lose the foot, though it will take a while to heal."

As she spoke she used the gift she'd been born with to meld shattered bones back together again. "And," she continued, her voice soft and low, weaving a spell of its own, "no doubt step in front of another horse." She smiled softly. "Make certain it's the other foot next time."

She gently laid the injured foot down upon the pallet and slowly released his thoughts. He stared at her blankly for a moment, then blinked several times, as though emerging from sleep.

"It don't hurt at all," he exclaimed as his mother burst into tears of gratitude beside him.

The woman seized Meg's hand between her two hands and clung to it. ''Thank you, mistress. Thank you.''

But as Meg gently withdrew her hand, she felt the stickiness of blood on her own. The boy's wound had stopped bleeding and was firmly bound. She curled her fingers over the palm of her hand in a tight fist concealing the stickiness of blood as she explained the care of the wound.

''The bones must have time to set and grow strong, and the bandage must be changed daily,'' she told the woman, wrapping her other hand about her clenched fist as the bleeding continued.

Eventually they left and Meg plunged both her hands into a basin. Water swirled at her fingertips as though stirred by an unseen hand. Images stirred in the shimmering depths of the basin, shifted, and then gradually took form.

She sensed them, felt them, *saw* them in the old way—images of blood and death, brilliant crimson swirling in the water and covering her hands, then slipping through her fingers like the sands of an hourglass; like life, precious and dear to her, that she could not hold on to. Within that vision of blood and death, a single image took form, as clear as if she was sighted . . . Connor.

She cried out as pain like that of a knife twisted deep inside, and as the vision sharpened and became more clear it seemed that it was her blood that drained out of her and swirled into the bowl.

''What is it, mistress?'' Cynwin asked with rising alarm. Then she saw the blood that filled the bowl.

''You've injured yourself!''

She seized a thick cloth and attempted to wipe the blood from Meg's hands. But it soaked through the thick cloth. She looked up at Meg with growing helplessness and fear.

''I cannot stop the bleeding! You must tell me what to do.''

Nor could Meg make it stop. There was no wound and yet the blood flowed. Grendel was immediately beside her. Alarm twisted his features, making him seem even more like a wizened gnome.

"Tell what must be done."

Meg calmed Cynwin's fears even as her thoughts reached out to Grendel with but a single word—*Monmouth*. And in that word conveyed all her unspoken fear—*there is danger at Monmouth*.

"Find Tristan," she whispered. "We must return without delay."

The distance normally traveled in a half day was crossed in barely more than two hours. They saw the spiral smoke of fires before they entered the Monmouth valley.

Even then Meg hoped and prayed against what she had seen in the swirling water of the basin. Even as she sensed when the watchtowers of Monmouth came into view, shrouded in the smoke of those fires, she still held out hope and refused to accept the images that tormented her thoughts.

But she knew as surely as if she was sighted. She sensed the violence of battle that still clung to the air, along with the smoke from those fires; just as she sensed the blood and death foreseen in the vision within that basin.

She reached the gates only a few strides ahead of Tristan and his men. She flung herself from the saddle. No guards called out from above to announce her arrival. There were no guards at all, and the gates stood open.

Meg stumbled and fought her way through the destruction and debris that had been her home. In spite of Tristan's shouted warning, she made her way across the yard toward the inner courtyard and the walled gardens as she had a thousand times in the past.

She stumbled over a body, recoiled instinctively, then *saw* with her gift of inner sight and pushed back to her feet with but one thought—it wasn't Connor!

She saw everything as she had seen it the first time Connor had brought her there all those years ago. Before her encounter with Morgana.

It was here they first became lovers, and it was here they had returned when she left the immortal world for the last time to be with him.

All the years in between she had learned every stone, each step, each cool, sheltered place within the garden she had planted where a kiss might be stolen and pleasure found.

It was just such a place where Connor often found her tending her flowers and herbs; a special, hidden place among the arbors and fragrant blooming hedgerows, where they risked much on a warm summer's eve and took their pleasure of one another in slow, lingering kisses and equally slow, lingering caresses. Just such a place as summer waned and gave way to autumn when she told Connor that she carried his child. A child that was not to be.

She found him not far from that place, where he had fought the attackers to a bloody standstill inside the garden wall. His men had fought at either side as the battle spilled inside Monmouth. She stumbled over their bodies to get to him. Blood filled her hands and flowed through her fingers as she reached for him, like visions of blood and death seen in her dreams.

"You must do something!" Meg's voice rose in the chill predawn air that filled the chamber at Monmouth.

Across the pallet Merlin's somber gaze met hers. "I have done all I can."

Guided by the bond that connected them, she rounded the end of the pallet and stood before him.

"It is not enough! Heal the wounds," she demanded, her voice quivering with desperation. "Use your power." She grabbed hold of the front of his tunic.

"You can do it." Her hands closed into fists of helplessness and anger. Unable to strike at an unknown enemy, she struck at him.

"I've seen it a thousand times! Do it, brother! Heal him, now!"

The blows had little effect, yet he felt each one deep within his soul because her pain was his pain. His hands gently closed over hers, his words equally gentle.

"The wounds are deep and there has been much loss of blood."

Her sightless gaze searched his. In that ancient way that connected them, she sensed his thoughts and the words that went unspoken.

"No!" She tried to jerk away, but he wouldn't let her. Instead, he pulled her into his arms and held her tight as she gave in to the rage and helplessness. Then continued to hold her when she gave in to soul-wrenching grief, and eventually when she could cry no more.

"I wanted more time," Meg whispered against the front of his tunic. "We should have had more time."

"Time is our enemy," Merlin reminded her. "For those such as we, time plays out its cruel game. You knew it would be so. Be thankful for the time you have had." Merlin gently stroked her hair. " 'Tis more than many of us shall ever know."

She heard the sadness and pain in his voice, and something more that went unspoken, something he hesitated to tell her. Through the bond they shared she sensed a far deeper concern, and fear.

"What is it?"

"That which I have not sensed for a very long time."

There was something in Merlin's voice, a glimpse of a thought that lay hidden there, interwoven with the fear. A shared memory of the daughter she had borne and the choices made to keep her safe.

Now Connor was dying, and their daughter was no longer safe.

CHAPTER ONE

Shadows lengthened as night closed in, one bleeding into the other across the unfamiliar landscape, obscuring the stone marker on the old Roman road.

For five days they'd followed the road. Now, there would be no more markers to guide them through the wild and uncertain country that lay beyond the borders of Arthur's kingdom.

The wind came up, warning of the storm that had followed them throughout the afternoon. The gnome shivered atop the weary palfrey, dark eyes barely visible over the edge of the thick woolen mantle he'd wrapped about himself.

Dressed in brown tunic and leggings, wrapped in the dark concealing wool, he more closely resembled a dung heap than a man atop the ancient beast. And smelled like one as well.

"What does it say?" the disgruntled dung heap demanded, his disposition as foul as the stench that emanated from him.

Tristan's eyes narrowed on the small pile of unpleasantness. "You're asking me? You're supposed to know the way."

"I do know the way," Grendel replied from the layers of

wool that muffled his response but not his displeasure with the palfrey, the cold, and the merciless pace his companion had set since leaving Monmouth.

"But it has been a long time and I do not read Latin. 'Tis a cumbersome, difficult language. Reading one's thoughts is far simpler."

"Then read my thoughts," Tristan invited, silken words belying his murderous thoughts, all patience gone with the creature's incessant grumbling.

"Tell me what I am thinking at this very moment."

Grendel shivered from the cold and a glimpse at those thoughts. "You were once such an agreeable child," he retorted.

"Once you told jokes, conjured rabbits out of your pockets, and did not complain at every turn." Tristan made a sound of disgust.

"And what is that foul stench?"

Grendel's eyes gleamed. "Do you like it?"

Tristan snorted. "I've ridden twice the distance on this journey, circling around trying to avoid it."

"Just what I hoped for." The gnome grinned back at him with malicious satisfaction over the top of the wool mantle.

" 'Tis a protective concoction to ward off others, lest they become too curious about us in these far northern regions."

Tristan swung down from atop his horse, staying upwind of the creature as he approached the stone marker to see it more clearly in the fading light.

" 'Tis strong enough to ward off the devil himself."

" 'Tis not the devil you should fear, boy," Grendel replied. "There are other forces and powers at work here."

His dark gaze peered out from a shriveled brown face like a sun-dried apple and scanned the horizon where the last light of day briefly lingered before surrendering to the darkness.

"Blood and death." He whispered what Meg had foreseen in her dreams and he had sensed within her thoughts, as though fearful he might call those dark forces down upon them merely by speaking of them. He shivered inside his tightly wrapped cocoon.

"The likes of which I hoped never to see again."

Then, rousing from those unpleasant memories, he cocked his head and his gaze sharpened once more on the warrior.

"Well, *boy?*" he demanded. "Have you deciphered the letters? Or have you discovered that you should have spent more time at your lessons and less time on the end of that sword?"

Tristan swung up astride his horse, setting his teeth against another sharp blast of wind as he gauged with narrowed glance the distance between himself and the gnome against the length of the sword.

"At this moment the sword serves me far better." He swung his mount about, maneuvering the restless stallion upwind of the gnome. "We leave the road from here and continue northward. And do not call me *boy!*"

The gnome ignored him. "The storm will soon be upon us. We are near the Bedwyn Forest. Do we seek shelter for the night?" he asked hopefully.

"We do not," Tristan informed him with pleasure. "The sooner we find the place, the sooner we can return to Monmouth. I have no desire to linger in these northern climes with only a short, ill-tempered troll to guard my back."

Grendel bristled. "I am not a troll. And you could do far worse. *Boy!*"

Tristan refused to be goaded into further argument by the creature. He swung his horse about and set his spurs deep.

"Stay well back," he replied. "Perhaps your foul stench will offer some protection after all."

"There will come a day when you will be grateful for my company."

"Not bloody likely!" Tristan retorted as he sent the warhorse into a hard gallop and smiled at Grendel's wail of protest at the bone-jarring pace.

His foul temper was slightly mollified knowing the little man was as miserable as he. The little creature hated being forced to ride atop the palfrey almost as much as he hated the cold. And that was Tristan's revenge for being forced on this journey.

Then, as they had continuously throughout the journey, his thoughts returned to Monmouth. Over the past weeks there had been several isolated attacks about the countryside. But when he and his men arrived, the attackers had fled and disappeared. Each attack drew them farther from Monmouth, and away from any ability to defend Camelot.

Like the other attacks, this one had been well calculated. Unlike the others, it had not been against some remote village or hamlet, but had struck at Monmouth when many of their men were far afield. And he had not been there.

Connor usually accompanied Lady Meg to Camelot. But the daughter of a nobleman had caught Tristan's attention on a previous visit and he was eager to make a conquest.

He persuaded Connor to allow him to escort Lady Meg so that he might spend time with Mistress Alyce, who had more charm than she had sense. And while he had lain with her, Monmouth had been attacked and the man whom he considered a father had been gravely wounded.

Even now Connor might lay dead and cold in his grave, and he'd been sent on this fool's errand in the company of another fool! But when Lady Meg insisted that she could trust no other, he could not refuse her.

Five days since the attack! he thought with frustration. And each mile took them farther from Monmouth and whatever dangers they faced.

The urgency to return made him incautious. He did not see the tree that suddenly loomed before him out of the darkness. There was no time to check the pace of his horse. A low-hanging branch caught him across the midsection. The blow drove the air from his lungs, swept him from the back of his horse, and slammed him to the ground.

Grendel grinned down at him as he gasped for air and fought his way past the pain from the blow.

"Who is the fool now?" the gnome inquired with a smug smile from atop the ancient palfrey while Tristan glared up at him through the gathering darkness with mute fury.

"Do we now make camp for the night?" the gnome inquired. "Or would you care to ride a bit farther?"

When he was finally able to drag some air into his lungs, Tristan replied a wheezing, guttural, "Aye." It was all he could manage at the moment and sounded more like a murderous threat.

"Well, I suppose that will be all right," Grendel replied as he rode past where Tristan lay—*downwind,* of course—and made no attempt to hide his smile of pleasure or to assist him.

"What do you have there?" Grendel demanded some time later, when they'd made camp and Tristan returned with a guinea fowl he'd startled from the brush and snared for their supper.

He was still sore from his sudden encounter with the tree branch, and his mood was no better.

"It has feathers," he replied. "It flies and lays eggs. Father in heaven!" he exclaimed with great sarcasm. "It must be a bird!"

The gnome muttered a curse. "I can see that well enough for myself. 'Tis only that I was concerned whether it is truly a bird, or perhaps a shapeshifter." He glanced uneasily at the limp bird.

"A relative of yours, perhaps?" Tristan commented with particular pleasure as he held up the bird. Then he added with a devilish smile, "Be careful you do not end up the same way."

"It would serve you right, you know," Grendel replied. "Who would guide you then?"

"I would have no need of a guide," Tristan informed him.

"For I would immediately return to Monmouth and be done with this madness. But you have no cause for worry," he assured the gnome. "With your foul disposition, you'd make a bitter meal. Although," he added thoughtfully, "the idea has merit. It would save me crawling around the forest looking for supper." He dropped the bird on the ground before the fire.

"Make yourself useful, little man. Prepare supper."

"*Little* man?" Grendel muttered to himself as he cautiously approached the lifeless hen. "The day will come, *boy*, when you will discover 'tis not size that matters."

"Size always matters," Tristan informed him as he threw more wood on the fire, then found a comfortable place to sit and await his supper. And with a wink, "Just ask the fair Alyce."

The guinea fowl was roasted to perfection, but he would never have told the little man that. It would have made him impossible to live with, and he was near impossible already.

The fire burned steadily, warming them against the cold that settled all around them. Tristan washed a mouthful of food down with water liberally laced with wine, and tried to reconcile what he had always believed—that the child Lady Meg had borne all those years ago had died shortly after birth and was buried in the chapel yard at Monmouth—with what he had learned only a few days ago.

"What do you remember of the child?"

Grendel squatted on the ground before the fire wrapped in the thick wool mantle. A disgusting smacking sound emanated from the woolen shroud as he ate, occasionally accompanied by a loud belch. The wool shifted on the shrug of a rounded shoulder.

"What is there to remember? She was but a babe at the time. She was small, noisy, and foul-smelling."

Tristan cocked a brow and commented with a bemused expression across the safe distance of the campfire that separated them, "Ah, a kindred spirit. It seems you have much in common."

"Aye, a kindred spirit," the gnome snapped. "And much more. And best you remember it." Then he snapped his mouth shut and would say no more about the child, but muttered, "Curse the dark spirits, but 'tis cold."

"Why?" Tristan asked the gnome, as he watched him thoughtfully across the encampment.

Grendel expelled a sound of impatience that plumed on the frigid night air. " 'Tis winter's eve," he replied in a tone that suggested the most dim-witted dolt should be able to understand. "It usually happens this time each year."

"Aye, 'tis cold as a whore's heart," Tristan acknowledged. "And you are about as truthful. *Why,*" he repeated, so there would be no misunderstanding, "did Lady Megwin lie about the death of the child?"

For five days he'd ridden across half of Britain because Lady Meg had asked. She and Lord Connor were like mother and father to him after his own parents were brutally slain. They had raised him as their own. His devotion to them was stronger than blood. It was a devotion of heart and soul.

Out of respect and love he had not questioned what she asked of him. Now he wanted to know and he intended to find out. But again Grendel shrugged.

"She did not lie. She cannot lie. And well you know it."

As if the question had been sufficiently answered, the gnome seized another piece of roasted fowl, inspected it with great concentration, and then, evidently satisfied that he was not personally acquainted with the creature, sank his sharp pointed teeth into a leg portion.

Tristan could see this was not going to be easy, but he'd had much practice over the years matching wits with the little man who had been a childhood companion and then, in later years, taught him how to use the natural gifts he'd been born with, even though—as Grendel had pointed out—he'd been born a lowly mortal. As though it was a curse. But he'd had confidence that with Tristan's physical agility, quickness of mind, and uncanny ability with a sword that glaring shortcoming might be overcome.

The gnome had taught him how to use all his abilities and senses in a heightened awareness usually found only in animals. And though he had not the abilities of the gnome, Lady Meg, or Lord Merlin, he had developed a keen ability to read others, to sense things about their body language, mannerisms, and speech patterns when they were secretive or evasive, as the gnome was being now.

Grendel had taught him too well, for it was obvious that the creature chose to reveal as little as possible about this journey they were set upon. But just as Lady Meg was incapable of lying, so, too, was the gnome incapable of it, and Tristan had learned long ago the best way to learn something the little man didn't want known was to trap him with the truth.

"She must have been deformed in some way," he concluded, taking another long draught of wine-laced water.

Grendel's head shot up. "She was not deformed!" he replied indignantly. "She was perfect in every way."

"Then it must have been her eyes. No doubt they were crossed like poor Juno who works for the smithy. Or perhaps," he suggested, warming to the game, "she had one eye in the middle of her forehead."

"Her eyes were lovely, as blue as the stone in the sword Excalibur. Both of them!"

Tristan passed a hand over the scar at his chin where he'd taken a nick from a sword as a child, smothering back a smile at the little man's gullibility.

"Then it must be the warts all over her and the nose that hung down to her chin. Aye, that 'tis the reason Lady Meg sent her away."

"Her nose was finely made and she was fair as the morn with not a mark on her!" The gnome's eyes narrowed to slits.

"I know the game you play, *boy*. And you'll not have another word from me."

"Then you'll not have another mile from me on this journey," Tristan informed him. "You'll tell me the truth, now, all of it. Or I go no farther."

"Then go no farther," the gnome challenged him. "I do not need you to find the place. Remember, I am the one who knows where it is."

"Aye, you know it so well that you cannot even remember the road markers," Tristan pointed out. He stood, wincing slightly against the pain at his ribs.

"Then find it, if you can. I return to Monmouth, where I am needed."

"Tonight?" Grendel exclaimed, his head popping out of the woolen cocoon like that of a hedgehog startled from its burrow. "But 'tis dark."

"Aye, very dark. And cold." Tristan seized the blanket, his sword, and his leather pack and headed toward the horses.

" 'Tis foolishness to set off in the dark," Grendel reasoned, following after, the blanket discarded in a musty heap. "Remember what happened when you acted so hastily before. You will have bruises for days from that experience."

"Aye, I will," Tristan acknowledged, and then pointedly added, "but not the aggravation." Reaching the horses, he swung the blanket across the back of the black warhorse and prepared to saddle him.

Grendel wrung his hands. He hated the cold and he hated the dark. But more than either of those, he hated being left alone in a strange and distant place.

"Oh, very well!" he conceded, uncertain whether or not Tristan would carry out his threat and truly leave him there. Mortals were not at all practical or logical, and they were very unpredictable.

"But there is not that much to tell."

Tristan leaned back, laying an arm across the saddle, but making no further move back toward the encampment.

"Tell me what you know. All of it, or I will leave you in this forest and let the trolls have you."

He smiled to himself as he saw the little man visibly cringe at the threat. Grendel hated trolls, and although Tristan had never seen one and even doubted their existence, he didn't hesitate to threaten the gnome to get what he wanted.

Grendel shook his head and lamented, "You were always such an agreeable child. What have I done to deserve such treatment?"

"I can't imagine," Tristan replied. "Perhaps it has something to do with the time you abandoned me in the caverns below Monmouth as a child."

"There was no harm done," Grendel defended. "And it taught you to use senses other than sight."

"It got me so lost that even Mistress Meg feared I might not survive it."

"Not only did you survive," Grendel pointed out, "you found another way out."

"Which you knew nothing about. You could have gotten me killed."

"You are here to tell about it, aren't you?" the gnome threw back at him. "And a much better warrior for it, as well. So you see, it was good for you."

"And what of the time you threw me off balance when crossing the log across the Windemere River?"

"That was an accident. T'was not done deliberately. But you must admit, it had its advantages. You learned to swim."

"I almost drowned!" Tristan shot back at him.

"But you didn't. So you see, your complaints are for naught. Each lesson has taught you something you did not know before or improved your skills." Grendel shrugged. "It seems to me that I have done you a great service."

"Another child of less stamina would not have survived his childhood."

"Not only did you survive, but look at the warrior you have become."

"Aye, a warrior who should be riding with the king's men in pursuit of the murdering bastards who attacked Monmouth rather than playing wet-nurse to a child."

"This is of far greater importance," Grendel replied.

"Explain to me how it is of far greater importance," Tristan demanded. "Tell me now, or I leave for Monmouth this very night."

The gnome groaned. He had been entrusted with a grave responsibility and he had been bound to secrecy. He was also bound to tell the truth. And he had an intense dislike for trolls, which had him worriedly glancing about lest they were present even now, hovering at the edges of the meager light cast by the campfire.

"Kemflech!" he swore in the ancient dialect, a word that had not been used in the mortal world for more than a thousand years. Trolls were such vulgar, filthy creatures. He heaved a sigh of resignation.

"There is not much to tell," he replied hesitantly.

Without another word, Tristan slipped a foot into the stirrup and swung up into the saddle.

Grendel glanced wildly about, absolutely certain trolls lurked behind every tree and bush that surrounded them in the forest.

"All right! All right! I'll tell you what I know!"

Tristan did not dismount, but from atop the warhorse quietly demanded, "All of it."

The gnome swore again. But his dislike of trolls was worse than his fear of Meg's anger. The worst she might do was heave a pot at his head. Trolls were impossible to deal with. There was just no reasoning with them.

"Lady Meg wished very strongly to have a child, but Lord Merlin tried to convince her otherwise."

"Why?"

Grendel shrugged, "Who knows the ways of Lord Merlin's thoughts. Only once did I overhear a conversation between them. He argued most strenuously against it."

"With what reason?"

Having pots hefted at one's head was one thing, but crossing Lord Merlin was quite another. He decided on the side of saving his own hide, and shrugged. "I cannot say."

Tristan swung the stallion about in the direction of the trail they'd followed through the forest. Grendel lunged for the bridle. The black's head went up in alarm, nostrils flared wide. He had an instinctive dislike of the gnome and reared wildly, front hooves slashing out. The gnome dove for cover over the trunk of a fallen tree.

The stallion snorted wildly and would have taken after him if Tristan had not reined him in sharply. When he finally had him under control once more, Grendel slowly poked his head up over the fallen tree. He was wide-eyed and pale as fresh milk, which was quite remarkable, considering his natural dark coloring. No threats were necessary. He spilled his guts like a filleted cod.

"Mistress Meg is not like you or Lord Conner. In spite of her mortal appearance she is not truly mortal. No daughter of the light has ever joined with a mortal, much less conceived a child," he stammered a hasty explanation, all the while keeping a wary eye on the stallion.

"It was not known what powers such a child might possess."

"There is more to it than that," Tristan concluded.

"Aye," Grendel heaved a deep sigh. "There is more. Lord Merlin feared for the future of a child born with unknown abilities but of mortal form.

"He feared such a child would not find acceptance but be persecuted and feared. 'Tis the reason only a handful know the mistress is a true sister to Merlin. He has long known that were it not for Arthur's protection and support, he would be feared and persecuted as well. You mortals are not tolerant of those who are different," he added pointedly.

"But the child was born mortal."

"Aye, and there might have been nothing to be concerned about if not for a vision Lady Meg saw when the child was only weeks old."

Tristan did not dismount, but waited patiently astride the black. Grendel ground his teeth in frustration, knowing he would have to tell it all.

"She saw a vision of the Darkness."

Tristan's interest sharpened as it always did at mention of the powers of Darkness. As a child, he'd been raised on stories of great battles between good and evil, of dragons, trolls, gnomes, and sorcerers. And as a child he had believed them all, perhaps because he needed something to believe in after the death of his family.

But that was a long time ago, and he'd lost the naivete of a child, and along with it the willingness to innocently believe in things of myth and legend.

Grendel nodded. "After all these years, you still do not believe. What do you think it was that robbed Lady Meg of her sight? What of the standing stones? Do you think they just happened to be there, while there are no others of that size in all the land?"

"What do I care for stones? 'Tis only a story."

"Only a story!" Grendel slapped his own forehead in frustration.

"Why am I cursed?" he shouted to the night sky. "He demands to be told the truth, but when I tell him the truth he does not believe it." Then, "Yes, yes, I know. Because he is merely a mortal. Pitiful creatures. Well, I'll tell you this! 'Tis yourself who has the better bargain while I am stuck here with these fools."

"Who are you calling a fool?" Tristan demanded.

"You, of course." Grendel glared at him once more, and

warned, "You try my patience, *boy*. 'Tis truth you wanted. Are you too cowardly to hear it now?"

"I am not a coward," Tristan replied in a low, even voice, and then warned, "and do not call me *boy*."

"Aye, well, I see no man before me, for it takes a man such as Lord Connor to believe where other mortals show only fear, clutch at their crucifixes, and pray to their god for deliverance."

Tristan swung down from the saddle. He tethered the black but did not remove the saddle or bridle.

"Tell me."

Once more seated across the campfire from one another, Grendel told his story. Of the birthright of Lady Meg as a child of the Light, her journey through the portal that separated the mortal and immortal worlds, her deadly battle with the powers of Darkness, and the bargain she made afterward to live in the mortal world with Lord Connor.

"You were but a child," Grendel reminded him. "Arthur was not yet king. The powers of the Darkness were strong across the land. Much was at stake." More wood was thrown onto the fire, sending embers high into the night sky overhead like a swarm of brilliant flame-colored insects.

"The circle of stones has not always stood there. Once there was only a flat plain." He thought of Morgana, Arthur's half-sister, who wanted so much and was willing to sell her soul to have it. He shivered. Even now he could feel that coldness of evil to the depths of his soul.

"It was within the ring of stones that Lady Meg confronted the powers of Darkness, and it was there she defeated them. But victory had a price. She was blinded in the encounter."

Tristan had grown up on stories of the stone ring and the unusual happenings that supposedly took place there. To this day most people believed the ring of stones was haunted. Some said that sounds came from the ring of stones. Others said they'd seen strange things in the moonlight when venturing too near the stones. As a child, he'd once approached the stones, and Lady Meg had soundly thrashed him for it.

He'd been told that her blindness was from an accident suffered when she was gone those many weeks during the time Arthur was finally made king, and Lord Connor returned alone to Monmouth. But after she returned, she seemed hardly hindered by it. Most certainly he never got away with anything. In fact, she seemed to see things others could not, much to his misfortune.

"I remember when the child was born," Tristan recalled that night long ago.

"On Samhuin," Grendel replied, of the night when the forces of Darkness and Light are most closely aligned within the ancient universe.

"All-hollows eve." Tristan remembered it as a child who had no understanding of the more significant things that unfolded that night. "Bonfires were lit across the countryside. The horizon was aglow with them. Lord Connor was very happy."

"Aye." Grendel recalled the night very well. "As happy as any new father. Instant love it was, when he first held her. There could have been no more love for a son, so pleased he was."

"I was told the child had worsened and died."

"It was what everyone was told. It made the lie Lord Connor told about her death that much easier to believe."

"What happened?"

Grendel sighed. "One night the young mistress rose to feed the child and found her blankets soaked in blood. There was no injury. In fact, Lord Connor saw nothing when he rose at her terrified screams. There was only one other who saw the blood that soaked the child, even though he was far away at Camelot."

The gnome's gaze met his across the campfire, and Tristan

knew exactly who it was who had seen the terrifying events in a vision.

"Merlin."

"Aye," Grendel acknowledged. "Connected as they were by the powers both had once possessed, so too were they connected by the same vision. He arrived at Monmouth within a very short time."

Tristan's gaze narrowed. He'd heard many stories of Merlin's powers. Half he believed, but others . . .

" 'Tis a half day's journey from Monmouth to Camelot on the fastest horse."

"Aye." Grendel shrugged. "For mortal man astride one of those foul beasties." He gestured to the horses tethered nearby, then looked up at Tristan.

"But not for one such as him." He saw the doubt in the young warrior's eyes.

"Ah, you do not fully believe. But you do not fully disbelieve either. Too much have you seen of Mistress Meg's abilities to believe they are merely mortal skills." The beady little eyes sharpened with understanding.

"Methinks that perhaps you've seen something of Lord Merlin's powers." His eyes widened as his thoughts connected with Tristan's.

"Perhaps a young lad roused from sleep that night and saw Lord Merlin appear through clouds of swirling mist."

"At first I thought it was a dream," Tristan replied.

"It was real enough. You saw what few mortals have ever seen."

The fire had burned low once more. The cold pressed at their backs and seeped into weary bones.

"All these years I believed the child had died."

Grendel nodded. "It was easier to let everyone believe it. That way the child could remain safely hidden." His eyes gleamed with approval as he sensed Tristan's next thought.

"Right you are. If she sent the child away and had no knowledge of her whereabouts, the powers of Darkness could not use the knowledge to find the child.''

Tristan shot him a dark look and a murderous thought across the campfire. Grendel ignored both. He'd been sensing the boy's thoughts for a long time and used it to keep him safe on more than one occasion.

''She entrusted the babe to the woman Dannelore, who was once her servant, and her husband John,'' the gnome continued telling his story. If he was going to tell it, he was going to tell all of it.

''They vowed they would raise the child as their own with no knowledge of her birthright.''

Tristan frowned as he remembered back all those years before, seeing and understanding everything as he had then, through the eyes of a child. And with what he now knew to be the truth.

''It seemed strange that they left so suddenly with no fare-wells. John had promised to help me train a young colt.''

Grendel sighed heavily. ''There was no time for farewells. Mistress Meg feared that any delay endangered the child. It was done under cover of darkness one night. It was Lord Conner who let it be known that the child had died.''

Tristan remembered back all those years and recalled that dark, sad day and the days that had followed. A stone was set into the floor of the chapel at Monmouth. Words were spoken by the priest. Lord Connor asked that he not speak of the child because of the sadness it caused.

But it was Lady Megwin who had spoken of the child in odd moments, and the way she spoke of the babe in the odd turn of a phrase, it seemed as if the child was not dead at all. Now he understood the reason she had spoken of the child just so in those unguarded moments. And he understood the sadness that never seemed to dim with time.

It explained so many things, as well as the reason that no

other children were born in the years that followed. Tristan placed more wood on the fire.

"The child was only an infant when she left Monmouth. How will you know her?" Tristan asked.

Grendel's hand closed over the small leather pouch tied at his belt, the contents safely guarded within.

"I will know her. And she has a name. 'Tis Rianne."

Tristan had once known the babe's name, but over time and with Connor's admonition not to speak of the child, he had forgotten it. She was a few weeks old the last time he saw her and so he had not formed a lasting impression of her that lingered the way others had whom he had spent time with— his friends, the old Viking who had told him bloody tales of his own youth and taught him how to wield a seax, or even the gnome.

"One changes much over the years," Tristan said, thinking back to the events of his own early childhood that had a profound effect on him. Even now, years later, he still had dreams of the night his family was murdered and their home burned. Even now, all these years later, he woke in a sweat screaming for his father and brothers.

"She had the fairness of her mother, and the same blue eyes. She is also descended from the Ancient Ones." Grendel added with confidence, "I will know her."

"What if she will not come with us?" Tristan speculated. "Have you thought of that, little man? She has a life with those she believes to be her family. She may not so easily understand, nor willingly leave them."

"She will understand," Grendel replied.

"I would not understand if my family had given me over to another, no matter the reason."

"Of course you would not understand. You are mortal and very illogical." Grendel pointed out the obvious, as if that was all the explanation that was needed.

"She is half mortal," Tristan reminded him, more than a little pleased at the glare he received from the gnome.

"Aye, the part of her that comes from her father," he said with obvious disdain. "But Lord Connor is quite logical ... for a mortal."

Tristan smiled inwardly at the gnome's emotional response, a seemingly wholly mortal trait. If the little man was to be believed.

"She is a child, and a female at that. They are very unpredictable creatures. And you have no knowledge of her temperament. She may be very spoiled and disagreeable."

"Impossible! She was a sweet-tempered babe!" Grendel snapped. "No doubt she has grown to be an amiable young girl. And I do not wish to discuss it further!"

Tristan grinned. As a child he had been no bigger than the gnome and Grendel had taken advantage of his small stature with all sorts of pranks and tricks. But children have a habit of growing. Now, all Grendel could do was argue with him, and when he found himself unable to do that he simply refused to discuss the matter further.

"We shall see," Tristan told him as he rose to unsaddle the black.

When he returned, he found the gnome wrapped and snuggled into his blankets like a tick burrowed into a hound's hide. He'd quickly fallen asleep and made loud snorkling sounds that no doubt could be heard to the edges of the forest in all directions. If there was anyone about, they knew they were there.

"Why not blow a horn and announce our presence?" he muttered with disgust as the little man rolled over and added another sound to his assortment—the long, low rumble of escaping wind.

Tristan escaped once more to the far side of the fire and laid out his own blanket of thick fleece hide. He placed the long sword within easy reach. A smaller blade was concealed inside the fleece.

They were at the far reaches of Arthur's kingdom, and the power of his laws extended only so far. Thieves roamed freely in such places and thought nothing of slitting a man's throat for the finely made sword he carried, or their horses, which might be traded for tankards of ale, food, and a woman at the next inn, much less if it was known he carried gold coin in the leather pouch at his belt.

Sleep was a long time coming in spite of the fatigue from the long day's ride. But when it finally came, it was invaded by dreams that slipped silently upon him in vivid, familiar images of blood and death.

In those dreams he was a small boy once more, waking from other dreams of adventures with his brothers to the sounds of battle and death all about him.

A cold sweat broke out at those images of blood and death suddenly wrenched from the past, as though he lived it all over again—the terrified screams of his mother and sisters, the gleam of a war-ax, his father's fierce battle cry suddenly silenced. And then, amid the flames and smoke, the stench of death as he crawled over the bodies of his family.

He was soaked in their blood, their lifeless eyes staring back at him. Where there had once been love, joy, and laughter, there was only blood and death. He reached for a battle sword. But the hand he saw in his dream was not the hand of a child. It was the hand of a warrior, who pulled the sword from beneath the dragging weight of his father's lifeless body.

Just as he had that long ago day, he stumbled through the ruins of his home as he went from one lifeless body to the next, his father and brothers all dead, his mother and sisters brutally raped and then murdered. And just as it was that long ago day, he left the burning ruins of what had been his home. In the courtyard he plunged his face into the frozen water of the ancient fountain where his sisters had once played.

The water washed away the blood and tears, but not the memories that were forever etched into his brain. Then, like that long ago day, the water became still and calm once more. But unlike that long ago day the image that looked back at him from the surface of the water was not his face. It was the fleeting image of a young girl.

She was beautiful, with fragile, exquisite features, and eyes the color of rare blue gemstones. Flames surrounded her, but she didn't seem to feel their intense heat. Instead, she stared back at him with such profound sadness that it seemed a reflection of his own.

At first he thought that he must have seen her reflection in the water, that he had only to turn and he would find her standing beside him. Another, who had somehow managed to survive the blood and death as he had. But no one was there. He was alone.

Perhaps it was his own reflection that he saw. But when he looked back at the water in the fountain, he again saw those exquisitely beautiful features, and those brilliant, vivid eyes that stared back at him with such overwhelming sadness. Then she turned and the image faded. And it seemed that the flames that surrounded her, consumed her.

And, as he wakened from those dreams, she was gone.

CHAPTER TWO

A steady drizzle blanketed the forest. It soaked through heavy wool wrapped tight against the cold. It created a quagmire that sucked at the hooves of horses, bogged down the wheels of a cart heavily laden with barrels of ale, and sucked at one's boots.

Guttural curses filled the frigid air amid raucous laughter and crudely shouted suggestions from the inn's patrons. The driver of the cart snapped the whip over the heads of the horses as they lunged in their harness, straining to move the cart.

After several attempts the cart was more deeply mired than before. Someone handed the driver a tankard. It was quickly emptied, a sleeve dragged across a bearded face. Sides heaving, hides lathered, the horses stood in their traces. No amount of shouting, whipping, or cursing could move the cart.

Temper mollified by another tankard of ale that quickly followed the first one, the driver threw down the whip. He abandoned the cart and the quivering horses for the inside of the inn, a warm fire, a woman, a bit of gambling, and more of the heady brew he'd delivered only a short while earlier.

The inn was filled with smoke from the cookfire, the stench of stale food, spilled ale, and a quagmire of the worst sort of humanity that had ever gathered in one place. They came here to drink, to whore, and to find a game of chance at the cups or rolling the stones.

Garidor ran the lower floor of the inn near the river Wye and provided those necessities of life to pilgrims who traveled the forest road, local inhabitants who eked out a meager existence hunting and trapping in the forest and then traded the skins, crofters, and an odd assortment of disreputable and dangerous customers whose activities were best unknown.

Occasionally a traveler with gold in his pockets ventured into the inn for a hot meal, a tankard of ale, and a room. Neither the traveler nor his gold was ever seen again.

Mab was in charge of the upper floor of the inn, where another sort of comfort could be found for the price of a fox pelt, a piece of silver, or taken in trade. She was as wide as she was tall, had the disposition of a wild boar, and the looks to match.

Some said she was married to Garidor. Others said it was a business arrangement. And business was good, provided by young Kari, who had the ethereal features of an angel, the body of a young girl, and the wounded soul of someone far older.

No one knew where Kari came from. It was rumored that she was Mab's daughter, although there was nothing to suggest it on appearances. Other rumors had it that Garidor took her in trade to settle a debt, a debt on which he regularly collected interest upstairs in one of the rooms.

Then there was Ox, so named because he was as dumb as one, and made sounds very much like one as well. He was tall as an oak and kept order in the inn when customers became too boisterous or when arguments broke out over Kari or the games of chance run by the *boy*. No one argued with Ox.

The *boy* was the newest member of Garidor's little "family." He was small and thin, with the look of a beggar with his ragged clothes worn in thick layers even through the warmth of the summer, and smudged cheeks that gave the appearance that he was in constant need of washing. And this observation was made by Mab, for whom washing was no more than a seasonal occurrence as long as the season was mild and temperate.

But those beggar's rags and smudged appearance were deceiving, for beneath the layers of filth was a cunning survivor's instinct that belied the woeful expression in startling blue eyes that seemed to see everything that went on in the inn.

That cunning was first made known in the games of cups and stones that began innocently enough in a corner of the inn that early spring. The boy seemed to appear out of nowhere. One minute there was no one there, the next he was hunched down in the corner, three wooden cups upended and set in a row with an equal number of Garidor's patrons placing wagers on which one concealed the small, glistening crystal with those strange markings. If one of them guessed correctly three turns in a row, he won not only the amounts wagered but the unusual sparkling crystal as well.

Then, there was the game of stones that was even more of a favorite among his patrons. The stones were actually carved from the tusks of a wild boar. Each one was six-sided. On each side were different markings.

The three stones were placed in a cup, shaken with great enthusiasm, and then slammed down onto the planked wood table where those participating had gathered. A matched pair earned the one controlling the stones the right to keep his wager and another roll. Three different sides showing and he was forced to surrender the stones and his wager to the boy. If someone rolled three matched stones, he was paid three times his wager.

So far the crystal still belonged to the boy and he'd accumulated an amazing amount of trinkets, silver pieces, and baubles, although one would never know it by his appearance.

Early on, Garidor had realized the advantage of having the boy become part of his family. The more a patron gambled, the more ale he consumed, the more ale he consumed, the more he gambled. He cut a bargain with the boy for a portion of his take in trade for allowing him access to his patrons.

It was a fair bargain, especially when one considered how much his patrons lost to the boy—enough to fill the small pouch he wore at his belt most nights, but not enough that it turned his customers away.

Garidor's portion was healthy, but he knew the boy's portion was even healthier. He tried several times to learn where the boy kept his small treasure, but each time Ox followed him from the inn when he left after a day's wagering, the boy managed to elude him.

In fact, he could not say for certain where the boy lived, for no one saw him other than at the inn. Most likely he lived in the forest, Garidor concluded. He would have to give the search more effort, for there was a goodly sum to be had that the boy had acquired over the past months, if only it could be found.

It had occurred to him to have the girl Kari learn the location from the boy, for there seemed to be a special relationship between them. From the moment the boy arrived, the girl had seemed particularly taken with him. Whenever there was no one about wishing her company, she could be found with the boy, watching over one of the games of stones or cups, or talking with the lad.

She was the only one who exchanged more than a passing word with him. Or rather, it seemed that she did all the talking. Perhaps the boy was mute, Garidor thought with sudden inspiration. That would make it much easier when he eventually discovered the location of the boy's winnings at stones. There would be no screams to draw attention, although there was no one likely to come to the boy's aid.

For now, Garidor was content to let the arrangement remain as it was. He benefitted greatly from the boy's skills. But winter was near, and when it finally arrived and snow blanketed the forest there would be few customers to lay down their coins, baubles, or pelts for a game of stones.

Times were hard. Each winter there were some who did not survive to return to his inn come spring. But Garidor was a survivor and he would winter through quite well, especially when he found the boy's hidden treasure.

It would be more than enough to carry him through, perhaps to purchase a new draft horse to haul his own ale, and—his eyes gleamed—perhaps to purchase a new gown for Kari. He considered both the horse and a new gown an investment, for he had plans to expand. Garidor was a very enterprising man.

Garidor was a pig! the *boy* thought, glimpsing the lustful gaze that fell on Kari. Not for the first time, the boy expanded that thought to other thoughts of Garidor, trussed and tied to a spit, the flames of a cookfire licking at his flesh. Would he squeal like a pig as well? the *boy* wondered with a longing to discover if it was so.

Not yet, came the answer in cautious reply. *Bide your time.* There was still much coin to be bled from his patrons, who so foolishly squandered their meager coins, a trinket, or a soft pelt of fur. And too, there was the girl Kari. The *boy* could not leave her there when it came time to go.

His gaze scanned the smoke-filled inn. Eventually, *he* had grown accustomed to the stench of the inn—the amalgam of overcooked food that sat in the pot for several days afloat in a congealed mass of whatever it was that was not still crawling that Mab threw into the cookpot, the stink of so many unwashed bodies pressed into the small inn, the acrid smell of torches soaked in animal fat, spilt ale, and overall the smoke from the hearth that hung in the air and stung at the eyes.

"I've brought you something to eat," Kari said in that soft, sweet voice, startling him from his thoughts. He wasn't usually so careless, allowing someone, even her, to approach without warning. But there was something different this evening, something that seemed to hang in the air amid the smoke and smell of human decay that had distracted him.

"You must eat," she insisted, her eyes like that of a wounded angel peering from under the sweep of pale gold hair that half hid her features.

It was a habit, he knew. A way of disguising herself, shrinking within herself with the hope of making herself less noticeable. Perhaps then no one would ask for her. But there was always someone, and when it was not a paying customer it was Garidor.

"He takes the same portion of your winnings whether you eat it or not," she reasoned, and looking down at the grayish contents of the bowl, her eyes seemed to grow even sadder.

"It's not much, but you grow used to it. 'Tis easy enough to abide when there's nothin' else."

She wanted so to please him, her only friend, with those unusual blue eyes, a soft sensual mouth, and an equally soft touch, like that of a girl.

That was when he surprised her, reaching out for her wrist with a slender hand that was surprisingly strong. Equally slender fingers closed with gentle warmth that seemed to seep into her very bones. With his other hand he gently pried her fingers apart and dropped several soft, fleshy berries into her palm.

Her eyes grew as round as the plump, ripe fruit. "Wherever did you get them?"

The boy pressed a finger against his lips and with a glance toward the open doorway, where rain drizzled over the eaves, indicated the forest beyond.

"There are more where those came from," the boy whispered secretively, and gently folded Kari's fingers over the priceless treasure.

Then, without warning, the expression in Kari's eyes suddenly changed from childlike wonder to one of terror. Before the boy could react, her head snapped back from a blow that sent her sprawling into the filth at the floor. Garidor stood over her.

The boy should have seen it coming. But it had been so unusual to see a smile on the girl's face that he'd let his guard down for a moment.

The boy was old beyond his years. He'd lived by his wits and lived when others had died. Better than anyone he knew the low-life animal Garidor was. Not for one moment could one turn his back on him. But he had, just for a moment. And Kari paid the price.

"Upstairs with you!" Garidor snarled as he stood over her. "There's payin' customers waitin'."

Kari slowly picked herself up off the floor. Ducking her head to hide the vicious red marks that already appeared across a swollen cheek, she warily edged around Garidor and obediently headed for the stairs.

"Well, boy?" Garidor turned on the dirt-smudged lad wrapped in his beggarly clothes. "What yer lookin' at?" A lewd grin split his face.

"Maybe you think you'd like to have a little piece of that, eh?"

Raucous laughter erupted among the patrons of the inn. But none was so pleased with himself as Garidor.

"Bony as ye are, you'd have to strap a paddle to yer ass to keep from fallin' in. Think yer man enough, eh? Or do you prefer the lads?"

There was more laughter at the boy's expense. Garidor leaned close and laid a hand on the boy's shoulder, his breath fouling the air.

"Tell you what, lad. I'll give you a free one. No charge on accounta we're partners. That'll convince you, when you've got her moanin' beneath ya."

He squeezed the boy's shoulder, unaware of the slender blade that slipped so easily into the boy's hand concealed within the overlong sleeve of the stained tunic he wore.

"Would you like that?" Garidor asked, as if talking to a

child. "It's about time you had yer first piece. It'll make a man of you, and I swear there's no piece sweeter than that one."

His gaze wandered up the stairs where Kari had disappeared, and the expression in his eyes darkened as he thought of her slender body, the almost boyish hips, and the small high breasts that brought a fresh hunger to his gullet.

"Will it make a man of you, Garidor?" Mab asked to even more raucous laughter, drawing Garidor's attention away from the boy. Loathing burned in his eyes.

"Shut yer mouth, hag."

"Hag, is it?" Mab retorted with a wide, almost toothless grin. And then, loud enough for everyone to hear, "I looked just like 'er once. This," she jabbed a thumb at herself, "is what layin' with the likes of 'im will do to a girl."

"Shut yer face, Mab, or I'll shut it for you," Garidor threatened.

But Ox had come up and stood behind Mab like a large, silent shadow that easily outweighed Garidor and was several years younger. Some thought Ox was Mab's son, but there was nothing in the lumbering giant that bore any resemblance to Garidor.

"Will ya, now?" Mab said, that gaping grin widening with pleasure as Garidor eventually backed down and retreated to the corner of the inn where he dispensed ale to his customers.

Through the evening, he downed several tankards of ale himself. Not the watered-down supply he sold his customers, but a stout, full-strength brew he kept for himself. When he'd downed enough courage, he made his way over to those stairs and amid wild shouts of laughter and lewd comments, he staggered upstairs. A short while later the latest patron stumbled frantically downstairs, his breeches down around his ankles.

Mab grabbed the boy by the scruff of the neck when he would have headed up the stairs after Garidor.

"There's payin' customers waitin' to try their hand at stones, boy," she reminded him. Ox loomed behind her, a threatening expression on his wide, flat face.

He could have easily escaped Mab. Once beyond the reach of those fat, grimy hands, the boy would have quickly been up the stairs. But escaping Ox was another matter.

He might be dull-witted as an ox but he had the strength of one as well. If Ox caught him, he would break every bone in his body with a single blow. What then would become of Kari?

Mab shook the boy, grinning a toothless grin at the murderous glare he flashed at her.

"Get to it," she growled, releasing him with a hard shove.

With a glance at the stairs, the boy returned to his table. The stones were removed from the pouch and dropped into the wooden cup as the next customer laid his wager down on the table—a few small trinkets and a carved brooch of some value that had no doubt been stolen from some poor traveler. The boy hardly noticed as he rolled the stones, easily won, and mechanically scooped the trinkets into the pouch he carried.

Over the next hour, the stones were tossed many times. Wagers were placed. A few won, but most lost what they'd come with.

Eventually, Garidor returned, and the next man who'd been waiting for Kari moved cautiously past him up the stairs.

The stones were slammed down on the table with unusual force, and eyes the color of blue fire burned with hatred at Garidor. The boy waited.

When Garidor finally slumped into his usual drunken stupor and Mab and Ox dozed in a corner, snoring loudly, he made his way across the inn and slipped upstairs.

He found Kari huddled in the corner of the upstairs chamber. The roof leaked in a dozen places, water puddling on the floor, and the room was achingly cold. She was curled into a tight, miserable ball, the bruises visible through the tangled mass of her hair. She cringed when the boy gently laid a hand on her shoulder. Eyes that reflected all her misery gradually cleared and stared back at him with bone-deep sadness.

She shook her head pitifully and tried to crawl away, but the walls at the corner of the chamber trapped her with her shame and misery, preventing escape. And so she turned away, unable to look at the boy with eyes as blue as gemstones, a mouth as sensual as a girl's, and a tender touch that made her want to weep.

There was no need to ask if Garidor had hurt her.

"I'll kill him if he touches you again," he said, gently stroking the tangled hair back from a bruised cheek. Frightened eyes looked back at him.

"You must not say that. Garidor owns me. He can do whatever he wants with me."

The sensual mouth was set in a hard, determined line. "Then I will buy you from him."

"Buy me? How?"

"Let me worry about that," the boy told her, lightly stroking the swollen cheek.

Kari's eyes widened at the surprising warmth of the boy's touch that as before seemed to reach deep into her soul, filling all the cold places, easing the pain and misery of Garidor's abuse. She laid her head on the boy's shoulder.

"Don't leave me," she pleaded. "Please, don't leave me."

The boy wrapped an arm about her thin shoulders. "Sleep now," he told her. "I won't leave you, and I promise, no one will hurt you again."

Eventually, he felt the tension ease out of her painfully thin body, and her head grew heavy at his shoulder. There was nothing in the barren room that offered any warmth from the cold. No blanket or fleece, yet he kept her warm.

The *boy* did not leave, nor did he sleep, but stayed awake through the night, listening and protectively watching over her. A silent rage burned through him like a fire within his soul, his fingers clenched over the handle of the slender blade should Garidor waken and return.

"How much farther?" Tristan demanded.

It had rained since dawn. Now, hours later, he was tired, cold, soaking wet, and had a growing suspicion they were lost.

Grendel, huddled deeper in his sodden cocoon, and shrugged. "A bit farther."

Another rivulet of water slipped down Tristan's backside. The fleece-lined tunic molded him like a wet dog and smelled suspiciously like one as well. It was impossible to decide who smelled the worse, he or the gnome.

"You said that four hours ago," he said between teeth set against the cold. "How far is it, now?" And when there was no immediate reply turned in the saddle and glared at the little man.

"We're lost," he concluded with disgust.

"We are not lost," Grendel insisted, indignant at the thought as he drew up beside him on the weary, sagging palfrey.

Whereas mortals were constantly lost even in their own backyard, it was impossible for him to be lost. He had an uncanny way about such things, guided by the heightened instinct very much like that of a hunting hound.

However, at the moment, after riding almost an entire day and certain the entire last hour that they should reach their destination at any moment, he failed to sense anything familiar about their surroundings that even suggested they were near.

"Do you know where we are?" Tristan demanded, not at all pleased about spending the night out in the open. Lost. With no indication whether they were near the place they sought. Except for the determination and persistence of a creature no larger than a child and at times with the immature, fussy disposition of one as well.

"Not precisely," Grendel replied, his gaze scanning the cover of trees for a familiar landmark.

"A guess, then, perhaps." And as the gnome completely ignored him, "Do you have any notion at all where we are?"

"We are in the forest," Grendel snapped, his thoughts focused on something remote and yet at the same time very near.

"Trees, ferns, moss." Tristan slapped his hand against his forehead as though seized with sudden inspiration.

"By God! We *are* in the forest."

Grendel glared at him but did not reply. He was too busy concentrating on that illusive awareness as he reached out with his senses.

It was a connection of familiarity that was part of every creature of the immortal world. It connected them like a kindred spirit, reached out like a whisper, and was answered in just the same way. It was there now, just beyond the reach of his senses, like a scent carried first in one direction then in the other, but always just out of reach.

They were very near. The time and distance traveled was almost exactly the same and in the same direction as before. Yet, there was no cottage where there ought to be one.

"I do not understand why I cannot find the place," he growled with frustration.

"It has been several years," Tristan reasoned. "Things grow and change."

"It has to be here," the gnome insisted. "I will not leave until it is found."

Tristan swung down from the saddle. The horses were tired, he was tired, and if they didn't find the place by nightfall he had already made it be known that he was turning back at first light.

He'd kept his promise to Lady Meg. They'd come on this fool's errand because she asked it even though he sensed that they should remain at Monmouth.

"Where are you going?" the gnome demanded with rising panic. "You cannot leave when we are so near."

Tristan tethered the black to a nearby tree. "I had best leave now," he informed the gnome. "Or I will piss myself."

"Oh," Grendel replied with the surprise of one who is not bothered by such necessities. "By all means. Don't let me keep you."

"Thank you," Tristan replied.

The little man's outcry a few moments later ended any further necessity. Seizing his sword, Tristan returned to the small clearing where he'd left the gnome with the horses. The horses were there, but the little man was gone. Then that cry came again, more distinct this time and only a short distance from the clearing.

He followed the sound and found the gnome beside a stone wall almost completely obscured by ferns and tangled vines. He was frantically ripping them away.

"I knew it was here! This is the place! This wall ran along the side of the cottage to prevent forest creatures from getting to the garden Dannelore intended to plant. We've found it!" he announced triumphantly.

But what had they found? Tristan wondered as he helped the little man clear away the thick ferns and vines that had grown wild with neglect.

Where were Dannelore and John? And more important, where was Meg's daughter?

CHAPTER THREE

Tristan followed the wall to where it ended at the edge of the garden—a garden that no longer existed because the forest had long ago reclaimed it.

Beyond the garden the stone cottage with its thatched roof was barely visible. Trailing vines climbed the walls and draped from the eaves, making it seem one with the forest. They might never have found it if Grendel hadn't stumbled upon that garden wall.

Beneath the lowering sky that lay over the tops of the trees like a sodden gray blanket, there was only the sound of the rain, dripping from the trees amid the lonely, abandoned quietude.

There were no voices, no sounds of activity. There were only the darkened window openings that stared back at them like sightless, gaping eyes, and the sagging door that hung at a precarious angle from a single hinge.

"There has been no one here in some time," Tristan observed. "Perhaps there is another cottage nearby."

Grendel shook his head, his expression more deeply lined if that was possible. "This is the place."

"How can you be certain after all these years?"

The gnome offered no other reason than a simple, "I am certain."

Grendel wordlessly pushed against the lopsided gate that blocked the path into the garden. With time and the encroaching forest, the gate had become solidly wedged in the opening neither closed nor open.

Tristan tried to move it but could not. When he backed up and would have kicked it in, Grendel stepped up to the gate and with the lightest touch, slowly pushed it open.

"How did you do that?" Tristan demanded. But Grendel did not reply. He was already walking through the gate. Once inside the garden he stopped, head slightly angled, face lifted, like a hound on the scent of a rabbit.

It came to him in whispers. A sound out of the past that still lingered in this lonely abandoned place. A sound of pain and loss, anguish and despair, so brief and illusive that he might have convinced himself he had not sensed it at all. If not for the sudden, weighted heat of the pouch that hung at his belt. His bronzed, clawlike hand closed around the pouch.

"Aye, you were here," he whispered. "So long has it been, but I can feel you."

Tristan drew the short blade from the sheath at his belt and slowly approached the cottage. He peered inside.

He cut through the curtain of thick spiderwebs at the door that all but sealed off the opening and cautiously peered inside. It was dark inside except for the somber gray light that loomed at those gaping window openings.

The cottage had the unmistakable smell of neglect and decay about it, and overall the empty coldness of abandoned places he'd come across many times during the early years after Arthur returned to Britain.

He'd only been a child at the time, but there were some

things that were never forgotten. The slaughter of his family at the hands of Maelgwyn had left him an orphan who at first survived by hiding out in places such as this. Eventually, he was taken in by Lord Conner.

But that time on his own, when he survived only by his wits and some good fortune, or perhaps by the grace of God, left its mark on him. There were times when he still dreamed of it—the cold, the hunger, the fear, and at times the overwhelming loneliness of never knowing who he could trust and so therefore relying on and trusting in no one except himself.

He had quickly learned to be self-sufficient. He'd also become an expert thief who could lift something from a man's belt without him even knowing it. By the time his victim discovered his misfortune, Tristan had already disappeared like a ghost or invisible spirit incapable of being seen.

There were times that he thought of himself as an invisible spirit. It was much safer, and in his childish innocence—what little remained of it—he imagined that others could not see him, that he could move among them without their taking notice.

At first it was a game he played, a challenge with very high stakes if he was caught. It began with a crust of bread cleverly nicked right from under the hand of the man reaching for it. But by far his greatest accomplishment was the disappearance of a fine partridge right off the spit and out from under the watchful eye of the man who'd spent hours trying to snare the bird. One unguarded moment and the partridge was his, although admittedly he hadn't accounted for the fact that it was hot from the cookfire.

He'd almost given himself away when he seized the bird and burned his hand. Instinctively, he almost cried out, but instead sucked in his cheek and bit down to keep from making a sound. He made his escape, but success was marred by the painful burns on his hands.

It was a good lesson in using his head—and not relying on

his stomach—when it came to such matters, and stood him well when it came to others that could easily have cost him far more than a plump partridge. But in spite of the burns he'd received, no meal had ever tasted better. To this day he remembered the smell and taste of it.

No such smells lingered in the abandoned cottage. At the hearth layers of ash had hardened almost to stone. It had been a long time since a cookfire had burned there.

An accumulation of dirt and grime lay over everything. If there had once been any furnishings that might have offered comfort they were long gone, either carried off by the former inhabitants or scavenged.

A rat, no doubt a current inhabitant, glared up at him with beady eyes. Tristan caught it with the toe of his boot and launched it across the cottage. More than once as a child, after he lost his family, he had to fight the rats for food. He had a particular dislike for them.

He watched for other four-legged inhabitants as his gaze swept the inside of the cottage. With each passing moment he became more doubtful that this was the place they sought. No one had lived here in a very long time. The gnome must be mistaken.

Something moved in the shadows at the far corner of the cottage. He spun around and brought the blade up, every sense focused on that movement, too large for a rat.

"Have mercy!" a thin, quivering voice pleaded from the shadows. "You wouldn't harm an old woman, now would you, milord?"

Milord? He had not been called that in a very long time. Since he was a boy, before the loss of his family, home, and lands. Now he was merely a knight in service to Lord Connor. It seemed the old hag was as blind as she was foolish for lurking about in dark corners.

"Show yourself," Tristan told her, and as she stepped from the shadows added, "Slowly."

"I mean no harm," she said in a faint, quavery voice. "I am quite alone and defenseless." She spread her thin arms wide and revealed that she carried no weapon.

He glanced past the old woman to the corner of the cottage. He was between the corner and the doorway. She could not have followed him inside. How had he missed seeing her there?

She was frail and bent with age, her shoulders rounded, so that she was forced to slant a look up at him, and painfully thin, so that it seemed her bones would poke through the coarse wool of her gown. Her hair was streaked through in shades of silver and white, and hung in a mass of tangles. And her skin was like parchment, almost translucent and heavily lined. But in spite of the infirmities of age her dark eyes held a razor sharpness that gleamed back at him with unnerving calm, and he could not rid himself of the feeling that he had seen her somewhere before.

"How long have you been hiding there?" he demanded, unable also to rid himself of a warning tingle that leapt across his skin. Surely he had nothing to fear from an old woman who looked as if her bones would shatter at any moment.

"I was not hiding, milord." And then, in that quavery, thin voice, "Surely you would not begrudge an old woman the comfort of her home on such a miserable day."

Tristan was stunned. Home? But that could not be. The gnome was certain that this was the place they sought. And even though he found it difficult to believe that Conner's daughter would live in such a place, the little man was never wrong.

As if she guessed his thoughts, the old woman added, "And as you can see, milord, I am quite alone."

"Perhaps you know the people we seek—John Moore, his wife Dannelore, and a child."

The old woman shrugged a thin shoulder as she moved past him to the hearth and set a well-rusted pot over the cold hearth. He frowned as she stirred the bed of ash where a fire had not burned in a long time.

"I know of no one by that name," and then suggested, "Perhaps you would help an old woman with the fire?"

A few meager pieces of wood, laced with cobwebs, were stacked beside the hearth. As he laid them upon the hearth, she wrapped a bony hand around his wrist. Her grasp was unusually strong for one so frail and her hand was cold to the touch—colder than the cottage, colder even than the air outside—and for a moment he thought he glimpsed something in those dark eyes. Something equally cold that he had glimpsed somewhere before, and again the thought came to him that he knew the woman.

"Have we met before?"

That razor-sharp gaze fastened on his. Amusement and some other emotion glittered in the depths of her eyes.

"I would remember if I had met such a fine warrior before." And then gestured to the pile of wood. "A few pieces more, milord. To keep the fire going through the night."

He laid several more pieces of wood on the hearth. He could still feel the coldness of her touch, a coldness like death.

"Perhaps you and your companion will stay the night," she suggested as she added more wood to the hearth, though no fire was lit.

"It will be cold tonight and there is not much light left."

The thought seemed to implant itself in his brain, as if it was his own. He glanced toward the open doorway and the lowering gloom of night.

"Aye, perhaps." He hesitated accepting the old woman's offer, uncertain why he did so.

"Ask your companion," she suggested. "Surely a warm fire offers more comfort than sleeping on the hard, cold ground."

And again, as if it was his own thought, Tristan replied, "I will ask my companion."

The thought stayed with him as he left the cottage, like a voice that whispered through his thoughts until it became his only thought.

He found Grendel in a place apart from the cottage and

garden. The gnome knelt on the ground beneath the denuded limbs of a tree. His arm was outstretched before him, the fingers of his small hand flattened in the muddied earth.

He didn't look up, didn't so much as give the slightest indication that he was aware that Tristan approached.

"They are here," the gnome said. He was bent over the sodden earth, the hood falling forward and all but obscuring his features, his hand outstretched and flattened in the muddied earth.

"This is not the place. An old woman lives here. She knows nothing of John and Dannelore."

But again Grendel insisted, "They are here."

Tristan would have thought he must be daft if the little man had not looked up at him then. He had always thought the gnome incapable of emotion. But at that moment his face was etched with grief and sadness, his mouth set in a grim expression as he whispered, "They are dead."

It was then Tristan saw his other hand, clutched in a tight fist, and the blood that seeped through his fingers.

"You've injured yourself!" Tristan said with more concern than he would have admitted to anyone, particularly the evil-tempered little creature who derived such pleasure out of tormenting him.

"There's no cause for concern," Grendel assured him.

Ignoring the gnome's protests, Tristan pulled the woolen cloth from about his neck and seized the little man's hand. As he forced the fingers apart to bind the wound, something fell from the gnome's grasp.

The small object glittered in the fading light. When it fell to the sodden earth, the glow suddenly flared much brighter, then gradually faded, like a flame that slowly died.

Tristan picked up the small object and turned it over in his fingers. In the fading light, the marks etched into the smooth crystal gleamed dully. There was no glimmer of the light he'd seen only moments before, bright as a flame.

"I have seen this before," Tristan said with certainty as he held the crystal rune in his fingers. Even though the flame was gone, warmth remained like a memory of the fire. It spread through him, driving back the cold that had settled deep inside him at the old woman's touch, clearing his thoughts.

"It belongs to Lady Meg."

"Aye, one of several she has kept all these years," the gnome acknowledged, "sent to guide us to this place."

Tristan remembered as a child how the ancient runes fascinated him. But he had not seen them in many years and had thought them lost.

"The wound at your hand?"

"As you can see," Grendel indicated, turning his hand over in the fading light, "there is no wound. The blood you saw was theirs." Again his gaze turned toward the earth and he repeated, "They are here. It was the changeling's essence that joined with the power of the light within the rune crystal. It was their deaths I saw reflected there, their blood that appeared on my hand."

Tristan had always known that Lady Meg possessed an unusual gift. He had seen it countless times in her healing ways. Magic some called it. The dark arts, some whispered, but never in the presence of the Lord of Monmouth.

Once he had entered her chamber, dared by young companions to find out whether the rumors and superstitions were true. Wagers were made. He had to find proof of her magical powers and take it to them.

Upon entering the chamber through a servant's entrance, he discovered he had made a fateful mistake, for the lady was in her chamber. With no hope of escape, he hid in the shadows behind the tapestry at the wall. She could not have seen him, and so certain was he that his heart quit beating the moment he discovered he was trapped that he knew he made no sound that she might hear.

She gave nothing away by glance or deed. He was certain she had no knowledge of his presence. For hours he stood there, until his stomach gnawed with hunger, thirst clawed at his throat, and his bladder was near to bursting.

"Are you ready to show yourself now, young Tristan?" she had called out softly. "Or are you going to stand there the entire night?"

There was nothing to do but reveal himself and suffer his fate. And he was most curious how she knew he was there. He pushed back the edge of the tapestry.

"How did you know?"

He remembered her secretive smile, peering back at him from the face of an angel, golden hair spilling about her shoulders, her gaze steady in spite of the blindness that had taken her sight.

"I saw it in the rune crystals."

She had extended her hand wide over the glistening crystals spread out before her, the light from the fire reflecting in their clear depths, the pattern on each reflecting a pattern of light that played across the ceiling of the chamber. He could not help but be fascinated and had gradually slipped from his hiding place to stand beside the blanket spread before the hearth where she sat.

"The runes tell a story," she told him then, gathering them in her slender hands. Then she cast them out across the dark fur blanket once more. They fell like glittering stars in a midnight sky, each one filled with shadows and light in a stunning array of colors and patterns that drew him closer.

She explained the markings on each crystal, carved by ancient hands long ago. The gift was in the ability to read the crystals and the message they contained. She told him then of things that would come to pass in the very near future, frowning slightly, then commenting that she must warn John about the young stallion he had recently acquired for Lord Conner's stable, for the beast was of unusual spirit.

She *saw* other things in the rune crystals—the birth of a healthy child at last for the wife of the seneschal, a woman who had lost four babes at birth; some mischief she claimed Grendel was up to; a certainty that the coming winter would be long and hard; and a vision she had not shared with him but had kept to herself with a secretive smile, saying that she must tell Lord Conner of it first. Then she had asked if he would like to cast the crystal runes to see what they foretold for him.

He was most eager to learn what the crystals might know, especially when it came to his daily lessons, which bedeviled him. He hoped the crystals might reveal some magic to make the lessons easier. To his disappointment the crystals refused to tell him anything about them, but they revealed that he would someday become a great warrior in a great confrontation.

He thought Lady Meg made some jest at his expense, for he had told no one that he longed to train for the knighthood when he was older but was teased that he was too small and would never have the height or strength required. Yet she foresaw it in the runes, and as he stared down at them with her words softly moving through his thoughts, he almost believed that he could see those images in the crystals—of a gallant, brave knight astride his warhorse, a gleaming sword held in his hand.

Dream or imagination, the images faded. But even as they faded he sensed that she had entrusted him with something very special—the truth. Then, last but not least, the crystals warned of the friends who had sent him there that night.

"So," Lady Meg said, when the runes had revealed all that they could, "you have won your wager. I hope it was a good one."

He realized then that she knew even that, and he had hurt her deeply. She had always been as kind and loving as his own mother, and with the impetuosity and foolishness of youth, he had betrayed that kindness and love. At that moment, he had felt lower than a worm's belly.

"You were to take something back as proof, I believe," she said, startling him and making him wonder if the runes had revealed that as well. She handed him one of the crystals.

"Take this and they will know you tell the truth. But if you should choose to say nothing, the crystal will protect you."

He took the crystal. When he saw his friends the following day they asked countless questions about Lady Meg's chamber.

Were the walls smudged black from the witch fires? Did she turn into an old crone behind closed doors? Did she try to cast a spell on him?

For some reason their questions annoyed and angered him. He could have told them about the things Lady Meg saw in the rune crystals—that if not for the warning John might have been trampled by the young stallion that morning; about the healthy baby born to the seneschal's wife that very same day; of the early snow that blanketed the practice yard that morning, a portent of the early winter that descended upon them. He could have shown them the crystal rune Lady Meg had given him. But he said nothing of those things.

Instead, Tristan kept the secret of his encounter with Lady Meg. He said nothing of the crystal runes or the things they foretold; he said nothing of the images he had seen, or of the crystal buried deep in his pocket.

His friend William called him a liar and a coward. They did not believe that he had actually been inside Lady Meg's chamber. Confident in the power of the crystal hidden in his pocket, he bravely faced them all down.

It was a nasty brawl. Afterward, with a split lip, swollen eye, and covered in blood, he sat quietly while Lady Meg washed and dressed his wounds.

"You could have told them the truth," she reminded him while applying a foul-smelling concoction to his bruised cheek that brought tears to his swollen eye.

He fought back the tears. "Aye."

"You could have shown them the crystal."

"Aye."

"Why didn't you?"

He shrugged. "I changed my mind."

She looked at him then with a faint smile, as if she knew the true reason—that he could not betray her kindness; that he could not betray her.

"A high price methinks to pay for changing your mind."

He had grinned at her then. "You should see the other fellow."

She grinned back at him. "I did."

"Besides," he shrugged, "I had the crystal rune. You said it would protect me."

"Is this the crystal rune you speak of?" she inquired, retrieving the crystal from her own pocket. He gaped at her, then frantically searched his own pocket. It was empty. She had tricked him.

"Aye," she read his thoughts, "because I knew you had it in you to stand up for what you see as true and right. You needed only to be reminded of it, and a little courage along the way."

"I could have been killed."

"But you weren't."

"I could have been pounded to pulp."

"But you *weren't*. All right," she amended, "pounded just a little. But you found something of far more value than your friend's approval."

And he knew he had. Ever after, he always imagined that crystal rune snugged in his pocket whenever he faced a particularly difficult task.

Now he and Grendel faced the difficult truth that the ones they sought were dead.

"What of the child?"

Grendel shook his head. "I sense nothing." When he turned, his dark gaze fastened on Tristan's. "She is gone."

"How long?"

"Many seasons past," Grendel replied, as with eyes closed he held the crystal rune between hands pressed tightly together.

"How did it happen?"

"Only the child can tell us."

"Where is she now?"

"I have not the power to tell you that."

With a grim expression, Tristan seized the sword from his pack and turned toward the cottage.

"Perhaps the old woman can tell us."

"Do not!" Grendel warned, following after as fast as his short legs would carry him.

Tristan felt that coldness deep in his bones even before he reached the cottage. It reached out with an invisible hand and touched him just as she had. But when he reached the cottage, it was empty. The old woman was gone. And everything inside was just as he had found it.

"Come away," Grendel insisted. "We must go now."

"She *was* here. I saw her. I spoke with her."

"I believe you, but come away now." Grendel tugged at his sleeve. "We must leave this place."

The cold seemed to close around him, drawing him in, squeezing the air from his lungs so that he could hardly breathe. Tristan backed away from the cottage door, his sword held before him.

"Aye."

The storm was full upon them when they reached their horses at the edge of the clearing. The snow that had threatened throughout the day made good on those threats and fell in large swirling clouds that dusted the trees and muted the sounds of the forest around them.

Tristan turned in the saddle as they left the clearing. It seemed that the growing darkness and the snow closed around the cottage, making it all but invisible as the forest reclaimed it. As if it had not been there at all.

He did not see the solitary figure who stood in the sagging doorway, the snow falling all around but never touching, nor the dark eyes that watched, cold as death.

CHAPTER FOUR

"What news?" Grendel anxiously asked as Tristan returned to the horses. But even before he replied, the gnome sensed the answer that had been the same at each village and hamlet the past weeks—no one had seen the child or knew of her.

A smithy at a village they passed through only days earlier had recalled a man who had a special way with horses. But it had been at least five winters past since the man last brought his horse to be shod, and the smithy knew nothing of a child.

"And what of Dannelore?" Grendel asked, reading the warrior's next thoughts. "Did anyone recall a woman with healing skills who might have come to the village in the past?"

Tristan was hungry, cold, and hadn't slept on dry ground for the last fortnight. And he hated when the little man did that—as if his thoughts were not his own.

"No one knew anything of John or Dannelore."

"Did you ask the local healer? Dannelore might have sought her out to purchase medicants."

Tristan nodded. "She recalled no one."

"What of the village priest? They know everyone who passes through."

"I found him," Tristan replied, "though the man's godliness is highly questionable." He snorted with contempt. "My horse is more godly than that drunken fool."

"What of the merchant we were told of? The one called Oreck? Did you find him?"

Rapidly losing what little patience he had left, Tristan replied through tight lips barely visible through the thick growth of beard that had not felt a razor in more than a fortnight, "If you have so little faith in me, little man, feel free to enter the village and inquire for yourself."

Grendel blanched. "Nay! I cannot. You know very well people do not like gnomes."

"Then change into something else," Tristan suggested, and thought to himself, *"preferably something that does not talk incessantly or smell so foul."*

"I heard that!"

"Good," Tristan replied. "Then hear this as well," and he let the little man know in no uncertain terms that he had no intention of spending another night on the cold, hard ground with snow for a blanket.

Grendel's eyes grew even wider at the next thought. "An inn by the river? You know very well I cannot go to such a place."

"That is your misfortune," Tristan informed him. "You may freeze your arse off in the snow if it pleases you. I have no intention of doing so. I want a hot meal, a hot bath, and a dry bed. And a woman, if they have one with all her teeth," and added, "and who smells better than a gnome."

"Bah!" Grendel snorted. "All you think of is food and whoring. We are not staying at the inn. 'Tis too dangerous. There are all sorts of bad types about."

"It is not all I think of," Tristan informed the gnome as he seized the reins and swung astride the black Frisian.

"Travelers come and go daily at such a place," he explained logically, and watching for the gnome's reaction added, "Someone there may know something of the child."

Grendel groaned. "You would leave me here? Alone?" Panic rose in his voice. "There are wolves about. I might get eaten."

"Not bloody likely." Tristan snorted. "Not if the wolf has any sense at all." And without another backward glance sent the black stallion off at a loping gate toward the river.

Grendel stood in the middle of the road, his breath pluming in the frigid afternoon air that promised an even colder night.

"Keflech!" he muttered. "Why must I be burdened with a mortal on such a journey? Why could not the mistress have accompanied me?"

But he knew the answer. Meg would not leave Lord Conner so gravely injured. And so she had entrusted him with all her hope and faith to make the journey. And entrusted his care to a stripling lad who lived his life between his legs.

"Ah, mistress. You should have picked a more noble companion. This *boy* you sent thinks only of food and women."

Within his hand the crystal rune glowed with sudden warmth, as if in answer.

"Yes, yes, I know," Grendel grumbled. "I must trust him. But should he not also trust me, and not act so impulsively or unwisely? Can you tell me that?"

There was no answer as the crystal rune cooled once more in his hand. Or perhaps the answer was in the silence broken only by the gnome's complaints as he seized the reins of the palfrey and dragged the lethargic beast along behind him.

"The least you could do is cooperate," he muttered over his shoulder at the beast.

"This is the most disreputable establishment I have ever seen," Grendel said with disgust as he slipped into the shadows at Tristan's side. Once his mind was made up, he had caught up with him with amazing speed.

The aroma of simmering food mixed with the smell of ale, the warmth of a fire, and raucous noise. If one looked past the smoke, the overall filth, the crude, foul-smelling patrons, and the gaping, toothless smile of the huge woman who was no doubt the innkeeper's wife, it had a certain appeal. And . . . if one was desperate enough.

"At this moment, I will gladly take *disreputable* over another night in the open," Tristan announced and stepped into the inn. Grendel had no choice but to follow, or be trampled by a rough-looking man with a grisly scar down the side of his face who pushed past them in search of a tankard of ale in exchange for several pelts thrown down on the long bar. Grendel cringed as the lifeless creatures stared back at him.

With a glance at the lifeless pelts, Tristan commented, "Anyone you know? A cousin or uncle perhaps?"

Grendel glared at him. "No! Thanks be to the Ancient Ones." Then, added with disgust, "I would rather share company with creatures of the forest than the mortal creatures in this place."

Tristan was inclined to agree with him. He had never seen a more wretched gathering of humanity in his life. His hand instinctively went to the short-bladed knife sheathed at his belt. The sword, wrapped in soft leather, was carried at his back. If there was trouble, both were within easy reach.

"I do not like this place!" Grendel groaned.

"Then stay outside," Tristan suggested, and watched with amusement as the little man's Adam's apple bobbed precariously.

"I care for that even less."

"Then I suggest you find a corner to hide in and draw as little attention to yourself as possible."

"That's easy for you to say," Grendel retorted. "You're not the smallest creature about, and fair game for everyone who hates gnomes."

"You are a gnome," Tristan pointed out.

"That is no reason for everyone to pick on me. You have no idea what it's like."

Tristan smothered back laughter. "I'm much smaller than that fellow." He gestured toward a giant of a man who leaned against the stout timber that supported the bar.

Grendel's eyes widened. The man was huge, at least a full head taller than Tristan. He whistled softly through his teeth.

"That is one fellow you do not want to make angry."

"Aye," Tristan acknowledged as he moved through the crowded inn. Grendel scurried along beside him, keeping well out of the way of others.

They stepped over bodies of drunken patrons slumped across the floor, traders with animal skins knotted at their belts, and an odd assortment of low-life.

"Play the stones?" a boy called out from the corner as they passed by. "Any wager you want to make, sir. Any wager at all." And keenly eyeing the knife at Tristan's belt, "The pot is rich tonight."

The boy swept a slender hand over the assortment of coins and medallions before him that he'd taken from others that night. "Wager your blade against this fine prize," he challenged the stranger, attempting to draw him into the game. "And all will be yours." And when the stranger hesitated, "Or are you afraid to try your luck?" The boy baited him, tumbling the stones from one hand to the other.

Quicker than the eye and without any warning, Tristan leaned across the barrel, seized the stones, and rolled them. When they came to rest against the rim, he'd rolled a near perfect score. He scooped up the stones and, still leaning across the barrel, seized the boy's wrist, their faces only inches apart as he said with a flashing smile that gleamed in his dark eyes, "It's other sport I'm after tonight, boy." And dropped the stones into his hand.

"Where are you going?" Grendel demanded.

"To find a hot meal," Tristan announced and turned toward the bar, where tankards of ale were filled by the large, toothless woman. The gnome darted into the shadows. He dare not follow, for fear that he would be seen. Even though a wee bit of ale would have helped ease the chill from his bones.

"Fine!" he muttered, scurrying out of the way as a drunken patron slumped against the wall beside him and slowly sank unconscious to the floor.

"Great! This is just wonderful! He goes in search of food while I'm forced to hide out. How are we to find out anything about the child?" he muttered to himself as he hopped over another prostrate body, landed on someone, and quickly had the presence of mind to scuttle out of harm's way as a fist came flying in his direction and the man bellowed in pain.

He was jostled and shoved about amid a sea of legs, heavy boots, and various weapons as he made his way back to the corner where the boy rolled the stones.

Arriving relatively unharmed, he heaved a sigh of relief, while across the inn, Tristan was engaged in conversation over a tankard of ale. The gnome frowned. At this rate, a tankard per conversation, he would be too drunk to remember if anyone knew anything of the child.

Conversations, laughter, and occasional arguments surrounded the gnome. He was forced to content himself with the safety of his secluded corner and the occasional tankard of ale that was set aside and then forgotten. He would not have admitted it had his life depended on it, but the warmth of the inn was far better than another night in the freezing snow with only the palfrey to keep him warm.

The little man had acute hearing that rivaled any creature of the forest and no conversation went unheard. Gossip, jokes, lewd comments were heard as easily as the loudest spoken comment, mingled with the thoughts of these foolish, half-wit mortals, which he plucked from their brains like plump, ripe berries. Nothing escaped him, especially the distinctive rattle of *stones* in a wooden cup.

A born trickster and hustler with a penchant for a game that any mortal was foolish enough join him in, the sound of the stones immediately caught Grendel's attention and peaked his curiosity. While Tristan sated his appetite with food, drink, and a woman, what harm was there in sating his own appetite for sport?

The patrons hardly noticed as the gnome slipped among them and edged his way closer to the corner where the stones rattled with irresistible invitation.

None had ever bested him at the stones. Of course, it might have something to do with his unusual abilities. Most mortals thought him a simple-minded fool. They quickly learned who the fool was when they sat down at a gaming table with him and lost their coins.

He never cheated; that was a purely human failing. But he had been known to manipulate the outcome of a game of stones now and then. It was amusing to see the looks on the faces of his challengers—always so boastful of their luck—when they lost their last coin to him.

Tristan watched the game, the skill of the boy who threw the stones, and the ease with which he took the money of those who were either too foolish or too drunk to know better. He smiled inwardly as he caught sight of the gnome hovering at the edge of the game.

Tristan shoved his empty tankard across the scarred table toward the large woman, who moved with surprising agility when she heard the rattle of coins. Mab was her name, according to crude requests made by her customers. It was a disturbing thought that she might be someone's wife, mother, or lover.

He held out his tankard to be refilled and Mab obliged. She was as wide as she was tall and with each movement it looked as if a herd of hogs were battling beneath her voluminous skirt. Her face and hands were grimy. Straggly hair hung in her face and she had the smell, not of something unwashed, but of something no longer alive. Yet, disgusting as she was, she probably knew or had met everyone who passed this way. She might know something about the child they sought.

"Payment in advance," she told him when he shoved the empty tankard toward her. "No exceptions, not even for one as 'andsome as the likes o' you." With a wink and a leering grin that revealed two rows of rotted gums, she reached across the bar with a grubby hand and affectionately squeezed his arm.

Even though it was risky business in such a disreputable place, he tossed a gold coin down onto the bar. It immediately drew the attention of anyone within sight and set him up as an easy target for every low-life thief and murdering jackal, but it also sent the message that there might be more where that came from if they had what he wanted. Mab's eyes lit up like twin torches at sight of the gold.

"There's few in these parts have that sort of coin," she remarked, her tongue stroking hungrily over her lips. "Yer could buy yerself a lot with that."

"What I would like," he went through the list, "is food that hasn't been cooking in the pot for the past week, this tankard kept full of ale, a hot bath that twenty others haven't already pissed in, a clean bed for the night, and some tender young girl to warm it for me."

Mab's eyes gleamed. Her grin widened, revealing nothing but stumps and gaps where teeth had once been. She slapped his arm. "What would you be wantin' with some young piece? Ain't I good enough for ya?"

To prove her point, she scooped a huge, pendulous breast in a large, grubby hand and flopped it out for his approval. It was not a pleasant possibility. She winked at him.

"Yer won't find no better 'an this."

"Ah, Mab," he winked at her, fighting back equal amounts

of incredulity and amusement, "I don't think I'm up to the likes of you. I need something a bit tamer."

She snorted. "Ya do look a bit on the lean side." She leaned over the bar, as if sharing a secret. "Ya might find it a bit difficult to keep up." Then added thoughtfully, "There is the girl, o' course."

With a jerk of her head toward the end of the trestle table where drinks were served, she indicated a young girl who dodged the unwanted attentions of a customer who was pawing at her.

"She could use some meat on 'er bones," Mab said, obviously thinking he would find that less appealing than what she had offered. "But if you like that kind, I could send 'er up to the room at the top o' the stairs."

Tristan was inclined to think the girl could use more than a little meat on her bones. She was painfully thin, but that was the least of her problems. She had pale gold hair that swept forward and half-concealed her features. What he could see of those features was badly bruised, no doubt from the last patron who had preferred something other than Mab. There was also an ugly bruise on her shoulder, exposed where the sleeve of her gown was torn and gaped open.

She looked to be no more than a child and he wondered what misfortune had brought her to this place, for it was obvious that no one in the tavern could claim even the most distant relationship to the girl.

"What is her name?" Tristan asked, as a thought surfaced. The girl was close to the same age as the one they sought.

"Calls herself Kari."

"How did she come to be here?"

She shrugged. "Garidor found her in the village. She had no people, no place to go, no food, and hardly no clothes."

"We took her in, cleaned her up, and gave her a job," Mab said, as if it was something to be proud of.

"That was most generous of you."

"Like 'er, do ya?" Mab asked with a sly smile, and added, "It'll cost ya." She sent a glance in the direction of a pock-marked man who sat by the fire, "By the hour. Think you can go that long?"

Tristan had known men like Garidor all his life. They were crude little weasels and what they didn't have in size they made up for in cruelty. It explained the bruises on the girl's face.

He had no desire to bed her, but he did want to talk to her. If she'd lived on the streets in the village, she might know something about the girl they were looking for. He laid another coin down on the table.

"Have her bring the food up to the room."

Mab seized the coin with a grubby hand and grinned ear to ear. "Fer this, you can have her the entire night."

Grendel's attention was fastened on the game of stones and the boy who played with such skill and cunning that only one of equal skill would recognize or appreciate.

It was difficult to tell the lad's age or even discern his features for the layers of clothing he wore, which looked as if they might be cast-offs by the way they hung on his body. The hood of his tunic was worn low over his face. Occasionally the light from a torch fell across the lower part of his face, revealing a smooth, dirt-smudged face that had not yet felt the edge of a razor.

The only other visible features were the lad's hands. Beneath more grime and dirt they were slender and fine-boned, rolling the stones with a lightning quick flick of the wrist once the bets were laid down.

At first the boy won only a few more games than he lost, but the bets won in those games were substantially higher. As the evening went on and more ale was consumed, the boy's winnings improved. Grendel began to suspect it had not so much to do with with luck or skill as it did cunning.

The stones continuously rolled across the top of the barrel, hitting the rim with a rhythmic sound and delivering his opponents to their fate with an ease that was beautiful to watch.

When an opponent had bet and lost his last coin his place was taken by another eager to lose his valuable possessions. As another place opened up, another patron pushed his way through the crowd that had gathered around the barrel. Grendel recognized him as the one he'd encountered at the entrance of the inn. He angled a look up and in the light of a nearby torch saw the pale, gleaming scar that ran the length of the man's face from the corner of his eye to his jaw. It was a gruesome sight.

When no place was available, *Scar* made one and threw down a fistful of the dull metal coins he'd received for the skins he brought in. No one challenged him. In fact, several others vacated their places.

"Let's see if you can beat me, boy," Scar challenged.

Take great care with this one, Grendel cautioned, sending the boy his thoughts. *He didn't get that mark for filching pies from someone's kitchen.*

The boy's head angled as he caught the warning, uncertain where it had come from. A smile played at the corners of the boy's mouth, half hidden in the shadow of the voluminous hood that concealed the rest of his features. It was a smile of pure, complete confidence. As another patron left to spend the last of his coins on a tankard of ale in which to drown his sorrows, the gnome edged closer. Bets were placed and the game began.

The boy played with that same skill and confidence he'd shown before, refusing to be intimidated by Scar. After all, stones was a game of luck. They were rolled and fell as they may; there was nothing anyone could do about it. Unless, of course, the stones were weighted.

Grendel was an experienced player. He'd met all kinds, including those who gave themselves the added advantage of metal embedded in the core of the stones. The heavy metal made the stones roll with the opposite side up. When the roll could be controlled in such a way, bets were heavily padded.

At first he thought the boy played with weighted stones, so great was his skill and the number of games he won. But as he watched he discovered there was no pattern to the combinations of numbers that won. No sides of the stones that constantly rolled face up.

He continued to watch the boy play—every roll of the stones, the way he rolled them—and could discern no logical reason for such good fortune. Neither could *Scar*.

At first he'd won several games. The coins piled up before him. But then his luck changed. He was losing, and he didn't like it.

Be careful, Grendel silently warned the boy. But he played as before, with surprising skill and luck. He took one bet after another from the arrogant Scar, who became sullen and dangerously quiet, downing tankards of ale while he watched his pile of coins steadily disappear.

It grew quiet in the inn as everyone watched the game. Most others had already lost their money to the boy, or a good portion of it. Then Scar slammed his tankard down on the barrel-head, the contents sloshing over onto the stones.

"No one has that kind of luck!" he snarled. "I say you cheat."

The tip of the boy's hood lifted slowly. From the shadows that concealed most of his face, Grendel could almost imagine the defiant stare that looked back at the filthy, foul-smelling Scar.

By the expressions of those who stood nearby, it was obvious they thought the same.

The boy shoved the stones across the top of the barrel toward his accuser. "You roll the stones," he told Scar. "Then no one can say that I have cheated."

Scar picked up the stones and rolled them around in his

hand. Several others returned to the game and laid down their bets. They bet against the boy, certain that *Scar* could not lose.

With great confidence, he rolled the stones across the top of the barrel. They skidded across the surface and came to a rest against the rim. Those who watched stared in disbelief. Several moved away, perhaps seeking a place of safety. Scar had rolled the stones himself and lost.

Grendel had watched it himself and could not believe it. It seemed the stones had a mind of their own. In fact, one had rolled against the rim and teetered on one edge. Then, as if nudged by an invisible hand, it rolled back onto its flat side, completely changing the outcome. By the unwritten rules of stones, the score wasn't final until all three stones rested on flat sides.

Scar was furious. A huge fist slammed down onto the top of the barrel, rattling the stones and a fair amount of teeth of those who stood nearby.

"You cheated!" he accused with a thunderous roar that drew the attention of everyone in the inn, including Mab and the drunken, lecherous Garidor.

A little fear might have been wise, but the boy wasn't in the least intimidated.

"You threw the stones yourself," he reminded Scar.

Scar leaned over the barrel, and Grendel was genuinely concerned for the lad.

"That was a full season's work. I lost everything. Now I have nothing left for the winter."

The boy gathered all the coins before him. "Another wager, then?" he proposed.

Was the boy mad? Grendel wondered. Scar had nothing to wager with.

"A chance to win back what you've just lost on another roll of the stones," the boy offered.

It was more than generous. But Scar was not the sort who wanted part of anything.

"I could simply take it all from you, boy!" he snarled. "Who is there to stop me?"

Garidor pushed his way through the crowd that had gathered, the dutiful, mountainous Ox following in his wake. He glanced down at the coins the boy had won. He shoved a tankard of ale at Scar, who took it, downed the contents in one gulp, and slammed the empty tankard down on top of the barrel.

"It seems a fair offer," Garidor said. "The chance to win back half of what you lost." A deadly grin spread across his face. "Then Ox won't be forced to smash in yer head."

Like the creature he'd been named for, Ox stood like an immovable force beside Garidor. At mention of his name he smiled, an affable expression that had all who stood nearby scrambling for cover. Grendel was swept along with them, helpless to do anything but watch. Obviously Ox had a certain reputation that not even Scar was willing to challenge.

He was not pleased, but neither was he stupid. He nodded. Coins were counted out and the wager made. Garidor handed the stones to Scar, who took them and rattled them ominously in his large hand. Even Mab joined those gathered about, a hand resting on the large shelf of her hip. Scar rolled the stones.

Everyone seemed to be holding their breath, dreading the outcome. The stones slammed against the rim of the barrel and then tumbled backwards. One teetered precariously, then fell over onto its side. There was nothing but silence in the inn as everyone strained to see the outcome. A few slipped out of the tavern, while other enterprising souls filled their tankards from those that had been abandoned. There was a sudden sigh of relief. Scar had won.

"Step this way," Mab said, pounding Scar on the back. "I'll fill that tankard. And it won't even cost ya."

Scar had won back half his money and a tankard of ale, and he'd live to wager other games. With a disgruntled sound, he collected his winnings, stuffed them into the pouch that hung at his belt, and followed Mab and that offer of ale. Ox followed along like a dutiful shadow. But Garidor remained behind.

"Half," Garidor demanded.

As the crowd dispersed to find their drinks, Grendel watched as the boy poured out the contents of his pouch and portioned off half to Garidor. That explained Garidor's interest in the outcome of the game.

If there'd been a brawl everything might easily have been lost in the straw and dirt on the floor, grabbed by whoever could find it. But if Scar was appeased with a portion—what man wouldn't be, after losing everything—then a brawl was avoided. And Garidor collected a portion by prior arrangement with the boy.

It was not an uncommon practice. By sharing a portion the boy was allowed to run the game without fear of reprisal from unhappy patrons, and both went away with their pockets heavier. Especially if the boy was able to control the roll of the stones and the outcome, though Grendel had not yet figured out how he accomplished it.

What wasn't explained was the amount the boy had emptied from the pouch. Grendel had kept track of the boy's winnings the past hour, including what he'd won off Scar. The amount he portioned off to Garidor was far less than half his winnings for the last hour, much less the entire evening. His respect for the boy deepened, though it was a dangerous game he played—this game with Garidor. And where was the rest of the money if not in the pouch?

As the crowd thinned, Grendel cautiously moved closer and laid a metal coin on top of the barrel. The best way to learn how the boy did it was to play a game.

From the shadows of the hood that all but concealed his grubby features, the boy looked up. Grendel expected him to refuse to play with one of the little people. But to his credit the boy did not refuse. Instead, he picked up the stones and rolled them in his slender hands.

"That was very brave," Grendel commented, watching the boy's hands to see if there was any substitution of stones made. That might explain the unusual outcome of the games the boy had rolled through the evening.

"He was very stupid," the boy commented. "It is easy to win when people behave stupidly. He deserved to lose."

Wise words for one so young. His features were so obscured by shadows, dirt, and the layers of clothes that he seemed to hide himself in, not to mention the meager light within the tavern, that it was impossible to determine his age.

"Ah, but you would have lost far more had he not won back a portion of his money with that last roll of the stones," Grendel reasoned. "He is a very disagreeable fellow."

"I do not like to lose," the boy replied. "And I would not have if Garidor had not interfered."

"Confidence is an admirable quality. It is good to have confidence. It can make all things possible," Grendel replied. "With a little good fortune."

"Good fortune?" The expression on the boy's mouth was slightly bemused.

Grendel shrugged. "There are many who believe in luck."

Again there was that bemused smile. "Very well, little man. If that is what you wish to believe."

Grendel's eyes narrowed on a suspicious thought that had nagged him from the beginning as he watched the boy play.

Was it possible that the boy was able to control the outcome of the game?

The gnome watched every roll of the stones as the game progressed. The wins and losses were evenly balanced. He could determine nothing that might have influenced the outcome earlier. Then he scooped up the stones.

The boy gave nothing away either by expression or gesture, but instead inclined his head slightly in acknowledgment. Grendel rolled the dice, and when one tilted against the rim of the barrel nudged it over with a powerful mind-thought that tumbled the stone over onto its other side and altered the outcome.

It was not for the money. Such things had no meaning or value for Grendel. He was curious to see what the boy's reaction would be. He rolled several more times, losing his meager winnings as he let the game continue. Eventually, all the coins were gone.

The boy watched with cool detachment. But beneath it Grendel sensed fascination and a growing curiosity. Then, with lightning-quick reflexes, the boy snatched the stones back.

"No coins, no game," the boy told him.

It had been a game of sport, for Grendel had nothing more to wager.

He shrugged, turning his pockets inside out. "I have nothing of value." Then, on a sudden thought, he took the crystal rune from the pouch at his belt.

"Only this."

He laid the slender crystal with the ancient markings etched down the length upon the top of the barrel. The boy's hands suddenly went very still.

The game was momentarily forgotten as the boy reached out and tentatively touched the gleaming crystal that seemed to reflect the light from a nearby torch. He jerked his hand back.

"Surely it is worth at least one game," Grendel said.

"And if you lose?" the boy asked.

Grendel smiled with supreme confidence in his own skills. "If I lose, then the crystal is yours. But if I should win . . . ?" he added suggestively.

The boy shoved three coins toward him that he'd taken from Scar. The gnome shook his head.

"The crystal is worth more than that."

"Perhaps to you," the boy reasoned. "But 'tis worth nothing to me."

"It is a magic crystal," Grendel informed him with a secretive smile. "See how it glows."

" 'Tis only a reflection.''

"It glows in the dark, like a lantern, to show the way."

The boy looked down at the crystal skeptically. "How do I know you are telling the truth?"

By the Maker! the boy tried his patience. Grendel seized the crystal. Covering it with his other hand, he gave the boy a glimpse of the glow that still remained. The boy added three more coins to the others.

"Ten," Grendel demanded. "No less."

The boy made a sound that might have been frustration or a curse as he shoved four more coins across the top of the barrel. Grendel smiled.

"Now we can play."

The game that followed was fast and furious. Grendel took the first round only by the luck of the Ancient Ones, thereby saving the crystal and winning the small stack of coins. The boy won the next two rounds. By the third round, Grendel knew he was in trouble.

Keflech! but the boy was good. He was better than good. Grendel had never seen anyone, mortal or otherwise, who could match the boy for skill. There were times he sensed that it was almost more than skill. And the times he won, he had the nagging feeling the boy let him win. The boy faltered only once, and then when his concentration was suddenly broken.

Grendel followed his line of sight to the bottom of the stairs, where Mab spoke with a pale-haired girl. She was young and slender, almost painfully so, with a vicious, ugly bruise on one cheek. She dutifully nodded her head, took the trencher of food Mab handed her, then slowly started up the stairs.

The boy stared after her. It took no special gift to realize the girl's lowly status. For the cost of a few coins she was there to please the customers. No doubt that was the reason she'd been sent upstairs. The boy shoved the stones toward him.

"You cannot leave," Grendel protested. "What about the

game?'' There were several who had gathered about, eager to play now that Scar was gone.

''You may play. Whatever you win, you may keep,'' the boy announced. ''The split with Garidor is the same.'' Then the boy made the announcement to those who had gathered about to try their luck with his *apprentice* who would be rolling the stones for the next game.

Before Grendel could protest further, the boy slipped into the shadows and disappeared, and Grendel was staring up at Scar.

The gnome hastily gathered up the carved stones and tried to escape. He was stopped by a big meaty hand that halted any further retreat.

''I really must be going,'' Grendel told him in a quivering voice.

''I don't like little people,'' Scar informed him.

Grendel swallowed hard. ''All the more reason why I should leave.'' And found himself picked up by the scruff of his neck.

''I intend to win back everything I lost.''

Scar had too many tankards of false courage than was safe to argue with.

''Are you good with the stones?''

Grendel was indignant, but dangling off the ground by several feet was not the best position in which to attempt to take a stand.

''The boy is far better,'' he truthfully admitted.

''Good,'' Scar replied, obviously satisfied with his answer. ''Roll the stones, little man.''

Grendel had no choice. As he rolled the stones he couldn't help but think of Tristan, that trencher of warm food, and a warm bed. It was going to be a long night.

The *boy* kept to the shadows as he crossed the inn, his gaze fastened on Garidor. He had the manners of a boar and the cunning of a fox. If he was seen there would be trouble, for above all else Garidor valued the portion he made each night off the winnings at stones and cups. There would be trouble if he discovered that another rolled the stones in his place.

Garidor thought of himself as a businessman with various enterprises, all for the purpose of bringing him more wealth. The inn was one enterprise that provided food and ale at an exorbitant price to those who traveled the north country and the river.

Furs and trinkets were traded or bartered. The back room of the inn was filled with a sizable bounty of items that Garidor and Mab collected.

The girl, Kari, was also one of Garidor's *enterprises*. She'd been orphaned just as the boy had, taken off the streets by Garidor and promised food, lodging, and a coin now and then in exchange for work. But she was young, pretty, and innocent compared to Mab, whom he doubted was ever any of those. With no one to turn too and only the clothes on her back, Kari did what she had to in order to survive.

Garidor took her the first time in the storeroom behind the barrels of ale. She was terrified, with no knowledge of what to expect. It was brutal and degrading. She bled for days afterward. Eventually the bruises went away, to be replaced by others. Those were the physical marks he gave her. There were others that never went away, glimpsed in her eyes and heard in her tears late at night.

She wanted to die, but the *boy* convinced her that she must not. He promised that he would take her away from there when he had enough money. And it was a promise that would be kept, but they needed money.

After that first time, whenever Garidor wanted her, she was told to meet him upstairs. When she wasn't upstairs with Garidor, she was expected to make money from those who frequented the inn. She never received any coin for it; Garidor saw to that. She was told she was lucky to have the clothes on her back and a warm meal once a day.

Mab didn't seem to care what Garidor did. But she didn't

want any more mouths to feed. It was only a matter of time before Kari discovered she was with child. Perhaps it was a blessing for both that she lost the child. After that Mab made certain the girl knew the precautions to be taken to prevent it happening again. It was the one kindness she ever showed the girl.

The boy's skill at gaming was another of Garidor's *enterprises*. He'd found the boy in the village, after a noticeable decline in business. Many of his customers were spending their coins or trading their goods for a chance at cup and stones, their pockets almost empty by the time they found their way to his inn.

With Ox at his side, Garidor proposed a partnership—he would provide a corner in the inn where the boy could safely ply his trade in exchange for a portion of the boy's earnings each night. The unspoken had been that if he did not accept Garidor's offer, he wouldn't live to see another day.

The boy wasn't afraid of him. He'd seen his kind too many times before to be afraid. Garidor was greedy, slovenly, and cruel. But the boy was wise enough to know that what was paid to Garidor each night was a pittance compared to what could be made for himself in such a place. And when it was time to terminate the partnership, the boy would simply move on. And take Kari with him.

He reached the stairs and with a skill learned from living in the shadows, slipped upstairs unnoticed.

There were two rooms on the second floor of the inn. Garidor and Mab shared the larger room at the end of the narrow hall. A smaller second room was tucked beneath the eaves of the gabled, thatched roof.

For a price either room could be had for a night's lodging, since Mab more often than not fell asleep downstairs by the fire and Garidor fell asleep over his ale. Kari often slept in the smaller room, where she barricaded the door against Garidor's nightly wanderings.

On nights when both rooms were occupied, she slept in the storeroom with the boy. It was then they made their plans to leave when the boy had hoarded enough money from his winnings.

Tonight the smaller room was occupied by the tall, lean stranger who carried that unusual knife and the sword wrapped in leather. And Kari had been sent to him.

The stranger had consumed several tankards of ale. He had been most amiable by the time he sought the stairs, and the hot water he'd ordered for a bath would add to his lethargy. With any luck he was in a drunken stupor and Kari could make her escape unharmed. If not . . .

The boy's hand closed over the handle of the knife as he eased it from the top of his boot. Then they would be forced to leave the inn that night.

The door to the room was ajar. The boy toed it open with his boot. Steam rose from the tub of water on the chilled air. Light from oil lamps quivered across the wall. The boy heard the sound of water splashing and the stranger's voice as he called to Kari

"Come here, girl. And bring more water. It will take every bucketful to rid me of this filth and stench."

The boy toed the door open farther and caught a glimpse of the wooden tub used for bathing, the wet floor where water had sloshed over the edge, and Kari. She stood just behind the stranger, who was chest deep in the tub.

His head rested on the back rim of the huge half barrel, the thick mane of dark hair spilling wetly over the edge, his eyes closed above the shadow of dark beard. His arms were splayed along the sides of the barrel, the rest of him submerged in the murky water.

The boy stepped just inside the door on soft leather soles. Kari looked up with a startled glance, no doubt expecting to find Garidor lurking in the doorway. The boy pressed a finger against his lips, warning her to silence.

"Where is that hot water?" the stranger demanded.

"Right away, sir," Kari hastily replied, and poured the bucket of water into the tub.

The stranger sighed, his mouth curving in a smile of pleasure. "Bring the cloth. I have dirt in places I didn't know existed."

Kari looked over at the boy with rising panic. Her face was ashen and her hands trembled violently. She was terrified to be so close to a man after the things Garidor had done to her. But if she refused, the stranger would complain and it would go badly for her. After all, she'd been paid for.

The boy motioned Kari away from the stranger, then picked up the cloth and slowly approached the tub.

"And some of that lye soap your mistress sent up," Tristan added, eyes still closed. "It's worth losing a little of my skin to be rid of this filth."

"Yes, sir." Kari's voice trembled as she exchanged worried glances with the boy. He seized the cake of strong lye soap and the cloth and was about to toss both into the water.

"Give a hand, girl," Tristan said. "This water is getting cold and I've no desire to freeze my arse off. Or anything else, for that matter." His mouth curved in a teasing smile, knowing she was standing right behind him. "I wouldn't want to deprive you."

She made a small strangled sound, confirming his first suspicion that she was not accustomed to seeing a man at his bath, since the company she was forced to keep obviously was not the sort who bathed with any sort of frequency.

The boy angled a glance at the man's tunic and pants, thrown over the chair. He'd seen the glint of gold the man had given Mab. There might be more. It would offset his losses at stones that evening, as well as his decision that they must leave that very night. He nodded a look at the stranger's clothes and Kari moved toward them.

"Lather up that cloth, girl," the stranger said. "And be quick about it. I'm ready for my bath."

The boy realized the stranger intended for Kari to bathe him. He glanced over at her. He had to give her time to search the stranger's clothes for the gold. Clamping his teeth tightly together, he began to lather the cloth with the lye soap.

"Don't be shy now," Tristan coaxed, sensing the girl's hesitation. She was such a timid little thing. He had no intention of bedding her, but a bath couldn't hurt. Then he would send her on her way with several coins she needn't tell the hag about.

The girl began to wash his shoulder in hesitant, circular motions, but ventured no farther. At this rate he would have a very clean shoulder and little else.

"You can do better than that," he told her, one corner of his mouth curving upward at her obvious dilemma. He seized her by a slender wrist and forced her hand lower as he added with a wolfish grin, "I promise not to bite. At least not very hard. And you might like it."

Slippery as an eel, the boy escaped the stranger's grasp. With his other hand he gave a firm shove, sending the man beneath the surface of the water.

When Tristan surfaced amid much thrashing of arms and legs, and sputtered curses, he confronted not the timid girl, but the menacing glint of a blade leveled at his throat.

"Not bloody likely!" the boy hissed.

CHAPTER FIVE

Tristan stared down the length of that lethal blade into the feral blue gaze that peered back at him from the concealment of the hood his assailant wore.

His own gaze narrowed. He recognized the overlarge tunic worn over layers of clothes and belted at the waist with a length of rope, the too-long leggings stuffed into the tops of slender boots, and the hands that had exhibited such amazing speed and dexterity at the gaming table.

His assailant was the boy he'd seen earlier who gambled with remarkable cunning and skill for one so young, relieving the inn's patrons of their coins, and now relieving him of the pleasure of his bath and quite possibly a great deal more if he had his way.

Hell fire and damnation, he thought, as he laid his head back on the rim of the tub. The steam that rose from the water still smelled vaguely of the potent brew it had once contained. No doubt he would smell the same if he was allowed to continue his bath. Which at the moment was in serious question.

"It has been weeks since I bathed in anything other than a cold river or stream," he began almost conversationally, head still tilted back against the rim, eyes closed. He sighed.

"The last hot meal I enjoyed was a month ago." His head slowly came up, his eyes slowly opened, his dark golden gaze slicing past the blade and fastening on the boy.

"I cannot remember the last time I slept on anything other than the cold, hard ground." There was something equally cold and hard in his voice.

"This is no child's game." He gestured to the knife. "Someone could get hurt. Go back to your mama. No doubt she is looking for you."

The boy snorted. "Aye, someone could get hurt," he said, obviously amused. Then his voice hardened. The blue gaze narrowed, like twin blue daggers from the shadows of the hood that concealed his other features.

"But there's no need to concern yourself with my mother; she hasn't concerned herself with me since the day I was born."

The words were laced with loathing and contempt. He'd struck deep an old wound without even drawing a blade, a wound far too deep and old for one so young. And somewhere wrapped within the loathing and contempt, he knew was a longing for the mother and family that had been lost, whatever the circumstances. It was something Tristan understood all too well. A boy needed his family. After the loss of his own family, he'd been fortunate enough to find another that gave him kindness, love, and nurturing when he needed it most. But what of this boy's fate?

There were scores of children like him, orphaned by war and poverty, even in these times of peace and prosperity since Arthur became king. They saw them as they rode north, living at the edges of towns, villages, and hamlets. Like this boy, they lived as they could, begging, scavenging, and stealing to survive. Just as this boy was intent on stealing from him.

The boy's gaze darted to the pouch that lay among his clothes in silent communication to the girl. The girl seized the pouch from among his clothes and stuffed it into the pocket at the front of her skirt. The boy then waived her back a safe distance.

"There are places," Tristan commented, "the first time a thief is caught he loses a hand. If he's caught stealing a second time, he loses the other hand."

"Only if one is caught," the boy replied with far too much confidence.

"Aye," Tristan grimly acknowledged. "Only if one is caught." He suddenly lunged out of the water.

The boy had not expected it. Tristan could see that in the stunned expression on his face. But he quickly recovered and using those lightning-quick reflexes Tristan had seen at the gaming table, sidestepped and thrust with the knife, slicing Tristan across the chest.

He wasn't certain who was more surprised, himself, the girl Kari, who squealed at the sight of a naked man, or the boy, whose eyes were round as gourds.

The wound wasn't deep; he'd received much worse in the practice yards at Camelot during mock battle with Arthur's other knights. It was more aggravating than anything, to be bested by a mere boy, not to mention the fact that it was cold in the chamber and he was naked and dripping wet.

The rounded eyes narrowed as they scanned the length of him with an avid interest that had his stomach tightening.

"Make another move and I'll slice off something vital," the boy threatened, his gaze aimed just below Tristan's midsection.

"By God, that is enough!" Tristan swore, and in a move that was far more experienced and quicker, stunned the knife from the boy's fingers, clamped a hand around a slender wrist, then doubled it behind the boy's back, and hauled him off his feet, his other hand clamped around his throat.

The boy's head snapped back so hard that the hood spilled to his shoulders, revealing a startled expression amid smudged features and a mass of thick golden hair that tumbled down the boy's back.

Kari shrieked in dismay. "Yer no boy! Yer a girl!"

Tristan stared in disbelief at the smudged features framed by the mass of radiant golden hair, like a brilliant yellow flame, that swirled around the boy's shoulders.

Impossible! But it wasn't impossible. Not when he got a good look at the *boy's* features in the light of the oil lamps. They were far too delicate: the angle of high cheekbones, the slender nose above a well-curved mouth, the delicate angle of that small chin that was presently thrust out in defiance, and the anger in searing blue eyes the color of the heart of a flame. Not to mention the soft curves felt through all those layers of concealment as he held her against him.

She was spitting mad in spite of the arm pinned behind her back and his hand clamped at her throat. But along with the anger and defiance was an equal measure of surprise.

Caught, trussed, helpless. Not feelings that she liked. It made her vulnerable. And she'd vowed never to be vulnerable again. Not to mention her indignation at being wrestled and then pinned against a naked man.

Her fingers itched to feel the cool reassurance of the knife in her hand. But he'd efficiently relieved her of it. It lay on the floor several feet away and was of no use to her. Nor could she count on Kari for any help there. The poor girl was struck dumb at the sight of her, so complete had her disguise been that no one, not even the girl she'd befriended, had any sense that she was anything other than what she wanted them to believe.

But if surviving on her own all these years had taught her anything, it had taught her to be resourceful. And she was a survivor.

Her hands were of no use to her pinned behind her back. The harder she struggled, the tighter he held her. So, instead of fighting to get away, she attacked, sinking her teeth into his shoulder.

The taste was startling, that combination of strong lye soap, the faint metallic taste as she drew blood, and something else that lingered on her tongue.

She quickly recovered as he yelped with pain and surprise, and as his grasp momentarily loosened she brought her knee up hard.

It was a glancing blow but it was enough to loosen his hold completely.

Slippery as an eel, she dropped to the floor and scrambled for the knife. He cursed the air blue, the only words he was able to manage between lips curled back in a snarl of pain and fury.

She might have made it if her aim had been better. Instead, like a wounded animal, he was still alive and even more dangerous.

She felt his hand at the neck of her tunic. Then she was spun around and shoved against the wall of the chamber.

"Make one move and I'll separate your head from your shoulders."

She was out of breath, humiliated, and furious. But she was not foolish. She swept the thick tangle of hair back from her eyes and suddenly went very still as she stared down the length of a deadly, gleaming sword.

Blood beaded along the neatly sliced wound she'd opened at one shoulder. A perfect set of tiny teeth marks had drawn blood at his other shoulder. Her gaze wandered lower as she contemplated the next wound. Then immediately retreated back to the safer territory of his face.

Yes, she thought with growing certainty, aware of the heat that flared at her cheeks. A nice mark across a cheek would alter that smug, handsome expression. Or perhaps a smile . . . slit from ear to ear!

She would have to think how best to accomplish that at a

more opportune moment, when there wasn't the tip of a sword pressing against her own throat.

"Keflech!" Grendel exclaimed from the doorway as he stared at the disheveled chamber. "What happened?"

The chamber was a mess. Considering the overall condition of the establishment, it was remarkable that anything could be considered worse.

A small table was overturned, the tankard and trencher of food scattered across the floor along with their contents. A chair had been knocked over backwards too near a small brazier. The chair hit the brazier as it went over, sending a stream of molten embers across the wood flooring covered with straw.

Disaster had been averted as water from Tristan's bath washed over the edges of the tub and doused the small fires that had erupted in the straw.

Here and there small fires smoldered in the damp straw. The air was filled with the stench of strong lye soap, burnt straw, and the acrid smell of singed wool. The boy he'd followed up those stairs was nowhere in sight.

Kari cringed in the corner, none the worse for wear except for the blackened eye and swollen cheek she'd sported earlier. But the most intriguing sight of all was the warrior Tristan de Marc.

He was naked as the day he was born, one foot still firmly planted in his bath, the other firmly planted on the bare floor, straddling the edge of the low barrel between.

His height was even more impressive without the thick padding of tunic, vest, and leggings. And lean muscles flexed and bunched across his shoulders and at his arms as he held the broadsword angled overhead, poised to strike. His wet hair lay plastered to his head and shoulders, the muscles of his clean-shaven jaw were tightly clenched, blood was smeared across one shoulder at a neat wound, and the expression in his eyes was cold as death.

Even naked, when most mortals would have felt their most

vulnerable, he was a formidable sight. He seemed completely oblivious to his nakedness as he stood with the battle sword leveled at the young girl sprawled on the floor amid the smoldering straw, overturned furnishings, and spilled food.

Her chest rose and fell with each breath she dragged into her lungs. Tangled hair spilled forward and framed vivid, flushed features, brilliant blue eyes gleaming with defiance. But where was the boy?

Grendel had followed him up those stairs. This was the only place he could be. His sharp gaze returned to the furious, defiant girl. He scrutinized the clothes, the angle of her head, the slender smudged hands that groped for the blade that lay several feet away.

The clothes were the same. As were the slender hands. He had seen those hands swift as lightning at the gaming table. And the angle of the head was equally familiar. Had he not seen it angled just so as his opponent concentrated on cups and stones?

Impossible, the mortal instincts he'd acquired told him. This could not be the boy. But the evidence was there, the rest easily enough hidden beneath those layers of clothes belted about a thick waist that was inconsistent with the slender hands and equally slender legs.

It was deception, as clearly as any he'd conjured himself, including the body he presently occupied. But why disguise herself?

The answer came to him in the next thought. Beneath the filth and layers of soiled clothes the girl was no doubt comely enough. The evidence was there in the tumble of shimmering golden hair that fell about her shoulders and the delicate features beneath the dirt. Like Kari, she was alone, with no one to protect her, for he had seen no other with her in the inn.

It was not safe for a young girl to be alone in a place such as this. Even Dannelore and John had not been safe. Then something more slipped across his senses in the old way; almost unrecognized, so long had it been since he had felt it. Like something forgotten and at long last remembered. It was recognition of a kindred spirit.

"Keep your eye on the other one," Tristan muttered. "Thieves the both of them, and in it together. This one tried to cut out my heart."

"I was aiming for your throat!" the girl hissed back at him.

"Then you shall have to practice more."

"Gladly!"

Her fingers itched to feel the coolness of that knife in her hand. Grendel knew it as surely as he sensed her rage and the other emotions that were like an assault on his senses: the deep bond of friendship for the girl, Kari; the protectiveness this girl felt that was almost like that of a wild creature for its young, so fierce was it that he knew of a certainty that if she could reach that knife she would gladly risk her own life for the girl; and other emotions. The pain of great loss, bitter hatred, and a glimpse at the wounded child within. It was a brief glimpse, revealed as those other emotions battled within her. Then carefully hidden away beneath the cunning and fearlessness that had helped her survive.

"A lesson, I think," Tristan concluded as he angled the blade beneath her chin.

"Stop!" Grendel cried out, sensing he might very well carry out his threat. "You must not."

With a single thought, he concentrated his energy, and with outstretched hand, knocked the blade of the sword aside.

Furious, Tristan rounded on him. "What are you doing? She tried to kill me."

It was all she needed. Grendel sensed her thoughts, sensed the murderous rage that coursed through them as she lunged for the knife and drove back to her feet. The knife gleamed in her hand as she struck.

Tristan felt it as well with that warrior's sense of survival. He instinctively brought his sword arm up in a defensive move.

Instead of plunging the knife into his chest as she intended, the blade struck a glancing blow across his forearm. Tristan grabbed her by the wrist, jerking it back hard.

"Perhaps it would do you good to lose a finger or two," Tristan threatened, his face only inches from hers.

"Perhaps it would do you good to die!" she spat back as she beat at him with her other fist.

Once before Grendel had seen such fierce strength and courage in the face of overwhelming odds. Only once, these many years he had lived among the mortals.

The truth whispered to him. A truth of the ancient ways that moved through him, something glimpsed in that unmistakable courage . . . something glimpsed in those brilliant blue eyes.

"Stop! You must not! You don't understand!" But they didn't hear him.

Grendel saw the raised fist with that gleaming sword. He moved with surprising speed for one so small, terrified that Tristan would carry out his threat.

There was no time to transform, no conjurement quicker than the sword. The gnome launched himself from his meager height, hit the girl at the knees, and rolled her to the floor and out of harm's way.

"Damn! You little weasel!" Tristan exploded with anger. But the gnome paid no heed as he rolled with the girl.

The momentum rolled them in the direction of the knife that had been knocked to the floor. She was quick and agile and scrambled to retrieve it. But the gnome was quicker and not hampered by the need to use mortal strength or skill. And he had not as far to reach.

He went after her. But instead of fighting her for the knife, he clasped a hand around her arm.

The knife fell from her numbed fingers. The tingling sensation shot all the way up her arm. Then the little man touched the side of her neck. Warmth spread across her skin and through her blood. Darkness crowded at the edges of her vision. She tried to fight it, tried to hold on to the image of the warrior, but she could not. She felt herself falling. She tried to stop it but could not. Then there was only that enveloping darkness.

The girl slumped to the floor at Grendel's feet.

"What the devil are you doing?" Tristan demanded.

"Preventing you from suffering a more grievous injury," the gnome speculated.

"I had everything under control."

"I can see that," Grendel said, angling a glance at the various injuries the girl had inflicted.

"It would have done the little thief good to lose a finger or two for attempting to cut my throat. No doubt she cheats at gaming as well."

"Aye, she cheated," Grendel acknowledged, now certain exactly how she had done it and quite amazed that he had not realized it sooner.

"But it might not have gone well for you if you had sliced off a finger or two."

"What are you talking about?"

Tristan was in no mood for the little creature's games. His bath and supper were ruined, and his clothes were soaking wet. By the acrid stench in the chamber, the fire had burned more than just a few handfuls of straw, and the wounds at his shoulder and chest were beginning to throb, not to mention the further damage she'd inflicted with a well-aimed knee.

He thought fleetingly of Lady Alyce and wondered if he'd ever be able to please her again for the grinding ache in his groin that spiraled all the way up to his belly and had nausea backing up in his throat. He leveled the sword at the gnome.

"What are you *talking* about?" he demanded again through clenched teeth.

Grendel angled a glance down at the girl slumped on the floor. "I am talking about Meg's daughter."

CHAPTER SIX

"You're mad!" Tristan told the gnome. "That," he emphasized with the tip of his sword in the direction of the unconscious
girl, "is not Meg's daughter."

"I have not the time to argue with you," Grendel told him.
His head came up, and like a hound casting about for a scent,
he frowned.

"We must leave this place. Now." And with a glance at
Tristan, he said, "I suggest that you dress."

"My clothes are wet," Tristan pointed out. "And by the
stench in this room very likely burned as well."

Grendel shrugged as he bent over the motionless girl. "The
choice is yours, of course."

"You cannot be certain this is the girl."

A flicker of doubt crossed the gnome's face. He should have
sensed it sooner, yet he had not. Only when her emotions were
exposed and vulnerable had he sensed the truth. What did it
mean? Did she possess so little of her mother's powers that he
had not sensed them? Or was it something more?

"Where are her powers if she is Meg's daughter?" Tristan demanded, almost as if he could read the little man's thoughts.

"Why did she not know who we were? Can you answer that?"

"I cannot. But I *am* certain she is Meg's daughter." That much was true. "We are taking her with us."

"Just how do you propose to accomplish that, little man? Are you going to put her in your pocket?"

Grendel swore under his breath. "You are going to help me."

Tristan lowered the sword. "And if I refuse?"

"I could turn you into a toad, or a wort on the buttocks of that great hulking oaf they call Ox," Grendel threatened.

"That didn't work when I was a lad of ten years. It won't work now."

"Don't try my patience, boy!" Grendel warned.

A sound from the stairs drew their attention.

"It's Garidor!" Kari cried out. "He'll kill me for certain."

Grendel's eyes sharpened as his gaze met Tristan's. "What is it to be, then?" he demanded.

Tristan's gaze flickered to the terrified girl who cowered in the corner. She was Garidor's property. He would blame her for what had happened and she would be punished. From the look of her bruised face, she might not survive the next time.

He retrieved his clothes from the floor and ordered the girl, "Bar the door."

She hesitated, as if uncertain where the greater danger lay, in that chamber or with Garidor.

"Bar the door!" Tristan repeated. Her decision made the girl sprang to her feet and slammed the cross bar down across the door opening.

His pants and tunic were wet, the fleece vest slightly singed. Tristan quickly pulled on his boots and stuffed the pouch with the coins the girl had thought to steal into the front of the vest. Then he sheathed the sword in the leather scabbard at his back.

He picked up the knife from the floor and shoved it into his belt as he strode toward the window opening. With a look of regret at the soft bed against the wall, he threw open the shutters.

It was bitter cold outside. The drizzling rain had turned to sleet. There would be snow by morning. He made a sound of disgust at the thought of the warm brazier, a warm supper, and even an empty bed, which would have been far preferable to what waited for them beyond the inn.

It was a long drop to the ground below he thought with a vengence. He wondered if he was quick enough to simply thump the little man upside the head and pitch him out the window. It would be daylight and they would be miles from the inn before the gnome discovered what he'd done.

"I heard that," Grendel replied as if he'd spoken aloud, then informed him, "You're not quick enough. "Now help me tie these blankets together. It's a long drop to the ground."

They tied two threadbare blankets together, but still it was not enough. The girl, Kari, approached hesitantly. She removed the heavy woolen shawl from about her shoulders and handed it to Tristan.

"You'll have nothing to keep you warm," Tristan said gently, for if they used it there was no way of returning it to her.

"I'd rather be cold," she timidly replied. "Garidor gave it to me."

Tristan gently patted her shoulder and took the shawl. He knotted it onto the end of the blanket. She jumped as that pounding came again at the door.

Tristan tied one end of the blanket around the post at the window opening, then tossed the other end out the window.

"It will have to do." He nodded grimly to Grendel. "You go first. I'll lower the girl to you."

Grendel's eyes narrowed. "Make certain you do," he threatened.

Tristan made a dark comment as he slowly lowered the gnome to the ground below.

He made a sling of the shawl and slipped it over the unconscious girl's shoulders. She was no child, he thought, as his hands brushed the softness of a breast beneath the layers of clothing in which she'd disguised herself. And in spite of her filthy appearance, her hair was clean and smelled like the forest.

Dark gold lashes lay against her cheeks, concealing eyes that had glared at him with hatred. Her lips were softly parted, her breathing shallow, when only moments before she had sworn to kill him.

Was she Meg's daughter?

He found it impossible to believe, and yet the proof of it was there in the soft gold of her hair, the tilt of her small nose, and those remarkable eyes that had all but gleamed with blue fire. But the strong chin, the arch of her brows, and that reckless courage reminded him of someone else: the man who had found him more dead than alive beside his murdered parents. The man he thought of as father, brother, friend, and more. The man he'd sworn his life to.

He gently lowered her through the window opening as the pounding at the door changed to the distinctive sound of ax against wood. There wasn't much time. Soon Garidor would be through the door.

He scooped up the loaf of stale bread from the floor and swung his legs over the window ledge. With the bread firmly clamped between his teeth, he lowered himself hand over hand down the blanket rope.

"What of the girl Kari?" Grendel demanded as Tristan stuffed the loaf of bread into the front of his tunic. It was likely all the food they would have for the foreseeable future.

"You can't mean to leave her. You know what Garidor will do to her."

"Perhaps you would like to take along the old hag to cook for us," Tristan suggested through tight lips. "And what about the trapper? We could use someone like that! Why not announce to everyone in the inn that they may come along as well?"

Grendel sighed. He would never get used to mortals and their odd sense of humor, for surely the warrior was jesting with him.

"We cannot leave her," he said adamantly.

"We have two horses," Tristan pointed out. "How do you propose to travel if there are four of us?"

"You intended to purchase another horse when we found Meg's daughter." Grendel shrugged. "You will simply have to purchase two."

By the sounds that came from the chamber above, there was no more time to argue the matter. Grendel let out a soft, low whistle.

Kari appeared at the window above. He motioned for her to follow. She hesitated, then as the door gave way made her decision and scrambled over the ledge. It was a precarious journey to the ground. She lowered herself halfway, then dropped the rest of the way to the ground.

"You must come with us," Grendel told the girl as he untied the shawl from the rope and wrapped it about her shoulders. When she glanced uncertainly at the tall warrior, the gnome assured her, "It was his idea. He was most adamant about it."

They had tethered the horses in the shelter of nearby trees. They rode until they could go no farther, doubled up on the tired horses. Eventually the storm closed around them, and even Grendel's powers were of no use as the sleet turned to swirling snow that blinded his ability to see where others could not just as surely as it blinded the horses.

They eventually took shelter in a shepherd's hut they stumbled upon. It was small and the cold seeped through gaps in the sagging walls. But there was a roof overhead that kept out the snow and protected against the wind.

"What a wonderful smell!" Tristan commented as he calmed the black stallion, uneasy in such close quarters with the foul-smelling sheep.

"And to think I could have had a warm bed and hot meal at the inn."

"Aye," Grendel acknowledged as he tethered the exhausted palfrey. "And no doubt a knife in your back as well."

It was dark as a tomb inside the shed. Grendel rummaged around in the pouch he carried at his belt and found the crystal. He pressed it firmly between both hands and closed his eyes, concentrating his limited powers.

The crystal grew warm in his hands. When he opened them, the crystal glowed with a light that spread through the darkened hut.

"Ohhhh!" Kari exclaimed as she slipped from the back of the palfrey and cautiously edged closer to see.

"How did you do that?"

Grendel shrugged. He was not in the habit of revealing too many of his talents. It could prove dangerous, for there were those who were simpleminded and easily frightened by such things.

But there were times when necessity demanded his skills. This was one of those times. While he had no difficulty moving around in the dark, he didn't want to have to listen to Tristan's complaints or have that nasty black stallion stomping on him. And he sensed he had nothing to fear from Kari. She was a good-hearted girl who'd fallen into bad circumstances.

"It's a special crystal," he explained, not caring to get too technical about the source of his powers. "It catches the light and reflects it, like the surface of a pond on a summer day."

Tristan snorted as he tethered the Frisian. "He's really a gnome. He casts spells with foul-smelling concoctions and wild incantations."

Grendel glared at the warrior as a particular incantation came to mind at that precise moment, one used to silence noisy jackdaws. Kari looked at him warily and edged no closer.

"He is simpleminded," Grendel explained in a low voice, and touched a finger to his own head to indicate that Tristan was addlepated. "However, they make perfect warriors because they blindly follow orders with no thought of their own. Pay him no mind."

"And you are remarkably outspoken for one who is so short." Tristan eased the unconscious girl from the back of the Frisian and lowered her none too gently into the straw.

"Be careful, you oaf!" Grendel admonished. "Do not hurt her."

"By all means," Tristan replied. "She is such a delicate, fragile creature. Her mother and father will be so proud. If she is who you say she is."

"I tell you, she *is* Rianne," the gnome insisted. "I do not make mistakes about things like this."

"Why did you not realize it earlier?"

That same question had plagued Grendel through the long, cold hours since their escape from the inn. He had no answer though he was still adamant.

"She is Meg's daughter. You will see."

Tristan removed the saddle and harness from the Frisian and dropped them into the straw. With a faint smile, he warned Kari, "Do not make him angry. He has a foul temper. He's been known to change people into toads when they aggravate him."

Uncertain whether he told the truth or merely jested, she stepped farther away. Grendel glared at him. "I should have turned you into a toad."

He suspended the crystal from a peg on a nearby timber. It glowed softly throughout the hut, reflecting in the sleepy gazes of the sheep who huddled together for warmth.

The gnome bent over the unconscious girl. The extra layers of clothing she wore as a disguise had protected her against the cold, but her hands were near frozen. He frowned. The cold should not have affected her so. Was it possible he was wrong about her?

Her features were Meg's, but there was nothing else about

her that even hinted at the unique heritage to which she'd been born. He reminded himself that she was also part mortal as he made a bed for her of the straw on the floor of the hut.

She possessed heightened senses, of that he was certain. That would explain her extraordinary skill at the gaming table, far better than any mortal's. Far better than his own.

Indeed, it seemed she had sensed the outcome of each round and bet with ruthless cunning. Or perhaps she had manipulated the outcome. His eyes gleamed with pride. If it was so, then she was a child after his own heart.

He gently laid a hand against her cheek. He had not seen her since she was a babe. He mentally counted the years. A lifetime had passed since then in terms of time as mortals knew it. In truth she was not a child at all, but a young woman full grown.

What had happened to Dannelore and John? How long had she been on her own? What had happened to her in the time in between? And what did she know of the legacy she'd been born to?

He sensed the power within her, like a resting flame, tentative and uncertain. Yet it was there just the same. It reached out to him, connecting in a way that bound all creatures of their world together in unspoken thought.

Kari edged closer, and glanced uncertainly at the unconscious girl curled in the straw.

"Will *she* be all right?" she asked tentatively.

Grendel sensed that she wanted to draw closer, but she held back. Like himself, she was still trying to get used to the fact that the boy she had known was not a boy at all.

"Aye, she'll be well enough in the morning. But 'tis better to let her sleep for now." He looked up as Tristan approached and frowned as the warrior stepped past him and bent over the sleeping girl.

"What are you doing?"

Tristan took a length of leather and bound it around her wrists, tying them securely.

"I am taking precautions." He jerked the leather knot tight. She did not stir.

"Precautions against what?" Grendel demanded. "She cannot escape. I would know if she did."

"Precautions against a knife in my back," Tristan replied, tenderly rubbing the cut at his shoulder. "Even if she is Meg's daughter, you cannot be certain what she might do. You know nothing about her. And it's clear, she knows nothing about you." The gnome glared at him.

"And if you release her, I'll douse you with salt." Tristan threatened.

"That is nonsense!" the gnome replied. "Foolishness and old wives' tales. Salt cannot harm me any more than it can hurt you."

"Then perhaps a bit of dragon's horn mixed with bat blood," Tristan suggested.

Grendel blanched. "What do know you of such things?"

"Something Mistress Meg mentioned once. Something about the best remedy for quarrelsome gnomes."

"You're bluffing. And badly, I might add. 'Tis a good thing you are not a gambler, Sir Tristan."

"Ah, but I am a gambler."

Grendel snorted. "Where would you come by such things, even if it was true?"

"The old hag, Mab. It seems she had some knowledge of the black arts. It also seems she doesn't like gnomes."

"You lie," Grendel said with disgust. "I sensed nothing about the woman."

Tristan nodded. "There you see. She was so skilled in the arts that not even you were aware of her abilities." He frowned. "It's most disturbing to think what she might be capable of."

"Bah! You are a fool. True, the woman was most foul. But she possessed no powers."

Tristan stood. He shook his head as though deeply worried. "That is what she wished you to believe." And concealing a grin, he spread his blanket in the straw some distance away while the gnome muttered to himself.

"I am plagued by half-wits and practical jokers. Why could the mistress not send a true, brave knight on this journey? But no, she sends a reckless fool who thinks more of pleasure than duty. Dragon's horn and bat's blood? Bah! Everyone knows dragons do not have horns."

He bent over the unconscious girl and tucked his blanket around her shoulders. And then, not at all typical for a creature of his world, offered a silent prayer for what was to come in the morning.

Rianne dreamed old dreams; of places she had seen and others she had not; faces of people she could not remember; and a voice that called to her from the mist. She dreamed of fire, blood, and death. She saw herself within the flames. She saw the dead lying all around her. She felt a sudden warmth at her hands. When she looked down, they were covered with blood.

"You cannot escape," the voice whispered in her dreams. *"Destiny awaits."*

It was always the same. She held her hands before her as the words reached out to her through the mist. Blood spilled through her fingers. She thought she must have injured herself, but there was no pain. There was only that voice and the blood that slowly disappeared until all that remained was a single drop of blood. She stared at it as it slowly transformed into a smoothly polished stone set in a large ring at her finger. And as she stared at it she became aware of the image of someone walking toward her through the mist.

It was a man, and yet it was not. He was tall, with long, flowing dark hair, and then the mist swirled around him and he seemed to disappear. Then it shifted once more and he was much closer. So close she could see his eyes.

They were brilliant blue like the heart of a flame, and seemed to look deep into her soul. Then it was herself she stared at, *her* eyes that looked back at her, and she reached out through the mist . . .

Rianne jerked awake.

Slowly, like the mist that burns off beneath the heat of the morning sun, the dream receded, and those images receded back into the shadows of sleep.

She gradually became aware of her surroundings; the smell of hard, damp earth, the dry rustle of the straw beneath her cheek, the pungence of animals, the scratchy texture of the wool blanket, and the deep breathing of those who slept nearby.

Her eyes gradually adjusted. Through the surrounding darkness she eventually noticed the shades of gray that filtered through the walls and at the corner of the roof overhead.

It was cold. Her breath misted in the shadows. And the smell of newly fallen snow was sharp in the air. Her hands were cold. She tried to rub them together and immediately felt the restraint of the leather bonds.

Where was she? What had happened?

Memories of the night before at the inn came back; the tall stranger, the gold he'd handed over to Mab. She'd interrupted his bath. She had thought to wound him and take the gold. She'd been quick with the knife. He was quicker still.

He'd come out of the water like a demon and sprang at her. Even now she could still see him, completely naked, glistening wet, stunning, terrifying, fascinating.

She'd seen men without their tunics before, but never one without his tunic and pants. He seemed oblivious; for all he stood there, boldly naked, he might have worn the finest battle armor instead of nothing at all.

Even now she remembered everything about him; the heavy muscles that corded under golden skin at his arm as he wielded the sword with deadly ease; the taut flatness of his stomach as if he had been cast from iron, and the thick swell of muscle at his chest.

She remembered how he had not even flinched when she cut him, nor even later when blood beaded at the wound. And she remembered the taste of him.

Even now the memory stirred, as if it had only just happened and she could taste him still. That strange, unsettling essence of male.

She had drawn blood there as well. She had been more startled by the sight of the teeth marks at his shoulder than the cut she'd inflicted with her knife, perhaps *because* she tasted him and found it strangely pleasurable when all she had wanted was to cut out his heart.

She willed the memory away and concentrated on the bonds at her wrists. She easily escaped them and continued to listen to the sounds around her as she silently rubbed warmth back into her numbed hands.

Two others slept nearby. She heard their deep, rhythmic breathing. She lay there for some time as the feeling gradually returned to her hands and the gray dawn penetrated the walls.

As the sky continued to lighten, she made out the shapes of those who slept nearby. She was fairly certain one was the little man who had accompanied the warrior to the inn, and she experienced a sinking feeling. If he was here, then his companion was not far away. How many more were there?

The person who slept closest to her was painfully thin and huddled beneath a thick shawl. Straight pale hair spilled over the edge of the shawl. Her heart sank as she realized that her captors had also taken Kari, although she drew some comfort that they were together and far from Garidor. But what now was to be Kari's fate?

Who were these strangers? And why had she and Kari been taken captive? Certainly, all this wasn't because she'd tried to lift the stranger's gold. It made no sense.

Were they traders? Or slavers, perhaps? Even in Arthur's kingdom, such things existed. Especially here in these far northern climes, where each man made his own laws.

She crouched in the shadows. The smaller man slept nearby. He made a low, snicking sound as he slept undisturbed. Across the shed she made out the humped shapes of the sheep who had taken shelter there. One of the animals stirred, then settled itself with a deep sigh. In the far corner she made out the taller forms of two horses.

Only two? Where was the tall stranger? No doubt he slept with the horses, leaving the little man to guard her and Kari.

She remembered nothing after the little fellow came up behind her in the chamber at the inn. Only that sudden lethargy, that falling sensation, like drifting off to sleep, and then darkness.

She glanced back at Kari and the little man, wincing slightly at the dull ache at the back of her head that worked its way around to her eyes.

Had the little man struck her? She didn't recall a blow, only the light pressure of his hand at her shoulder and then that consuming darkness that had swept over her.

The little man slept on undisturbed. She silently crept toward Kari and clamped a hand over the sleeping girl's mouth.

Kari awakened instantly, eyes wide with fear. Then, as they adjusted to the meager light in the shed, her eyes widened with recognition. Rianne saw the confusion and the questions that filled the girl's gaze. She pressed a finger against her lips and motioned her to silence.

There was no time for questions or lengthy explanations. Escape was now their biggest concern, for she had no intention of lingering about to learn what their captors intended for them.

She gestured toward the opening of the shed. Kari nodded with understanding. As the girl stood and brushed straw from her gown, Rianne realized with some surprise that Kari was not bound as she had been. She slipped a hand around the girl's wrist and moved toward the opening of the shed.

Beyond the hut, snow blanketed the ground beneath the pearl gray dawn. Her breath plumed on the frigid morning air. They had no provisions and no weapons, only the pouch of coins and baubles tucked inside her tunic. She frowned, unable to comprehend these captors, who had not taken the pouch while she was unconscious.

The newly fallen snow was soft underfoot, muffling their footsteps and concealing their escape as they slipped into the shadows at the edge of the hut.

There was a pen at one end of the hut, no doubt where the shepherd penned the flock during shearing season. Beyond was the gentle slope of rolling hillsides spiked with the trunks of trees barren of any leaves. The land sloped away from the hut in a narrow expanse that connected to a heavier line of trees. Here naked trees were intermingled with pine at the edge of the forest.

She'd often taken shelter in forests rather than villages or hamlets. The forest offered shelter and cover. It would be almost impossible for anyone to find them until they were far away.

She gauged the distance to the edge of the forest. It was no more than a few hundred yards at most. Inside the shed, the little man's snoring rattled on undisturbed. Again, she motioned Kari to silence.

They set off across the snow-covered expanse toward the nearby line of trees. Her own clothes were warm enough, and the boots she wore kept her feet dry. But Kari's clothes were pitifully threadbare and she wore only thin slippers at her feet. She was soon soaked through, teeth chattering between blue tinged lips.

They had almost reached the line of trees. Rianne quickened her pace, eager to reach the safety of the forest. Kari was right behind her.

They moved quickly and silently. Rianne was now confident

of their escape. Reaching the line of trees first, she turned and frantically motioned for Kari to hurry before it was discovered that they were gone. She wanted to put as much distance as possible between them and their captors.

Kari tripped over the hem of her wet gown as it molded about her legs. Rianne went back to help her. They had almost reached the cover of trees when Kari looked up, stared past Rianne, and suddenly gasped.

"What is it?"

The look on Kari's face was frozen with terror. Rianne whirled back around to see what it was that had frightened the girl and came face-to-face with their captor.

In the cold light of day, standing between them and freedom, he seemed more formidable, more intimidating, and even a little frightening as he casually leaned against the trunk of a tree, boots crossed at the ankles, arms crossed over his chest, those tawny eyes glowing with amused satisfaction at having caught them like a cat that had caught a mouse.

"Good morning," he said, those tawny eyes watching her intently. "What are you doing here?"

Rianne saw no reason to lie or try to convince him otherwise. And she most certainly wasn't about to let him intimidate her. She'd known far too many others who were far more intimidating than him.

"We are escaping," she calmly announced. And then bluntly demanded, "What are *you* doing here?"

"I was relieving myself," Tristan replied, equally blunt.

He smiled inwardly as her eyes widened slightly. Last night she'd caught him off guard. He'd just turned the tables on her.

He glanced past her to the shivering girl who huddled behind her. She was poorly dressed for such weather, let alone travel afoot about the countryside. Her lips were already turning blue and she was thin as a stick, with an unhealthy pallor at her cheeks. Unprotected with only the thin gown she would not survive long.

" 'Tis cold out here," he commented. "And there's another storm on the way." Then he added, not unkindly, "Return to the hut and warm yourself."

Kari hesitated, clutching at her arm, uncertain what to do.

"Go," Rianne finally told her, knowing there was no hope for escape. At least for the time being. "Everything will be all right," she assured her.

She watched as Kari returned to the hut, worriedly glancing back from the doorway. Then she went inside.

"I tied the rope securely," Tristan commented, when they were alone. "No man could have escaped. You are most resourceful." Her gaze met his. There was no fear there, only defiance and courage.

"It is necessary to be resourceful when it comes to survival." Her gaze lowered to the knife secured at his belt—the same knife she'd cut him with at the inn.

Even now he suspected she plotted ways to separate him from that knife, and possibly a limb or two, considering the wound he'd received the first time. He had no intention of that happening, but her bold defiance in the face of such overwhelming odds intrigued him. It was reckless, even foolhardy.

"You'd like to have this back, would you not?" he speculated, his hand resting lightly on the handle, watching for her reaction in those magnificent eyes.

That unusual blue gaze met his with undisguised loathing and hatred. The color was not the light azure of summer sky or the darker blue of still, deep waters. It was the shimmering blue found at the heart of a flame.

With that same boldness and candor, she replied, "I'd like to cut out your heart."

CHAPTER SEVEN

Tristan threw back his head and laughed. He laughed until tears welled in his eyes and threatened to roll down his cheeks.

In the cold predawn, with her long golden hair spilling about her shoulders and a murderous expression on her lovely face, she looked like some fierce warrior princess in the stories his grandfather had told him when he was a child. By heaven, he hadn't thought of them in a very long time.

The only thing missing was a war shield clutched in one hand and a sword in the other. And he had experienced firsthand her skill with a blade, he thought, as he rubbed a hand across the tender spot at his shoulder where she had cut him.

It was not exactly the reaction Rianne expected or intended. In the very least she expected to be beaten, then dragged back to the shed at swordpoint, and bound and gagged. Her anger demanded no less, for then she could justifiably hate him and plan her next attempt to escape. But his laughter caught her off guard and confused her. What sort of captor was he? she thought furiously.

"Hold, milord! Do not be angry!" Grendel called out with alarm as he plunged through the snow toward them. On much shorter legs he was forced to make bounding leaps in the knee-deep snow, occasionally sinking in up to his waist.

" 'Tis but a simple mistake. The girl meant no harm."

Fear propelled him. He'd awakened a short while earlier, roused from sleep by a prescience of foreboding, to find both girls gone and himself quite alone in the shed, except for the sheep they'd sheltered with, the poor, miserable palfrey, which looked as if it might have perished and been frozen standing upright, and that damnable black beast Sir Tristan rode in a mood fit to bring the shed down around his ears.

He was not greatly surprised that Rianne had fled. in spite of the fact that Lord Tristan had bound her the night before. For someone as skilled as she with her hands and with unknown powers, escaping the bonds was mere child's play. What had surprised him was that he had not sensed her leaving.

They shared a bond in the powers that flowed through her, powers that he also possessed, limited though they were. They were kindred spirits. A kinship that allowed those such as themselves to recognize the bond in another. What worried him was that he had not sensed it when they first encountered her at the inn. There had been no sense of connection. Was it possible that her powers were so limited, that what she had inherited from her mother was so meager as to almost not exist?

True, she had shown uncanny skill at the games, but as he had feared earlier, it might be the skill of any common thief.

Now she had attempted to escape and been caught at it. It might have been almost amusing if not for the dangerous expression on Sir Tristan's face.

" 'Tis no mistake, little man," Tristan said evenly, his golden gaze locked with hers. The expression on his face made Rianne uneasy.

"She intended to escape and would have, had I not caught

her in the act. So much for your assurance that she would not attempt it.''

'' 'Tis most fortunate that you found them.'' Grendel tried to make light of their attempted escape. ''However did you happen to come upon them?''

''He was relieving himself,'' Rianne replied, with characteristic bluntness.

''And that is not all of it by half,'' Tristan informed him. ''She would like very much to cut my heart out.'' His eyes narrowed. ''Her mother would be so very proud of her. That is, if she is who you say she is.''

Grendel paled. This was not going at all as he'd planned it. First the discovery that John and Dannelore were dead these many years, and Meg's daughter disappeared. Then to find her in that dreadful place, disguised as a boy, living like a common beggar. Or perhaps *thief* was the more appropriate term. He was still not certain how she had bested him at cups and stones.

She was not at all what he expected or had hoped for. She was neither demure nor quiescent, well educated, nor apparently even the least bit aware of the legacy she'd been born to. Instead she had survived in the worst hellhole, matching wits and skill with the worst elements at the fringes of Arthur's kingdom, had the manners and temperament of a hedgehog, not to mention a bluntness and crudeness with words that rivaled any man.

If she was Meg's daughter.

She favored Meg in so many ways, yet there were other ways in which she was very different. He had hoped for time alone with her so that he might gradually tell her the things she must know, carefully reveal the bond that linked their lives together, and probe her inner thoughts so that he might learn her true abilities and the extent of her powers. But that hope disappeared as she turned on him.

''What is he talking about?'' Rianne demanded. ''What do you know of my mother?''

Grendel sensed her rising anger and attempted to assuage it.

"All in good time," he replied. "Come, let us return to the shed. 'Tis much warmer there."

Rianne defiantly refused to move. "I am not cold."

"You may wish to stand here and argue, but I do not," Tristan informed her. " 'Tis cold, and you *will* return to the hut."

"And if I do not?" she demanded.

He leveled his sword at her. "Then I will be forced to cut off something significant."

It was more than a threat, it was a promise, and with the memory of their previous encounter and its outcome still vivid in her thoughts, Rianne decided that for the moment wisdom perhaps served her better than anger or stubbornness.

"One day I think we will finish this, *milord*," she vowed between small, perfect, clenched teeth.

He bowed his head, as if she was some titled lady and he was a royal knight there to do her bidding.

"I eagerly await the hour, *milady*. But for now, you *will* return to the hut."

It was not a request but a command and, under the circumstances, one which she had no choice but to obey.

Kari sat huddled in the far corner, legs bent at the knees, arms wrapped about them, trying to keep warm. She looked up, relief flooding her face, at sight of Rianne as they entered the hut.

It was barely warmer inside the hut. The fire had gone out and wind from the coming storm knifed through the gaps at the walls. Rianne removed the oversized tunic over her head and offered it to the girl. It was fleece-lined and in spite of its outward appearance, stained with mud and grime, it offered considerable warmth.

Kari's expression was owlish, her eyes wary, as if she expected Rianne to transform into something else at any moment.

"Take it," Rianne said gently. "There's no sense in your freezing to death when I have more than enough clothes to keep warm." A patent understatement, considering the layers of muslin and wool with which she'd disguised herself. Kari tentatively took the tunic and slipped it over her head.

It engulfed the girl, sagging at her shoulders, the tips of the sleeves hanging past her fingertips by at least two hand lengths.

" 'Tis very fine," Kari murmured her gratitude.

" 'Tis not fine," Rianne replied, hating the way Kari ducked her head, as if she expected to be beaten at any moment. "But it will protect against the wind and cold."

"No one has ever cared if I was cold before," Kari said, tentatively. "Thank you."

"There is no need to thank me. 'Tis my fault you're in this situation. If not for me, you would be . . ."

"With Garidor at the inn," Kari said. Her voice faltered and she said no more, as if merely speaking his name was more pain than she could bear. She fidgeted with the folds of the tunic, her eyes downcast.

Rianne found the leather with which the warrior had bound her in the straw on the floor nearby. She pushed Kari's hands aside and slipped it about her waist, cinching in the extra folds of the tunic so that it fit better. The girl stared at her as she tied the belt and she knew the question that plagued her.

"You lied to me," Kari said in a small, meek voice as if she still could not believe the transformation from grubby boy to young woman.

"I lied to no one. You believed what you chose to believe, 'tis all," and in the silence that followed also sensed the girl's disappointment and pain.

In the weeks since she'd first struck her bargain with Garidor a close friendship had grown between her and the girl. She felt protective of her in a way that she might feel protective of a younger sister. But she sensed that Kari's feelings had become confused with a different affection based on that deception. She owed Kari an explanation.

Rianne sighed with exasperation and no small amount of

guilt. So long had she been on her own that she was not used to this obligation of emotions. Since she was a small child she had kept to herself, trusting only in herself. These feelings of friendship for another were new and difficult to deal with. But not nearly as difficult as the confusion and pain she knew Kari struggled with.

"I was very young when I lost my family," she explained and as she spoke of things she had not even thought of in a very long time, images of that long ago time flashed through her thoughts. Images of blood, death, and unbearable loss.

"I was alone and had no one to turn to. In the weeks and months afterward, I saw things I will never forget. Life is hard for children, harder still for a child without anyone to protect her." She saw the look of empathy in the girl's wounded expression.

"A girl is considered worthless until she is of a certain age," she said, recalling other things she had seen.

"And forced to do the bidding of whomever thinks he owns her," Kari added, the words filled with bitterness.

Rianne nodded. "Disguised as a a boy, I became invisible to others. No one paid any attention to me. I was able to move about as I pleased, without fear of being harmed by anyone. I was safe." As always, she tucked the painful memories away into the past of childhood.

"And your skill at games?" Kari asked.

Rianne smiled. "It was much safer than stealing."

"But Garidor took half of everything."

"Aye, that is what he thought."

Blue eyes glinted slyly. "He had no way of knowing how much I won at the games, and his customers had no desire to brag about their losses."

Kari grinned with delight. "You lied to him!"

"I never lied. I tricked him. He believed what he wanted to believe. The amount I paid Garidor was a pittance compared to the amount I kept hidden."

Kari was stunned. "What if you had been caught?"

"I've never been caught. And I had no intention of Garidor catching me."

Kari glanced past Rianne in the direction of the warrior. "What will happen to us now? They will surely kill us."

Rianne shook her head. "If that was their purpose, it would already be done."

"What then? Why have they done this?"

Rianne twisted her hair into a long braid that lay over her shoulder. She angled a glance at the warrior, who tended to the restless stallion tethered at the corner of the hut. He seemed to pay them no heed as he spoke in low, soothing tones to the great black beast. Yet she was not deceived. His sword was close at hand and her own knife secured at his belt. She would have to find a way to get it back.

She pushed to her feet and brushed straw from her leggings. She tossed the heavy plait of hair back over her shoulder.

"I do not know, but I shall find out."

Tristan watched them talk among themselves. It was obvious the girl, Kari, had been as surprised as anyone to discover that her companion was not a boy at all but was, in fact, a young woman not much older than herself. Eventually, she seemed to lose her wariness and they huddled together in whispered conversation. He suspected escape was the primary discussion and was not surprised when the girl who Grendel insisted was Meg's daughter approached him.

What would it be? he wondered. Tears or threats?

Both seemed inherent to all females. Young ladies, highborn or low, used both with the hope of obtaining what they wanted—usually a proposal of marriage.

When they discovered tears could not gain what they sought they attempted other schemes and tricks, which he was more than happy to take advantage of. Lady Alyce had sought to obtain a proposal of marriage by luring him to her bed and then arranging for them to be discovered.

Caught in the act by no less than a half dozen people, including her own father, dear sweet Alyce dissolved into tears and assumed the role of the innocent who'd been lured to his bed with promises of marriage.

Her father, Lord Alston, who closely resembled a puffed-up partridge—more so when he was angry—immediately demanded that Tristan do the right thing by his daughter.

He did. Without a stitch of clothes or the least embarrassment, he rose from atop the lovely Alyce of the innocent expression, tear-swollen eyes, and luscious breasts, picked her up naked as the day she was born, and threw both her and her father out of his chamber.

Alyce and her father left Monmouth the very same day amid much indignation and tears, both of which he found very amusing. Needless to say, relations with Lord Alston were strained for some months. Not so his relations with sweet Alyce. Within a fortnight, upon a visit to Camelot, she was back in his bed.

Now he watched with some amusement as the young woman approached, and wondered which it was to be, tears or threats. It was neither as she approached the stallion quietly yet unafraid, then extended a hand toward the glossy, silken head.

"The last one who attempted that lost three fingers," he warned, waiting for her hasty retreat.

The stallion angled a large black head toward her, dark eyes watching her with intense interest. Tristan watched with equal interest. She did not retreat but moved closer, laying a slender hand against the silken neck and slowly stroking the stallion with a light, gentle hand. Instead of becoming agitated or baring his teeth and taking a nip out of her, the Frisian nuzzled her shoulder.

The black stallion was a magnificent creature. He was obviously well cared for. She had seen other horses, beasts of burden like the lumbering oxen, harnessed to the heavy draft wagons, and others like the palfrey the little man rode. She also had memories of a fine cinnamon-colored mare, but the memory was like so many others, lost amid the blood and fire that returned only in her dreams. She had never seen such a fine creature as the black.

She swept her hand down over a muscular shoulder and felt the warmth of blood and muscles that quivered beneath her touch. There were small scratches and nicks in the velvet hide, marks of a long journey since last time this fine beauty had felt the comfort of a stable.

To her surprise the tiny wounds were clean and none festered, no doubt due to the care of the little man who still had not returned. He was an odd little creature. It was difficult to determine if he was a servant or an equal of the warrior.

"Oil of yarrow will heal the wounds more quickly and without scarring," she said as she lightly ran her hand down a foreleg.

Tristan was aware of the healing effects of yarrow on both man and beast alike. More than once, Lady Meg had applied healing salves to his many childhood injuries.

"But difficult to come by buried under several inches of snow," Tristan replied. That unusual blue gaze met his in a measuring look.

"Not if you know where to look." She continued to run a hand over the silken hide that quivered with pleasure beneath her touch.

"I would not have thought to find one who wields a sword with such skill to be knowledgeable of healing herbs and medicants."

"I was not always so skilled with the sword," Tristan admitted, passing a hand over the scar at his chin. "But the most painful lessons are the ones not soon forgotten. I learned early the benefits of oil of yarrow."

She was not prepared for the self-deprecating charm or the

smile, and forced herself to remember that this same man had threatened to separate her head from her shoulders.

"Aye," she said, the memory of old dreams surfacing with images of blood and death. "The most painful lessons are not soon forgotten."

There was something in her voice—something unexpectedly vulnerable and he suspected unintentional—that gave a glimpse he had not anticipated. Then it was gone, hidden behind the cool appraisal in those vivid blue eyes.

"I have some gold and silver coins hidden away," she said matter-of-factly. "What is your price to release myself and the girl?"

Neither tears nor threats nor emotional demands, but a business transaction. Coins for their freedom. He experienced again that stunned surprise he'd felt when he'd discovered that she wasn't a boy at all but a breathtakingly beautiful young woman, albeit a grubby, smudged young woman.

"Do not bargain with that which is not yours," he cautioned. "You forget, milady. You are our prisoners. Whatever belongs to you," he gestured to the pouch that hung from her belt, "belongs to me. You have nothing to bargain with."

There was no outward sign of distress, nothing betrayed in either that bright blue gaze or her voice as she turned and continued stroking the stallion's silky neck.

"There is more," she calmly told him. " 'Tis safely hidden. Do you think I would be so foolish as to keep it with me?"

No, he should have realized she would not. She had proven herself to be resourceful and cunning, a survivor who had survived on her own terms, no one else's. Not even Garidor's.

" 'Tis not a matter of gold, milady," he replied. " 'Tis a matter of duty and honor."

She looked at him incredulously. "What would you know of duty and honor? You are nothing but a thief and a blackguard."

He bit back the urge to burst out laughing at her. "Is that not a little like the pot calling the kettle black?"

She was caught off-guard by the laughter she saw in his eyes, not to mention the insult he'd very handily thrown back at her.

"No more so than those who call King Arthur wise, fair-minded, and merciful." That succeeded in wiping the smile from his face. The golden eyes narrowed.

"I serve Arthur the king," he pointed out.

"Ha!" she exclaimed, her gaze measuring him from head to foot. "In what capacity do you serve the king? As head pig-keeper?"

Tristan refused to be baited into an argument. Instead, he smiled. "Aye, 'tis the reason I am so skilled with the sword. When 'tis necessary, I can carve the ham for the master's table."

He was being absurd and maddening, and she was no closer to gaining freedom for herself and Kari.

"Name your price," she repeated, certain that one such as he couldn't even count, much less think beyond a few gold coins to buy ale and his next woman.

"I wish there was a price," he replied with silken charm. "I would gladly name it and be done with this. But I cannot."

"Why not? 'Tis a simple matter."

"Because the little man yonder has decided otherwise." He cut a glance toward the doorway of the shed as Grendel returned.

"Him?" she gaped incredulously at the little man, who was dusting snow from his shoulders. "Are you also a coward?"

"I am no coward, milady. But I have learned that there are things in this world that are to be respected and heeded, especially when they come in such small packages." And he left her to the mercy of the black stallion whom he sincerely hoped would take a nip out of her backside.

"I could hear you quarreling from the edge of the forest," Grendel admonished as he threw down several skins of water that he'd filled at the river. His expression was grave.

"We must leave this place. 'Tis not wise to remain so near the village."

"Aye," Tristan agreed. "When the storm has lifted. It would be dangerous to set out in this."

"Now!" Grendel insisted. "I have a bad feeling about this place."

"What is it?" Tristan demanded, all senses now alerted. "Did you see something at the river?"

The gnome nodded gravely as he plucked a feather from his sleeve. "Beyond the river."

The transformation had required all his skill and concentration. These things were almost beyond his limited powers. But necessary after what he had sensed at the cottage deep in the forest. And then among the smoldering ruins of Garidor's inn. He wrapped a small hand around the crystal rune, safely hidden in the pouch at his belt, and felt its answering warmth.

"We must leave."

It stopped snowing just after midday. They did not stop but pressed on, doubled up on the two horses. It would have been impossible for Grendel to prevent it if she suddenly took it into her head to escape, so Rianne was forced to ride with Tristan astride the black stallion. Kari would not attempt to escape without her. She rode with Grendel astride the pitiful, ancient palfrey.

Several hours later they still had not stopped. The palfrey made a dreadful wheezing sound with each step it took, and Kari sagged wearily behind Grendel. Rianne felt as if her bladder was about to burst.

"May we stop now?" she asked between clenched teeth as she attempted to maintain her precarious control, which was jarred with each step the stallion took over uneven terrain hidden beneath the smooth blanket of snow.

"Not yet," Tristan tersely replied. "There are a few hours of daylight left. We need to cover as much distance as possible."

Grendel gave no details of what he'd seen while he was gone, but Tristan understood the little man's moods and sensed whatever it was had been most serious. That urgency communicated itself to the stallion, who had been edgy and restless all morning, and required all Tristan's attention just to keep the two of them from being unseated. Not so the ancient palfrey, who fell farther behind as the creature struggled through drifts of snow that were knee deep in some places.

"We must stop now!" Rianne insisted.

"Not yet," came the reply, setting her teeth on edge. "We will stop when there is sufficient shelter for the night."

"No!" she replied, hauling back on the reins he held in gloved hands "We stop now, or I will piss my pants!"

Startled, the stallion sidestepped, mouth sawing at the bit. As Tristan fought to keep them both from being unseated, she slipped from his grasp and dropped to the ground. She quickly gained her footing and trudged off through the snow and thick pine foliage, a low-hanging branch whipping in her wake.

The palfrey halted wearily in its path. Kari bit anxiously at her lip as the warrior dismounted, tethered the stallion to a nearby tree, and tore off through the trees after Rianne. Grendel jumped to the ground.

He had no concern that Kari would attempt to escape. She was deathly afraid of the palfrey, her hands clenched white-knuckled at the edge of the saddle.

He lumbered off after Tristan and Rianne as fast as his short legs could carry him, genuinely concerned for Rianne for he sensed Tristan's thoughts, filled with murder and mayhem, all of it focused on Rianne.

CHAPTER EIGHT

It occurred to Rianne to keep on going. She could have easily eluded them. But she had no food, no horse, and no sense of where she was.

It was not the first time she'd been on her own with only her wits to save her. She would survive, of that she was certain. She had before. But then she thought of Kari.

The girl had suffered much at the hands of Garidor. She had no one in the world to protect or look after her. Yet for all the misery she had suffered, she had offered Rianne kindness and friendship, and asked nothing in return.

Rianne had promised to take Kari to the abbess at Glastonbury, where she had heard sanctuary might be found far from people like Garidor. She intended to keep that promise.

Tristan burst through the trees and undergrowth, sword in hand, a string of curses announcing his arrival.

"What the devil are you doing?" he demanded as he caught up with her.

Then he stopped, almost falling over her in the thick undergrowth. She looked up at him with cool composure and announced without a hint of embarrassment, "Relieving myself."

He could have joyfully strangled her. Instead he turned around, embarrassed quite possibly for the first time in his life.

"You could have gotten us both killed," he informed her through his teeth."

"You already said that," Rianne announced as she stood and hitched up her leggings. She cut around him as she exited the underbrush. "Do you always repeat yourself?" And stalked back in the direction they'd left the horses.

"Impossible," Tristan muttered as he skewered a partridge he'd killed on a green stick and set it to roasting over the fire.

Grendel shuddered. He could not bring himself to eat meat of any kind. Instead he nibbled on nuts and berries he'd foraged, his gaze fastened on the girl who sat across the fire from them, huddled in deep conversation with Kari.

"They are probably planning their escape," Tristan speculated.

"They are discussing the girl's need for warm clothes and," the gnome added, angling a glance at the warrior, "Rianne's intense dislike of you."

"How can this girl be Meg and Lord Connor's daughter? She is brazen, uneducated, and completely without manners or scruples. And she is an accomplished thief," Tristan argued.

"She has been on her own for some time," Grendel pointed out. "She has had no one to rely on but herself. I seem to remember another who had a wildness about him and might have ended the same if he had not been taken in as a child by a kindly lord and his lady." He angled a sharp look at the warrior.

"How is it she knows nothing about her parents?" Tristan argued. "What of her powers? There must be something of

Lady Meg in her. And yet, we have seen nothing in this girl that would even suggest a bond with Meg beyond a remote resemblance of features."

"We shall see," Grendel ruminated as he sipped the hot brew he'd made from leaves he'd gathered. "We shall see."

He sensed Tristan's growing doubt and knew well that they could not return to Monmouth with a young woman who might very well be an impostor.

It was so simple in the beginning. All they had to do was bring Meg's daughter back to Monmouth to be reunited with her parents before it was too late. Through Dannelore and John she would know her parents and the powerful legacy she'd been born to.

But John and Dannelore were dead these many years past, and Meg's daughter had been left on her own to survive. How much did she know or remember? Had there been any time at all for Dannelore to tell her of the things she must know? Of the legacy of the powers of the light that bound her to the netherworld? Of those who had gone before? Of the Ancient Ones? The counsel of the Learned? Or Merlin, who was the son of the past and the guardian of the future?

She seemed to know nothing of these things. There was only her unusual skill at games, which might be something she merely learned for survival, and the unusual color of her eyes.

Meg's eyes had once been that color. Or very near it. But all that changed with her encounter with Morgana in the ring of standing stones. She'd been blinded that day by Morgana's powers of darkness and could no longer see in the mortal way. And her eyes were no longer the color of blue flame, but a pale, sightless color.

Even though she had never seen her child in the mortal way, she had seen her with that unique power of inner sight that guided all creatures of the netherworld.

It was for that reason that he could not return to Monmouth, with Lord Connor so near death, and not be certain that the girl was in fact Meg's daughter. He must not fail his mistress.

Rianne felt that thoughtful gaze from across the fire and glanced at the little man. Several times she'd caught him watching her just so and wondered at the thoughts behind that thoughtful countenance.

He had called her Rianne, and the sound of it seemed to whisper from out of the dreams that haunted her sleep. No one had called her by name in a very long time, yet she instinctively knew it was her name.

She did not remember meeting the little man before but sensed that she knew him. It hurt to think of it, forcing open a door on the past. The door that opened onto her dreams and images of fire and blood and death.

They crowded at her now, flashes of images in the flames that mingled with the flames at the cookfire, the sound of distant voices that overlay the murmur of voices now, the sound of her name suddenly cried out in warning, and the screech of some wild creature that entwined with the screams of the dying.

Grendel saw those same images in the connection of his same thoughts with hers. They were only fragments, painful and raw, torn out of the past in fleeting glimpses that stunned him. And then, just as suddenly, they were gone, and all that remained were silent tears—tears wept alone in the darkness.

Grendel was not prone to mortal emotions, nor was he affected by them. He was a creature of the netherworld and such things were not part of him. Yet, at that moment, he experienced such heart-wrenching sadness and pain for the girl that tears welled in his own eyes. And for the first time since he'd journeyed through the portal that joined the mortal and immortal worlds, he felt human emotion.

"I am here, child," his thoughts whispered to hers.

Rianne looked up. It was as if someone had spoken to her. Yet, beside her, Kari silently nibbled on some of the berries the little man had found. Across the encampment, the warrior poked at the fire and stirred the coals beneath the roasting partridge, lost in his own thoughts. Only the little man watched her.

He nodded in acknowledgment, and it seemed his voice whispered through her thoughts. *"You are not alone."*

She stood abruptly, suddenly restless and uneasy. Tristan also rose, his hand on the knife at his belt. Grendel laid a restraining hand on his arm.

"Let her go."

Tristan was incredulous. "Are you mad? She will escape."

"Let her go."

She glanced from one to the other. Neither made any attempt to stop her. She took a tentative step away from the fire. Still neither made a move to prevent her leaving.

"Bring the blanket and the food," she told Kari. The girl looked at her with confusion and then quickly obeyed, scooping the berries and nuts into the corner of the shawl and tying it off. She also seized a skin of water.

Wordlessly, she backed toward the perimeter of the encampment, taking Kari with her. As they reached the perimeter of the camp, Rianne turned and pushed Kari ahead of her into the gathering darkness of the forest.

The girl was frightened. Rianne could hear it in the deep gulps of air she dragged into her lungs. And she felt it, like a fear of her own moving across her skin. Except that she was not afraid.

She was never afraid. Not since that long-ago night. And even then it was not fear she had felt. It was anger and rage as she saw those she loved slain before her eyes. She blocked the images that flashed through her thoughts once more and concentrated only on the path that lay ahead.

She saw it clearly in spite of the growing darkness, the tree that suddenly loomed in front of them, a turn and the thick undergrowth that blocked their way, the heavy cover of trees where the path seemed to disappear altogether, yet it was there.

She saw the path as she had always seen things, with an awareness that wasn't sight at all—a lost trinket that could not be found; the certainty that someone had been injured and needed help; the growing darkness of the storm that long-ago day.

She stopped suddenly, out of breath from running. Kari clung to her, equally out of breath, her frightened sobs mingling with gasps for air. She wanted to keep running, but felt her thoughts pulled back to that clearing, as clearly as if the gnome spoke to her. She took Kari by the hand and led her back to the encampment.

Tristan looked up. He would not have bet on their return. Kari, settled by the fire, shivering as she hovered near its warmth. She gratefully accepted a leg of roast partridge and tore at it hungrily with small white teeth. Rianne huddled a distance apart. Her gaze met Grendel's.

''Who are you?''

The fire grew low and the cold settled around them. Tristan placed more wood on the fire. Kari had long since fallen asleep, curled into the warmth of the blanket Rianne had given her. Neither Grendel nor Rianne seemed to notice the cold.

He told her everything. Of Merlin, his friendship with Arthur, and the powers of Darkness and the Light. He told her of the portal that linked their world to the mortal world, the journey Meg had made through the portal long ago, and the price she had paid to remain in the mortal world with Rianne's father.

He explained the powers Meg had once possessed; that she was not a mortal creature at all, but an immortal who had transformed herself to journey into the mortal world. He spoke of visions that opened a window on the future, of her healing power, and her ability to summon the forces of nature—earth, wind, and fire.

Then he told her about the child that had been born to Meg

and Lord Connor. A girl child of rare and fine beauty who resembled her mother, but who also possessed her father's spirit. Even as a babe she had shown these things, ready to seize the world and make it her own. A child of unknown powers and abilities.

He spoke too of the terrifying vision Meg had when her daughter was only weeks old. A portent of blood and death that reached out to the child, and her heart-wrenching decision to send the child away to a place of safety in the care of a trusted friend.

Finally, he told her of the attack on Monmouth only weeks earlier, the wounds Connor had received, and Meg's decision that their daughter must be brought back home before it was too late.

"My mistress sent this," he said, removing the crystal rune from the pouch at his belt.

It caught the light from the fire, flames gleaming in the hidden facets of the shimmering crystal, as if the flame burned within.

Grendel angled a glance at the girl. Her gaze was fastened on the crystal. As if in a trance she continued to stare at it, the brilliant flames that gleamed at the crystal reflected in the brilliant blue of her eyes. And for a moment Grendel was certain he sensed a connection like that of a window opening— a window on the past.

Something deep within Rianne reached out to the things he said, the lonely child within her who longed to find a connection to family and home. But there was another part of her that refused to accept the things he said because she had been alone so long and learned that she must trust only in herself.

Just as suddenly as he had sensed it, the connection was gone. The window was firmly shut. Disappointment lay heavy upon his heart. The only sound was the stirring of the wind overhead in the tops of the trees, and the hiss and crackle of the fire as the heat found pockets of sap in the wood.

"These things you speak of," she said after a while, "the powers of Darkness and Light? Transformation? Visions of the future?" She shook her head. "They are stories told to children at bedtime. They do not exist."

"The doubt is the mortal in you talking. You must reach out with that part of you that is not mortal."

She shook her head, tossing the shimmering gold plait over her shoulder. The expression on her face was equally closed.

"The things you speak of are most impressive," she told him. "Think of the things I could do if I possessed such powers." She smiled at him then and angled her head.

"I could conjure a spell and have anything I wished. You must show me how it works. What words must I say? Is there a magic potion that I can use on my enemies?" She warmed to the game now.

"Perhaps I will turn them all into toads. No! I have it. I will turn them all into two-headed toads! With warts!" She seized a slender stick from the edge of the fire and stood, striking a pose.

"I think I will give Garidor an affliction." She looked across the encampment at Tristan, who leaned back against the large trunk of a fallen tree, legs crossed before him at the ankles, arms folded across his chest, a thoughtful expression on his face as he watched her.

She angled her head thoughtfully. "Something very dreadful." At the other side of the encampment, Kari had sat and now stared at her with a worried expression.

"A hump, perhaps. Or two. No! I have it," she said with great excitement as if struck with sudden inspiration. "Boils."

Kari's eyes widened. Grendel could only shake his head. Where had he gone wrong?

"Big, painful, pustulate boils," Rianne went on, warming to the idea. "Everywhere. And for Mab . . . I think I will turn her into a sow so that she can root around in the dirt and muck for her next meal, and wonder if *she's* about to be the next meal for someone's table."

Tristan smothered a smile behind his hand as he watched her performance, while beside him the gnome looked as if he'd swallowed something crosswise.

"Oh, and I mustn't forget *Ox*," Rianne continued with a wicked sparkle in her eyes. "Since he already resembles one of those great lumbering beasts, I will turn him into one."

"Enough!" Grendel exploded. "I do not want to hear any more!"

Tristan was shocked at the gnome's outburst. He was usually calm, logical, and reasonable. For someone who claimed that he wasn't vulnerable to human emotions, he'd just exploded with them, including a few profane words that Tristan recognized and several he didn't.

Across the encampment, Kari cringed into her blanket at the gnome's outburst, while Rianne stared with amusement at the little man who at present looked at if he'd swallowed a hedgehog.

"You are right!" he told her. "You cannot possibly be the one I am looking for. You are ill-mannered, rude, and completely without any redeeming qualities. Not to mention that you look like a beggar and smell like one as well. I would not take you within a league of Monmouth Castle!

"Keflech!" he muttered, stomping off across the encampment, where he wrapped himself in his blanket and lay down in a disgruntled heap, grumbling to himself.

Rianne looked at Tristan with wide, innocent eyes. "Was it something I said?"

Tristan looked at her thoughtfully. For all his unique ability to sense things in others and know their thoughts, the little man had one glaring fault—the inability to understand mortal emotions. Especially female emotions, an area where Tristan had far more experience than he cared for—most recently with the lovely Alyce.

But he had to give her credit: One moment she was the

vision of an angry, irate captive, the next she held them both captive with her outrageous performance.

"It was quite possibly several things you said," he replied as he unrolled the fleece blanket and spread it upon the ground near the fire with a disgusted gesture at the thought of spending another night on the cold, hard ground.

"I suspect he believed everything you said."

In the next moment he expected indignant outrage and her protestations that it was not a performance at all, and that she had meant every word of it. Quite possibly she would flutter her lashes at him in the process, for she was a striking beauty and had no doubt learned to use that to her advantage as well.

"Then there is no reason to hold us captive," she reasoned, surprising him again.

She retreated to a place near the other girl and unrolled the fleece blanket he had given her.

"The girl and I will leave in the morning," she announced as she pulled the fleece up over her shoulders and turned toward the warmth of the fire.

Her gaze met his across the glowing warmth of the fire, and for a moment it seemed as if the fire burned in the brilliant blue depths of her eyes. Then they closed as she drifted off to sleep.

It was dawn when Tristan awakened, the first silvery light filtering through the trees to the east while overhead the sky was that deep pearlescent color of night that still clung to the sky. It rapidly grew lighter with each passing moment as the dawn drove back the night.

There had been no more snow through the night. Instead the sun appeared on the horizon, warming the earth, sending streamers of mist rising in the frigid morning air.

He threw off the heavy fleece and stood, stretching sore muscles against the stiffness that had set in through the night. He crouched low before the glowing embers that were all that remained of the fire. He rebuilt it, coaxing a meager flame as he fed in pine needles, leaves, and small twigs, then larger pieces until flames leapt higher and pungent smoke spiraled overhead.

He squinted through the smoke and rising heat as he laid larger pieces on the hungry fire. Across the encampment, the gnome continued to sleep, curled into a tight ball within the thick fleece like a little ferret burrowed into its lair. Then his gaze angled across the encampment and he immediately stood. They were gone.

He immediately seized the short broadsword and crossed the camp. He knelt in the soft snow and immediately found fresh tracks. It would have been foolish to set off in the dark; they could not have gone far. He was immediately on his feet and following those soft imprints in the snow as they led through a clearing in the trees and toward a nearby lake he'd glimpsed through the trees the day before as they made camp.

She had told him they would leave in the morning. He simply had not thought they would be so careless or foolhardy as to set off alone on their own. He should have known better than to leave either of them unguarded and unbound.

The tracks followed a path through the trees, up a small rise, beyond the tree line, and to the edge of the lake. Here they disappeared altogether as the edge of the lake gave way to frozen shoreline. He glanced in first one direction and then the other. His eyes widened in disbelief.

Rianne stood on the edge of the shoreline where a finger of land extended out into the water then curved back on itself, creating a small pool of shallow water.

She had removed the woolen tunic and several more layers beneath. They lay over a nearby tree branch. She was dressed only in leggings, boots, and a sleeveless muslin shift. The tail of the shift was tucked into the leggings. The muslin was so thin that it offered no protection from the cold, but that did not seem to bother her in the least.

She knelt at the water's edge and dipped a cloth into the icy water. She scrubbed at her skin everywhere it was exposed, down the length and under each arm, her neck, hands, and then scrubbed at her face.

He silently edged closer as she continued her washing. Her skin glowed golden with the rising sun. It framed her, caressed the curve of a slender jaw, the arch of her throat, the sweep of high cheekbones, tipped dark gold lashes, then exploded in the gold satin of her hair as she shook it free of the heavy plait.

Like a creature, wild and free, she tossed her head, shimmering gold hair fanning loose about her shoulders and tumbling past her waist. And it seemed that she became the sun—golden, silken fire that beckoned a man's hand.

He realized the moment she knew he was there. Not by anything that was said, but by something subtle, instinctive, known in the way of all wild creatures. He saw it in her sudden stillness, the change in her breathing, the slight angle of her head, and then in those unusual blue eyes as she turned and her gaze met his.

The muslin shift was so thin he could see the gold of her skin through it, the outline of her breasts and the darker skin of her nipples where they puckered against the thin cloth.

There was no shyness in her, nor was there the coyness of other young women he'd known as he slowly approached. Nor did she turn and flee. Instead she stood her ground and returned his gaze measure for measure without guile, without deceit, or the least embarrassment. He lifted a tendril of hair from her shoulder.

"Do you always go bathing when there is snow on the ground and ice at the water's edge?" he asked, stroking the silken strands between thumb and forefinger.

She pulled the strands free with a little jerk of her head. "If it suits me, and most particularly if I'm accused of smelling like a beggar."

Water beaded her skin. It ran in tiny streams of molten gold that shimmered in the sun, disappeared beneath the neck of the shift, then reappeared in the dark places where it lay wet against her skin.

She did not smell like a beggar. She smelled like the heat of the sun as it warms fresh rain, like the whisper of the wind on a summer day that brings with it the sultry scent of the earth, flowers, and time suspended, like the tender caress of the mist as it lingers just at the edge of dawn.

Nor did she look like a beggar. His fingers skimmed along the curve of her shoulder and slipped beneath the thin gold chain. His hand glided downward and cradled the slender crystal that hung about her neck.

"This looks very much like the crystal rune Grendel carries with him," he commented.

Her breathing became very quiet and still. But the pulse at her throat quickened. She retrieved the crystal, her fingers closing around it as those unusual blue eyes angled away from his.

" 'Tis nothing more than a trinket I found," she replied.

His fingers closed around hers, refusing to let her or the crystal escape that easily.

"Where?" he demanded. She wasn't cold at all, but seemed to possess the warmth of some inner fire that flashed with anger in those unusual blue eyes.

"I do not remember."

He was about to call her a liar when a terrified scream shattered the morning stillness.

"Kari," she gasped, her gaze frozen as she stared past him toward the shoreline where it curved away from where they stood. Then she was pushing past him and running back along the shore toward the place where the smooth surface of the ice had broken away, exposing the cold gray lake beneath and the frantic girl who flailed helplessly in the frigid water. She had ventured out onto the frozen surface and the ice had given way beneath her.

She clawed at the edge of the ice, trying to gain a handhold, but it broke off in pieces, disappearing beneath her fingers so that she had nothing to hold on to.

Her screams had roused Grendel, who stood helplessly at the water's edge.

"A rope!" he shouted at Tristan. "We must have a rope. It is her only chance."

"There is no time," he shouted grimly as he flung himself down on the embankment and edged out onto the ice in a desperate attempt to reach her. But she was growing weaker with each effort to save herself, the cold numbing her arms and legs.

Tristan knew well that in these cold climes death could come in a matter of minutes. He edged across the surface even as it crumbled beneath him, and plunged an arm down through the opening in the ice. His hand brushed hers once; then she sank away from him. Each time he reached for her, more of the ice broke away beneath him.

"You must do something!" Rianne cried out, grabbing hold of Grendel's arm. "She will die!"

The little man's gaze locked with hers. How many times had she seen him looking at her just that way? As if he saw inside her . . . as if he saw inside her soul.

He knew that he was taking a great risk. But he had to know. He could not believe that he was wrong. And the Ancient Ones willing, the girl would not die.

"I cannot," he said, throwing his arms wide in a gesture of helplessness. "I cannot swim. But you can save her," he told Rianne. "You have it within you."

"You are mad. I cannot. 'Tis impossible." But each moment she argued with him was one more moment that Kari's life slipped away.

The surface of the water had grown very still. Tristan was soaked, his breathing ragged as he continued to search below the surface for some sight of the girl. But she was gone.

"I cannot," Rianne whispered, her throat aching with unshed tears.

CHAPTER NINE

Tristan tore off his tunic and boots and prepared to go into the water.

Rianne stared at him incredulously. In the very next moment he would be in the water, risking his life for Kari. She was stunned. Life meant so little among those she'd known. No one had ever been willing to risk his life for another.

Grendel knew the moment she decided. It was as if her thoughts opened to him at last, and within those thoughts he glimpsed everything she was; the pain of the past, the loss, the loneliness, the part of her that was mortal with very mortal emotions, and the child within—that part of her that she had denied, but that had guided her through all the days and years of loneliness—the legacy she had been born to, the power of the light that was as much a part of her as the blood that flowed through her veins and the heart that beat within her. Yet, she denied it even as she pulled off her boots.

"If you are wrong, little man, then you shall have both our

deaths on your hands.'' She tore off her boots. "And I swear I will haunt you until you are dust.''

Before Tristan could stop her, she was in the water. Then she slipped beneath the surface.

The cold knifed through her in a spasm of instant pain that drove the air from her lungs. Every instinct she possessed made her want to kick back toward the surface.

"You can do this. You have it within you. I have seen it." The words came unbidden, moving through her thoughts like the warmth of the sun.

"Open your thoughts, open your senses. Let go of what you believe. Accept that which is within you." The words moved through her even as she tried to push them away. *"Reach for the light within. Let it guide you. It is part of you.*

"You do not feel the cold. You do not need air within your lungs. Open your eyes. Reach out. The strength is there. Use the strength. Use the power of the Light." She kicked out with all her strength, reaching out through the depths of the murky water.

"You fool!" Tristan turned on Grendel. "You interfering, meddling fool! You simply could not accept that she is not Meg's daughter.''

He was furious. Of all the things the gnome had done; all the tricks when Tristan was growing up; all the hard lessons learned; all the inexplicable things that the little man somehow justified in his own way—nothing justified this. He was sacrificing the girl, to prove something that did not exist.

The crystal was a coincidence, along with the other things he had imagined, as was her resemblance to Meg. He had said it himself—he could find a score other young women with blue eyes and golden hair. It did not make her Meg's daughter.

He shoved past the gnome, sprinting back toward the encampment. He seized the black stallion by the halter and ran him back to the water's edge. There he hastily unwound a rope and tied the end about a rock.

It had only been moments since the girl fell through the ice but it seemed like eons. If either of them were to have a chance at all, it was this.

He secured the other end of the rope about the stallion's neck and prepared to drop the rock through the opening in the ice. The weight of the rock would anchor the rope to the bottom of the lake and offer a life-line back to the surface. He seized the rope in one hand and prepared to go into the water.

Far below the lake surface Rianne focused on the glow of warmth that began as a small pinpoint of light. Like opening a door on the past, the glow of light slipped beneath the door and around the edges. In her thoughts she turned toward the light, reaching out for it.

It spread like liquid fire through her blood, driving back the cold, easing the pain that squeezed at her lungs.

"You have it within you. It is part of you. It is who and what you are. Accept it. Take hold of it. Become one with the Light."

The words guided her, taking her back through the eons of time before there was a kingdom, before the forests and lakes, into a world of beginnings, through a portal in time to another world that had existed long ago, when she and those like her first began, first felt the fire burning through them, first seized the power of the Light and became one with it.

It was like walking through cool mist. One step, then another, searching through the darkness beyond the mist. Then she saw Kari.

She was only inches away, unmoving, suspended in the cold water, eyes closed, arms spread wide in those last moments as she had struggled to reach the surface and the strength failed her.

Rianne reached for her. A hand, then an arm. She was pulling Kari toward her, then moving toward the surface with her in strong, powerful kicks.

She found the line that sliced down through the water, seized it, and followed it to the surface. Then strong hands were reaching for them, closing around Kari and dragging her the rest of the way to the surface.

The ice broke and crumbled beneath their weight as Tristan held on to the lifeless girl. With his other hand he held on to the rope and shouted commands at the black stallion, who slowly backed away from the water's edge.

It was painstaking and torturous. The stallion lost footing, dug in, and continued to back away from the edge with Grendel pulling frantically on the harness. Eventually, they reached a place where the ice was solid. Tristan inched back onto it, felt it solid beneath his shoulders, then his back, finally dragged all the way back onto the shore at the lake's edge.

Tristan released Kari, and started back for Rianne. She was clinging with both hands to the rope, still in the water, and struggling against the cold. He reached the edge of the ice, and half fell in as he thrust a hand toward her.

"Take my hand!"

Her hair molded her head and shoulders like liquid gold. Her skin was flushed instead of blue-tinged like Kari's, and the hand that reached for his was warm with surprising strength.

"I won't let you go." He slipped his hand around her wrist and pulled with all his strength.

Rianne held on, her strength combining with his as she fought the dragging weight of the frigid water and crawled up onto the ice. They stumbled and fell together, then slowly crawled toward the embankment.

Grendel had wrapped Kari in thick fleece and frantically rubbed at her hands and arms, trying to force warmth back into her frozen limbs. Her lips were blue, as were her eyelids. No heartbeat could be found at her throat.

"Damn you!" Tristan cursed the gnome. "You could have killed them both."

"There is no time for this now!" the little man snapped as he looked anxiously at Rianne.

"You can still save her. You've seen the power of the Light. Use it now."

"I don't know how!" Rianne replied. "I haven't the knowledge or skill!"

"It is within you. As much a part of you as breathing. Draw on the power of the Light as you did when you went after her," Grendel replied.

"Let it guide you. You have only to let go of your doubts. It is here," he took hold of her hand and turned it over between his.

"You possess the ability in your touch. You have only to reach for that spark of life still within her, connect with it, give her your strength, give her the beat of your heart. Imagine it, dear child, and it will be."

Precious seconds slipped away. If she did nothing, Kari would die. She had seen it before, once when a child had been pulled from a river. Lifeless, unresponsive, the child slipped farther away while his distraught father wrung his hands with helplessness.

Imagine it and it will be. She bent over Kari, torn with doubt.
You have only to let go of your doubts. It is here within your touch. . . . Rianne opened her hand and laid it over Kari's heart.

Give her your strength. Give her the beat of your heart. Imagine it and it will be.

The words whispered through her thoughts as she closed her eyes and imagined—the pool of light that shimmered within, the expanding glow as it spread through the connection of her hand, the faint, thready sound that gave way to a flutter, then the solid beat of a heart, the warmth of blood that moved through frozen veins, and that first shuddering breath followed by a gurgle of water from the girl's lips.

Kari would live. Even now she recovered, bundled in thick fleece before a warm fire, with little memory of anything after she fell through the ice. If only Rianne didn't remember. But she remembered everything, in vivid, terrifying detail.

She did not sit before the fire but a place apart, distancing herself as she struggled to understand the truth of who and what she was.

What was she? Witch? Sorceress? Conjurer? Changeling? They were words that had no meaning for her except in stories told at bedtime to frighten little children.

What was the truth? For so long she had asked those same questions. But there were no answers. They were lost in those images of fire, blood, and death when her guardians—the ones called John and Dannelore—had also been lost.

She had closed it away along with the pain of that loss, refusing even to think of it. Now the door to the past had been opened when she was forced to save Kari.

It was like opening a floodgate on the memories she had locked away and refused to see except in her dreams, where they came to her unbidden.

She remembered it all; the unusual restlessness of the hounds that long-ago night, Dannelore's uneasiness framed in small gestures—the way she angled her head, as if she listened for something, her apprehensive glances toward the door—the sudden rising of the wind beyond the shuttered windows, then finally, Dannelore's decision to send Rianne to the secret place where they gathered things in the forest.

She had not wanted to go. She was not afraid. Fear was not something she understood. But Dannelore insisted. And so she left, following Dannelore's instructions that she must not look back no matter what happened, no matter what she heard, and she must not remove the crystal rune from about her neck.

She had always worn it. Dannolore told her that it protected her, and she had believed it with the trusting innocence of a child. It was with that same trusting innocence that she left the cottage that night, the crystal rune about her neck to keep her safe and Dannelore's strange parting words in her thoughts.

She left, instinctively sensing that she must not disobey. But as she huddled in the secret place, she heard sounds that she would never forget—the screams of terror and dying. Then flames illuminated the night sky and she experienced fear for the first time in her young life—fear for those she loved.

In spite of Dannelore's warning she ran back to the cottage, but by the time she reached it, it was too late. John and the hounds were dead in the gardens outside the cottage. Dannelore had died inside. And there was nothing she could do to help them.

The wind howled about the cottage, whipping at the thatched roof, the limbs of the sapling trees Dannelore had planted, the flames that leaped at the cottage, and the dark mantle of the one who stood at the edge of the fire watching.

She could not see his face. It was concealed by the hood that covered his head. But from the depths of the shadows within the hood she saw those eyes of death, like the remnants of burned-out stars, cold, desolate, void of any light, void of any life.

He did not see her. Eventually he turned, his dark robes whipping in the ghastly light cast by the flames that consumed everything, and disappeared as if he had not been there at all.

Afterward, standing there alone, filled with the pain of loss, she had felt something warm in her hand. When she looked down she saw blood.

Her hand was covered with it. It dripped from her fingers. She frantically tried to wipe it off, but it reappeared each time. Then it suddenly receded, slipping from her fingers and across the back of her hand, coalescing to a single point, a single drop of blood that transformed into a brilliant crimson stone that shimmered at her hand.

Traumatized by what she had seen, she was certain she had imagined it. Something that appeared only in her dreams, a child's fancy plucked from the nightmare of death.

"You did not imagine it," Grendel said as he came up behind

her, his thoughts connecting with hers. He sensed her pulling away from the past, returning to the present as images of recent events spun through her thoughts, several of them from those moments past at the water's edge.

"It was a vision of the future," he gently explained. "No doubt you've had others and not recognized them for what they were. You will easily recognize them in the future, just as you discovered other abilities this afternoon. I knew you had it within you," Grendel went on. "I knew I could not be wrong. But you needed to realize it yourself."

He rolled his eyes. "Those in your family possess an unusual amount of stubbornness that I cannot understand at all. But everything turned out very well. Very well indeed." He grinned with satisfaction.

Rianne turned on him, her anger an invisible, powerful force, like a blow that sent him tumbling head over heels across the encampment where he landed in a stunned heap in a pile of pine needles.

"You miserable little worm!" she exclaimed. "You tricked me!"

Grendel gently probed his head. It appeared to still be attached, although it throbbed badly and there was a nasty bump on it. He slowly got to his feet.

Miserable little worm? She had no cause to call him that when he was only looking out for her best interests.

"It was a small deception. But necessary," he explained quite rationally, picking pine needles from his clothes and hair, and squirming uncomfortably as he seemed to have several down his backside.

"Necessary?" her voice was low and menacing. "You deliberately risked Kari's life!"

The pine needles could wait. He definitely sensed hostility— a dangerous thing in one who possessed powers such as hers, those powers completely undisciplined. Very dangerous indeed, he thought, as he recalled another with a stubborn, reckless spirit. Her mother.

"There was no real danger," he hastened to explain, his eyes never leaving hers as he moved a safer distance away. He did not like the look in those eyes, and having been on the receiving end of her mother's temper on more than one occasion, he sensed he might be best advised to find a safe hiding place.

Rianne sensed his game and closed in on him. "No real danger?" she replied, "I suppose there was no real danger when she fell through the ice and could have frozen to death?"

"Barely none," Grendel nervously explained, circling away from her with the distinct impression that he was being stalked.

In the small clearing some distance apart, Tristan heard their arguing and approached with curiosity. He silently watched the confrontation, thinking with some amusement that the little curmudgeon had probably outdone himself. This time, he'd met his match. More than his match, since it seemed the girl was in fact Meg's daughter.

She was furious, and quite possibly the most beautiful creature he'd ever seen. He leaned a shoulder against the trunk of a tree and watched the confrontation with great enjoyment.

"And I suppose there was no danger when she slipped beneath the surface of the water?" Rianne closed in on the gnome. "What harm in that?"

"Precisely," Grendel replied very logically, and immediately sensed he should have chosen something a bit more compassionate for an answer.

"You little wretch! She could have died! How could you play with someone's life as if this was a game?"

"I would not have let any harm come to her," he replied indignantly. "She was never in any real danger."

She advanced on him, her eyes narrowed. "And you did nothing to help her."

He didn't like the way this was going at all. "Of course I

did," he quickly replied as he backed up several more steps and cast a glance at Tristan, with the hope that he might intervene on his behalf. No hope there, Grendel realized. The warrior was enjoying all of this far too much.

"What if you had been wrong?" Rianne demanded, the force of her anger like a hand that shoved the little man back several more paces.

"What if I did not possess the ability to save her?"

Grendel was pushed back several more paces by that invisible power so recently discovered and now used against him. He tripped and fell over a downed tree limb.

"What then, little man?" she demanded as he scrambled to his feet and quickly sidestepped out of the direct line of her anger.

"But I was not wrong," he pointed out, inching toward a large rock where he might hide. "Everything turned out well as you can see."

"You manipulated everyone for your own purposes." Her gaze narrowed even further as she saw the direction of his escape. She blocked it, throwing an invisible barrier directly in his path as she warmed to her newly discovered abilities.

He was thrown back, clambered to his feet, and wildly glanced about for a new place to hide.

"It was necessary. I had no choice."

"As I have no choice now," she replied, launching a pine-cone in his direction. It circled around the clearing overhead, like a lethal missile seeking out a target. And the target was the gnome.

When he changed direction, it changed direction. When he ducked beneath a low-hanging branch, it followed. It was like a game of chance, except that all bets were stacked against him. Another pinecone whizzed dangerously close to his head. His eyes widened.

"You tried to hit me."

"Absolutely," she confessed as another low-flying cone

flattened him to the ground. He flung his arms over his head to protect himself.

"A bit high and to the right," Tristan said as he came up behind her and sighted the angle of the shot from her shoulder to the target.

Grendel's head popped up. "Who's side are you on?"

Tristan angled his head. "A little to the left."

"I protest! This is highly unfair."

"Now," Tristan told her, and the pinecone shot across the clearing and barely missed the gnome as he dove for cover. When he eventually emerged, he had streamers of moss clinging to his hair and clothes.

"You go too far, mistress," Grendel scolded and was forced to dive for cover again as another pinecone skimmed the air much too close for comfort.

"You most certainly go too far," Tristan repeated as he leaned over her shoulder, and took great pleasure in the little man's plight,

"Not quite far enough," she replied, as she launched another cone that all but parted the hair on the gnome's head.

"Stop this at once!" Grendel demanded from the pile of pine needles, leaves, and mud where he'd landed. "You are getting far too much pleasure from this," he scolded. "What would your mother think?"

But from experience he knew exactly what Meg would think. She would laugh at the uncanny resemblance between mother and daughter and take great pleasure at his expense, for she had been known for just such hijinks in her youth.

"You are *getting far too much pleasure from this,"* Tristan repeated as he learned close, the warmth of his breath tickling her cheek in a very pleasurable way.

"Aye." Rianne couldn't help but smile in spite of her anger. The sight of the little man dodging pinecone missiles was very funny indeed. She didn't really want to hurt him; she merely wanted to teach him a lesson. Now he was the one on the receiving end of someone's *manipulations*, and the boot didn't fit very well on the other foot.

"You might consider sparing his life," Tristan suggested. She angled him a sideways glance, that gleamed with mischief and slipped beneath his defenses. It glittered in her magnificent eyes and curved her mouth into a devilish smile.

"Give me one good reason."

"I can give you two good reasons."

A new missile hovered just above the ground several feet away. Grendel was frantically looking about for some place of safety where he might hide himself.

"What is the first one?"

"I'm told the little creatures make a dreadful mess, much like a pile of goat droppings."

"And the second reason?"

"They smell very much like a pile of goat droppings as well."

She considered the logic of his suggestion. Her expression was most serious. "Two very good reasons."

Across the clearing, Grendel watched them warily, his head cocked, as if he heard every word, which in all likelihood he did with his abilities and acute sense of things that allowed him to know everyone's thoughts.

"I suppose I should let him live," Rianne concluded, the pinecone lowering to the ground once more.

"After all, I wouldn't want his death on my hands." She watched as the gnome relaxed his guard, confident from his eavesdropping that she'd decided to spare him. He stood up, adjusted his tunic, and bent over to dust off his pants.

"However," she added, eyes twinkling with merriment, "I think one more for good measure." And on a single thought sent the pinecone flying low across the clearing at breakneck speed. It hit the gnome square in the backside and sent him tumbling head over heels.

Laughter bubbled into her throat and the anger evaporated

as Grendel quickly rolled to his feet and ran for cover, hurling protests over his shoulder and waving his hands above his head to ward off any renewed attack from flying pinecones.

"That should keep him for a while," she said with satisfaction as the gnome dove for cover among the trees and underbrush at the edge of the clearing and refused to come out.

"You really are very much like your mother," Tristan said as she scattered the rest of the pinecones at her feet with the toe of her boot. The smile disappeared from her face and the eyes that looked back at him were a somber shade of blue and filled with soft gray shadows.

"Do you believe in the things Grendel speaks of?" she asked. "The powers of the Light and Darkness? Transformation? Another world that lies beyond a portal?"

In spite of their initial encounter, she found that she valued his opinion on things. He was a warrior, a knight to King Arthur. No doubt he had confronted matters of life and death many times. Such a man would not be given to the fanciful notions the little man seemed to believe in.

"When I was a lad of ten years, I had an encounter with a creature I shall never forget." He thought back all those years to that fateful day.

"A creature of such pure evil that I know such darkness exists. It was an evil that sought to destroy everything that is good and true in this world, leaving behind only death and destruction in its quest for power. I also encountered a creature of unbelievable goodness, truth, and love. Someone who was willing to give her life so that others might live in a world free of that evil.

"She brought such happiness and joy to those around her, and possessed the ability to heal both body and spirit with a single touch of her hand."

He passed a hand thoughtfully over the pale scar at his chin, a gesture she had seen before.

"And she truly had the patience of a saint with a young boy

who managed to get himself into more mischief than any ten lads. She helped heal the painful wounds of loss with her gentle spirit and courage.'' His expression softened.

"Yes, I believe in such things, for I have seen them. I cannot explain what I have seen, but I know it is real.''

She knew he spoke of Meg. Her mother. A creature of magic and great power, much like Merlin, counselor to the king. *If* one believed in such things. And how could she not believe? All her life she'd been aware that she was different.

She heard things others could not hear; sensed things others were unaware of. And then there were the inexplicable incidents throughout her childhood—the first time she discovered she could move things without touching them, her ability to sense things before they happened, the fact that she was bothered neither by the heat nor the cold. And many more things Dannelore had promised to explain to her in time. But, sadly, she had died before she could pass on that knowledge.

"Your father is dying,'' Tristan said gently, his chest constricting at the thought of losing the man who had been a father, brother, and friend to him.

"Surely you wish to see him before it is too late.''

There was no emotion in the clear blue gaze that met his.

"The bonds you speak of are made of memories. I have none of those. The man I remember as my father died several winters go. I do not know the man you speak of, nor the woman Meg.''

She walked past him to return to the encampment. He stopped her with a hand on her arm. His touch was gentle yet strong, the warmth of his fingers felt through the soft wool of the tunic she'd donned after rescuing Kari from the frigid waters of the lake.

That amber gaze searched hers. There was a gentleness in his voice that surprised her and slipped beneath her defenses, touching something vulnerable deep inside her.

"I do not fully understand the choices that were made all

those years ago. But I do understand what it is to lose one's family." He again felt the pain of an eight-year-old boy as he peeled back the layers of memory.

"I saw my family butchered as a child and I have felt that loss and pain every day of my life since. But your family is alive. You have the opportunity to regain what was lost. There is not a day that passes by that I wish I had that opportunity."

She sensed the emotions he felt. It caught her off-guard and connected with her own profound emotions at the loss she'd suffered. But she did not know the people he spoke of. They meant nothing to her.

"My family sent me away," she reminded him.

"To protect you."

"Aye," she said, her voice filled with bitterness. "To *protect* me." That choice seemed ridiculous now in light of the outcome.

"Is there nothing I can say to persuade you to return to Monmouth?"

"Nay, milord. There is not. I promised to take Kari to Glastonbury. I intend to keep that promise."

"Very well." Tristan accepted her decision. For now.

"But we will accompany you. Monmouth lies in the same direction, and it will be safer if you do not travel alone."

CHAPTER TEN

Smoke spiraled from the roof of the inn. A patron lay where he had fallen, apparently drunk. Except that his eyes were wide open, staring with a horrified expression forever frozen on his face, his mouth gaping open in a silent scream that no one heard.

Inside the inn, Garidor lay where he had been brutally slain. Ox sat slumped against the far wall, blood from the gaping wound at his throat staining the front of his tunic. Mab lay across the serving table, her eyes wide with disbelief in those last moments before death, certain that she could be spared when she'd told the stranger what he wanted to know. Then she had realized too late that her fate was to be the same as the others.

The smoke billowed from the doorway and curled from the second-story window as fire spread and consumed everything. The stranger watched from the shadows of nearby trees. He watched the inn burn, eyes as cold as death from the depths of the hood that shrouded his features.

Cries of alarm came from the nearby village as people rose from their beds and discovered the inn on fire. He watched their hopeless, futile efforts to put out the fire. Then, as dawn rose over the village, he turned and disappeared in clouds of swirling mist.

"Lame," Tristan said as he stood and patted the neck of the exhausted palfrey.

"Keflech!" Grendel muttered. "What are we to do now?"

"Walk," Rianne replied as she slipped from the back of the black stallion. It seemed a simple matter to her, and one she was accustomed to.

"I hate walking," the gnome complained. " 'Tis slow and cumbersome and this is not a place to linger."

Rianne shrugged. "Then do not walk. Stay here if you like. Though 'tis rumored trolls live in this part of the forest."

"Trolls?" Grendel shuddered. He had a particular dislike of trolls, and searched the surrounding trees and hollows for sight of any that might be lurking about.

The little man swore again. "Foul, nasty creatures. You cannot trust them. They steal everything." He cast furtive glances over his shoulder as he jerked on the palfrey's reins, urging the beleaguered beast to a faster pace.

"Trolls?" Tristan grinned, as he returned to adjust the harness, so that the stallion might be led.

Rianne shrugged, not quite meeting his gaze, even as her mouth twitched with a suppressed smile. "It seemed the most likely way to avoid an argument. He is a most contrary creature. And 'tis not exactly a lie. People believe all sorts of creatures live in these woods."

They'd retreated to a truce the past several days, since the girl's brush with death at the lake. She was determined to continue to Glastonbury. He was determined to deliver her to Monmouth.

"Be careful he doesn't suspect you of tricking him," he warned. "He has an uncanny way of knowing one's thoughts. And a foul temper."

" 'Tis not *his* thoughts I should be wary of," she replied, meeting his gaze with a directness that made him think she knew exactly what he schemed.

But he'd had much practice in such things, and long ago Merlin had taught him the way of concealing one's thoughts from one with abilities such as hers. It had proven most useful in escaping reprimand as a child when caught by her mother at some misdeed.

"What is to be done now?" the gnome grumbled. "We are still four days' ride from Monmouth, more than twice that afoot."

"The city of Bath is not far," Tristan replied, recalling the road they had traveled only weeks before. "We will find horses there."

Grendel frowned. "I do not like such places. They attract all manner of strange disreputable, creatures. 'Tis a dangerous place."

"Aye," Tristan acknowledged with amusement. "Strange creatures indeed."

Bath was an ancient city. Its origins were Celtic, British, and Roman, with influences of all three found in the carved stone edifices that decorated the houses, public rooms, and buildings of the town center, situated at the heart of several streets that converged like the spokes of a wheel.

Here all manner of craftsman, merchant, and miscreant could be found, plying their trade or wares by day, by night filling the inns, ancient pleasure houses where the faces changed through the centuries but the trade was the same.

In the marketplace all manner of food, product, tool, or utensil could be found, brought up the Tamar River from the seaport at Bristol. There were exotic spices, fabrics, and foods, pigs, chickens, and sheep traded or sold.

It was a lively place where all manner of strange things were seen, from dancing bears to acrobats, mummers, and those who performed magic tricks.

Tristan made several quick purchases as they moved at the edge of the market, hiding Kari's features beneath an overlarge tunic with a hood.

"Do not remove your hood," he ordered Rianne. "We do not want to draw attention to ourselves. 'Tis safer for others to believe we are simple pilgrims on our way to the west country."

"If we are in danger, it would make sense to return the knife to me," Rianne pointed out.

He jerked the edge of her hood low over her face in reply. "And do not say anything. I will do the talking."

They kept to the side streets, passing an ancient stone building with a wide portico, columns, and Roman edifice, a faintly sulfuric smell permeating the air.

"What is that smell?" Grendel complained.

"The Roman baths," Tristan replied, with a fondness of memory for several days spent there with a particularly nubile young creature who would do anything, for a price.

Grendel shuddered. "Baths? Filthy habit."

Eventually they found the the stables near the edge of the market. They slipped inside, tethering the horses as the spirit of the marketplace took on a new and different sound of revelry and merrymaking. Several other horses were also tethered in the stables.

" 'Tis the celebration of Sulus," Tristan announced as he returned from his search for the proprietor of the stable. "A Roman holiday marking the winter solstice."

"What of the proprietor?" Grendel asked, eyeing the scrawny, pockmarked youth who had returned with him.

"He is the boy's father," Tristan explained. "He takes his meals at a nearby gaming house. The boy says he has horses for sale but refuses to name a price. He will take us to his father. He claims it is not far.''

The boy, a gangly youth with grubby features and horse dung caking his boots, watched them with a sharp-eyed intensity that belied the slack-jawed expression on his face. Rianne had encountered many like him. She edged Kari behind her as the boy's curiosity intensified.

"Let us see what deal may be made,'' Grendel said. "I have no desire to remain here any longer than necessary.''

"Remain here with the others,'' Tristan told him with a glance toward Kari and Rianne in silent communication. The little man swallowed his objections as he saw the wisdom of it.

Tristan turned to the boy. "Take me to your father. If I strike a bargain with him, there's a piece of gold in it for you as well.''

The boy's eyes lit up, all traces of ignorance vanishing, replaced with the cunning of greed. "Most likely drunk, he is, by now,'' the boy said matter-of-factly. "Or at the games. There ain't no talkin' to him if he's at the games. Not until he loses. Then he gets mean.''

"Then you had better hope he's not at the games,'' Tristan replied as he followed the boy from the stable.

"Stay here,'' Rianne whispered to Kari. "You'll be safe.''

"Where are you going?'' Grendel demanded.

"To see a man about a horse,'' she said, stroking the black stallion's gleaming neck. He lowered his head and gently nuzzled her.

"Oh, no,'' Grendel informed her, rounding behind the stallion while he wagged a finger at her as if she was a child who had misbehaved.

"I forbid it. 'Tis not safe. We will wait together for Lord Tristan's return.''

As he approached with determined expression and purposeful

stride, she nudged the stallion backwards with a gentle touch of her hand at the heavily muscled neck.

Grendel squawked with alarm as the large beast threatened to step on him. Then, to avoid being trampled, fled to the wall of the stable and promptly found himself pinned by those lethal hooves, and a black, feathery tail snapping the air with malicious intent.

"You must not!" he called out. All further protest was smothered as the stallion pinned him against the back wall of the stable.

The street outside the stables was filled with people, carts, and animals. Amid the noise, smells, and jostling bodies that closed in on her from all directions, she eventually sensed the direction Tristan and the boy had taken and set out after them.

Night had descended on the city. Outside some establishments, oil lamps had been lit. Outside others, torches burned brightly, illuminating painted signs on walls and at posts with the mark of a boar or bull's head, a hound, or a pair of fighting cocks.

From open doorways raucous noise spilled out into the street: curses, drunken conversation, a woman's shrill laughter, and wagers being made at some game.

The sword was in the scabbard at his back within easy reach, and his hand was at the shorter knife at his belt as Tristan sharply watched for any danger—some trick or deception, an establishment they already passed by, a street corner that was suddenly familiar—any indication that the boy led him on a fool's errand.

He was just about to cuff the boy along the side of the head when he turned and mounted the steps of an establishment. The sign painted outside was the image of a fox and a hare, indicating that both food and games could be found inside.

It was a place not unlike many he'd been in, including the inn where he'd found Meg's daughter. Except for the assortment of customers. Bath was an ancient city. A score of civilizations had plied their trade and influence here.

Along its streets could be found the architecture of each of those ancient cultures built helter-skelter alongside each other; simple Celtic dome structures were side-by-side with columned Roman buildings and two-story houses whose walls surrounded ancient gardens, patios, and fountains. Within its establishments could be found the miasma of those ancient cultures in patrons with rounded Celtic features, the sharp blue-eyed features of Norse invaders, as well as the aquiline features of Roman ancestors.

Smoke from the cookfire permeated the air, amid the acrid stench of torches, and ale and wine for those with the purse to pay for them. Crude comments and shouts of laughter mingled with the loud crowing of a cock as bets were taken on the next cockfight.

He followed the pock-faced boy to a long table, where a new game of stones had begun, a handful of players eagerly placing their bets on the outcome. The boy sidled up behind a fat, squat man, the remnants of his supper staining the front of his tunic.

"What yer doin' here, boy? Yer s'pose to be mindin' the stables," he grunted. Then turned and glanced at Tristan as the boy bent low and whispered to him.

"Go away. I'm closed for business."

"A game, then," Tristan suggested.

"Wot yer got to wager, stranger?"

Tristan pulled the pouch of coins from his belt. He dropped it onto the table with a dull thud. The eyes sharpened in the fat face and a grin spread amid a sea of heavy jowls, revealing the cause for the stained tunic; few teeth remained in the gaping gums.

Rianne slowly made her way through the shadows from the doorway to the table where Tristan was engaged in conversation with a patron who appeared to have already been most fortunate at the games that night. Several metal coins were piled before him.

Others sat about the table, their misfortunes apparent in their faces and their dwindling piles of coins as they cursed their losses and shouted for more ale.

The cup was metal instead of wood. The stones were not stones at all, but small square-cut cubes made of hand-carved boar tusk with markings painted on each side. The squinty eyes gleamed in the fat face.

"Aye, a game," the stablekeeper agreed, barely able to take his eyes off the pouch.

"Name yer wager?"

Tristan sat down at the bench vacated by another patron. He opened the pouch and poured the contents onto the table. Gold and silver glinted among dull metal coins. Tristan wagered a silver coin and the game began.

The owner of the stables nodded. "House rules," he bellowed, slipping a knife from his belt and driving the tip into the badly marred surface of the table.

Tristan nodded. "Agreed."

Rianne watched with fascination as she discovered that he was quite skilled at the game, and blessed with a certain amount of good fortune. He took the first two rounds. But as the game progressed he lost more and more of the coins.

A crowd had gathered. As another round ended, more ale was called for. A pitcher was brought and tankards filled as a woman with striking dark features made the rounds of the table.

Dark brows angled over sharp dark eyes, and she lingered as she slowly bent over the table to refill Tristan's tankard, the soft muslin of her bodice gaping away from full, ripe breasts.

Her mouth was curved in a soft smile as she said something to him, her unbound hair and the neck of her gown falling off one shoulder in open invitation. Rianne watched with growing curiosity as the woman leaned closer still, slipped a hand behind his neck, and kissed him.

These were not the quick, stolen kisses Rianne had witnessed between flirtatious young boys and girls. Nor were they the pawing, sloppy kisses Kari had been forced to endure from Garidor. These were different. They were slow, deep, and fully savored by both the woman and Tristan. And when she finally drew back ever so slightly, Rianne realized far more had touched than their lips.

The woman's cheeks were flushed. She stroked her tongue across her lips and kissed him again, a look of such pure hunger and need in her glistening eyes that it seemed she would devour him.

With a few softly spoken words she could not hear, Tristan gently pushed the woman away. With a sultry pout the woman retreated, but not without a final, all-too-clear message as she bent low and brushed her full breasts against his arm.

Men were all alike, Rianne thought with disgust. She had been so certain he was different. He had shown such gentleness and concern for Kari.

A pox on them all!

She considered returning to the stables and setting out alone with Kari. She'd been alone most of her life. She had no doubt they could find their way to Glastonbury. But the meager coins she'd managed to hoard were also in that pouch. He'd cleverly taken them from her. As a *guarantee,* he'd called it, that she wouldn't take off in the middle of the night.

That small hoard was all she had in the world. Without it, it would be impossible for them to reach Glastonbury, and they might well find themselves in a place very much like this again. She moved closer, elbowing her way through the crowd that had gathered as the handsome stranger bet against the stable owner, who was obviously well known for his skill at games.

Shouts of encouragement were heard around the room, and as she watched the next game progress, Rianne began to sense the source of the stable owner's good fortune, which seemed to have turned so dramatically.

As one who had played countless games and admittedly influenced the outcome of many, she sensed it was the only explanation. No doubt the stones carved from boar tusk were weighted, guaranteeing a predictable outcome. The swine had probably switched them after allowing Tristan to win the first few rounds. The original stones were probably stuffed up his sleeve, in his tunic, or in a concealed pouch at his breeches.

She continued to watch as Tristan lost more coins. He was a skillful player and also seemed to sense that fortune had suddenly turned against him as he watched the stable owner intently.

She had realized early on that in order to keep suspicion at bay when at the gaming table, it was necessary to lose a round every once in a while. But greed overruled caution as the stable owner scooped another round of bets from the table into the pouch at his belt.

"You've only two coins left," he pointed out. Two gold coins gleamed from the table in front of Tristan, the last of their combined wealth.

"One last game," he wagered.

Tristan was neither reckless nor a fool. But she had reason to believe he might be both as he removed a silver chain from about his neck. A ring dangled from the chain. It was finely made and also of silver, with a gleaming blue stone set in the middle.

"The gold coins and this against everything in that pouch and two of the finest horses in your stable."

He must be mad. To wager everything, when surely he must know the man cheated, was more than madness. Unless he knew something she did not. Unless he intended to expose the man for what he was.

It was dangerous and reckless. In such a place it was difficult to know where the sympathies of others lay. No one knew it better than she.

The gaping grin widened as the piggy eyes narrowed. "Aye,"

the stable owner agreed as he swilled down more ale and then wiped his mouth with the back of his sleeve.

"I just hope me luck holds."

Rianne's eyes narrowed as she saw a shadow moving at the perimeter of the crowd that had gathered. She sensed who it was even before she caught a glimpse of the pockmarked face in the quivering light of a torch at the wall behind Tristan—a further guarantee that the stable owner would not lose as his son slipped into place behind the warrior.

The game began. The stones were tossed. To no surprise, the outcome was the same as before. As the stable owner reached out to claim his winnings, Tristan leaned across the table.

"What is this?" he asked with such beguiling charm and innocence that Rianne almost burst out laughing. As she'd learned, he was much quicker than she'd given him credit for.

In the blink of an eye he'd drawn her knife from his belt and sliced across the front of his opponent's tunic. A small leather pouch fell out onto the table, drawing the attention of everyone.

"It's me winnings," the stable owner explained, snatching at the pouch. But Rianne was quicker. She seized the pouch and emptied it. Five stones made of carved boar tusk tumbled across the table.

One of the others at the table seized a stone from each group in each hand. He rolled them around in each hand. Then he laid one down onto the table. He seized a metal tankard and slammed it down over the stone.

It cracked into several pieces, exposing the piece of metal that was embedded inside.

Shouts of outrage exploded amid accusations. The stable owner seized Rianne by the front of her tunic and the hood fell back to her shoulders. For a moment everyone was silent. The stable owner's shock was almost as great as Tristan's. Then chaos erupted.

As Tristan came across the table, the boy attacked, throwing him to the floor.

"Bitch!" the stable owner swore as he realized what everyone else now knew. His hand closed around her throat. Her own hand closed around the handle of the knife he'd embedded in the top of the table.

She pulled it from the wood and drove it into his other hand, pinning it to the table. He let out a howl of pain and immediately released her.

As air rushed back into her lungs, Rianne dropped to the earthen floor and dove beneath the gaming table. She quickly crawled to the other side.

Coins that had scattered when the fighting began gleamed dully in the dirt beneath the table. She scooped them up and stuffed them inside her tunic. Her knife had also fallen to the floor when the fighting began. She scooped it up as well.

Tristan still had the longer sword in the scabbard that hung at his back but refused to draw it against the boy, who was gangly and no match for him. But he was tenacious. It was obvious that Tristan did not want to hurt him. Then the boy drew a knife and lunged at him.

"I'll cut your heart out," the boy told Tristan. "And roast it on a spit."

Tristan almost burst out laughing. Except for the added touch about roasting on a spit, he'd heard this threat before, and not long ago. At the thought of it, his gaze scanned the inn and the embattled patrons who fought over coins that had fallen to the floor, spilled ale, and anything else that occurred to them to steal.

Where was she?

The distraction was enough to give the boy a momentary advantage. He saw an opening, lunged with the knife, and slashed Tristan's arm. Now the boy had his full attention.

Someone staggered against the table and upended it. The stable owner let out a howl of pain as the blade was wrenched free of the table. While clutching his wounded hand, he saw Rianne. With a bellow of rage, he charged after her.

Keflech! she thought, sprang to her feet, and headed for the boy.

With one clean slash she severed the belt at the boy's waist. The voluminous pants had no doubt been inherited from his father. The boy was reed thin and the pants plummeted to his ankles, revealing pale skin with a sprinkling of spiky dark hair knobby knees, a bare arse, and little else. Very little else.

Rianne gaped with surprise. The boy screamed with humiliation as he dropped the knife and grabbed for his pants.

Tristan grabbed Rianne and propelled her toward the door of the inn. Then they were out the door and running down the darkened street. Noise exploded from the inn as patrons spilled out behind them, including the stable owner and his son, who clutched at his pants to keep them from falling around his ankles.

Tristan pulled her down yet another street. She had lived her life simply, traveling from village to village. The numerous cobbled streets, houses, and establishments that all looked alike left her confused and disoriented. He seemed to know where they were going, as did those who gave chase behind them.

They had to get back to the stables, but she had no idea where that was. He pulled her down yet another street, across a stone courtyard, and through an opening into a passage that led down several steps and into a large, dimly lit chamber. The smell of sulfur and the damp heat of the air hit her. Then she heard the sound of lapping water.

"What is this place?"

"The ancient Roman baths. They were built centuries ago."

Her eyes widened at the sight of the huge pools in the cavernous room. They shimmered phosphorescent in the light of the torches at the walls and revealed that they were not alone. Then widened even further at the sight of a man and woman entwined in the glowing depths of the water, their bodies intimately joined, and oblivious that anyone watched.

All she could think to say as she stared at their glowing, entwined bodies was, ''Where does the water come from?''

He would have burst out laughing if he hadn't wanted so badly to strangle her.

''It's fed from underground channels,'' he hastily explained as he pulled her along the wall toward the other end of the large room. '' 'Tis said the baths reminded the ancient Romans of their home. 'Tis also said they have healing powers.''

''Ah, so that is what they're doing,'' Rianne said, with one last backward glance at the man and woman in the pool.

She gasped as they emerged from the ancient building and the cold night air hit her skin. After the warm, sulfurous air of the baths, it was like being dropped into the icy depths of the lake. It stung at her eyes and made them water.

Tristan pulled her into a narrow passage. They heard voices close by. Light from several torches played across the opening. They squeezed deeper inside the passage.

He pressed her back against the wall, shielding her from the opening, the sword held low between them so that it would not catch the light of the torches and give away their presence.

Light from more torches appeared at the opening, then faded as their pursuers passed by. She slowly let out the breath she was holding.

''That was very foolish.''

''Aye,'' she admitted and smiled. ''A knight of the king should know better.''

He laughed. His breath was warm against her temple. His body was warm against hers. And like that day at the lake, when they'd both fought to save Kari, she was suddenly aware that she had changed from the child who once had donned a boy's clothing for a disguise.

So long had she worn them that she had ceased to think of herself as a girl, or as a woman. But that day at the lake she was reminded that even though she wore the clothing of a boy, she was not one. And at the inn, when the woman kissed him, her curiosity had not been the curiosity of a boy, but that of a woman for something she'd never experienced.

"And most dangerous." His breath tickled at her cheek.

"Aye," she agreed. "You could have been gravely wounded."

He didn't know whether to rebuke her or paddle her until she couldn't sit down. Rianne solved the dilemma. She kissed him.

CHAPTER ELEVEN

Rianne slipped her hand behind his neck, then angled his head down and pressed her mouth against his just as she had seen it done.

She sensed surprise, then tasted it in the sudden expulsion of his breath mingling with hers. He tasted of ale, cool night air, and something dark, illusive, and powerful.

She instinctively leaned into him, holding on, reaching out for that something else. Her body fit all the sharp, hard angles and edges of him; her mouth fit the hard angle of his mouth, her hands lightly stroked the hard edges of cheekbones and the rough texture of his beard over the sharp edge of muscle at his jaw. She closed her eyes as she found that something else.

His mouth moved against hers with sudden heat, power, and mysterious need; like warm honey—sweet and illusive on her tongue, like a powerful hand stroking deep inside to touch in dark places, finding the need deep inside her.

Then he was pushing her away. She sensed the anger and

saw it on his face as the light of passing torches angled across the planes of hardened features, like a stone mask.

His fingers bruised as he pushed her away. He swore, a hard sound that whipped at her from the shadows in the passage. But it was more than anger. She sensed pain, bitter disappointment, and a loathing that was worse than if he'd struck her.

"Are you through with your foolish little games, milady?"

She flinched. The color drained from her face, then returned to blaze across her cheeks. Her eyes flashed with blue fire and pain.

"Aye." Her chin hitched slightly. She set her jaw. "I was merely curious, as I have never kissed anyone before. But in truth, methinks 'tis highly overrated."

"Overrated?"

She shrugged. "No doubt it holds interest for certain women," she bit off.

"But not you?"

"Not in the least." Especially not now.

She jerked out of his grasp and pushed past him toward the opening of the passage. He hauled her back as the light from another torch flared across the walls at the opening.

Several men passed by as the search continued. As the light gradually faded, she wrenched free and slipped out into the street. With a softly muttered curse, Tristan followed.

"I hope you did not hasten on our account," Grendel remarked peevishly as they returned to the stable and slipped inside. Kari stirred and sat up, blinking the sleep from her eyes.

"We will take two horses," Tristan snapped, ignoring the little man's quarrelsome comment. "We leave at once."

Grendel's eyes widened. "You're stealing them?"

"Let us just say that I *negotiated* the price with the stable owner," Tristan informed him, seizing the saddle and swinging it atop the black stallion.

He jerked the cinch into place with a less than gentle hand, causing the black to flatten his ears and snort with disapproval.

The gnome glanced from the warrior to Rianne as she stiffly stalked past and seized a bridle. It was obvious there was anger between the two of them, but he could not sense the cause of it.

"You will ride with me," Tristan informed her, as if he was giving orders to his men.

She refused to respond, giving her answer instead in stubborn silence and her determined efforts to harness one of the other horses.

He jerked the harness from her hands. Her head snapped up, eyes ablaze with a cold blue fury that had Grendel backing away. He'd seen anger very much like that before in her mother and knew when it was perhaps much wiser to hide.

Tristan had experienced it as well but wasn't the least intimidated. "You have neither the skill nor the strength to ride alone. You'll be on your arse in the dirt with one misstep, and I have no desire to play nursemaid to a mewling child."

"One more word and *you'll* be on your arse where you stand!" she exploded, meeting him toe-to-toe, nose-to-nose, even if she did have to look up to do it. Quite a ways up.

"I have not the time to coddle you. You will ride with me, or I will tie you across the saddle!"

"Several men approach!" Grendel warned, before there was an explosion of cataclysmic proportions. "We must leave at once!"

Caution tempered her anger. That, and her promise to see Kari safely to Glastonbury. She would not break that promise simply because at the moment she would rather see Tristan of Monmouth roasting on a spit. She seized the black stallion's reins, and with an efficiency that amazed even herself, vaulted astride. She glared down at him.

"You're wasting time."

His fingers itched at the imagined feel of that slender throat as he swung up behind her. The stallion snorted with disapproval, the gleaming dark head swinging around. The animal's lips pulled back as it worked the bit between large white teeth.

"Silence, you lop-eared nag!" Tristan warned. "Or I'll stake you out for crow bait!" And jerking Rianne back hard against him, he sent the black charging out of the stables.

Grendel scurried to keep up with them, with dire thoughts of the journey that still lay ahead.

They rode for several hours, the moon guiding their path while clouds of a coming storm raced across the sky. They stopped sometime after midnight as clouds blanketed the sky and made riding any farther dangerous. They made a cold camp in a heavily wooded area where dense foliage offered concealment and shelter from the coming storm.

Rianne huddled with Kari under a thick fleece blanket in the shelter of a downed tree, while Grendel curled into a tight ball nearby. Tristan remained with the horses.

It seemed they had slept only moments before Tristan was rousing them. There was little time even for the barest of necessities, and then they were again astride the horses.

"I have to stop," Rianne informed him through clenched teeth several hours later, keeping her back rigid so that as little of their bodies touched as possible.

It was near midday. They'd ridden nonstop since before dawn, drinking from the skins of water carried over the saddles. Her backside hurt, her legs hurt, not to mention the fact that every step jostled her already full bladder, threatening dire consequences if they did not stop.

"Later." With a firm hand on her hip, he hauled her back against him.

Rianne ground her teeth together in frustration. "You said that last time, and the time before that."

"And it will be the same next time."

She squirmed and again put distance between them, with the same results.

"We have been riding for hours. We must stop."

"Two more hours."

It took all her self-control not to turn around and claw that cold expression off his face.

"Kari is not well."

"She is well enough. There are no healers out here. It will do no good to stop."

"She needs to rest," she adamantly insisted. "She has not the strength for this."

"She can rest in a few hours."

This was getting her nowhere. She tried for diplomacy. After all, he was a knight of the king. Surely he knew of such things.

"*Please,*" she said, almost choking on the word, and braced herself for another curt response.

That one little word no doubt cost her dearly, he thought. He had no desire to meet up with anyone who might have followed them from Bath, nor did he have any desire to be the cause of more harm to the girl.

"We will stop briefly," he finally replied. "There is a wooded area some distance hence that offers shelter and game. We will make camp there for the night."

He felt the subtle change in her body, her hips and thighs snugged between his in the saddle. For hours she'd carried herself stiff as an oak before him. The slightest contact of their bodies caused her to stiffen and immediately pull away, as if he had the plague. The stiffness in her spine eased, causing her to relax against him.

"Will there be trouble?"

He shifted as well, against the sudden tightness in his groin at the softness of her bottom pressed against him. The body disguised in the boy's clothes was most definitely a woman's.

" 'Tis always possible so far from Arthur's landhold. And the stable owner did not exactly agree with the price I offered for the horses." When he reined in, she slipped from the saddle with deliberate care, moving stiffly from so many hours in the saddle.

"But Arthur is king. There is no war," she replied, words laced with sarcasm. "Surely no one would dare attack a knight of the king."

"Aye, so we thought at Monmouth," he grimly replied.

Monmouth. A name, a place, nothing more. It held no meaning for her. Only a vague recollection from stories Dannelore had told her. She had tucked them away along with the other memories of her childhood, which had ended on that night of blood and death.

Unwanted feelings surfaced—old fears, unanswered questions, and along with it the longing of a child for family, mother, father.

"How much farther to Glastonbury?" she asked, blocking out those painful thoughts and needs.

He heard the quiver of emotion in her voice, along with the steeliness that followed, making him think that she perhaps felt more than she let on.

"Two days, possibly three."

The respite was brief. No sooner had she and Kari returned from a few moments of privacy than they were again astride the horses, holding to the pace he set.

They made camp that night at the edge of the Bodmin forest. They were all weary, the horses' heads sagging in their harnesses. As Rianne slipped to the ground, her legs went out from under her. Tristan's hands tightened at her arms and prevented her from crumbling to the ground in a pathetic pile of useless muscle and bones.

They were hard hands, more accustomed to the feel of the sword or war ax, capable of snapping slender bones. But unlike the last time, he didn't push her away.

"The feeling in your legs will return shortly," he said sympathetically as he steadied her.

It returned in a flood of searing heat as blood rushed into her legs and other places where their bodies brushed.

He slowly relaxed his hold with a gentleness that was even more disturbing than the anger. This time *she* pushed him away as she slowly walked past him and willed her knees not to go out from under her.

They were all exhausted from the long ride, but Kari more so than anyone else. Too long she'd been used and abused by Garidor. She was too thin, little more than skin and bones. She had not the reserves of strength that Rianne possessed and she worried about her. She'd seen too many die from wasting sickness, in Arthur's kingdom where peace and prosperity abounded.

Bah! she thought. Where was the prosperity for those like Kari?

She had no needs of her own; she had always been able to take care of herself. But those like Kari were ill-equipped to take care of themselves in a world where they were invisible. Except to the likes of Garidor.

"You are not to blame for Kari's circumstances," Grendel said, startling her as she realized he had read her thoughts.

"There are others who must bear that burden."

"Perhaps," she conceded as she and the little man gathered wood for the fire. "But she offered friendship when I had no one. The least I can do is keep my promise. She will be safe at Glastonbury."

And afterward? The words moved through her thoughts as clearly as if he had spoken the words aloud.

"Perhaps I shall stay there as well," she replied. "The peaceful life of the abbey holds a certain appeal. . . ."

She suddenly stopped as she realized that the little man hadn't uttered a single word. Not in the way others usually spoke to one another. She had sensed his thoughts and responded as easily as if they conversed aloud.

Grendel had wondered if she possessed that particular trait, as did so many of her kind, including her mother and Merlin. In those brief, unguarded moments, he'd realized for the first time that she did indeed possess the ability of thought transference. Hope flared anew that if she possessed that trait, she might possess other abilities inherited from her mother. If only she would open herself to that possibility instead of stubbornly denying her legacy.

She walked over to him and dumped the armful of wood that she'd been gathering at his feet. One particularly large piece fell on his foot. He jumped back, howling with pain.

Read my thoughts, now! she silently dared him. *And by the way, how is your foot?*

"Partridge tastes better if it is cooked," Tristan hinted broadly as he watched the little man struggle to start the fire he'd laid.

Rianne too watched with amusement as Grendel labored over the fire, mumbling all sorts of incoherent incantations interspersed with an occasional curse while he huffed and puffed in an attempt to coax flame from a thin feather of smoke.

"The wood is wet," she pointed out. "That happens after a rain."

The little man glared at her. "Thank you, mistress, for that enlightening bit of information."

Then his gaze sharpened on a sudden thought. She refused to accept who and what she was. However, her one weakness was the girl Kari. She might be persuaded to explore her other powers if she thought the girl might benefit from it.

He shook his head, as if with deep regret. "Master Tristan is right. Without a fire there will be no food to eat."

Tristan looked up with sudden curiosity. It wasn't like Grendel to agree with him on anything. What was the little beggar up to now?

Rianne sensed his game as she approached where the little man knelt before the wood that had been laid for the fire. She saw the sly expression on his face. She leaned over the neatly laid fire and, smiling to herself, struck the small flat stone she carried in her pouch against another dark rock.

A spark ignited, smoldering among the dead leaves and bits of pine bark. A small flame appeared. It caught at the leaves and pine needles, quickly consuming them, then sent fiery fingers reaching upward toward larger pieces.

She sat back on her heels with an expression of smug satisfaction. " 'Tis not so difficult, when you know the way of it."

Grendel frowned. "Anyone can do that."

"Apparently not," she replied, angling a sharp look at him.

The gnome muttered to himself as he fed more wood onto the growing fire, thwarted once again in his attempt to draw her out and force her to use her powers.

The fire burned steadily as night descended around the encampment. All that remained of the partridge were a few scattered bones.

Grendel contented himself with dried berries and eggs he'd scavenged in the forest. He'd cracked them open and sucked out the contents. His aversion toward consuming fowl obviously did not extend toward eggs.

Rianne had steeped a concoction of herbs and dried berries, carried in the pouch at her belt, and had given it to Kari. Already the girl's eyes grew heavy-lidded; her head nodded forward and the wooden cup slipped from her fingers.

"You have a surprising knowledge of curatives," Grendel commented, thinking that praise might succeed where his other schemes had failed.

Rianne looked up as she took the fallen cup, mistrustful of the little man's attempt at casual conversation. As she was rapidly learning, there was a reason to everything he said and did.

She shrugged. " 'Tis a small thing. No more than the next person who must learn of such things to survive."

Grendel smiled inwardly. Her selflessness toward the girl

was so like another. Meg had that same quality, that same nurturing and caring spirit.

" 'Tis no small thing in the hands of a healer such as my mistress. She also has a healing touch."

Tristan looked up as he listened to the direction of the little man's conversation.

"Then you are most fortunate," Rianne told the gnome. "Perhaps she can heal your sore foot when next you see her."

The little man pulled a face at the reminder about his throbbing foot and just how it had come to be injured.

"Perhaps," Tristan concurred as he joined the conversation "Although she has been able to do little about his *sore disposition.*"

"I do not have to listen to this," Grendel informed them.

"I was only trying to be helpful, and this is what I get for my trouble—a knave of a knight who lives his life between his legs and an ungrateful child with the temperament of a hedgehog. Well, you won't always have Grendel to push around."

He grumbled and fumed and made dire imprecations about those who made jokes at the expense of others as he poked at the fire, feeding in larger pieces of wood.

The flames leapt higher as the heat found pockets of sap and pine tar, then exploded in a shower of sparks and live embers. Grendel howled with pain as the sleeve of his tunic caught fire.

Tristan seized a blanket to smother the flames, but Rianne reached the gnome first.

He had no warning to protect himself. Just as he had no warning of the healing power that flowed through the connection of her hand at his arm, taking away the pain and healing the burned flesh.

Tristan was immediately beside them, and he cut away the tunic in spite of the gnome's protests. He stared down at the small muscular arm. There were no blisters or singed skin. In fact, the skin was unmarred except for the goosebumps that quivered across the gnome's skin and set the tiny hairs on end at the sudden loss of his shirt. Tristan seized her hand and turned it over in his.

"You're not burned."

Her fingers curled into a fist as she tried to free herself. "My good fortune," she replied, lightly dismissing it as she sensed his thoughts.

Tristan seized her other hand and turned it over. There were no marks on the pale skin, yet he had seen her smother out the fire with her bare hands. The scar at his chin tingled with the memory of another who possessed the ability to heal with the gentle touch of a hand.

"Most fortunate indeed," he murmured.

Aware that Grendel watched with intense interest, she pulled her hand from Tristan's.

"I will have to be more careful in the future," she replied and retreated to the fleece bedroll she'd laid out beside Kari.

Rianne slipped from the warm fleece. The sky lightened over the crowning tops of the trees, as dawn broke over the encampment. Kari stirred beside her, rubbing sleep from her eyes.

"Is something wrong?"

" 'Tis nothing. Go back to sleep."

Kari caught her by the arm. In that surprisingly strong grasp, she sensed the girl's alarm.

"I won't be gone long."

But the girl was insistent. Rianne consented rather than argue with her and risk waking the others. They silently slipped from the camp.

She'd greatly depleted her supply of medicinal herbs and hoped to find more in the forest to replenish them. And she needed time to gather her thoughts and make a decision about her own future as they neared Glastonbury.

* * *

Tristan suddenly jerked awake. It was dawn. The fire had burned low. Only embers remained, glowing brightly on a shifting current of air. Mist lay over the encampment, wrapping around the trees, shifting in one direction, then another, as he'd seen it a thousand times.

All was quiet; no one stirred. As the mist shifted again across the camp he saw that only the gnome lay curled asleep before the fire. He immediately came to his feet. Rianne and the girl were both gone.

He found the soft impressions in the loamy soil at the edge of the encampment. He shifted the sword to the scabbard at his back. As the sky grew lighter he followed the tracks that led deeper into the forest.

Rianne found star thistle near the water's edge, growing in the shelter of some rocks. When brewed the leaves produced a tonic for fever. She picked several handfuls and deposited them into the pouch at her belt. The dragon herb was not as easily found.

It was effective against fevers and helped stimulate the appetite. When they had the opportunity she would brew a tea for Kari for she was far too thin.

The girl followed along behind, gathering acorns and hickory nuts in the hem of her gown, her voice soft and ethereal as she hummed to herself. In spite of the hardship of their journey, a peacefulness seemed to have come over the girl with every mile they put between themselves and Garidor.

Rianne knew she was right in her decision to take the girl to Glastonbury. There she would hopefully find a measure of peace that had been lacking in her life.

She found a small dragon herb at the edge of the clearing. Kari came up behind her as she snipped off only a small portion of the leaves, leaving some for the next one who needed it, just as Dannelore had taught her.

Kari's eyes widened at the knife she held in her hand. "Where did you get that?"

"From Grendel," Rianne replied with a conspiratorial smile. "For one who supposedly has many unusual powers, he is greatly lacking in common sense." Her grin deepened. "I lifted it from his belt."

"Master Tristan will be displeased," Kari said fearfully.

"That is why there is no need for him to know about it. I feel safer with it. Say nothing," she told the girl. "It will be our secret."

"You take a great risk," Kari fretted. "He has a horrible temper."

"Bah!" Rianne snorted. "His bark is worse than his bite. He does not frighten me." She picked through some of the taller undergrowth, noting each stalk, leaf, and slender reed with a practiced eye. She was looking for comfrey, which usually grew in abundance in such places.

"Do you believe what the little man says of your family?" Kari asked as she trailed along behind.

"I have no family," Rianne replied, closing off all thought of such things. "They are dead to me." Then her eyes lit up as she spotted the telltale gray-green leaves.

"There it is!" she exclaimed as she bent down to pick several sprigs.

She had almost given up finding any of the herb so late in the season. As a child, she and Dannelore had gathered enough herbs to last them through the winter. When steeped, dried leaves, seeds, and stalks they collected throughout the spring and summer produced a variety of elixirs that provided curatives for fevers, injuries, and other complaints.

But it had been many years since she had lived within the safe walls of the forest cottage with the sweet, pungent fragrance of herbs that hung in tied bundles from the rafters.

Satisfied with her find, she was about to turn back to the encampment when something across the clearing drew her attention.

At first she thought it was a trick of the light and the swirling clouds of mist as dawn filtered through the tops of the trees. She was certain it was only her imagination, even as her senses sharpened and told her it was not.

Then shadows shifted and mist swirled around the solitary figure who stood across the clearing. The creature seemed to have no substance at all but drifted on currents of air. Then the mist shifted again, the creature slowly taking shape and form.

It seemed to glide over the ground as it drew closer. And Rianne realized that the swirling shadows were the folds of the mantle the creature wore, the edges drifting on those currents of air, the hood worn low over his face, the features hidden.

Behind her, humming in that singsong voice, Kari was unaware that they were no longer alone. She suddenly stopped singing as she came up behind Rianne.

Rianne immediately sensed her fear, and it became her own fear in the metallic taste that backed up into her throat, the sudden chill that broke out across her skin, and the dread that moved through her blood, as voices whispered to her from old dreams.

The herbs she'd gathered fell from her fingertips. With the knife in one hand, she motioned to Kari with the other as she slowly backed up.

"Leave!" she whispered fiercely. "Go back!"

Kari seized her by the sleeve. "I will not leave you."

With a fierce protectiveness, Rianne shoved the girl away from her.

"Run!" she told her. "Do not look back no matter what you hear!"

The words were as fierce as they were that long-ago night when Dannelore had sent her running from the cottage.

When the girl hesitated, Rianne thrust her away with a single, fierce thought, like an invisible hand. Kari turned and fled the clearing.

"The child has become the woman," the creature said, its voice disembodied, human and yet not human in the low, rasping whisper that carried to her on an icy wind.

"Who are you?" Rianne demanded. "What do you want?"

The features faded and the creature took on the form of a woman. Her hair was long and black, flowing about her. And the eyes that looked back at Rianne were the eyes of death.

"You know who I am."

"Nay, I do not."

"We have met before."

"I do not know you."

Eyes as cold as death gleamed back at her. *"Ah, but you do know me."*

The words pierced her thoughts like the blade of a knife as images flowed back across the years from childhood. Once more she saw through the eyes of a child, as she stood beside the ruins of her home, the flames leaping into the night sky, smoke mingling with those clouds of swirling mist. Once again, she saw the images of blood and death. The smell of it choked at her throat. And once again she felt the blood at her hands.

Kari ran headlong into Tristan. She was terrified, near hysterical, and would have fallen if he hadn't caught her. She grabbed the front of his tunic.

"You must help her! She'll be killed!"

He disentangled the girl's fingers. "Return to camp!"

Then she was forgotten as he turned toward the clearing and followed the tracks left in the muddied earth.

Something was terribly wrong. Grendel sensed the evil. He smelled it, then felt it in the smothering weight that pressed down on him, making it difficult to breathe; his bones ached, and thoughts spun from his head even as he struggled to waken.

He heard the sound of wailing, eventually realized it was Kari, and reached for the knife at his belt. It was gone!

It took several moments to clear the lethargy from his muddled thoughts. By then, Kari was pulling at him. Tears were streaming down her cheeks.

Tristan found Rianne at the edge of the clearing. He saw no one in the clearing or in the trees beyond. He moved to within a few feet and called out to her.

"Do you see it?" she cried out. "We must kill it!"

He scanned the clearing again and saw nothing. "There's nothing there."

She adamantly shook her head. "It's there! I saw it! We must kill it!"

He scanned the clearing once more. He had no idea what she had seen. Whatever it was, it was gone now. He came up behind her, grabbed her, and dragged her back against him.

"There is nothing there!"

CHAPTER TWELVE

Tristan released her. As she spun away from him, the knife fell to the ground at her feet. She ignored it, refusing to feel guilty about having been caught with it.

"You must have seen it!" She was trembling, furious, eyes bright with anger.

For a moment he thought he had seen something but couldn't be certain. When he looked again, whatever it was he thought he'd seen was no longer there. If it had been at all.

"I saw nothing."

"Nothing?" She was incredulous.

He had seen her many moods—and disguises. This was neither. The fear and anger were real. She had seen . . . something. Kari had seen it as well. The girl had been terrified. But whatever they had seen was now gone.

"I saw nothing," he repeated, not unkindly. "But we will take greater precautions from now on. 'Tis for just this reason I didn't want you going off on your own."

She groaned, a sound of frustration and helplessness. "It was there. I saw it. It's still out there."

"What is still out there?" Grendel demanded as he finally reached the clearing.

Rianne swept past him, her thoughts now turning to Kari. The girl must be terrified and she was alone back at the encampment.

"Nothing!" she fumed. "There is nothing there!"

It took all Tristan's considerable self-control not to go after her. Instead, he retrieved the knife and tossed it to Grendel.

"Try to keep this out of her hands."

The gnome was confused. He almost injured himself as he caught the knife. On top of that no one would tell him what had happened.

"Will someone *please* tell me what is going on?"

"Nothing!" Tristan snapped as he returned to camp. "Nothing happened!"

They were ready to leave by the time the sun was full up. The black stallion seemed to sense his master's foul mood. He swung that glossy head about as Rianne prepared to climb astride, velvety muzzle pulled back over large teeth.

Rianne would have preferred his master, but failing that likelihood, she was willing to accept whatever opportunity presented itself and doubled up a slender fist.

"Not even so much as a nibble, you lop-eared nag," she threatened, fully prepared to carry it out.

The black tossed his head and stretched against the restraint of the bridle but made no further attempt to take a chunk out of her.

"You have a way with him," Tristan commented drily as he gathered the reins.

"We have an understanding."

He swung up behind her, almost smiling to himself as she scooted as far forward as possible. His long arms pinned her, making escape impossible. Everywhere she turned, each shift she made brought her into intimate contact with him, so that she eventually gave up trying to escape and sat still as stone in the saddle before him.

"What did you see in the clearing?" he asked.

Seated before him, it was impossible to gauge his mood. She wasn't certain whether he humored her or truly wished to know. But if he made idle conversation at her expense, then she would dump him on his arse in the roadway and not regret it for a moment!

"I thought I saw someone."

"Who?"

She heard the doubt in his voice. "I thought it was a man at first, but then . . . There were a great many shadows. It was dark. I can't be certain."

"If not a man, then what?"

"A woman."

Eventually he urged the stallion forward. He said nothing for a very long time, so that she was certain he was no longer interested in what she had seen.

"What did she look like?"

Rianne angled a glance at him, uncertain whether he truly cared to know or merely humored her.

"She was not very tall, whereas the man was tall."

"Was it a man or a woman?"

She frowned. "I don't know. . . . I saw both."

"At the same time?"

"No. First the man. Then his features changed and I saw the old woman."

"Did you know him?"

"I've seen him in my dreams," she replied hesitantly. "He's there amid the blood and death. . . ." And she shivered as those vivid images returned. "He is blood and death."

"And the woman? Is she in your dreams as well?"

She shook her head. "No, but I know her. I don't know how, but I know her." And then she stunned him. "She has long dark hair and cold dead eyes."

Grendel stared after them as the dung-colored mare plodded behind the black stallion. He shivered as he withdrew from her thoughts, his own memories making him quail in the saddle.

A woman with long dark hair and cold dead eyes . . .

Two days later they reached Glastonbury. The light from the abbot's tower guided them through the pouring rain as night fell. They were cold, wet, exhausted, and covered with mud.

All rancor and animosity had disappeared hours earlier. It required all Rianne's concentration just to remain seated in the wet saddle as the black stallion struggled for footing over uneven terrain.

She no longer fought to maintain that precious distance between them, but gladly accepted the solid strength of Tristan's hard-muscled body at her back and the sheltering comfort of the fleece he wrapped around them rather than find herself pitched into the mud beneath the stallion's hooves.

She slumped wearily as they dismounted in the abbey courtyard and would have collapsed if those strong hands hadn't caught her.

"A fine soft evening, is it not, milady?" Tristan commented. "We shall have to do this again."

The fight had gone out of her hours earlier, revealing an almost amiable disposition that he would have bet all the gold in Arthur's kingdom did not exist.

She was more the young girl he had hoped to find, unaffected by the experiences of all the years in between. He was surprised to discover that he missed the spirited side of her.

She was wet through to the skin in spite of the thick fleece he'd wrapped around them. Mud was splattered across her cheeks and her hair was molded to her head like wet gold. She looked like a drowned kitten, but he reminded himself that kittens have claws as her gaze met his, brilliant blue like twin flames amid the grit and grime.

"Again?" she croaked. As if they had just returned from a casual afternoon ride about the countryside.

"Not on your life, Tristan of Monmouth. Come near me with that horse again and I swear I will gullet you like a cod."

"That's more like it," he quipped. "I was concerned you might have taken ill. 'Tis not like you to let a decent word past those lips when a vicious one will do instead."

Her eyes narrowed as feeling burned down through her legs and feet, and several words formed on the tip of her tongue only to be swallowed in frustrated silence as a young monk approached them. While she had no particularly devout feelings, still she respected them in others.

"We have been expecting you," Brother Timothy greeted them.

And as Rianne joined Kari, she heard Tristan ask, "What news of Monmouth?"

She could not hear the young monk's reply as she and Kari were escorted into another part of the abbey. There was no need as the light of the torches played across Tristan's somber features.

"Come in, little man," Father Dunstan invited Grendel. "No need to go lurking about in hallways. All are welcome in God's house." Grendel finally slipped into the abbot's private chambers.

"And close the door behind you," Father Dunstan called out. " 'Tis drafty on such a terrible night."

Grendel perched in the corner, where he could watch without being watched and could listen to both the words spoken and the thoughts that went unspoken. And besides, it was the same corner where a fire burned warmly at the brazier.

The room was spartan, as befitted a man of the abbot's position and calling. The one extravagance was the precious journals and manuscripts upon the shelves and at the reading table. There were volumes written on the sciences, astrology, history, and even a volume of ancient Latin text, several hundred years old. And another in which the abbot had been making entries of his own.

When Tristan commented on it, the abbot smiled secretively. "I have taken to laying down my thoughts of events as I have seen them unfolding. These are most interesting times we live in."

As a learned man he accepted that there were many things between heaven and earth that were not easily explained. Such was his acceptance of Lady Meg and Master Merlin. In fact, a keen respect had grown between the two men, each willing to accept the other for his beliefs. It was also Father Dunstan who had christened Connor's infant daughter.

"We received word you might pass this way and have been watching for you every day," Father Dunstan informed Tristan as he poured a healthy draught of mulled wine for each of them.

He offered none to his companion, having learned long ago that the little man did not drink. Then the abbot settled into his own chair, wine shimmering in the goblet cradled in both hands.

"You were overlong in returning."

Tristan hesitated, choosing his words carefully. Father Dunstan's beliefs were firmly rooted in the concept of God, and absolutely unshakable. He could attest to the depth of that belief, for the good father had been called upon by Lord Connor on many occasions to pray for Tristan's soul.

But he was also a learned man, attested to by the volumes of priceless manuscripts that lined the walls of his private chamber in the abbey.

"The journey was not as anticipated," Tristan replied— a mild understatement—and explained their discovery of the abandoned cottage and that Rianne had been on her own for a very long time. He said nothing of his unusual encounter with the old woman at the cottage.

Father Dunstan shook his head with sadness as Tristan finished relating the story. "What do you believe? Is the girl Lord Connor's daughter?"

Once again Tristan answered carefully, for it delved into matters most delicate where the abbot was concerned. "Grendel believes that she is. And there is a resemblance of feature."

He left off telling the abbot that there were an equal number of qualities that baffled him about her, or any reference to her more accomplished skills at thievery. He only prayed she kept her hands off the ornate fixtures in the abbey church.

"What does *she* believe?" Father Dunstan asked.

Therein lay the heart of the problem. "She has been on her own a very long time," he explained. "Her life has not been easy."

" 'Tis difficult for many," the good father replied. " 'Tis how she chooses to live her life that matters—that and her steadfast belief in God. How has she fared these past years? Is she educated?"

In a manner of speaking, Tristan thought, recalling her extraordinary skill at gambling. He squirmed slightly as he stretched the truth.

"She is resourceful and very skilled with her hands."

"Ah, needlework," the abbot assumed. "Most appropriate for a young woman of noble birth. Lord Connor and Mistress Meg will be pleased."

Pray God, he hoped so, Tristan thought. He wasn't about to point out that her skills hardly fell within the area of domestic acceptability.

"There is the matter of the other girl who traveled with us," he went on to explain. "An unfortunate orphan who seeks the shelter of the church. She has suffered greatly and been sorely abused. But she has a kind heart and a good mind. Rianne hoped the girl might be given sanctuary."

"Ah," Father Dunstan lit up with a hopeful expression. "So our little Rianne has a generous, benevolent heart as well. It pleases me to hear it. I had feared the worst for her temperament, not to mention her soul, when you spoke of the death of the woman Dannelore.''

The worst was quite possibly exactly what it was. And as for her benevolent spirit, Tristan almost burst out laughing at the thought of their first encounter, when she'd been most benevolent and spared certain of his bodily parts at the end of her blade.

"The girl is most welcome," the abbot assured him. "We shall find a place for her. It will be a comfort for Rianne to have her friend so near."

With matters of Kari's immediate future settled, Tristan's thoughts turned to home.

"What news is there from Monmouth?"

The abbot frowned, his expression grave. "Most grave, I fear. In spite of Meg's best efforts, Lord Connor's wounds have not healed. He is much wasted by fever. I have been deeply concerned that you might not return in time."

"What of Merlin?"

The abbot shook his head sadly. "My friend has not been able to help him." He rose then, his face heavily lined, and laid a hand on Tristan's shoulder.

" 'Tis good that you have returned. I fear there is not much time. My heart is heavy for Lord Connor and Mistress Meg. Their daughter's return will most certainly be a comfort to them."

Tristan sincerely wished that he shared the abbot's faith.

"How far do ye s'pose we've come?" Kari asked, her voice echoing softly off stone walls in the sparsely furnished chamber that adjoined the lady chapel. Light from a single oil lamp glowed softly across those walls where trailing vines had been painted in a natural motif that softened the harshness of stone.

Each day that had taken them farther from the inn and Garidor, Kari had asked the same question. And each day the answer was found in the landmarks they passed—villages and hamlets, the dense barrier of the Bodmin forest, the gleaming ribbon of the Tamar River, the ancient city of Bath, and farther. And still the question was there.

"Far enough," Rianne told her as one of the women who had brought them to the chamber returned with a trencher of food, a basin of water, and clean clothes.

"You are safe," she assured the girl. "No one will ever hurt you again."

When there was no response she turned around to discover that Kari had fallen asleep as they talked, the food before her untouched, her head cradled on her bent arm.

"You are safe," she quietly repeated as the girl slept peacefully for possibly the first time in her life.

She removed Kari's sodden clothes and boots, and covered her with a thick blanket. Then she made her own bed nearby. But sleep was long in coming.

She could not remain at Glastonbury. Tristan was determined to take her to Monmouth, and she was equally determined not to go.

There was nothing for her there. These people meant nothing to her. She had no memory of them. The bond—if in fact it had ever existed—had been severed long ago. In the years since she had learned to live on her own, and she had found truer friendship and deeper loyalty with Kari than with those she supposedly shared a blood bond.

Her promise to Kari had been kept and, as much as she regretted the loss of that friendship, she was consoled by the fact that the girl was now safe. Garidor would never hurt her again, and when morning came Rianne would be far from Glastonbury.

She rose before dawn. In the cool, steeped shadows of the chamber she silently bid the sleeping girl farewell, then made her way along the passages and across the abbey hall to the courtyard.

She passed several of the monks at their morning prayers, but they paid her no heed. Once outside the abbey hall she made her way to the stables.

Though her skills at riding were limited to the past few weeks, she would put more distance between herself and Tristan if she was astride. When she no longer needed the horse, she could sell it.

She had no provisions, only the clothes on her back. But she'd lived most of her life with no more than that. She did, however, have the small pouch with the coins she'd won at gaming and her skill. She would be able to take care of herself, just as she always had.

The horses caught her scent as soon as she entered the stables. Nearby a dark head suddenly appeared over the top railing with equally dark, inquisitive eyes fixed on her. She sought the docile roan Kari had ridden and quickly moved past the stall.

Harness and saddle presented a problem she hadn't considered, but she thought she pretty much had the way of it from having seen it done countless times. The trick seemed to be in cinching the belly strap tightly enough so that she and the saddle didn't end up in the dirt.

She spoke softly to the roan as she moved around it, stroking a hand over the silken hide. Ears pitched back and forth as she made gentling sounds.

The black stallion snorted from the adjacent stall, a sound that might have been a greeting or disapproval.

"No one asked your opinion," she informed him, as if they conversed in some ancient language. "And I certainly do not need your permission."

The black shook his head as if he heartily disagreed.

"Nor did anyone ask my opinion, or my permission."

Rianne whirled around and came face to face with Tristan.

He leaned against a support post, arms folded across his chest, one booted foot casually crossed over the other. But there was nothing casual about the narrowed gaze that fastened on her.

Which would it be? he thought. A lie? Or some carefully contrived story? Not a lie, but not quite the truth either. She was, after all, incapable of lying. If she was Meg's daughter.

She gave nothing away either by word or gesture, but calmly returned his look measure for measure. The consummate gambler who revealed nothing about the game she played. He reminded himself, she'd had a great deal of experience at disguising her emotions and her thoughts.

Her breath exploded in the frosty morning air. Those emotions perhaps were not completely disguised, he discovered, as those unusual eyes gleamed like blue flames.

She offered neither excuses nor explanations. "I do not need your opinion or your permission," she replied as she led the roan out of the stall.

"Ah, but you do, Rianne," he assured her. "You have been entrusted to my care. You may not leave without my permission."

Blue flame turned to blue ice as that unusual gaze met his.

"By whom?" she demanded, facing him down, hands planted on slender hips.

"Your father and mother."

"I have no mother or father," she defiantly replied. "They're dead."

"They're very much alive," Tristan assured her. "And make no mistake about it, you are going to Monmouth."

The entire journey from the northern lands he'd struggled with the uncertainty that this girl was Connor and Meg's daughter. There was nothing in the defiant, dirt-smudged girl that even suggested the bond of kinship.

Surely not in the anger that curled the slender fists at her sides, the curses that fell too easily from her lips, nor the bruises she had inflicted with such undisguised pleasure. Except for the color of her eyes, a startling contrast amid the dirt, grime, and anger.

Meg and Connor longed to see their daughter, a child raised in obscurity in the care of a trusted guardian, gently reared and protected, who embodied the traits of both her parents, whom Tristan loved as his own. But Dannelore was dead, the girl was no longer a child, and she hadn't been gently reared or protected.

She'd been left to fend for herself, oblivious to the legacy she'd been born to, with a survivor's instincts, the anger to go along with it, and absolutely no notion of the power she possessed. Or the desire to be reunited with her family.

She was understandably mistrustful, suspicious, and resentful. It was probably safer for him that she had no idea of the powers she possessed. If they were even one-tenth of the power her mother had or that which Merlin wielded, he would have been turned to stone during their first encounter.

How could he possibly take this girl back to Monmouth? It would have been easier and perhaps better for everyone if he simply told Meg and Connor that he was unable to find her. But he could never lie to Meg. She would know the truth in spite of her blindness, and the pain of that betrayal would be worse than the pain of the truth. Therefore he intended to see the matter through.

"You cannot make me go with you," she informed him. "And I won't change my mind. 'Tis my choice. Not yours to make for me, nor that of people I cannot remember, who have no need of me except to suit their own purposes."

She refused to be intimidated or told what she could and could not do. In spite of the set angle of his jaw, which suggested she'd perhaps been pushed too far and the instinctive warning that slipped across her senses.

He sighed deeply as he pushed away from the post and slowly advanced on her. "I thought that was what you would say."

"Stay away from me," she warned, standing her ground

with a bold defiance that almost made him laugh. As if she was defending the castle mount with an entire army to back her up. There was something about that anger, stubbornness, and reckless defiance in the face of overwhelming odds that reminded him of Lord Connor and persuaded him all the more that she was going to Monmouth.

"You have two choices, Rianne," he informed her. "Either astride that horse, or across it like a sack of grain. But," he assured her, "you are going to Monmouth."

Now it was her turn to laugh. It bubbled into her throat and curved her lips. Surely he jested. She'd learned much since he and the gnome had come into her life.

She focused her thoughts and on a burst of energy launched it at him. Her intention was to send him sprawling into the straw, as she had sent the gnome sprawling across the clearing in the forest. But she immediately learned another valuable lesson about size and weight.

Tristan was taller and far outweighed the little man. Instead of sending him over backwards and providing an opportunity for escape, the blow caught him at the chin, barely more than a well-landed punch.

Those dark eyes glittered as he rubbed his chin. Then he smiled. The transformation caught her off-guard. The smile transformed his features, gleaming at those dark eyes with stunning heat, riveting her gaze to the beguiling sensuality that curved his lips when she should have been watching his hands.

"You give me no choice, milady." Like a fox pouncing on a hare, he came after her.

The momentum sent them sprawling into the straw of an open stall. Before she could react, he was on her. She was flipped over onto her stomach, her face buried in the straw. Then she felt his knee at her back as her arms were dragged behind her and bound.

As Tristan stood, she flipped over onto her back, spitting out straw and several vile curses—many he'd heard and several he hadn't.

"What was that you said, milady?" he remarked, his smile curving into a smirk. "There is no need to thank me. You're most welcome. After all, I wouldn't want you to injure yourself on the ride to Monmouth."

"You bastard!" she screamed at him, leveraging herself so that she sat facing him. "You pig! You miserable son of a . . ."

"Aye, well, that should just about do it as far as animals are concerned," he replied, cutting her off as he entered the next stall, seized the saddle, and flung it over the back of the black stallion.

She spit out more straw, then informed him in a low voice that sent the air rippling with heat, "I refuse to go to Monmouth!"

"That hardly seems worth arguing at present," he pointed out as he snapped the cinch strap into place and led the stallion from the stall.

"What is this?" Grendel demanded as he entered the stable and glanced from Tristan to the stall, where Rianne sat in a pile of straw. "Has something happened?"

Pieces of straw clung to her clothes and hair. Other disgusting substances stained her clothes. She was filthy and pathetic, except for those eyes, which gleamed like twin pools of blue fire.

"I will cut out your heart!" she threatened. "But first I think I'll start with your throat!"

Tristan merely nodded. "Aye, we've heard that before as well."

"Perhaps 'tis best to be gentle, milord," Grendel suggested, hoping those bonds about her wrists were securely tied. There was, however, no restraint on her thoughts, and though her powers were unskilled that perhaps made her all the more dangerous.

Rianne knew where her best chance for freedom lay as she turned that threatening gaze on the gnome.

"Put an end to this or I will turn you into a dung heap."

He gestured helplessly. "I wish that I could, mistress. But I dare not."

Ignoring the blistering look she aimed at him, Tristan seized her by the shoulders and hauled her to her feet.

"Aye, and you will turn me into a goat," he commented drily.

"A goat is too good for you!" she hissed as she aimed the toe of her boot at his shin with barely more reaction than the first blow.

"Warming your backside is more appealing by the moment."

"Not if you wish to keep your manhood!"

"Sweet Jesu!" he swore vehemently. "You have a mouth that would make any warrior in Arthur's army cringe."

"Let me go and you will not hear another word," she bargained.

It was tempting. A sound thrashing was also tempting. Instead he seized her by the shoulders and kissed her. Not experimentally, as she had kissed him, but thoroughly, deeply, and absolutely without any mercy at all.

The kiss was stunning. It burned through her like wildfire, fast and hot, searing every nerve ending . . . setting *her* on fire so that her fingers curled into tight fists where they were bound low at her back. She longed to touch him, to hold on to that heat until it consumed her.

Tristan pushed her away. Her mouth was slightly bruised and her lips tingled. And for the first time she was completely speechless. He lifted her like a sack of grain and tossed her across the front of the saddle.

What little air was left was slammed from her lungs as she dangled head down, backside up in front of the saddle. Then he swung up behind her, his knee banging into her ribs.

She arched her back in an attempt to throw herself off and

received a stinging wallop across the backside. She screamed with frustration and pain, several more curses on the tip of her tongue, as she angled him a murderous look, the kiss almost forgotten.

"The choice is yours, milady," Tristan warned in a silken tone, with a hand poised above her curved bottom, a thoroughly wicked smile on his lips.

She clamped her mouth shut, but the expression in her eyes was murderous.

"Excellent choice, milady," Tristan complimented her as he dug in his heels and sent the black stallion charging from the stables at a bone-jarring pace that prevented any further curses.

Grendel stared after them, horrified, as he imagined what would happen when they reached Monmouth. Then a slow, wicked grin spread across his face.

He led the roan from the stall, crawled up the cross bars of the stall like a ladder, and then vaulted into the saddle. The very thought of riding a horse again after the past weeks was enough to make him shudder. But he couldn't wait to see this!

CHAPTER THIRTEEN

"What news is there from the eastern army?" Connor shifted against the pain that was a constant presence, his skin damp with a cold sweat that broke out.

"I did not come to talk military strategy," Arthur replied from the chair opposite as they sat before the roaring fire in the smaller chamber off the great hall.

"Then why did you come?" The wasting sickness from the wound he'd received several weeks earlier had not dimmed those sharp eyes.

"To see my friend," Arthur said with honesty, carefully chosen words, and humor that was sorely needed. "Since you are far too busy to come to Camelot."

"To see if I was still alive?" Connor struck at the heart of the matter with a bluntness that caused Meg to look up with concern.

"To hunt," the king countered bluntly with the easy comaraderie they had shared since their youth. "Your forests are far richer with game than those surrounding Camelot."

Only once had there been an estrangement between them, when Arthur had left England with Merlin as a youth, and England had been left in chaos. Those left behind, Connor among them, had endured the wars and civil strife that had ravaged the kingdom waiting for Arthur's return until hope was almost lost.

When he finally returned, Arthur found a country in ruins, those he loved dead or held for ransom, and the friend who had once been as a brother to him a man full grown who had endured the loss of family, home, and all hope that Arthur might ever return.

It had been difficult, but they had found their way through the anger and mistrust and discovered a new friendship bound by honor, blood, and hope for the future.

Many had been lost along the way. It was something they accepted as warriors. But Arthur knew that no loss would be as great as that of this friend, who was dying little by little each day. And no one could seem to stop it. Not even Merlin.

''The location of Camelot was your choice,'' Connor pointed out, enjoying the companionship of his friend, who spoke with plain words and simple truths and did not coddle him with falsehoods that he would soon be better, or leave the room weeping as others did.

Death was a part of life. Every man who carried a sword into battle accepted that his life could end at any moment. It had been deeply ingrained since he had first held a sword in his hand, and it was no different now. There was but one regret, and his gaze softened as it sought and found the slender creature who had shared his life and passion all these years since Arthur was made king.

The years had not changed her. If anything Meg was more beautiful now. There was no hint of the pain or sadness that she had endured at the loss of the beloved child they were forced to send away, nor of the truth they now shared with death so near.

That truth had always been there, for she was not bound by the laws of the mortal world as he was. Always it had been part of their life together that the day would come when he would grow old and die, while she would not.

He accepted it with the certainty that the love they shared would remain as long as one of them was alive to remember it. She looked up now, having sensed his thoughts, and her own reached out in the way that had bound them one to the other from the very beginning.

He felt her love reaching out to him, and his reaching out to her like an invisible hand that needed to touch and be touched. Always it was so that whatever task they were at, no matter the distance that separated them, all that was needed was a tender thought that reached across the time and distance between. So it would always be.

But there was an apprehension there as well. He saw it in her eyes. The blindness that had robbed her of sight could not hide the emotions within. Or perhaps it was that he had come to know her so well. A look, a touch, a thought, a gesture. All of them, all of her as much a part of him as breathing.

He knew her apprehension was because yet another day passed and still there was no word from Tristan. He too was apprehensive, for these were uneasy times in which they lived.

The attack on Monmouth weeks earlier had been but the first of many attacks. The hard-won peace of Arthur's kingdom had been shattered by an unknown enemy who moved with lightning swiftness, and left death and destruction in his path.

"There have been at least a score of attacks along the frontier," Connor went on, his thoughts returning to matters that were of grave importance to them all. For soon he would no longer be there to protect Arthur. Plans must be made.

"Shall we speak of the true reason that brings you to Monmouth?"

Once Connor had been his war general. In recent years he had commanded the largest contingent of Arthur's army. It seemed that in spite of his failing health, his friend still commanded a knowledge of everything that went on in Arthur's kingdom.

The king angled a glance at Lady Meg. He deeply respected her and valued her friendship, and in spite of the fact that he was king, he held no illusion that he wielded any power within this household. As if she sensed his thought, she shook her head.

"Do not hesitate on my account." She tried to keep the anger from her words but failed.

Wasn't it enough that Connor had served him all the years during his reign and even before, during the time when Arthur was gone and there was doubt he would ever return? Now her husband was dying and still Arthur needed him. And still Connor gave of himself. She did not understand these mortals, even though she had lived these many years among them.

She kept her thoughts to herself, for it would do no good to argue the matter. It was an argument she always lost and she did not wish to cause Connor more distress with bitter words. But her thoughts were not hidden from everyone.

Though she could not see his expression and no words were spoken, still she sensed Merlin's disapproval in the powerful thoughts that joined with hers.

"You have a sharp tongue, sister. Do you understand so little of the man whose life you have shared these many years that you do not realize the safety of the kingdom is in many more ways more precious to Connor? To lose it all now would mean that his life has been for nothing."

As though she had never been blinded, her gaze lifted and fixed on that point across the room where she knew Merlin stood at the window opening, as he had throughout the morning.

It was a truth she could not deny. For as much as she knew Connor loved her, she also knew that he loved Arthur in a way she could never understand.

It was the reason he had continued to fight long ago against the usurpers who would have destroyed the kingdom even when Arthur had abandoned England. And therein lay the simple truth that those qualities that made him the man he was, were the very qualities that she loved in him. To deny them was to deny that love.

"If he wishes to speak of war, then by all means," she said, tossing up her hands.

"He will not rest when he should anyway." She rose from the chair and threw her yarnwork into the basket at her feet with amazing accuracy.

"He is my husband, but he will always be the king's general!"

With that same ability that had guided her in spite of her blindness, Meg twitched the hem of her gown aside and headed for the door.

She slammed it behind her, the sound echoing off the stone walls in the cavernous main hall and helping assuage some of the anger and feelings of helplessness.

Merlin let her go. He did not try to stop her with words or thought, or even a hint of what he'd sensed even as they argued—that invisible energy that charged the air around them. Until he knew the cause of it, he chose to say nothing.

"If I had a legion of warriors such as she, there would be no threat to my kingdom," Arthur mused thoughtfully at her heated departure.

"You are a fortunate man to have such a loyal and spirited creature in your life."

"Aye," Connor agreed, smiling. "She is a passionate woman."

Merlin left the chamber as their conversation turned to matters of strategy and war, while his thoughts returned to that unusual presence he had sensed while standing at the window opening.

* * *

Every bone in Rianne's body ached. The edge of the saddle thrust up under her ribs and her leg muscles cramped. Her hair had come loose, blinding and smothering her all at once. And with every jarring step, her head was slammed against a hard muscled thigh.

She was past the point of anger, past humiliation and indignation. But not past the point of cursing. This must be what a chicken felt like all trussed up for the spit, she thought.

With teeth tightly clenched together to keep them from being rattled loose from her head, she swore at Tristan and told him exactly what she thought of him, her family, and the king. And received a stinging wallop across her backside that brought her head up with stunned disbelief.

"Touch me again . . ." A second wallop stung at her backside, while tears stung at her eyes. She decided against cursing him and concentrated on surviving.

Monmouth lay a half day's ride to the west of Glastonbury, over the old Roman road. They reached it in less than half that time by cutting across open fields that lay muddied beneath days' old snow, fording several streams, and plunging through heavily wooded forest and deep undergrowth.

When they paused at the crest of the hill overlooking Monmouth and the small valley below, the stallion trembled with exhaustion.

Tristan's gaze sharpened as he saw the banners that flew from the uppermost tower. Arthur's colors flew alongside those of the Duke of Monmouth. He prayed they were in time as he sent the black stallion charging down the slope toward the heavily fortified keep.

The main gates were opened as he approached. He signaled a greeting to the master of the gate as he charged through. The main yard was crowded with horses, warriors, and mounted calvary. With only a cursory nod of acknowledgment he rode ahead to the gated courtyard of the main hall.

He reined in and dismounted. The black was heavily lathered, steam rising from quivering muscles on the chilled air. A stable-boy appeared and seized the reins. Like a sack of grain, Tristan seized his companion by the scruff of the neck and threw her over his shoulder. She landed with a smothered sound that assured him that she was still alive.

The gate of the courtyard was thrown open. Guards stared as he crossed the yard and mounted the steps. As he reached the top step, the door of the main hall opened.

Without ceremony and non-too-gently, Tristan heaved his slender burden off his shoulder and dropped it at the feet of the imposing man who stood there.

"Lady Rianne of Monmouth," he announced, introducing the disheveled heap who lay at Merlin's feet.

Rianne levered herself up on one elbow, then managed to work her legs under her. She was bruised, exhausted, and furious, and it took what little strength she had left to sit upright.

She blew at her hair in an attempt to get it out of her eyes. It was wet, tangled, and muddied.

She was equally wet and filthy. Her clothes were covered with mud and grime, and every cockleburr, thorn, and thistle that grew between Monmouth and Glastonbury. On a furious sound she finally managed to blow the hair out of her face, revealing features that were equally smudged with mud, grime, and other suspicious elements that presented a grim sight and an even worse stench.

"You whoreson!" she spat at Tristan. "You pig! You pile of goat excrement!"

Tristan smiled at Merlin with grim satisfaction. "She is all yours. I wish you good fortune, sir. You will need it." And turned and left her there, cursing for all the inhabitants of Monmouth to hear.

Merlin could have stopped her with a single thought. But he

was fascinated by the creature that squirmed with fury at his feet.

He'd sensed their approach after so many long weeks but said nothing to Meg because he wanted to be certain that the one who returned was in fact Meg and Connor's daughter.

It was almost impossible to tell based on appearance. There was absolutely nothing about this foul, wretched, loud creature that suggested even a remote bond to either Meg or Connor. She was dressed like a common beggar and had the disposition of a shrew. On top of that she smelled like the floor of a stable.

The guards hesitantly approached. It was not necessary for him to wave them back. One whiff of the disheveled heap and they instinctively backed away.

"Who the devil are you?" she furiously demanded, turning on him, revealing eyes as bright as blue flame amid the grime and stench. Then those unusual blue eyes widened, and whatever foul words she had been about to hurl at him were suddenly silenced as her awareness connected with his in the ancient way.

"Ah, so there is hope after all," he commented aloud as his thoughts connected with hers and discovered the familiar bond in spite of all outward appearances to the contrary.

She was gifted. The powers of the Light were strong within her, if unrefined and ruled far too much by her emotions.

"I feared you were only capable of making that foul noise. I see you are capable of learning. Not exactly what I had hoped for, but we will have to make do. Your education will be second on the list."

Education?

"And what is the first?" she demanded, her thoughts instinctively responding to his in spite of her wariness and anger.

"A bath," Merlin announced aloud. "Perhaps several of them. Whatever it will take to rid you of dirt and grime."

"One will do nicely," she informed him, her skill increasing with each thought.

And Merlin responded firmly, *"I will be the judge of that."*

"Why did you not tell me?" Meg demanded, pacing across the room. "Is it necessary to learn from the guards that my daughter has returned? I should have been told immediately." She stopped pacing and whirled around.

"Where is she? I want to see her. There is so much to say. . . ." Her voice trailed off. "I had given up hope. I had no dreams, no visions that told me of this. Why is that?" Then fear closed around her heart. The journey had been long and perhaps dangerous. After what had happened at Monmouth . . .

"She has not been harmed in any way?" she asked anxiously.

"She is safe enough," Merlin replied, reaching out with his thoughts to calm and reassure her. He closed his thoughts to other things that he would tell her soon enough.

"And what of Tristan and Grendel? Why did they not bring her to me straightaway? Where are John and Dannelore? Did they return as well? It has been so long since I last saw them." She whirled away from him, hands clasped together, cheeks ablaze with an excitement and happiness he had not seen in a very long time.

"There are plans to be made," she went on. "A special meal to be planned. We will celebrate. That won't be too hard on Connor?" At the mention of his name, her plans changed.

"No, it would be too tiring for him." And then on the next thought, "Tell me about her. Is she tall? What color is her hair? Is it light, or dark like Connor's? What color are her eyes?"

"They are blue," Merlin replied. "She has her mother's eyes."

"Is she sentient?"

"She has certain abilities. But 'tis too soon to know how much ability she possesses. After all, she is half mortal." He paused and knew he had not kept his apprehension from her.

"There is something else you are not telling me. What is it? What has happened?"

She must be told, for soon enough she would know and he wished to ease the shock of it.

"Dannelore and John did not return," he paused, struggling with the gentlest way to explain what she must know. He had always thought mortal emotions difficult and cumbersome, more hindrance than advantage. He still believed that, more so after the past months.

"Something has happened to them."

He knew she had sensed his thoughts, the images gleaned from his encounter with Rianne. As he had searched her thoughts for her essence, learning her, he had also learned of the tragedy of their deaths, the lonely, desperate years that followed, and the life that she had lived.

They were only fragments of images, brief thoughts, memories that were hidden away inside her. But a glimpse was all that was needed to tell him that she had endured a great deal. She had not been gently raised, protected, and sheltered. She had been left on her own, surviving by her wits, drawing on strengths both mortal and immortal, and had become the young woman she was now. A young woman far different from the image his sister had held in her heart and thoughts all these years.

"Aye," he said gently, opening his thoughts completely, letting her see with that ancient way what her daughter's life had been.

Meg sat down on the chair before the hearth in her private chamber. A hollow ache opened up inside her chest and seemed to swallow her heart, so that all she felt was pain and sorrow.

"What have I done, brother?" she whispered as tears spilled down her cheeks.

He laid a comforting hand on her shoulder and tried to console her. "Your only thought was to protect her. You made the only choice you could make. You had no way of knowing what the future would hold."

Meg laid her cheek on his hand at her shoulder. "What must she think?"

"There is a great deal of pain," he told her with blunt honesty. "She is angry. She has endured much and learned to hide her feelings away. She does not trust easily."

Meg smiled softly as she thought of Rianne's father. "Very much like someone I knew a long time ago, who learned to trust and to love. If there is enough of him within her, then perhaps we can find a way to open her heart to us."

"Did I also mention that she is unusually stubborn, single-minded, highly intelligent, very logical, and extremely emotional? She also possesses a most unusual vocabulary."

"A volatile combination," Meg commented with a soft smile. Perhaps there was something of her in her daughter after all.

"There is so little time." Her voice became wistful as she thought of the time perhaps marked by no more than days or hours as Connor's strength slipped farther and farther away.

"How do we reach her? How do we heal the pain of the past? Where do we begin?"

"I suggest a bath."

"What are you doing?" Rianne suspiciously demanded as the two women advanced on her.

There was no escape from the small antechamber near the kitchen, except through the door behind them. This did not bode well at all. She thought of Merlin's promise and immediately cursed that she had believed him when he said she could leave whenever she wished to.

Merlin. The name conjured up thoughts of the myriad stories

she'd heard of the king's counselor. Enchanter, some called him. Conjuror, wizard, sorcerer, others whispered.

Some said he was capable of changing himself into different creatures. Others said he had the gift of knowledge that allowed him to see far into the future. Still others whispered that he was not a creature of this world at all, but a spawn of the devil. Admittedly, those stories were told by Arthur's enemies. But nothing prepared her for the man who had stood over her when she finally shoved her hair out of her face.

He was tall with lean, handsome features and long dark hair that flowed to his shoulders. He had high cheekbones and a sensuous mouth that was curved into a frown as he stared down at her with that intense blue gaze.

She wasn't afraid. It wasn't about fear. It was about connection, much the same way Grendel had connected his thoughts to hers, only far more intense.

It was an invasion of heat that moved through her thoughts like fingers of liquid fire, exploring, probing, delving into the deepest part of her, learning her secrets, memories, everything that she'd experienced, everything she was. Learning her.

But the connection had flowed both ways, and in that bond she sensed the power in him, the accumulation of all thought, all experience, all knowledge, and glimpsed a secret that lay heavy on his soul.

He had removed the rope at her wrists then. Her first instinct had been to escape.

"Go, if that is what you wish," he said with an indifference that made her suspicious.

" 'Tis no trick," he replied as he read her thoughts. "The guards will not stop you. Although I cannot speak for Sir Tristan. You seemed to be at odds with one another." He'd held up a hand in a sign for silence.

"Yes, I know. There is no need to go through all the names again." He chuckled then, surprising her again. "Very colorful indeed. Not what I expected. Nor what Sir Tristan expected either.'' His expression changed and she sensed the change in his thoughts as well.

"But if you should remain, there is food and comfort, and safety. This is your home, after all. It will take some getting used to for all of us. Unless, that is," he paused with a lengthy perusal of her disgusting attire, "there is something better that awaits you elsewhere."

There wasn't, of course, and he knew it.

This connection of thought was going to take some getting used to. It was far different from Grendel's tentative probings.

"And if I wish to leave?" she demanded.

"You may leave whenever you choose," he had assured her.

"No tricks?" she asked, still suspicious.

He smiled then, persuading her with his thoughts. "No tricks."

She sensed that persuasion, of course, and with a smile of her own severed the connection and blocked all further thought. It was a challenge, and she had never been one to turn down a challenge.

"Very well," she agreed, with no great desire to be atop a horse again that same day. "I shall stay the night. But I intend to leave in the morning." She shuddered. "And I will need a horse."

He had agreed to all her demands and made none except that she stay. This was not part of the bargain, and he was not even there for her to argue with over it.

"You're to be given a bath," the woman named Hedda informed her in a kind voice.

"I am capable of bathing myself," she informed them. "I only have need of a basin of water. There is no need for all of this." She waved a hand across the assorted jars and bowls of herbal concoctions and pungent unguents set on the table beside the large metal tub.

The two women looked at one another.

"Master Merlin insisted," Hedda informed her not unkindly, shifting a little uneasily as she added, "And said that if there was any complaint he would see to the matter himself."

It took two baths to rid her of all the filth and grime she'd acquired on the journey from Glastonbury.

Warm water was an amazing experience. Even more amazing was the pleasant-smelling herbal soap. It smelled of forest pine, crushed fragrant leaves, and, oddly, of rose blossoms.

She was told that Lady Meg, the mistress of Monmouth, prepared the herbal soap and all medicants that were used at Monmouth and in the king's household.

Lady Meg . . . her mother.

The thought brought back all those feelings of betrayal and abandonment, of unanswered questions, loneliness, and uncertainty. It also brought back all the longings of childhood.

What was her mother like? There was no memory that stirred. She had been only an infant when she was sent away. Dannelore explained that she had been sent away to safety. But in the end there was no safety. Only blood and death, and those who were dearest to her had been brutally slain.

There was a great deal to think about as she soaked in her bath, then as she sat drying her hair before the fire.

Her thoughts of her parents conjured up vague images that lay in the deepest part of her. Images that had drifted back to her in old dreams. Then she ceased to dream of them at all. They did not exist for her. She had not lied when she told Tristan they were dead. To her it was as if they *were* dead.

The woman named Hedda left and another returned, moving quietly through the chamber. She was slender and moved with a quiet grace. Her clothes were finely made, suggesting that she was perhaps of higher rank among the household staff.

Rianne had never experienced such things, but she had heard stories of the lords and ladies of Arthur's court and the fine homes they lived in, with servants and stables full of horses, and packs of sleek hunting hounds.

The woman had brought food, but instead of plying Rianne with extravagant things meant to persuade her to stay, the food was simple yet ample—several slices of meat from a haunch of venison, warm bread, boiled eggs, and peaches with honey. After living off charred partridge and stale crusts of bread, it made her mouth water.

"Come, child," the servant said when Rianne had downed the last honied peach. "You must dress, and then I will braid your hair. Master Merlin wishes to see you."

Rianne made a face. She was beginning to rethink this bargain she'd made. But it was only for a few more hours and then he would be forced to keep his part of the bargain. She looked around for her clothes, piled in a disheveled heap while she bathed. They were gone.

She whirled around. "My clothes . . ." And saw the gown and tunic the woman held before her.

The gown was pale blue and loosely woven with soft gathers about the neck and at the edges of the sleeves. Rianne had never seen anything so fine or soft. It felt like goosedown. The tunic was made of a heavier fabric, to be worn over the gown.

It was slender about the shorter sleeves, bodice, and waist, the skirt falling in wide panels. Intricate stitchwork decorated the edge of the bodice, the sleeves, and down the front panel of the tunic.

"I have no need of such things," Rianne announced, wondering idly where the rest of the garments were. Such as pants.

"Ah, but you do," the woman said with a gentle smile that reflected in her pale blue eyes. "Your clothes were burned."

Rianne was stunned. "Burned?" How dare they? Those were her clothes. Even if they were a little dirty. Well, they were more than a little dirty. But they were still hers. These clothes were not hers.

She clung defiantly to the damp linen with which she'd dried herself. As a logical, pragmatic creature it was quite obvious she had two choices: She could wear the linen or she could wear the clothes the servant offered.

She decided that the clothes offered decidedly more coverage than the thin linen towel. "Oh, very well," she conceded. But she would have a conversation with Master Merlin immediately about some more suitable clothing. There was nothing at all suitable or practical about the pretty blue gown and tunic.

Then, as the tunic was slipped over her head and laced at the back, she discovered they offered barely more coverage than the linen cloth. The swell of her breasts was discreetly exposed above the neckline of the tunic. She kept pulling it up.

"Where is the rest of it?"

"The rest of it?" The pretty woman looked at her with confusion.

"Aye, the pants. Where are the pants?"

The woman smiled gently. "There are no pants, little one."

"What do you wear underneath?"

The woman smiled again, except this time Rianne could have sworn she struggled not to break out laughing.

"There is no need for anything underneath."

"Aye, there is," Rianne insisted, swishing the hem of the tunic this way and that as she walked about the room, trying to get used to the dragging weight of the skirt.

"There's cold air whistling up my arse."

The poor servant suddenly choked and began to cough violently, as if seized by a sudden spell.

"And I am not wearing those." She pointed to the small leather slippers. "I'm not about to freeze my feet as well."

"I will see what I can do about a pair of boots," the woman replied, dabbling at the tears that streamed down her cheeks amid her struggle not to laugh.

By the Ancient Ones, she thought. The girl was a rare, spirited lass.

"Now, will you allow me to plait your hair, mistress?" she

Take A Trip Into A Timeless World of Passion and Adventure with Zebra Historical Romances!
—Absolutely FREE!

Let your spirits fly away and enjoy the passion and adventure of another time. With Zebra Historical Romances you'll be transported to a world where proud men and spirited women share the mysteries of love and let the power of passion catapult them into adventures that take place in distant lands of another age. Zebra Historical Romances are the finest novels of their kind, written by today's bestselling romance authors.

4 BOOKS WORTH UP TO $24.96— Absolutely FREE!

Take 4 FREE Books!

Zebra created its convenient Home Subscription Service s
you'll be sure to get the hottest new romances delivered
each month right to your doorstep — usually before they
are available in book stores. Just to show you how
convenient Zebra Home Subscription Service is, we woul
like to send you 4 Zebra Historical Romances as a FREE
gift. You receive a gift worth up to $24.96 — absolutely
FREE. There's no extra charge for shipping and handlin
There's no obligation to buy anything - ever!

Save Even More with Free Home Delivery!

Accept your FREE gift and each month we'll deliver 4 bran
new titles as soon as they are published. They'll be yours
to examine FREE for 10 days. Then if you decide to keep
the books, you'll pay the preferred subscriber's price of jus
$4.20 per title. That's $16.80 for all 4 books for a savings
of up to 32% off the publisher's price! What's more...$16.8
is your total price...there is no additional charge for the
convenience of home delivery. Remember, you are under
obligation to buy any of these books at any time! If you ar
not delighted with them, simply return them and owe
nothing. But if you enjoy Zebra Historical Romances as
much as we think you will, pay the special preferred
subscriber rate of only $16.80 each month and save over
$8.00 off the bookstore price!

We have 4 FREE BOOKS for you as
your introduction to
KENSINGTON CHOICE!

To get your FREE BOOKS,
worth up to $24.96, mail the card below.
or call TOLL-FREE 1-888-345-BOOK

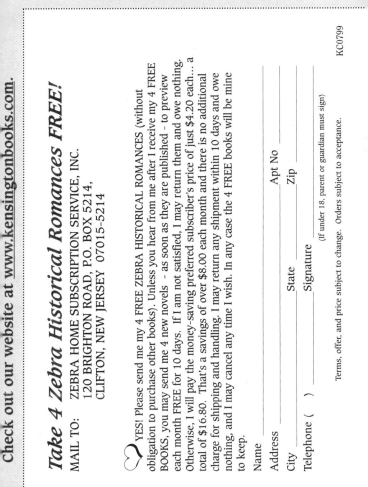

Check out our website at www.kensingtonbooks.com.

Take 4 Zebra Historical Romances FREE!

MAIL TO: ZEBRA HOME SUBSCRIPTION SERVICE, INC.
120 BRIGHTON ROAD, P.O. BOX 5214,
CLIFTON, NEW JERSEY 07015-5214

YES! Please send me my 4 FREE ZEBRA HISTORICAL ROMANCES (without obligation to purchase other books). Unless you hear from me after I receive my 4 FREE BOOKS, you may send me 4 new novels – as soon as they are published – to preview each month FREE for 10 days. If I am not satisfied, I may return them and owe nothing. Otherwise, I will pay the money-saving preferred subscriber's price of just $4.20 each... a total of $16.80. That's a savings of over $8.00 each month and there is no additional charge for shipping and handling. I may return any shipment within 10 days and owe nothing, and I may cancel any time I wish. In any case the 4 FREE books will be mine to keep.

Name _____

Address _____ Apt No _____

City _____ State _____ Zip _____

Telephone (   ) _____ Signature _____

(If under 18, parent or guardian must sign)

Terms, offer, and price subject to change. Orders subject to acceptance.

KC0799

4 FREE
Zebra
Historical
Romances
are waiting
for you to
claim them!

(worth up
to $24.96)

See details
inside....

KENSINGTON CHOICE
Zebra Home Subscription Service, Inc.
120 Brighton Road
P.O.Box 5214
Clifton, NJ 07015-5214

asked, lips twitching with suppressed mirth. "Master Merlin is expecting you."

"Aye." Rianne sighed, squirming in the chair as she tried to get used to the skirt hanging about her legs.

The servant had gentle, sure hands, carefully plaiting the thick tresses as she spoke of things at Monmouth as if Rianne had any interest in them.

They were trivial things; a humorous story about the cook, a new foal that had been born, the king's visit from Camelot, and the rumor that he intended to court Lady Guinevere of Lyonesse.

It had an odd, soothing effect on Rianne. As if she had sat that way a hundred times before, listening to that soft, tender voice, while gentle hands wove ribbons through her hair. Or wished that she had.

Then the woman spoke of Lord Connor and Lady Meg's joy now that their daughter had returned; how much they had missed her and longed for this day; how much it meant to them to have her home once more, with Lord Connor taken so ill.

She was aware that the woman's hands had grown still and lay lightly on her shoulders. It was a pleasant feeling, not unlike being held. Something she had not experienced for a very long time.

Rianne pushed unwanted memories back into the dark corners of her thoughts.

"If my mother and father loved me, they wouldn't have sent me away."

She felt the hands stiffen at her shoulders. "Do not judge too harshly, young mistress," the woman softly said. "There are perhaps things unknown to you. Reasons you could not know at the time." A slender hand reached out and touched her hair. "But know that they loved you very much."

Rianne abruptly rose from the chair, her emotions suddenly in turmoil.

"I am ready to meet Lord Connor and Lady Megwin," she

announced, clinging to the pain and anger that had protected her feelings over the past years. And the silent thought she mistakenly believed that no one heard:

"And in the morning I shall be gone."

Tristan splashed water from the barrel over his face and shoulders, shivering in the midwinter air as he scrubbed away the filth and sweat.

After delivering Rianne to the main hall, he had sent word that he wished to see Connor, then returned to the stables and vented his anger and frustration in grooming the black stallion, until the beast complained by nipping at his shoulder and trying to stomp him.

They had a meeting of the minds, an adjustment in attitude. Eventually Tristan conceded and ceased to take out his frustration on the hide of the stallion, instead venting it in muttered curses.

Now the girl had him doing it. Well, may the devil take her. It was done. He'd kept his vow to Lady Meg. Now his thoughts turned to other, more weighty matters that had plagued him the entire time he was gone.

Connor was no better. Word from the household was that he weakened with each passing day. The injuries he'd received still had not healed and filled his blood with poisons. It was whispered that death was imminent.

Was that the reason, then, for Arthur's presence?

He leaned over the barrel, hands braced at the rim, and a memory stirred, as though reflected on the shimmering surface of the water.

It was shortly after he came to Monmouth. He was but a boy of nine or ten years. It was one of the countless times he had practiced at mock battle in the yard with the small broadsword Connor had made for him.

His opponent had been the Viking, a ruthless old bastard

who knew more of warring and fighting than any other ten men. He had been with Connor since he was a boy and had taken it upon himself to teach Tristan the ways of warring.

He'd gotten right well bloodied that day, a slice here, a nick there. But he refused to yield. It was a matter of honor, or perhaps more a matter of pigheadedness. Connor had watched as he took the thrashing, barely escaping within an inch of his life. Or so he thought at the time.

After a time, Connor intervened. He had taken Tristan aside and explained that cunning and strategy are often equally as deadly a weapon as the sword. He pointed out that it was wise to study one's adversary, learn his ways, then strike at his vulnerabilities. He also pointed out that the Viking always led an attack with a strike to the right, the exact opposite of most warriors. His second point of advice was to use his own abilities to his advantage, rather than trying to match his opponent's abilities.

When the contest continued, Tristan heeded the wisdom of that advice. He led the attack with cuts and thrusts first to the left, throwing the rhythm of the Viking's attack off balance. Then, instead of standing and fighting to the last breath—and quite possibly the last drop of blood—when the Viking's greater strength overpowered him, Tristan dove through the old warrior's wide-legged stance, sprang to his feet behind the Viking, and declared victory with a thrust of his sword at the man's backside.

It had been a momentous occasion. One he never forgot. Afterwards, Connor scooped him up and carried him across his shoulder to the stables. There they had washed at the water barrel in the frosty morning air, the thrill of victory roaring through his blood.

It was that long-ago morning when he finally let go of the pain of the past over the loss of his family, and found acceptance with Connor, who had been his mentor, brother, father, and friend ever since.

"You should have waited for me!" Grendel's complaint returned him to the present. He was incredulous.

"You dropped her at Merlin's feet? Keflech! But I would like to have seen that."

The gnome had returned a short while earlier, afoot and worse for wear, with a story about a thicket of gorse and a low-hanging tree branch. He was covered with gorse and had a nasty bump on the head. The roan was nowhere in sight.

Tristan shook water from his hair and scooped it back. "You will get your chance. Lord Connor has summoned us to the main hall, no doubt to announce his daughter's return." His gaze narrowed on the gnome.

He seized the little man about his stout body, upended him, and dunked him headfirst into the water barrel.

It took several more dunkings and considerable scrubbing amid much cursing and dire threats, but at least the gnome smelled better.

CHAPTER FOURTEEN

Rianne had seen little of Monmouth when she first arrived—it was difficult thrown over the back of a horse dangling upside-down. And she hadn't seen much more of it when she was taken to the small private bathing chamber off the kitchen. Now, as she was taken to join Merlin, she stared at the imposing walls, arches, passages, and chambers of Monmouth.

She knew little of such places, only what she had heard gossiped about in taverns and inns. 'Twas said that Camelot was most grand. She could not imagine anything more imposing than Monmouth.

Her memory of home was the cottage where she had lived with Dannelore and John. Since then she had lived in stables, storerooms, an abandoned crofter's hut, hayricks, or under the open sky.

The longest time she'd spent in any one place was an old woman's cottage in the north country. The woman had no family and took Rianne in to help her through the winter. She died the following spring and Rianne moved on.

Her home after that was the wagon of a merchant. It was there she first donned the disguise of a boy, tried her skill at the games, and discovered her talent. The merchant saw it as a way to fatten his purse. She decided there was no reason he should keep all the money from the pots she won while she received only a thin crust of bread. She quickly moved on from there as well.

Then there was the healer in Tunbridge. The woman caught her stealing a handful of herbs in the marketplace for a poultice to treat a nasty cut. She took Rianne in, and she remained with her until the following spring.

The woman fancied herself gifted in the way of visions and spells. She was always brewing some foul-smelling concoction and then lapsing into some sort of fevered state where she claimed to see all sorts of strange creatures. One day she claimed she saw a vision of the future in a kettle of stewed fish heads. Rianne decided it was time to leave. Afterward, home was anyplace that provided shelter from the rain and snow.

The heavy skirt of the tunic kept wrapping about her legs and she constantly stumbled over the long hem. She was fast losing patience and rethinking the bargain she'd made with Merlin.

The woman who had helped her dress and plaited her hair had found her a pair of small leather boots. But there was nothing between the boots and the bodice of the gown. That and the fact that the neck of the bodice was cut rather low combined for a feeling that she was half-naked.

"This is the way of it," the woman indicated, as she took hold of the skirt of the tunic and lifted it several inches to prevent it being stepped on.

"The hem is a bit long. It's usually worn just at the top of the shoes, so that you don't step on it." Her voice caught softly. "I did not know your height to make the fit exact."

It was then Rianne realized the woman had made the gown and tunic for her. She had lived so long on her own, fending for herself, that the notion that anyone would do something for her was as unfamiliar as the gown itself.

"I've never had anything so fine." She spoke with the bluntness of sincerity that was inherently a part of her. "It will just take a bit of gettin' used to."

"Thank you," the woman replied with more than a little surprise. She obviously hadn't expected the gift to be appreciated.

Rianne took hold of the skirt and lifted it, immediately improving the situation. For someone who was used to the freedom of men's pants, the cumbersome gown did take some getting used to.

While the design was flattering and beautifully made, she was convinced that whoever came up with the idea of tying one into a gown was no doubt a man who had never worn one.

They crossed the main hall and Rianne paused, awed by the size of it. Her gaze was immediately drawn to the massive hearth. It was large enough for a man to walk through, and the logs that burned there were the size of tree trunks. Then her gaze was drawn upward, to the brightly colored banner that hung suspended at the wall over the hearth.

There was a design on it in the shape of large golden bird with spread wings on a field of deep blue. It was a fierce-looking creature that gave the impression of both power and strength.

A long table sat before the hearth with at least a score of chairs around it. The floor was made of stone rather than dirt. Fresh straw mixed with pungent herbs had been strewn over the stones.

Rianne recognized the scent of feverfew mingled with rosemary, willow bark, and pine. Tallow candles burned in wood holders as tall as a man, and oil lamps burned in niches on the walls, casting a golden glow throughout the large hall.

The woman drew closer as she explained. "There has been a Duke of Monmouth living here since the last Roman legion set sail for Rome. The first time I saw it, it had fallen into disrepair. No one had lived here for a very long time. There were animals nesting inside and it was dirty. But it did not matter.'' There was a sudden wistfulness in her voice.

Several other servants appeared as preparations were made for the evening meal. Platters of food were set out, along with large trenchers and bowls of steaming broth. Her stomach rumbled at the abundance and variety.

This, too, was completely unfamiliar to Rianne, who had survived on meager crusts of bread, a wedge of cheese, and a cup of milk when she had the means to purchase them, or stolen when she did not. When neither possibility existed, she went hungry.

''Your life has not been easy,'' the woman commented, startling Rianne, as if she sensed the hunger that gnawed within in spite of the food she'd eaten.

''I am sorry for that.''

The woman reached out as she had once before, when she plaited Rianne's hair. It was a tentative, tender gesture, a touch of the sleeve, no more. Then her slender fingers curled into her palm, as if she had no right.

'' 'Tis no concern of yours,'' Rianne replied as she thought of Kari. ''There are others who have suffered far more.''

''Aye, each in our own way,'' the woman whispered with a poignancy that made Rianne look at her.

She was so very lovely and yet there was a heartbreaking sadness in her expression that touched something deep inside Rianne; a connection of pain and loss so deep and wounded that she felt the need to comfort her.

It was a small thing, just a brief touch of her hand, but the woman looked up at the contact, her eyes glistening with tears.

Rianne instinctively stepped back, unsettled by the woman's sudden emotion and things she could not understand.

''Will Lord Connor and his wife be there?'' she asked, turning her thoughts to Merlin and his invitation to join him.

The woman's expression changed then, her features pale and fragile. "Aye, and the king as well. Do you not wish to meet them?" She seemed to hold her breath expectantly, almost as if she feared the answer.

"I have never met a king before," Rianne replied, uncertain how to reply about the man and woman who were her father and mother. She reminded herself that this woman's loyalties would lie with them and she must take care in how she responded.

"I have heard that he is as wide as he is tall and cannot even sit his horse but must have his knights lift him atop," she repeated what she had heard at Garidor's inn. "And then the poor beast is so overburdened, its knees buckle. I have also heard it said that he is bald and wears a head cap made from the tail of a horse to seem as though he has hair. And the reason he has not taken a queen is that he prefers young boys."

Her companion made a strangled sound that sounded very much like laughter.

"By the Ancient Ones! Tristan warned me," her companion said, and Rianne wondered if she had gravely erred. She reminded herself that the Duke of Monmouth was loyal to the king. Had she gravely mispoken?

"He warned you?" she cautiously asked.

The woman smiled. "He said you were most . . . outspoken."

It was better than telling the girl what he'd actually said. That she had the mouth of a common soldier, the manners of a scullery maid, and the temperament of a shrew.

But she was inclined to disagree at least in part. Outspoken? Aye, the girl was that, but in a refreshingly honest manner. As for her manners, it was no fault of her own that she was not familiar with the propriety of things when one considered what her life must have been like. There was certainly no need for fine manners when one lived by one's bravery, tenacity, and wit.

And as to her temperament, she found the girl most amiable

and pleasant, with a mischievous sense of humor that she thoroughly enjoyed.

She wanted to delay joining the others, but knew they could not any longer. She leaned close and laid a hand on Rianne's arm.

"Remember one thing," the woman told her. "Arthur is very clever. He did not become king by being fat or foolish. And," she smiled, "I have it on good authority that he prefers the ladies."

Guards stood at the door of the antechamber. They looked most intimidating. Rianne wondered if they were to protect those within or to prevent her leaving.

"A necessity since Monmouth was attacked," her companion explained, as if she sensed the direction of Rianne's thoughts. "There for your protection as well."

"I would rather see to my own protection," Rianne replied, and thought silently to herself, *"and the devil take the bargain I made with Merlin."*

She held back now that the time was near. Damn Tristan! If not for him she would not be here now.

That logical part of her argued that this meant nothing to her. These people meant nothing to her, just as she had meant nothing to them all these years. They were strangers. She'd lived her life among strangers with no bond, nor any need of one, to anyone. Except perhaps for her friendship with Kari.

It was the emotional part of her that hesitated, pain, anger, and uncertainty washing over her. She tried to hold on to the pain and anger. It was better that way. They had protected her all these years and they would protect her now from these people and whatever it was they wanted from her.

Her companion pushed open the heavy door. As she melted into the shadows at the edge of the chamber, Rianne felt the gentle pressure of the woman's hand on her own. Then she was gone.

Rianne felt the collective gazes of those within the smaller chamber. In the gown and tunic with the lacings cinched tight, Rianne felt like a partridge all trussed and ready to be skewered and roasted over a spit.

She had but one thought. *Run! Get as far away as possible, before it is too late.* But it was already too late as Merlin approached her.

He smiled to himself as he sensed her thoughts. It seemed their spirited falcon had the heart of a dove. Then her thoughts closed to him like a door firmly shut in his face, and the smile deepened.

Where the main hall had been impressive in its size, massive furnishings, and opulent tapestries, the smaller antechamber was impressive for its intimacy and lack of formality.

A fire burned at a smaller hearth. Two high-backed chairs sat before it. Ornate tapestries covered the walls and, amazingly, the floor. The guards at the door had been fully armed with gleaming broadswords and knives at their belts, the light in the passage gleaming off their breastplates and mail tunics. But there were no broadswords or breastplates here.

Merlin had been imposing as she stared up from where she lay at his feet upon their first meeting. He was equally impressive in the midnight blue tunic with silver medallions across the shoulders and sweeping across his chest. The color was like the blue of his eyes and the silver medallions were like dozens of tiny stars that winked at her.

His smile was enigmatic, as if he knew or sensed something, and she reminded herself of all the things she had heard about him—sorcerer, enchanter, conjuror. He seemed no different than any other man. Except for his eyes. They were a deep fathomless blue, filled with shadows and light, secrets and laughter that reached out to her as if they saw deep inside her.

It was a disconcerting feeling at the same time as it seemed the most natural thing in the world, like a connection of spirit, thought, and essence. As if they were somehow bonded.

Was he stealing her mind away? Her soul, too, perhaps? That, too, she had heard about him.

Yet he seemed no different from any other man. Warm flesh and blood as his hand reached for hers and he drew her further into the room.

"It is not true, you know," he said as he bent his head low beside hers.

"What is not true?"

"I do not steal souls." He winked at her as her startled gaze met his.

"I have found it is much too cumbersome carrying them all around with me. I gave that up long ago."

She didn't know whether to laugh or take him seriously. After all, he obviously had the ability to read her thoughts.

"And I can read your thoughts," he continued, and finished with a thought of his own, *"but only when you allow it. Just as you have the ability to read mine."*

Now she was certain that he was jesting with her. She had thought it a trick that Grendel played with her. Was it more than that? More than the ability to sense the outcome of a game of cups and stones?

"There is much that awaits you, Rianne," Merlin said as he escorted her across the room. "If you will only allow it."

What did he mean by that? she wondered. But there was no opportunity to question him as they approached the others in the room.

She braced herself for what was to come, reminding herself that these people meant nothing to her. She would keep her promise to Merlin and be done with it.

One man was seated in one of the high-backed chairs before the hearth, while another man of imposing height stood opposite. They both watched her intently. One was her father.

She knew of his injury and assumed that the man seated was Lord Connor of Monmouth. He was dressed in fawn-colored tunic, leggings, and boots. His rich auburn hair was close-cropped about his head. A full, neatly cropped beard covered his face. It was that same deep auburn color, and the blue eyes above were sharp, speculative, measuring.

"Daughter."

But even before she heard the word, she had already sensed that the man seated before the fire was not her father. And already her gaze was turning toward the man standing.

He was tall as an oak and broad-shouldered. There was nothing weak or infirm about him, unless one looked in his eyes. She saw it there, the heat of the ever-present fevers, the pain that he stubbornly refused to yield to, and the shadows that dulled the gleam of fiery spirit.

It was then, when she looked closer, that she realized his tunic hung a little too loosely, his color was too pale, and saw the effort it took just for him to stand. But she sensed that he would not have had it any other way. He would not have her find him weak and sickly. He was much too proud.

Nor was the hand that closed over hers weak. It was strong and warm, exuding the power of the warrior who had wielded a sword in service to his king, and at the same time amazingly gentle. And she also sensed that this man who had feared nothing in life, feared her.

He tried to prevent it, but he could not keep himself from staring at her. Rianne. His daughter. After all this time. Emotions overwhelmed him, threatening to send him to his knees.

So many years, so much lost time. He had all but given up hope of ever seeing her again. But now she was here.

He remembered the infant, only weeks old. Countless times he had imagined the child. But he could never have imagined the beauty she had become, so like her mother. And yet he saw others in her as well, a glimpse of his sister in the challenging look in her eyes, and a glimpse of himself in the angle of her chin. A rare beauty who would give no quarter and ask that none be given.

What to say? How to say it? A thousand times he'd gone

over the words, cast them aside, and then begun again. Now they all seemed inadequate. His hand tightened over hers.

"Welcome home, my child."

Welcome home. Simple words. Not some contrivance or meaningless pleasantry. Two simple words that tore at her defenses as nothing else could, scattering them like leaves before a bitter wind.

Rianne had convinced herself that she felt nothing for these people. She was certain she could keep her bargain with Merlin and then walk away.

She had expected cold, cruel, autocratic people who had sent her away without thought or concern. But she saw neither a cold nor cruel man before her, only a man who was dying.

He knew it and yet he stood before her, proud, strong in conviction if no longer strong in body, defiant against death, honest in the emotions she felt in the hand at hers. And in all those things she glimpsed something of herself.

Welcome home. More than words. It was a connection she had been seeking all her life. And it was there, so simply, in the warmth of his hand, reaching across the years, across the pain and loneliness that she saw too in his eyes. And it humbled her.

All the anger and defiance drained out of her. She wanted only to hold on to that warmth and strength.

She wanted to tell him that. She wanted to say words that would somehow comfort him as those simple words had comforted her, but before she could say anything she felt a presence at her side, and a strong hand clamped painfully around her arm in silent warning.

"If you say or do anything to cause either of them even a moment's anguish, I will break your arm," Tristan whispered low against her cheek. To all outward appearances it no doubt seemed that he offered some small last encouragement. Only they knew different.

"And then I will break your neck."

The gaze that met his was vivid blue, flashing with anger, the color high across her cheeks. Gone was the grimy, smudge-faced thief dressed like a boy with the manners and temperament of a hedgehog. The boy had been replaced by a slender beauty with striking features. It was amazing what a little soap and water could do.

She was her father's daughter in the high cheekbones, the angle of her jaw, and the stubborn curve of her chin. But she was her mother's daughter in those wide, expressive eyes, the color startling as she glared at him. Merlin must be mad to bring her here.

Rianne hadn't seen him when she first entered the room. Her concentration had been focused entirely on Merlin and those near the hearth. She wouldn't have recognized him now except for the look in those dark, golden eyes—simmering like the warning glow of embers at a fire before they explode into flame.

He was dressed all in black in a tunic stitched with silver threads that molded his wide shoulders, black leggings that molded his lean, muscular thighs, and black boots that gleamed in the light from the fire in the hearth. Long dark hair, still beaded with water, fell to his shoulders in glossy, silken waves.

She had never seen him clean-shaven. Without the growth of beard he seemed less the lowlife but no less threatening with tightened jaw, the pale scar at his chin, that hard expression in cold, handsome features, and the warning look in those golden eyes. His fingers tightened, and she thought her bones would snap. If only she had a knife.

"Sir Tristan, we owe you a debt that can never be repaid. You have our undying gratitude for safely returning our daughter to us."

A slender woman stepped from the shadows and joined Lord Connor. She laid a hand gently on his arm. The gesture was tender and familiar, even intimate.

With some surprise, Rianne recognized the servant who had helped her dress. She frowned in puzzlement. Then the woman's clouded gaze unerringly found hers. Her expression was a mixture of both hope and uncertainty.

"You have eased our pain and brought us much happiness," she continued. "My heartfelt thanks, Sir Tristan."

Rianne immediately realized the foolish mistake she'd made. She had assumed that the woman who had helped her dress and had plaited her hair was one of the servants. But the woman standing beside Lord Connor was no servant at all. She was her mother!

Countless emotions swept over her, not the least of which was a feeling of betrayal. But when her gaze met Lady Meg's there was no laughter or ridicule there, only sadness.

"I should have told you."

"Yes," Rianne replied, "you should have." And felt Tristan's hand tighten at her arm.

"Forgive me," Meg slipped into thought. *" 'Tis only that I wanted the chance to see you alone. It has been such a long time."*

"Yes, it has been," Rianne coolly replied, and then firmly closed her thoughts. She immediately sensed Meg's painful reaction.

This growing awareness of other's emotions was something new. It gave her a certain power over them. Was this part of what Grendel had spoken of?

She should have been elated at this newfound power and control over others. Instead she frowned as her thoughts turned inward. She'd waited for years for just such a moment. She'd dreamed of confronting the parents who had sent her away, and then turning away from them. But she discovered that it gave her no pleasure to cause another such a deep, wounding pain. Especially one who had shown her only kindness.

"The evening meal is being served," Meg announced, giving nothing away by either word or gesture of the hurt Rianne had inflicted with those private thoughts.

As they started to leave the chamber, Lord Connor suddenly stiffened. His face had gone ashen and was drawn with pain.

Meg immediately slipped an arm about his waist, easing his weight onto her slender shoulders while Arthur supported him from the other side. Together, they eased him down into the chair.

"What is it?"

Tristan heard the alarm in her voice. She wasn't even aware of it, or the fact that she had instinctively reached out toward her father.

"It will soon pass," Meg assured them, then looked up at Tristan, "Please go on to the main hall. We will join you there shortly."

Tristan seized Rianne by the arm. This time his hand was much gentler, though no less insistent.

Her own features were equally drawn and pale as she reluctantly allowed him to escort her from the chamber.

"What is wrong with him?"

Tristan glanced at her at the sudden catch in her voice, a soft, wounded sound he doubted she was even aware of. Of all the reactions he might have expected, this was not one of them. Was it another disguise?

"The wound has never healed properly. It fills his body with poisons that are slowly killing him." He felt her fingers tighten on his arm, as if holding on.

"Can nothing be done?"

"They mean nothing to you," he reminded her, curious about this sudden concern.

Her gaze met his. There was something in the expression in her eyes, something exposed, naked, wounded. And in the brief moment that it was revealed, he recognized it from his own childhood. That fear of letting anyone get too close . . . the fear of losing everything dear in life all over again.

His own anger at her slowly disintegrated. For a moment he had glimpsed the wounded child within and it tore at him as nothing she had said or done could. Then it was gone. The door to her emotions firmly shut once more.

" 'Tis only that I assumed with his extraordinary abilities surely Master Merlin could heal the wound.''

"Everything that can be done has been done,'' he assured her. "But not even Merlin's vast knowledge of healing ways seems to help.''

"But he will recover.''

In spite of her attempt to conceal her emotions he heard the thread of hope in her voice.

"He is dying,'' Tristan solemnly replied, "though he would never admit it to you. He could not bear for you to see him weak and sick.''

His hand closed over hers as he led her and the others into the hall. Her fingers were icy. The hand that had wielded a sword with such strength and had skillfully threatened to unman him trembled within his hand.

Eventually Lord Connor and Lady Meg joined them. He sat at the center of the long table surrounded by his guests, with Lady Meg to his left and the king, an honored guest, to his right. Rianne was seated directly across from them, with Tristan beside her.

Lord Connor seemed much recovered. But there were deep shadows beneath his eyes and sunken hollows at his cheeks. And even though Lady Meg's manner was casual, she never left his side.

She gave nothing away of the pain and fear she felt for him. The only outward sign of concern was the occasional touch of a slender hand, or a look that passed between them.

But Rianne sensed the pain and fear just the same, a bond of unwanted emotions that connected them. And as much as she willed against it, she found her gaze constantly drawn back to Lord Connor.

"Be careful,'' Tristan warned as he leaned close. "Someone might think that you actually cared about your father.''

He saw the denial that flashed in her eyes. But it never reached her lips. She slowly smiled instead. He should have realized he was in trouble.

With a sudden burst of thought, Rianne tipped over his goblet of wine. It thudded to the table, the contents spilling across the sleeve of his tunic. Her mouth curved in an impish smile.

"*You* must be careful, milord."

Supper was an experience that Rianne was certain she would not soon forget. She had never seen such an abundance of food. For someone who had often gone hungry, with no prospect of where her next meal might come from, it was a dizzying experience.

Platters were carried from the kitchen in an endless stream, laden with roast pig, venison, roast fowl, and a vast array of breads, puddings, cake, fruits, and some foods she couldn't even name.

A trencher was filled with food and placed before her. The aroma of roasted meat and sweet sauces set her stomach to rumbling. But her gaze fastened on the slender knife beside the trencher.

Tristan's hand covered hers. Strong fingers wrapped around her hand with a bruising strength.

"Do not even think about it," he warned.

Her eyes widened. Was the man capable of reading her thoughts as well? That was a very disconcerting. She shielded her thoughts while she attempted to extricate her hand.

"Let go of me!" she hissed furiously.

"Let go of the knife," he suggested with a charming smile, while beneath the silken words was an unmistakable threat.

"You're hurting me."

"I'll do worse than that."

She let go of the knife and his fingers loosened about hers. "I won't think about it at all the next time," she assured him with a radiant smile. "I will simply do it and take great pleasure in watching you bleed to death." Then she turned her attention to the meal before her and ignored him.

She wanted to taste everything. But as Rianne glanced down the table she discovered a new problem.

Eating had always been a necessity of survival. It was usually a crust of bread or a piece of roast fowl filched from someone's cookfire, then torn apart and quickly consumed, usually only a few paces ahead of the rightful owner.

The knife was handy whether it was for protecting herself or skewering bits of food from a cookfire. But here each person also used a small ladle for scooping stew and broth, rather than simply picking up the bowl and drinking from it.

It was a little disconcerting to discover that a warrior had better manners than she did. She eyed the spoon doubtfully, fingertips drumming lightly on the table surface. It did not seen all that complicated.

She seized the spoon with grim determination and plunged it into the bowl. It was more complicated that it looked. More of the broth ended up back in the bowl than made it to her mouth, and she came dangerously close to spilling it down the front of her tunic.

"Use your left hand," Tristan suggested, his voice low beside her. "And hold it like this. Or you can simply wear your supper dribbled down the front of your gown, if it pleases you."

"It does not," she replied, at battle with herself whether or not to take his advice.

Heat burned across her cheeks. It should not have mattered to her that she was as clumsy and inept as a child. It should not have mattered whether or not she spilled food down the front of her clothes. But it did. Suddenly, for the first time in her life, it mattered very much.

Her agonized gaze met that of Lady Meg's across the table. She did not see laughter or ridicule in that gentle blue gaze, but a sadness of compassion that was perhaps worse. She slammed down the spoon and would have fled the table if Tristan hadn't stopped her. His hand closed gently over hers, his fingers threading through hers as he wrapped them around the handle of the spoon.

"You are naturally left-handed, though you use the knife with your right hand," he explained with a self-deprecating smile.

"I noticed it that night at the inn, when you threatened to cut off a certain bodily part. You wielded the sword with your left hand." His fingers closed over her left hand. "It will seem easier to you." He held her hand just so, fingers angled around the handle in a firm grasp that did not wobble.

"Relax your hold," he suggested, "just as you would hold the sword. If you hold too tightly, it will spill."

He was right, it was much easier with her left hand. She refused to look at him, certain she would see that arrogant, mocking expression. Still, it was not in her to be ungrateful.

"Thank you," she murmured.

"What did you say?"

"Thank you," she repeated a little more loudly.

"I didn't hear you."

Her gaze snapped up and met his amused one. He had one hand cupped behind his ear. Her anger evaporated. She found it difficult to hold on to it when he looked at her that way, the light from the torches burning in his dark golden eyes, a teasing smile curving just one corner of his mouth exactly the way it had that night in Bath, when they hid from the stable owner in the darkened passage.

He had heard perfectly well. She suspected he wanted her to say it so that everyone would hear her.

" 'Tis a pity, Sir Tristan," she replied instead, in a voice loud enough for all to hear. "I didn't realize you were so old." And then, even louder, her smile deepening, "You should see someone about that. Perhaps Master Merlin can help you."

She was delightfully wicked. A breath of fresh air compared

to the women, both young and not so young, whom he'd spent time with during the past few years. He rapidly tired of them. He doubted he would ever tire of her, simply because he could never be certain what she would do next.

Throughout supper Rianne was aware of the scrutinizing gaze from across the table. Several times she looked up and her gaze met that of Arthur.

Here was a man of ambition and power, who humbly acted the part of the casual supper guest. But that scrutiny was anything but casual.

As she had openly commented to Lady Meg when she had mistakenly thought her to be a servant, she had expected someone short, fat, and bald. Arthur was neither fat nor short. Nor was he old; he appeared to be the same age as Lord Connor. And, as she studied his full head of hair, she was almost certain it wasn't made of horsehair.

"It is quite real." The thought connected with her own, and Rianne knew it could be no other than Meg. She looked over at the woman, and they exchanged a brief smile.

"But there is a man at Arthur's court who wears a head-cap made of horsehair. 'Tis a dreadful thing. I will have to point him out to you. He is most pompous. He resembles a strutting peacock."

Rianne had never seen a peacock, in fact had absolutely no idea what one was. But the word conjured up rather extraordinary images. She laughed outright, causing Merlin to look at her oddly.

"Is there something amiss, my dear?"

"Not at all," she replied, and heard a strangled sound very much like laughter as she narrowed a look at Merlin's dark flowing hair. Though blind, Meg had known the exact direction of her thoughts.

Midway through supper there was a commotion at the main entrance of the hall. The hounds made a dreadful noise until they were chained in the corner. A shadow named Grendel slipped along the wall and appeared at Meg's side.

Several of Lord Connor's men appeared, escorting one of the king's men, who had just arrived. His boots and mantle were caked with mud.

"Forgive my intrusion, your grace," the knight greeted his king. "But I have just returned from the borderlands and I bring word of matters there."

In the corner, the hounds had set up a terrible noise and would not be quieted. Lord Connor eventually ordered them removed from the hall.

"Join us, Sir Longinus," Arthur invited him. "We will speak of these things after you have eaten. And your men?"

"They are being fed as we speak." The knight's gaze swept the table and fixed on Connor.

"My gratitude for your hospitality, milord."

He removed his mantle and chest plate. He was tall and moved with that same economy of movement and restrained power. He nodded greetings to those about the table; then his gaze rested lightly on Rianne.

Connor made the formal introductions. "My daughter, Lady Rianne, recently returned to Monmouth."

Longinus bowed low, his dark gaze fastening on hers. "You seem well enough after such a long journey, milady. You encountered no difficulty?"

It was on the tip of her tongue to tell all of them precisely the difficulty she'd encountered, but she felt that warning pressure at her wrist.

"I arrived safely," she replied.

"Then we are most fortunate." Again he bowed his head, this time with a faint smile that emphasized his handsome features, then joined Arthur's knights at the far end of the table.

"I do not like that one," Grendel hissed as he suddenly appeared at Tristan's elbow.

"You do not like anyone," Tristan pointed out.

Grendel shrugged. "True. But I do not like him more than anyone else."

Tristan watched the knight from the length of the table. He had met Longinus on the practice field on more than one occasion and found him to be a noteworthy opponent. But he knew very little about the man.

His family was obscure, it was said, with a link to the old Roman nobility that had dominated Britain five hundred years earlier. But that was true of many, including Arthur.

His family was gone, killed many years earlier during the years before Arthur's return. It was not uncommon. Britain had suffered through much civil strife and warring, when one usurper after another fought to seize the throne.

His own memories of that time were those of a child. Longinus had been older and his memories no doubt were much stronger, but he never spoke of that time.

Longinus was highly respected as a warrior, but there were none in the closely knit brotherhood of Arthur's knights who claimed to know him.

He was not affable like Gawain, nor congenial like Bedevere. Nor was he curt and brusque like Agravain, who never smiled. And he was not the sort who gambled or played at games, and perhaps therein lie Grendel's dislike of the man, for he had never had the opportunity to lighten his purse.

"Perhaps you should tell him," Tristan suggested with a bemused smile.

"Perhaps one day I shall," the little man grumbled, filching a tart from the table when no one was looking, then disappearing underneath to hide once more in the shadows.

Rianne listened to the conversation around her with great interest. She had learned long ago that there was much to be learned by listening attentively to the conversations of others. She glanced down the length of the table at Longinus. His gaze met hers and he nodded in acknowledgment.

He was handsome, with fair features, a high brow, a long

nose, and a sensual, full mouth. By contrast his eyes were dark, contemplative, even a bit disconcerting in the way they lingered on her. But it was his hands that fascinated her. They were slender and fine-boned, whereas Tristan's hands were callused and scarred like those of his fellow warriors.

As the evening progressed conversation was of politics, matters of government, the delicate balance of power among the nobles whom Arthur was forced to constantly deal with, and the current uprisings along the borderlands.

"You have just returned from the north country." Arthur turned his attention to her. "What think you of these matters?"

She knew that he indulged her. He did not really expect her to have any thought of them at all, and he was right.

"I do not think of them, milord," Rianne replied, with blunt honesty and simple logic, and then added, " 'Tis difficult to contemplate such weighty matters when you are hungry."

He nodded. "You encountered much adversity, but surely there were those you could rely upon, those who cared for you."

"I learned to rely upon myself. When you have no one, you do what you must."

She regretted the words as soon as they were out of her mouth, for she immediately sensed the pain they caused Lady Meg and Lord Connor.

"It was not so difficult," she went on to explain, hoping to ease the sting of her words, again at a loss to understand why it mattered to her that she had caused them pain.

"When I had means of providing for myself, I hunted. There is abundant game in the northern forests."

Tristan listened fascinated as another of Arthur's knights pointed out to her, "The northern forests are the king's land. You killed the king's deer?"

She shrugged. "I was hungry."

The expressions of those around the table ranged from incredulity to humor. Merlin was most intrigued of all.

"How did you hunt?"

"I trapped small animals and birds in snares. I hunted larger animals with a bow," she replied matter-of-factly between nibbles at a crust of bread.

"A bow?" Lord Standford asked, the edge of the table cutting into his ponderous gut as he leaned forward to stare down the length of the table at her.

He was one of the noblemen whose support Arthur needed to put down this latest range of skirmishes. He was as wide as he was tall, and in spite of his fine clothes and fur-trimmed tunic, his teeth were badly rotted at the gums. He was Lady Alyce's husband.

"Do you prefer one particular bow over another?" he asked, poking at his companion with a fat elbow.

"I prefer the Welsh longbow," she replied matter-of-factly. " 'Tis best for distance and accuracy."

Standford winked at the man beside him. "I have heard of this bow. Perhaps you will show us the advantages over the bows used by the king's archers."

Rianne sensed the ridicule in his tone. She had met many men like him, such as Garidor. It didn't matter the finery of his clothes, they were much the same.

"The Welsh bow is very rare," Tristan interceded, giving her a sharp look.

Rianne glared at him. "If one can be found, milord, I will be happy to show you the advantages."

"But surely it was not necessary for you to hunt for your own food all the time," Lord Standford responded, still in that mocking tone.

"Oh no, milord," she assured him as Tristan attempted to silence her with a warning look. She ignored him.

"Most of the time I provided for myself from my winnings at the gaming tables."

CHAPTER FIFTEEN

"Ha! Lord Connor!" Lord Standford exclaimed. "Your daughter is a rare beauty and with a sense of humor as well." He turned to her.

"And what games, pray tell, milady, do you prefer?" He winked again at the man beside him as he leaned forward with great interest.

Merlin leaned forward as well so as not to miss any of their conversation. Since she had closed her thoughts to him, he was forced to listen as others and he was most curious what her answer would be.

At the center of the table, Meg's slender hand closed over Connor's with sudden uneasiness. She knew Lord Standford from Arthur's court. Outwardly, he was pompous, gregarious, a man of appetites that matched his prodigious size. But beneath the courtly exterior was a man of ambition and cunning, for whom the loss of his family holdings over eighteen years earlier, when Arthur seized the throne, was not forgotten.

Outwardly he had made his peace with Arthur and increased

his wealth by tenfold, becoming a strong ally to the south. But Merlin had warned Arthur about those ambitions and that cloak of affability and loyalty.

"Hold your allies close," he had told Arthur and Connor all those years ago of the perilous balance of politics that lay ahead of them. *"But hold your enemies closer."*

Arthur had kept Lord Standford very close.

Merlin sensed Meg's apprehension. *"Be of faith, sister,"* his thoughts connected with hers. *"Have you so little faith in your daughter's abilities?"*

"Sadly, brother, I do not know her abilities," Meg answered pragmatically. *"But I do know Lord Standford. The man is a viper. He allows his own wife to whore herself with Tristan with the hope of forging an alliance with Monmouth."*

Merlin looked down the length of the table with a thoughtful expression. *"There are no vipers in Britain, sister,"* he reminded her with a bemused expression, already sensing the outcome.

"Aye," she snapped. *"There is one. And I do not wish Rianne to feel his sting. She is too young and does not know of these things."*

Merlin smiled. *"Methinks she knows of many things you do not, sister."*

An expectant silence filled the hall. Rianne was aware that Lady Meg seemed distressed, but Lord Connor restrained her with a hand at her wrist.

The gesture confused her. She thought surely he would put an end to the conversation.

"I have some experience with cups and stones," Rianne modestly replied, sensing something in Standford that she did not like. An avarice that belied the genial demeanor. This was no affable fool, but a cunning fox in the guise of a fool.

"But I prefer rolling the stones."

"Ah, a game of chance," Lord Standford remarked.

"There is no such thing as chance," Rianne replied. " 'Tis a matter of skill."

"And you are skilled at rolling the stones?" he burst into laughter.

Tristan watched as those brilliant blue eyes gleamed. He glanced at Connor. Why didn't he put a stop to this? Standford was no novice at the games. Not like the drunks at Garidor's tavern who wagered their last coin.

While others preferred a challenge of physical skill, he preferred the games, and not just the victory over his opponent but thorough humiliation as well. And no doubt most particularly if that opponent was a woman.

His disregard for women, including his much younger second wife, was well known. Tristan was not in love with Alyce. Their affair was one of mutual appetites, nothing more. And while he had decided it best to end the affair, still he was fond of her. Which was more than she received from her husband.

Rianne smiled. "Aye, milord."

"I have beaten every man at this table. Do you think you could best me?"

"I could lift your purse in three hands."

Her skill at seeking out the thoughts of others constantly improved. It was like eavesdropping on whispered conversations and revealed a great deal.

All about the table, the reaction of the other guests was amusement. She knew they considered her to be nothing more than an outspoken child. But she discovered that it was far more for Standford. It was the opportunity to affront Lord Connor in a very personal way for reasons not immediately known.

"I would like that very much, my dear." Standford congenially accepted the challenge and turned to Connor.

"What say you, milord? Will you allow the child to entertain us?"

Entertainment? Hah! Humiliation was what he intended. It

was as clear to Rianne as if he had spoken it aloud. She saw it in that thoughtful gaze. And Lady Meg clearly objected. When she would have spoken those objections aloud, Lord Connor gently silenced them with a hand at her arm.

She expected Lord Connor to put an end to the matter. No doubt he had no desire to risk embarrassment before the king and Lord Standford.

"I have great faith that my daughter will uphold the honor of this house, Standford," he replied.

Then he smiled, and for a moment Rianne glimpsed the man he had once been, before the wasting sickness robbed him of his strength and vitality.

"Be forewarned," he added with a smile that hid his own cunning, "her mother is a very clever woman, and she is as much her mother's daughter."

"Perhaps," Standford replied. But his thoughts belied the careful reply. "Then you have no objection?"

Rianne's surprised gaze met her father's. And in the silent connection with his thoughts discovered trust, faith, and unconditional love that humbled her as no words could have.

"I have no objection."

"And you will vouch for her losses?"

"I will vouch for her."

Emotions threatened to overwhelm her. She had not expected his support, much less the unconditional love that reached out to her. She tried to close her thoughts to those emotions but found she could not. They were so new to her. It was like a door opening that she had closed long ago.

"Then let the games begin," Standford announced jubilantly, his eyes agleam in anticipation of victory.

The table was cleared and the guests gathered round as Standford's squire produced a set of cubed stones with the familiar markings on each side.

Merlin moved to her side. The impression was more the warrior than the king's trusted counselor. She realized that he was not much older than the king, who was still considered to be a young man.

"You do not need to go through with this if you wish otherwise. Your father, as well as the king, will support your decision. None will think the less of you. Standford is a worthy opponent. Nearly every man present has lost to him at one time or another."

She glanced past him to Lord Connor. The feelings of betrayal and bitterness were not so easily understood as they once had been. She had not counted on kindness. She had not counted on caring about him. He had given her kindness, but he had given her so much more. He had shown his faith in her.

"I would like very much to beat him," she replied.

Merlin nodded. "I would like very much to see you beat him."

A slender brow arched upwards, the exact expression he had seen on her mother's face countless time. She sensed far more that went unspoken.

"You must not interfere," she said adamantly. "He will suspect it. And if others believe it, then he has won anyway. You must let me do this."

"And if you lose?"

Her smile deepened and reached all the way to her magnificent eyes. "I do not intend to lose."

"I suspect he cheats," Merlin gave her parting advice.

"Then we will have to make an honest man of him."

One of the long trestle tables was separated from the others and turned sideways. Arthur's men gathered round. To a man they had all lost money to Standford, and the mere thought that Lord Connor's daughter had challenged him drew them to the table.

"I have no stake," Rianne pointed out. She had nothing to her name, not even the clothes on her back.

"Is there anyone who will stake Lady Rianne?" Standford inquired among those who had gathered round to watch.

If she hadn't the coin to meet the initial bet, then she defaulted the game. Why hadn't she sensed his scheme? It was so very clear. Or was there more to it than that? What dark ambition lay beneath the jovial demeanor?

She saw the way his eyes gleamed as he looked over at Lord Connor. But before he could respond, Tristan's voice rang out across the hall.

"I will provide her stake."

"Ah, the young warrior." Standford's eyes gleamed and his voice became silken. "By all means."

Rianne sensed there was more here than the simple challenge of a favorite game. There was something that passed between Tristan and Standford in looks that were exchanged that suggested it was far more.

Several of Connor's guests, including Merlin, the king, and the king's knights gathered about the table. Lord Connor remained seated, choosing to watch the game from his chair. Lady Meg remained with him.

Wagers were placed. Tristan placed several silver and gold coins on the table before her. It was a substantial sum, far more than she had ever seen before. He leaned close.

"You had best win. That is all the coin I have to my name." His amused gaze met her startled one.

"You can beat him, can't you?"

She felt insulted. "I will give it my best."

"Good. I would like very much to see him lose."

"Is there anything else you wish to say, milord?" she replied, making no attempt to keep the sarcasm from her voice.

He smiled, that same smile glimpsed in the tavern when he had challenged the stable owner, that same smile when he'd kissed her, then thrown her over the back of his horse. A dangerous smile that made her blood heat.

"You are most beautiful tonight, milady." And then added, "It is amazing what a little soap and water can do."

Her mouth dropped open. She snapped it shut again, cutting

off several curses as he quickly moved beyond earshot of those curses.

Milady? He said it in a most irritating way, as if he was about to burst out laughing.

"Swine!" she sent him the thought on a single word.

"Does this mean that you care for me, milady?*"*

Only days ago she had threatened to cut out his heart. What was it that had changed since then, so that the word that immediately leapt into her thoughts and almost escaped before she could snatch it back, was *yes!*

He looked at her as if he had heard something but perhaps not clearly. Rianne held her breath. She could not say why it was important that he had not heard it, only that it was. That uncertainty came from the same place as her response—a place deep inside that she kept carefully protected and allowed no one to see.

Standford was a most worthy opponent. He rolled the stones with skill and confidence. He liked to win and had no intention of losing. All the more so because she was Lord Connor's daughter. The reason, she finally sensed, as she saw the cunning look when the king was not aware of it, lay in their shared past.

The stones passed from one to the other several times. Bets were placed on each roll of the stones. Control passed to the one with the highest total score of each roll. At first, Rianne won as many rolls of the stones as she lost. But she was aware that Standford gradually increased the bet with each roll.

Then it seemed she gradually began to lose more than she won. When next she picked up the stones, she sensed the reason for the change in her "luck." The stones felt different in her hand. It was subtle, but she sensed these were not the stones they had first played with.

"Is something wrong?"

She looked up. Her gaze met Merlin's. *"Nothing that cannot be made right,''* she replied through the connection of their thoughts as she concentrated on her next throw of the stones.

She rolled them loosely in the palm of her hand and then tossed them down onto the table. They rolled heavily, confirming what she had sensed when she first picked them up. Two of them were weighted. As the last stone rolled to a stop she gave it a small nudge with a burst of energy that she had once used on Grendel. The stone tumbled onto its side, changing the outcome.

Across the table, she saw Lord Standford's subtle surprise. The stones were gathered up and handed back to her. She rolled again. She won again with a slight nudge of the outcome. This time Standford's reaction was less subtle as his eyes narrowed. She deliberately lost the next roll of the stones, allowing them to pass to Standford. She sharpened her thoughts as a small shadow appeared at her side, barely high enough to reach the edge of the table.

"He cheats!" Grendel's thoughts connected with hers. He had sensed it as well.

"Aye," she replied with an amused glance down at the little man beside her. *"But then, so do I."*

"Then cheat well, mistress. I have no desire to see this one win."

"I intend to."

She allowed him to keep control of the stones through several more rolls. He won a substantial amount of coins. Most of them were Tristan's. She glanced across the table where he stood beside Merlin, dark brows drawn together in a worried frown as he watched more and more of the coins leave her side of the table. She smiled secretly to herself.

Standford won two more rolls. Practically all of Tristan's coins were now gone. He looked miserable. She had mercy on him. On the next roll of the stones, she gave the two weighted stones an extra nudge and altered the outcome of the game. Standford frowned at the unexpected loss.

"It seems that it is your turn at the stones, milady." He shoved them across the table toward her.

"I hope I will have as good fortune as you, milord," she replied with a smile.

Standford smiled in return, except that it seemed more like a grimace of pain mixed with agitation. He had not expected to relinquish the roll of the stones, and she sensed that even now he was quite beside himself trying to figure out why the outcome of that last roll had not gone in his favor.

She wished him no ill will, merely the return of everything she'd *lost* to him, plus a substantial portion of his coins. She scooped up the stones, rolled them in the cupped palm of her hand, and then tossed them down onto the table.

She smiled to herself as they rolled exactly as she wished them to. Standford's expression never changed, but he paled noticeably. The stones were returned to her, she rolled, and won again. His expression went from discomfort to incredulity as the stack of gold and metal coins before him continued to dwindle.

Best to let him win one, she thought. And on the next roll, let the stones roll as they would, turning up a loss.

"Aha!" he exclaimed as he retrieved the stones. "Now we shall see who is the better player. Now we shall see."

He rolled the stones in his large, meaty palm, weighing the feel of them, reassuring himself they were the same ones he'd substituted. He smiled at her, an expression of confidence in spite of the beads of moisture that had popped out on his forehead.

He rolled the stones and promptly lost. His face drained of all color, then flushed bright crimson. Rianne thought he would have apoplexy.

"Most unfortunate," she said, then added, "But your misfortune is perhaps my good fortune."

It was not her intention to humiliate Lord Standford. She merely wanted to relieve him of a good portion of his coin.

As she reached for the stones, an image flashed through her thoughts

It was brief and lasted no more than a second, but it startled her. Beside her, yet hidden beneath the table, Grendel sensed her hesitation.

"Is something wrong?" his thoughts connected with hers.

" 'Tis nothing," she assured him and prepared to roll the stones.

Again the image flashed through her thoughts. Her fingers tightened over the stones as it invaded her thoughts. It was the image of a hand—her hand. Even as she stared down at the flesh and blood hand that held the stones, she saw that other hand from her dreams.

Again she heard the concern in Grendel's thoughts. *"Mistress?"*

She squeezed her eyes shut, forcing the image from her thoughts. *" 'Tis nothing."*

When she opened them again the image was gone. She rolled the stones across the table. With the same precision she'd used to let Standford win, she now turned the game against him.

He watched helplessly and with growing frustration and anger as she used his stones to reclaim the small fortune—his fortune—in gold and silver coins, and even a substantial amount of the odd-shaped metal issue that had become the common coin of the realm.

She was about to scoop up the stones and roll the next round when another image flashed through her thoughts in an explosion of flames so real, so intense, she could feel the heat and instinctively jerked her hand back.

Tristan watched as she rolled the last round. Something was wrong. Merlin also sensed it, his intense blue gaze fastened on her. He made his way around the table to where she stood.

She leaned against the edge of the table, her slender fingers curled over the edge, her nails digging into the wood. Her eyes had gone dark, the brilliant blue thinning to narrow bands that encircled black centers that gleamed like black pearls.

Her skin was pale, bloodless over fragile bones. Her breathing was ragged between equally pale, bloodless lips. His thoughts reached out to hers. Instead of feeling that familiar resistance his thoughts easily joined with hers. What he saw stunned him.

Through the connection of their thoughts, he saw the flames that burned at the edges of her vision and the blood at her hand. Then the blood gradually disappeared and in its place was a magnificent shimmering stone the color of blood.

Rianne heard her name. The sound of it moved through her thoughts and the images fled, receding to the edges of her vision, and then disappeared completely.

The torches burned steadily at the walls once more, and the faces that stared back at her no longer peered at her from the shadows of terrifying dreams. They were the faces of those who stood about the table, waiting expectantly for the game to continue.

Merlin felt the door to her thoughts being closed once more as the images fled. She was no longer pale, and the eyes that looked back at him were a clear, brilliant blue once more. She had returned from wherever it was that she had gone for those brief moments. Now it was as if nothing had happened.

It was not a disguise. Merlin would have sensed if it was. Just as she had closed her thoughts to him, she had also closed the door on those memories, refusing to remember anything that had happened, now or in the past.

All traces of those terrifying images were gone now. She seemed completely recovered, as if nothing was amiss. If he had not seen them for himself in the connection of their thoughts, he would never suspect anything had happened.

Did she truly not remember? Or was it that she could now control her thoughts and hide them away from him once more? It was an intriguing possibility. More intriguing, even disturbing, were the images he'd seen in that brief connection.

Images of things she'd no doubt experienced, and along with them an image of something he'd learned of long ago—the image of a stone transformed from blood. The Ancient Ones called it the Bloodstone.

Stories of the Bloodstone had been handed down through countless generations of those who possessed the power of the Light. Its origins were shrouded in the mists of antiquity. It was the mark of the Chosen, those who first entered the mortal world. It had not been seen in more than a thousand years.

Rianne sensed when Merlin moved around the table and stood very near. Their first encounter had been an uneasy one. Her uneasiness increased. She expected him to lecture or counsel her. Perhaps even Arthur had told him to order her to lose in the name of diplomacy. She braced for a confrontation.

"You might allow him to win at least one more round before he explodes."

She looked at him with surprise, identical blue gazes meeting in an understanding that was felt rather than spoken, something that moved through her senses with familiarity and surprise.

Merlin shrugged. "Then finish him off."

She expelled the breath she was holding on a soft ripple of laughter. "Be merciful?" she asked.

He shook his head, his expression solemn, as if he did indeed lecture her. But behind the solemn expression a smile gleamed in that shimmering gaze.

"Prolong the torture. He's handed out his fair share over the years."

"And the end?" she asked.

"Swift and deadly."

Rianne let him win the next round, the stones passing back to him for several rolls. But his jubilation was short-lived. He won just three rolls of the stones, then lost them again. He made a strangled sound. The veins stood out in his neck and his face turned bright purple.

"No mercy?" she asked, her eyes sparkling with mischief and the thrill of impending victory.

"Absolutely none." Merlin hadn't enjoyed himself so much in months.

The stones tumbled across the table and came to rest in damning defeat for Standford. He was livid. He scooped up the stones and hurled them against the wall. They broke into several pieces and fell into the rushes at the floor.

Grendel scurried over, dug among the fragrant grass, and scooped up the shattered pieces. He displayed them for all to see.

"Oh, look!" he exclaimed with mock seriousness. "There's an iron lug in the middle of this one!" All gazes turned to Standford.

"Preposterous!" he exclaimed, rounding the table to examine the pieces of stone. Rianne sensed the lie even before he spoke it.

"Someone must have switched the stones. Who would have done such a thing?"

"Who, indeed?" Tristan asked as he took the broken stone and examined it closely. "It's one of yours, Standford. This piece has your mark on it. Most of us are familiar with it."

"I cannot imagine who could have done this!" he exclaimed. "It is a plot to discredit me." He turned to Rianne. "I assure you, mistress, the scheme was none of my doing. When I find the knave you may be assured he will be punished."

"Do not punish him too severely," Rianne replied, and pointed out, "after all, I did win in spite of it."

Standford paled several shades lighter, his skin taking on a greenish hue. "Of course. I don't suppose you would consider a rematch in light of this most unusual outcome."

It was unusual and not at all what he'd expected. Rianne wasn't fooled that his solicitous words were for her benefit. She sensed the resentment and anger that burned within him at the humiliating loss he'd suffered. And she sensed his gaze slide past her to the king, who listened with much amusement.

She scooped her winnings into the pocket of her tunic, noting the incredulous expression on his face as he realized that she intended to keep every last coin.

"A rematch it is, milord." She smiled radiantly as she dropped the last coin into her pocket. "Now that I have my own stake. You have only to name the day and the hour."

He looked as if he might have ruptured something. Or in the very least swallowed something bitter and vile. But as Lord Connor joined them and with the king looking on, he could do nothing but acknowledge her acceptance.

"You are most gracious, mistress. My thanks for a most . . . interesting evening."

"Thank you, milord." She struggled very hard not to burst out laughing. She glanced at Tristan. He struggled with that same emotion. She saw it in his eyes, which glittered with laughter even as he fastened a serious expression on his face that battled with the smile that threatened at his lips.

Standford hesitated as silence drew out. He waited for someone to suggest that the monies from their competition be returned. But no one, including Arthur, even hinted at the possibility, and he could not very well demand it without being made to look more the fool.

"Aye, well, then it is settled. Now I must find the unfortunate soul responsible for tampering with the stones. I assure you, mistress, he will be punished."

He turned and left in a disgruntled huff, his seneschal and his squire following dutifully in his substantial wake.

"He won't be satisfied until one of his squires has been punished," Tristan commented in a low voice, some of the humor gone.

Rianne was incredulous. "But you cannot mean that he will punish another. 'Tis clear who weighted the stones."

"The guilt will be laid upon another," Merlin explained. "He cannot afford to be seen either as a fool or a cheat."

"The one chosen for the punishment will be dismissed, of course," Connor explained as he joined them, proving that nothing escaped his attention.

"We have seen it before. The lad will be given a place here at Monmouth if he wishes."

His movements were slow and made with great pain. But the hand that reached for hers was strong and steady. He tucked her hand through his arm.

"Walk with me, daughter."

There was something in his voice, something in the way he said the word *daughter* that pulled at something inside her and made her powerless to refuse him.

She glanced at Lady Meg, and sensed her silent agony. In spite of his hand on hers, he was not strong. Each effort cost him what little strength he had left as he slowly lost the battle against the wasting sickness. But she said nothing. Instead, her thoughts spoke the words she feared Rianne would not listen to.

"Do not turn him away. He loves you so, my daughter."

Rianne nodded, unable to answer, barely able to comprehend the reasons she could not, when only a day earlier she had been so certain of her ability to turn away from him, and her mother.

Through a door near the entrance to the main hall, they climbed the steps to the battlements. Rianne feared that his strength would fail him. But just as he had cheated death so many times, Connor of Monmouth held it at bay a while longer.

Occasionally they paused and he would lean upon her; then in the quivering light of the torches at the walls she saw that weak but determined smile as he spoke.

"I climbed the steps first as a boy of three," he told her, pausing once more for breath, then continuing.

"I know every stone, each timber, every hidden corner. I hid there on more than one occasion." They paused again as he pointed out a hidden alcove, and his expression shifted from that of the mischievous boy to the man who remembered other times he had hidden there with a beautiful young girl.

She sensed the thoughts that wove through the words, unfolding like a tapestry of life—his life. And hers. They continued on, finally reaching the top landing and the door that led out onto the battlements. And the thoughts continued on, revealing everything he was, everything he had fought for: his love for Arthur, a love of friendship that had endured much, more than friends, brothers in spirit; his deep, passionate feelings for Lady Meg; the pride he felt for Tristan, the son they could never have; and last but not least, the love that reached out for her.

It was a love that had been there all these years, across time and distance. A love that had endured the pain of sending her away, and then lived on the desperate hope that he might see her one last time.

Such was the curse of this gift she'd been born with that as much as she wanted to deny it, she could not. It was there in his thoughts, in his heart, in the simple touch of his hand on hers as they stood at the battlement walls.

It was cold. Even now clouds chased the moon. By morning the weather they had left behind in the north country would be upon them. There was the smell of it in the air. But tonight the stars and moon eluded the clouds, as he eluded death. For a while longer.

"This is what I wanted you to see."

Night spread before them like a velvet blanket, a canopy of glittering stars and a satin moon that painted the landscape in silvery light. The distant lowing of cattle and the occasional bleat of sheep mingled with the solitary call of a night bird. Here and there lights glowed as tallow lamps and candles were lit in the cottages and huts that spread to the forest beyond.

There were families in those cottages. Safe and warm. Just as she was safe and warm. It was a reminder that home was more than a word. It was a place. It was the daily lives of people who worked the land and lit those lanterns at night, who put their children to bed and sang songs to them in times of peace and tranquility. And sent them away to a place of safety in times of danger.

These were the things that lay in his heart, that he had waited a lifetime to say. This was what he wanted to show her. Home was not a place to run from; it was a place to run to.

"I know these years have not been easy for you," he said gently, stroking his hand over hers where it rested on his arm. "I have heard that you wish to leave. I will accept your decision whatever it may be.

"But it is important to me that you know I could not have asked for a finer daughter. You humble me with your strength and courage." He leaned forward and kissed her forehead.

"I hope that you will find it in your heart to stay."

She heard the weariness in his voice and felt it in the trembling of his hand. She sensed, too, that they were not alone. Then she saw the slender figure who stood apart in the light of the torches at the open passage.

Meg had followed them at a discreet distance, appearing now only out of concern for her husband.

"Come, husband," she said gently, slipping her arm beneath his. " 'Tis late, and well you know I cannot sleep in that large bed unless you are there beside me. There is time enough for Rianne to see Monmouth."

"Foolish woman," he scolded, but there was only tenderness in his voice as he closed his hand around hers. "You have slept without me during the wars."

"Aye, and for that very reason I refuse to do so now," she replied.

Her father chuckled, a soft, intimate sound filled with a subtle language that was theirs alone. He touched her mother's cheek with such gentleness. Instinctively, she turned and brushed her lips against his fingers in a ritual that was both old and new each time.

Rianne sensed the love that flowed between them. A love that not even death could diminish. A love that reached out to her in the gentle contact of her mother's hand, words unspoken yet heard. And deep inside felt the last stone in the wall of anger and bitterness that she'd built around herself crumble to dust.

She listened to the murmur of their voices as they returned down the passage; her mother's gentle whispers and soothing words, her father's reassuring response and tender laughter. Even now with death so near. Tears were hot on her cheeks.

She knew Tristan was there. She sensed his presence before he spoke, even before he reached out to her. She turned and went into his arms. She slipped her arms around his waist, reaching out for his warmth and strength.

"Please, hold me," she whispered.

Once, the angry child had lashed out at him. The child was gone, disappeared as that wall of anger had disappeared. In her place was the young woman who wanted only this—his strength, his warmth, his arms holding her. No questions, no anger, no threats, no words. Just the feel of him, filling all the lonely, empty places deep inside her.

CHAPTER SIXTEEN

The weather prevented her leaving. That was what she told herself. It gave her time to reconcile the decision so easily made in her heart that night on the battlements.

It snowed the next several days and the weather became Tristan's excuse as well, keeping him and his men far afield as they were needed in the towns and villages that surrounded Monmouth, before winter set in.

She sensed that he struggled with some inner turmoil and avoided her after the encounter on the battlements, even though their paths crossed occasionally.

Rianne had taken on the responsibility of seeing to the needs of the townspeople and villagers as well. Each day she and Merlin spent mornings together in the herbal at Monmouth. There he began instructing her in the healing ways that Dannelore had begun so long ago, the ancient art of blending and mixing herbal extracts with other natural elements that brought relief to the sick and injured of Monmouth.

He also began teaching her the ways of the immortals. Each

day she discovered more of the abilities she had been born with, far more than manipulating the outcome of a game or using her power to retaliate against pesky gnomes. A new, fascinating, and sometimes frightening world had opened to her. A world of extraordinary powers and profound responsibility.

Surely, she thought, with Merlin's great powers there was something that could be done for her father. Though he assured her that he had done everything that could be done, she refused to accept it. And if she also possessed this healing ability as well, then perhaps she might find a way to heal the sickness that was slowly killing him.

She spent most afternoons in the nearby villages as she assumed the responsibilities her mother now gladly relinquished so that she could spend more time with Connor. Late each afternoon when she returned, Rianne went directly to the small anteroom with its warm fire and soft candles. There she told her father everything she'd seen and heard in the village that day.

Meg joined them there. She was content to sit by the hearth, listening to their conversation as she worked at the tapestry, her fingers guiding the needle with unerring accuracy in spite of her blindness, occasionally asking about a particular complaint or illness that Rianne had encountered in the village.

It was a tentative beginning. Each moment was a small step forward, followed by another. They could not have back what had been lost, but they did have this time. And each day was a gift that they discovered together.

In these days and hours spent together Rianne discovered that her parents were not the cruel, unfeeling creatures she had thought them to be. As the anger and pain lessened with each passing day, she discovered the people Dannelore had spoken of when she was a child.

Her father listened attentively as she told him about the things she had heard and seen. On more than one occasion she thought he dozed off, head nodding forward, eyes closed. But then in a moment's silence he surprised her with a question that proved he had heard everything she'd said.

In spite of his illness, he knew everything that went on at Monmouth. Now Rianne became his eyes and ears. More and more each day he asked her opinion of matters; not only what she thought, but what she felt about a problem or concern that he'd become aware of.

It was an opportunity for him to learn firsthand of the needs of his people and at the same time gave father and daughter an opportunity to slowly build the relationship that had been missing from their lives. It flattered and humbled her that he placed such trust in her.

They discussed these matters of great importance as they sat across from each other at a large game board and he taught her a game that had been taught to him by his father. It was a game of cunning and strategy, each move effecting the next and the next, in an intricate pattern of moves and countermoves.

It could not be won by manipulation as she had manipulated the stones. It was not won by altering the outcome. And the strategy changed each time, making it impossible to know his thoughts ahead of time. It could only be won by thinking her way through it, learning her opponent, learning the patterns, and then positioning her game pieces so that she was protected from his advances at the same time she was in a position to seize his domain.

It was the most challenging game she had ever encountered. It was also frustrating, intimidating, and infuriating. That, too, she discovered, was part of the strategy—to unnerve one's opponent, expose his weaknesses, then use those weaknesses against him. It was a lesson she didn't forget.

The day she finally won a game, she moved her game piece with skill and decisiveness, eluded the enemy with cunning, and claimed her opponent's domain.

For several long moments her father said nothing. Then he looked up. For the first time she saw not fatigue and weakness in his face, but something else. An emotion that reached out to her from the expression in his eyes and the smile on his mouth. Pride in a handful of simple words.

"Well done, daughter."

It overwhelmed her. No one had ever been proud of her. For as long as she could remember there had been only herself. Only survival. Such things as pride, approval, love didn't exist in her life. Only in her dreams.

Her relationship with her mother and father changed irrevocably that day. She no longer dwelled on the pain of the past, but opened her heart to the future.

Tristan often joined them in the anteroom when he returned, bringing word from the outlying villages and hamlets that were under the protection of Monmouth. As the captain of the guard, Tristan was Connor's trusted right hand in matters of the protection of Monmouth.

When he was gone overlong, Rianne watched for his return from the battlement walls. Something had changed between them that night when she had first gone to the battlements and stood there alone after her father left. She had felt it in the way Tristan held her. She sensed that he also felt it, and that was the reason he stayed away from Monmouth.

One afternoon when she returned to the herbal, Grendel brought stunning news. Tristan had returned, and he brought word from a pilgrim who had recently returned from the north country.

An inn of particular notoriety and disrepute near the Tamar River had burned. The innkeeper and several others were trapped inside, their bodies found among the charred ruins. By the description the pilgrim gave the inn could only be Garidor's. And it had happened only days after they had left.

Fires were common. An ember from the hearth, a lantern knocked over during a drunken brawl had burned out of control, destroying everything and killing all inside.

She felt no sadness for Garidor or Mab. As far as she was

concerned they deserved their fate. Instead, she thought of Kari and wondered if the news might bring her any peace. When the weather cleared she would call on her. So much had changed since they'd parted at Glastonbury.

Or was it that she had changed? Or had she simply discovered who she was all along?

There were days when she was not certain which it was. Particularly when Merlin explained about the world beyond the mortal world.

She was part of that world. She possessed many of the powers he possessed, and others yet to be discovered. That part of her that was mortal found it difficult to accept these things. Impossible, she thought. Such creatures were not real. They existed only in myth and legend.

But Merlin was real. Her mother was real. And they were part of her. Their essence flowed through her. And each day as she discovered more of her powers and abilities, doubt gave way to that other equally mortal trait—curiosity. At times, much to Grendel's trepidation.

"I would not have believed it possible!" he exclaimed one afternoon as he swept up the remains of the latest pot she'd smashed against the wall.

"If anyone had told me such things were hereditary I would have laughed and called him a fool! But then, an immortal has never given birth to a mortal child. I should have been forewarned."

"Half mortal," Rianne corrected him as she focused on the task at hand. The tip of her tongue appeared at the corner of her mouth, a pink knot of intense concentration as she directed all her energy at the jars and pots lined up on the table.

The gnome blanched several shades paler as they all slowly rose from the surface of the table.

"By the Ancient Ones!" he muttered, abandoning his cleaning efforts and frantically searching for a place to hide as the pots and jars suddenly all took flight.

"We will all be killed!"

Rianne burst into laughter and the pots danced wildly in their midair flight, her power obviously effected by her emotions. Fascinated with this newest discovery, she thought of Garidor and his cruelty to Kari.

The pots suddenly shot across the room at a dangerous speed, careening at the edge of disaster. She thought of her father, and the pots steadied and moved with certainty and control. Then she thought of Tristan.

The pots suddenly spun in all different directions, in dizzying, loopy circles, soaring to the ceiling, then whipping frantically past her in a pattern of tumultuous, electrifying emotions.

As a pot swept past her at a thrilling, chaotic speed, the door to the herbal opened and Grendel seized the opportunity to escape. The pot careened after him on a burst of laughter, then without warning crashed into the wall beside the door opening.

It was difficult to say who was more surprised, her or Tristan, who stood in the doorway with a stunned expression at the chaos inside.

Rianne stared at him wide-eyed. Then the hilarity of it hit her, bubbling up inside her in rolls of laughter at the thought that a fierce warrior could be vanquished by a pot of herbs.

The last thing he expected when he opened the door was to find the gnome and a pot hurtling toward him at breakneck speed.

The gnome escaped through his legs, yelling some incoherent gibberish. The pot shattered against the wall beside his head. Several others collided in midair in an explosion of fragrant herbs that showered down over everything. He didn't know whether to draw his sword or dive for cover.

When it seemed that no more missiles were being launched at his head, Tristan glanced skeptically around the herbal. Then his gaze came back to Rianne.

She stood amid the broken pots and jars and drifting petals and leaves, like the queen of the forest. Her hair tumbled loose about her shoulders and fell in silken gold waves to her waist. The color was vivid in her cheeks. One was smudged with some unknown substance that gave her the appearance of a serving wench. Her eyes shimmered like brilliant blue flame and her mouth was curved in a startled expression that hovered somewhere between dismay and laughter.

He had never seen a more beguiling serving wench. Or any young woman, for that matter. She was an intriguing combination of mystery and mischief, whimsy and seduction. She was also Connor's daughter, and he had spent the better part of the last few weeks trying very hard to stay away from her.

Her parents had raised him as a son. She was almost like a sister. But the feelings and thoughts she had churned inside him from the moment he first confronted her at the long end of a sword were anything but brotherly.

"Failed that lesson, did you?" he asked, retreating to the banter that usually sufficed in keeping them at odds and at arm's distance from one another.

He knew she spent a good portion of each day here with Merlin. He had long heard the rumors about the king's counselor—that he was far more than merely an adviser to Arthur.

He had heard the rumors and speculation, along with the words *sorcerer, conjuror,* and *enchanter.* That Merlin possessed unusual intellect and abilities could not be argued. Nor could the strange events of long ago be ignored or denied, for he had been part of them as a boy, when Merlin had been seriously wounded and some darkness of evil threatened them all.

It was Lady Meg who had protected them all and had gone alone to meet the threat at a place where the stones taller than any man now stood on a barren plain. He also knew, as few others did, that Lady Meg was Merlin's sister. That Rianne had inherited some of their unique abilities there was no doubt. The only doubt was the extent of those abilities.

Fail? The word sliced through the laughter and joy at seeing him again like a battle sword.

Why was he forever finding fault with her? When he chose to speak to her at all!

It was a pity the other pots lay in pieces. At that moment she would have liked very much to heave them all at his head. And this time she would not miss!

"What are you doing here?" she demanded as she bent to pick up the larger pieces. " 'Tis unusual to find you in the herbal. Perhaps you've lost your way. The kennels are at the other end of the keep."

Her eyes still shimmered with that inner fire, but it burned furiously now, rather than with laughter. He'd hoped to put her in her place and somehow keep those disconcerting feelings she roused in him at bay.

He'd succeeded in the first but failed miserably in the latter. Bubbling with laughter or furious and hurling insults and pots at his head, she was the most beguiling creature he'd ever encountered. He was beginning to seriously rethink the wisdom in seeking her out for the wound at his shoulder.

He moved stiffly as he came away from the wall beside the door opening, and she immediately sensed that he had not come there to insult or berate her.

"You're hurt."

Not a question but a statement of certainty, so much like her mother in that way that was so natural to her. She was more like Meg than she perhaps was ready to hear yet.

" 'Tis a minor thing."

"A minor thing, yet you seek a healer?" She shook her head, pieces of dried flowers escaping the shimmering gold of her hair and drifting to the herb-strewn floor.

"The concoction for liars is a bitter brew."

"It would have to be," he replied, unable to hold on to the unpleasantness that had become his shield against her.

"Aye, most vile. So dreadful that the threat of it is enough to force most into a more pleasing and truthful mood.'' She pointed to a nearby chair as she kicked a path through the broken pottery.

"Have you perhaps taken some of it by mistake?" he asked, and smiled as she angled him a curious look from the table where she sorted through jars of other herbs.

"Was I that dreadful?" she asked.

"Worse."

"Aye, well, no worse than yourself," she informed him as she returned with a handful of healing balms and bandages.

"I seem to remember being trussed like a chicken and thrown over the back of your horse, and that was only the latest abuse," she reminded him, adding, "You will have to remove your tunic."

"Abuse?" he replied incredulously as he peeled off the tunic. "I still bear teeth marks where you bit me, I have bruises in places I haven't felt in years, and you threatened to unman me."

She shrugged. "A *minor* threat. But necessary at the time."

"I assure you," he informed her, " 'Twas not *minor* . . ."

His voice had gone low and rough, but it was the roughness of thick velvet and caused those uneasy feelings deep inside her—those same feelings that had sent those pots soaring wildly about the chamber, the same feelings she awoke with at night in her chamber.

"You must remove the shirt as well." Her own voice suddenly sounded husky, less angry, as he removed the shirt.

The wound was padded with a dirty, blood-crusted cloth, which she gently pried away with a wet herbal solution.

"You have a healer's hands," he said, his voice shades deeper, gentler.

Her fingers ached to touch more as she applied the solution. Her throat went dry as she remembered the taste of that skin— masculine, with a mysterious dark taste that lingered on the lips and haunted her dreams.

"Merlin says I have hands more suited to milking cows or strangling chickens," she said, trying not to think of how he had tasted. It was difficult with that naked expanse of chest and well-muscled shoulders.

"Or wielding a sword?" he suggested.

She smiled. "Perhaps."

"What is this?" Looking down, he indicated the toes of her shoes, which peered out from beneath the hem of her skirt. They were not the style typically worn by young maids.

She hitched up the skirt and revealed a pair of slender leather boots laced about a pair of equally slender ankles.

"Lady Meg had them made for me." She showed off the soft leather boots, unaware that his gaze lingered where the hem of the gown hovered above a slender exposed calf.

" 'Tis far better than freezing one's feet on stone floors. I'm working on a pair of *underpants* as well."

His brows shot up. "Underpants?"

"Oh, aye," she replied, with that bluntness that was so much a part of her.

"Pants and breeches are far more practical. I cannot for the life of me understand why women wear skirts and gowns with the wind whistling up their bare arse." For emphasis she swished the hem of the skirt back and forth.

" 'Tis most uncomfortable. And it could be most embarrassing in a high wind."

"Oh, to be certain," Tristan replied, struggling between laughter and a wicked curiosity to know whether or not she wore any *underpants*. And prayed for a high wind, even inside the stout walls of the keep.

"It goes well, then?" he said with mock seriousness.

She shrugged. "My needlework is somewhat lacking. I ruined the first pair. But I've been practicing and I've made adjustments to the fit."

That was indeed regrettable, Tristan thought.

Her head shot up. "Did you say something?"

"You've made progress, then?" he asked instead, lamenting the possibility.

She looked at him curiously, certain she had heard something far different. "Very slow progress, I fear. If I cannot get it right, I shall have to go back to wearing pants."

That was not altogether regrettable. He remembered the look of her in leather pants, the soft hide stretched taut across a shapely bottom occasionally visible in spite of her best efforts to disguise her appearance with layers of tunics and woolen shirts, and completely dispelling the notion that she was a man to anyone who looked closely enough. He had. More than once.

She finally peeled away the last of the soiled bandage and threw it in a pot of boiling water. The bleeding had stopped and the wound had sealed itself. A scar would remain, but she would try to lessen the damage with some of the special balm she kept for such things. She gently washed the wound with the herbal mixture, cleaning away debris and caked blood.

"How did you come by the wound?"

" 'Twas an accident. We encountered raiders in the forest and gave chase. In the confusion I took a blow from one of my men."

She looked up. "Your own man?"

He shrugged. "Aye, Longinus. It happens occasionally in the thick of battle. 'Tis often difficult to tell who is comrade and who is foe."

"I thought Longinus had returned to Camelot with Arthur."

"He and his men joined us at the river. Arthur thought it necessary due to the number of the raiders who were seen. It was thought they might be the same ones who attacked Monmouth."

Merlin had told her of the attack. Tristan had been at Camelot at the time and blamed himself for what had happened, even though Merlin assured her that his presence would not have made a difference. In all likelihood more would have died that day. She shivered at the thought.

"And Longinus?"

"One of my men intervened and he realized the mistake he'd made."

She gently pressed a clean bandage against the wound. "Hold this in place."

"I must dress my own wound?"

"I have only two hands and I need both of them to tie the bandage in place."

She knelt on the floor before him, wedged between those long muscular legs, recalling the long hours spent astride the black stallion, but under far different circumstances. Now he was her prisoner, in a matter of speaking.

She wrapped one end of a long strip of cloth over his shoulder and the other down across his chest and around his back to hold the bandage in place.

As she worked her hair brushed his shoulder. It was like cool silk, shimmering pale and golden in the quivering light of the oil lamps. He plucked a dried flower from the golden tendrils, some fragrant herbal remedy that now covered the floor, his fingers lingering around the silken strands.

Her fingers were gentle and soothing against his skin where she tucked in the ends of the bandage. Her voice was soft and tender, filled with resting shadows and sunshine laughter. Her breath was warm and sweet on a startled sound as he held on to that silken strand and refused to let go as she straightened from her chore.

Held prisoner by his hand at her hair, her gaze met his, eyes suddenly shades darker.

On the battlements, overwhelmed by new and unexpected feelings for the father she'd never known, she had asked simply that he hold her. Now, overwhelmed by far different feelings, she needed and wanted far more.

She sensed the fierce battle that raged within him, the conflict of duty and honor, the powerful emotions he tried to deny.

She could have demanded that he let her go and ended that

battle with a single word. Instead, she opened her thoughts to his and spoke with the need deep inside her.

"Touch me."

The words whispered through his thoughts, filled with silent longings that moved deep inside him and echoed his own needs and longings.

She held her breath, certain he would pull away. Then slowly let it out on a fragile, quivering sound of pleasure as he touched her.

His hand was a warrior's hand; powerful, scarred, more accustomed to the feel of a sword. Capable of killing in a single blow, yet warm, strong, protective; tender, gentle, and then trembling against her cheek.

She saw the fierce will to resist in his eyes, but she refused to show any mercy. A single need burned from her thoughts and through his.

"Kiss me."

His fingers skimmed across her cheek, then fisted in her hair. There was nothing gentle or tender in his kiss, only possession; powerful, bruising, and merciless as he forced her head back.

He tasted the surprise on her lips, then heat, then need as she kissed him back.

Heat exploded like an inferno in his blood, wild, feverish, and needy, burning from her through him. His hands were equally feverish and needy as they twisted in her hair, his mouth plundering, needing more with a hunger that deepened even as it consumed. She burned through him, as if she'd slipped inside him; part of him, in his thoughts, in his blood, in his soul.

It wasn't in her to be submissive or compliant. Her mouth was hungry beneath his, her tongue bold between his lips in a sensual game where the stakes were higher than any she'd wagered in some remote tavern or inn.

Gone was the cool calculation of the girl who played with such cunning and skill at the gaming table. Gone was the anger and defiance that she'd used as a shield around her emotions.

She was all fierce strength and equally fierce passions as she changed the angle of the kiss and took him more deeply inside the wet heat of her mouth.

Desire burned through her blood. The hunger grew as her body pulsed with deeper and darker needs—to touch him the way he touched her; to watch the expression in his eyes go from cool to dangerous, and then beyond; to feel the strength in his hands go from control to chaos in a single heartbeat; to taste him the way she'd first tasted him that long-ago night at the inn when she'd held him at sword's point.

He ended the kiss and on a ragged curse held her at arm's length. Her mouth was softly swollen. Her breasts rose and fell on short, choppy breaths. And the color of her eyes was like blue flame.

Her taste lingered on his lips and the look in her eyes burned in his blood. Only now was it possible for him to draw his first breath. His hands tightened on her arms even as he convinced himself to let her go.

The flames at the candles quivered as the door of the chamber opened. A wrinkled face with sharp, beady eyes cautiously peered around the edge of the door.

"What do you want?" Tristan demanded, his anger at her and at himself now focused on the gnome.

What he wanted was for people to quit throwing things at him—pottery and insults alike. His master had sent him on an errand and he dare not fail to carry it out.

"Master Merlin wishes to speak with the young mistress," Grendel replied, glancing uneasily from the warrior to Rianne.

"Is that all?"

Something was not right here, the gnome thought. Sir Tristan was angry. He wondered if his mistress had hurled a pot at his head.

"He insists on seeing her right away," he replied, still trying to sense what it was that lay in the air thick as heavy mist.

"He is needed at Camelot and must depart immediately."

Tristan released her. He donned the shirt and tunic, wincing as he pulled them over his shoulders. He welcomed the physical pain over the pain that gnawed at his insides, tearing them apart.

"The bandage will need to be changed regularly if the wound is to heal," Rianne reminded him, her voice wobbly, her thoughts even more erratic.

"The stable boy will change it," Tristan replied sharply.

His gaze locked with hers as he paused at the door. Moments before the gnome had thought the air in the herbal thick as mist. Now it heated, threatening to incinerate everything and everyone within those walls on just the look that passed between them. Then he was gone, the heavy door slamming shut behind him.

"Master Merlin is waiting. . . ." No sooner had he turned around and the words were out of his mouth than a small pot streaked the air very near his head and shattered against the closed door.

Several more followed as she gave into anger and frustration and a half dozen other emotions she didn't begin to understand, and sent the gnome diving for cover.

When several moments passed and no more pots came sailing through the air, he peeked tentatively out from under the low shelf where he'd taken refuge.

She stood in the middle of the chamber, hands on her hips, hair tumbling wildly about her shoulders, eyes ablaze. She looked around for something else to hurl at the door, but there was nothing left. The gnome slowly emerged from his hiding place.

The chamber was in shambles. Herbs and dried flowers were strewn across the floor amid broken pots and jars. He shook his head.

"If you dislike Sir Tristan so much, turn him into a toad," the gnome suggested what he thought to be a very logical solution for what seemed to annoy her.

"That would teach him a lesson."

Rianne didn't know whether to laugh or cry. She wanted to throw something, but there was nothing else left in the herbal. It was going to take a great deal of concentration and effort to set right the mess she'd made. But at the moment another thought had far more appeal. Her eyes gleamed.

"I think I shall turn you into a toad," she announced, smothering the smile that threatened at the gnome's suddenly horrified expression.

"Nay! mistress!" he exclaimed, heading for the door as fast as his short legs would carry him.

"Have mercy, mistress!" he croaked and grimaced at the sound. He hated toads. They were such slimy, detestable creatures.

"Do not! You are merely upset. You will regret it later."

"Then I will worry about it later," she replied and sent the little man scurrying out the door.

He didn't stop running until he reached the main hall, and only then because his short legs would go no farther. Cursed stairs, cursed unpredictable mortal emotions. With sudden panic he looked down at his legs, certain he would find slimy, green toad legs. He heaved a sigh of relief and collapsed against the wall of the passage at sight of his own legs.

What a day he was having!

CHAPTER SEVENTEEN

She had really done it this time, Rianne thought, as she felt the coldness of solid wall closing around her. She felt each coarse grain of the stone, each craggy seam, and then . . . she was stuck.

Panic started to set in. She couldn't breathe! She couldn't move! She was trapped!

Get a hold of yourself! she mentally chided herself. *Think! Remember what Merlin taught you!*

She concentrated her thoughts, focused on the image that she had started with, and then gradually took a breath. Then, still holding that thought and no other in her mind, gradually discovered that she could move. Slowly at first. Then as she continued to concentrate on that one thought, movement came more easily.

It was like taking that first step as a child on wobbly legs and uncertain feet. The second step came more easily, then the next, and the next, gathering momentum until . . .

She stumbled and half fell through the wall into the softly lit chamber.

It took a moment for her senses to make the adjustment, her eyes gradually focusing on the objects in the room—the carved wood trunk at the wall, the shelf with a shaving blade, brush, and basin of water, the high-backed chair set before a stone hearth, a table, and the wide, low bed covered with thick fleece blankets.

Then her other senses returned and she caught a familiar, stirring essence that moved through her blood with slow heat, and she knew that this was Tristan's chamber.

When they had returned to Monmouth, she had been given a chamber in the private quarters near her parents. His chamber was very near the top landing at the opposite end of the hallway that led to those private chambers.

Grendel had explained that he'd been given that chamber because it was strategic to defending the master's chamber and family. But her mother had later explained, with a secretive smile, that it had not so much to do with defending the keep as allowing Tristan easy access to his chamber when returning to his bed late at night after having consumed too much ale or wine in his wilder days, when he was first training as a knight.

Meg had then told her a particularly hilarious story of one misadventure when as a young lad of but six and ten years, his first year in training for the knighthood, he had returned to his chamber with whom he thought to be the gamekeeper's daughter with the intention of bedding her.

In his drunkenness he had seized the young maid from the cottage outside the gates and dragged *her* through the darkness to the keep. At some point in the darkness of the chamber and through the fog of drunkenness, something must have seemed amiss. He eventually lit a candle and discovered that the slender creature he was undressing was not the gamekeeper's daughter at all. It was the gamekeeper's son!

It had long been rumored that the young man preferred other

young men over women. He was both flattered and thrilled, for he had long admired Tristan.

In his drunkenness and shock, Tristan knocked over the candle and almost set all of Monmouth afire. Pandemonium broke out. In the midst of the confusion it was thought that Monmouth had been attacked.

The guards were called out. Several of his fellow knights and warriors stormed the chamber door. Light from a dozen torches revealed the gamekeeper's half-dressed son held at bay at the end of Tristan's sword.

Since the young man's preferences were widely known, it was assumed that he had chosen to reveal his affections to Tristan and had followed him back to his chamber. None of Tristan's fellow knights were aware of the true circumstances of the *mistake* that had landed the young man in Tristan's bedchamber.

He eventually revealed the truth to Connor. But only after several tankards of ale had been consumed and several years had passed.

Rianne lightly ran her fingers across the surface of the table as she imagined how surprised he must have been that night, and smiled to herself. After their last encounter in the herbal she had no doubt of his preferences in such matters. Still, she would liked to have seen his face that night.

A map was on the table. Landmarks, roads, and trails were painted on the muslin cloth that was then wrapped in a protective leather covering. She recognized the forest beyond Monmouth, along with towns, villages, and hamlets whose names she said aloud in the ancient Celt language that Merlin had been teaching her as well as Latin.

Marks had been made on the map, *X*s in series of two, three, and four at different locations with numbers that she wasn't familiar with. She traced the distance between the locations closest to Monmouth, then the distance to the next and the next.

She hesitated, her hand hovering above the map. For a moment it seemed as if the fabric was warm beneath her fingertips. She frowned, certain it was her imagination.

That was what traveling through stone walls did to you, she thought. No doubt it was because she still felt that coldness deep inside her and everything else seemed warm. But as she looked back at the table she could have sworn faint lines were visible where her fingers had traced, revealing several intersecting angles and lines.

Perhaps she had lost part of her brain on the journey through the stone. It would be very difficult to find again, she thought wickedly. Especially since she had no idea whatsoever how she had arrived here.

She had to work on this sense-of-direction thing or next time she might find herself in the midst of a very compromising situation that would be difficult to explain. After all, possessing a certain amount of skill at games and mixing healing herbal potions was one thing. Transforming and stepping through stone walls or materializing from out of thin air was an entirely different matter. According to Merlin, most mortals found such things very disconcerting, if not absolutely terrifying. For that reason, he and others like themselves rarely utilized the full extent of their abilities.

Dannelore had possessed limited abilities. As a changeling, born to a mortal, she was sentient but unable to alter her form or conjure visions. Rianne had learned there were many changelings in the mortal world. But there were a chosen few with powers such as Merlin's.

Once her mother had possessed such powers. But she had forfeited them so that she could live as a mortal, with mortal flesh and blood, in the mortal world. The injury that had robbed her of sight long ago remained. Not even her skill as a healer or Merlin's great power could give that back to her. If she chose to live as a mortal then she must live as one, with injury and sickness.

But she still possessed the ability to sense another's thoughts and to summon visions from the crystal runes she always carried. It was a terrifying vision of blood and death that had convinced Meg to send Rianne to a place of safety all those years ago. And as for the passage of time, though the years showed in the lines etched at her father's features and the silver that streaked his hair, Meg seemed barely older than herself.

It was most disconcerting for one's mother to be so young and still so beautiful. Except for the circles of sleeplessness and worry that rimmed her eyes, and the occasional redness that Rianne noticed, as if her mother had been crying. But she never let anyone see her tears.

What must it be like to love someone that way? Rianne often wondered as she watched her parents together. To know someone so completely that each thought was understood with a simple touch, a glance, a secret smile that only they shared, as if even now, when her father was so ill, they lived only in a world unto themselves where no one else could enter.

She suddenly pulled her hand back as she realized where she had wandered as her thoughts had also wandered. Tristan's brush and shaving blade lay on the shelf before her. Everything in the room—the room itself—was filled with his essence. That dark, mysterious, illusive taste that she sensed all over again at her lips and felt at her fingertips, so that she instinctively knotted her hand into a tight fist. As if she'd touched him, and as if that small act of defiance would make it all go away.

"Keflech!" she swore under her breath. " 'Twould be better for me if the man did prefer other men." But she thought that highly unlikely, given the rumors that traveled throughout Monmouth like wildfire. And this particular flame had a name: Alyce. Lady Standford, to be precise.

Tristan's affair with Lady Standford was common knowledge among highborn and low. She had summered the year before at Monmouth, preferring the rich, verdant valley and forest with its cool lakes and rivers to Lord Standford's distant keep at Bristol. Far too distant from the royal court at Camelot.

At Monmouth she was near Tristan and within only a day's ride of the royal court, which she preferred far and away to lonely, rough, remote Bristol. But it was the vast riches of Bristol, a crude shipping port, that provided the wealth she had become accustomed to.

Lord Standford, whom Rianne had already had the questionable pleasure of meeting, was a great deal older than his wife. It was thought he had not long to live, although everyone had been thinking that for quite some time. But when he passed on, it was rumored that Lady Standford had already selected her second husband. A man much closer to her age who also possessed substantial wealth—Tristan.

That thought roused feelings Rianne had never experienced before, somewhat akin to nausea, with a little loathing and anger thrown in for good measure. Very disconcerting indeed.

She was about to return the brush to the shelf but hesitated. The bristles were coarse and thick, and like the chamber itself smelled of his essence, that vague, illusive presence that surrounded her, that dark, mysterious, masculine scent that filled her senses, warmed her blood, and recalled that day in the herbal when he'd kissed her.

She shoved the brush back onto the shelf and was about to leave when she sensed something else in the shadows of the stone niche. Something that smelled faintly of faded summer days and wooded glens where mysterious things grew in shaded places.

Her fingers brushed against soft linen. When she retrieved it, she discovered that it was a small pouch tied with a length of yarn. It rustled faintly as she turned it over with her fingers, that faded essence of flowers permeating the air, and she realized that it contained dried flowers and herbs.

She smiled at the memory, recalling how they'd both been covered with dried leaves and flowers after her mishap with the jars and pots of herbal remedies. Or perhaps it was the feverfew that had such a soothing effect on her, for its essence was strong, mingled with dried rose petals, lilacs, and pungent starflowers.

She had been picking them out of her hair for days afterward. No doubt he had found several in his clothes as well and had kept them bound in the square of linen for some reason that eluded her.

She heard voices, not in the mortal way, but sensed them in that way that had become instinctive in such a short period of time.

She realized now that those strange instances that had been so disconcerting and upsetting to her as a child were nothing more than the natural abilities she had been born with but had little knowledge of. She had discovered limited abilities, such as her ability to control the outcome of a game of cups and stones, an awareness of things before they happened, and a keen insight into the ways of others that she now realized was the ability to know another's thoughts.

At first the voices came to her through the thickness of rock and timber at the stout walls, too thick for anyone with mortal ability to hear it. But now she heard those voices, loud and clear, just outside the chamber door. And one of them was Tristan's.

She could not allow him to find her there. What would he think? How would she explain being in his chamber?

There was no place to hide, no shadows that would conceal her. Panic was almost her undoing as the latch lifted at the door. As it was pushed open she whirled around and left the only way possible without being seen—the same way she had entered.

Tristan stopped just inside the chamber, his hand still at the latch on the door.

"Is something amiss?" Sir Roderick asked. He had been with Connor since the days before Arthur's return. He knew the countryside well for they had spent several years hiding out in the surrounding hillsides and forest, living off the land, hunted men with prices on their heads.

" 'Tis nothing," Tristan replied, frowning as he glanced about the chamber, not at all certain what it was he had seen. A shimmer of soft gold? A flash of light? Or a trick of the eyes?

Nothing was missing or out of place. A quick glance assured him that no one was in the chamber. Yet he was certain he had seen something.

It was brief, a fleeting glimpse of something at the edge of his sight. There one moment, gone the next. Or perhaps not there at all. Perhaps he had only imagined it.

"This is the map I spoke of," he explained, unrolling the linen so that it lay flat across the table. "I would like your thoughts on it."

As he pointed out different locations, he paused once more. The scent of dried flowers and pungent herbs seemed stronger than before. Or did he only imagine *that* as well?

Again, Sir Roderick asked, "Is anything amiss?"

And again, all he could answer was, "Nay, 'tis nothing."

Merlin realized with a mixture of frustration and pride that she was gone. Again. With such speed and mastery that even he was stunned.

He had merely paused between words, explaining the manner and means of the powers of transformation, and suddenly he had the distinct feeling that he was talking to himself. Again.

Quicker than the thought formed, he knew that she had escaped. And like an instructor seeking out a recalcitrant student, albeit a brilliant one, he went after her. Again.

That was the frustration of it, he realized as he slipped through walls, casting about for her essence in an effort to determine which way she had gone. She was impetuous and reckless.

That accounted for her skill at the games. But there were things in this life that she would encounter that were no game. And recklessness came with a price.

He knew well enough that wisdom came with age and experience. And not without a price. But those who possessed the power of the Light also possessed the ability to learn from and transcend such things. Such was the blessing and the curse of their immortality.

But this amazing and fascinating creature who was part of him in the unique and unusual essence they shared, just as mortals shared hereditary bloodlines, was not wholly a creature of the Light.

She was part mortal, with all the frailties and strengths that imparted, a combination of her mother and father, for Connor's blood flowed through her veins as well. As much as he sensed Meg's ways within her, he also sensed that part of her that she'd inherited from her father.

Connor's courage, his sense of honor and steadfastness to duty even in the face of overwhelming odds—those things that were as much a part of him as breathing—were within her. She also possessed her mother's wit, charm, sense of mischief, and daring, which had long ago fueled the curiosity that had sent her from the immortal world into the mortal world adventuring. And so far, the combination of all proved to be most exasperating.

He had sensed something else in her, something that was surprising and troubling at the same time. There was an essence of something glimpsed in the vision of blood she repeatedly experienced, like an echo from the distant past. His own past and beyond.

There were stories told among the immortals, legends and myths handed down much the same as those handed down from one generation to the next among mortal creatures. Their pasts were inextricably linked, but the origins of that bond were shrouded in mystery, secrets guarded by the Ancient Ones. His own past was obscure.

A well-placed rumor had it that he had been born to a Celtic woman who was given to visions and strange ways. But within his collective memory, which spanned more than three hundred years, there was no lingering essence of her as there was of everything he had experienced in this existence.

There were only fleeting images in all that time, glimpsed occasionally in a subconscious moment when he thought he sensed something that was not consciously known to him. Something akin to memory as mortals knew it. And like memory it never came to him as a whole, but in bits and pieces. And Rianne was part of that illusive memory.

It was there in something seen in a look, a flash of awareness that passed between them with almost frightening clarity, then slipped away. But he was certain with all the powers he possessed that he had known her before . . . before that brief time when she was born a mortal, flesh-and-blood child, before Arthur was made king, long before his own existence. And that certainty was bathed in images of blood.

He turned sharply and emerged from the stone in the hallway outside the private chambers. He sensed Tristan and one of his men very near, their conversation coming to him as if several feet of stone wall did not separate them. Their discussion was of the attacks the past several months. But within those same chamber walls he sensed . . . something.

She had recently passed this way, of that he was certain. Her essence lingered within the stone walls in an erratic, chaotic pattern that suggested no logical thought at all, but clear emotion. And that was the frustration and danger of it all. She allowed her emotions to guide her powers.

Keflech! Would the girl never learn to control her emotions?

Now she had him doing it. Giving in to his own frustration. By the Ancient Ones, he could have throttled her. Or in the very least taught her a lesson on the folly of such recklessness by perhaps casting a spell on her. If he could find her.

His frustration deepened at the nagging awareness that his time here was almost done. In the weeks since Rianne had returned he had taught her most of what she must know. Her ability to learn increased with everything she learned with almost frightening proportions.

Arthur wished his presence at Camelot. There were matters he wished his counsel on, not the least of which was his decision to take a queen. And therein lay Merlin's greatest emotional pain.

He sensed that he must leave Camelot soon. He could not bear to stay and watch the woman he loved with a frightening mortal passion wed to the man he loved as a brother.

It had been unwise to allow it to happen. He had sensed it and could have stopped it almost before it began. But he had grown weary of living his cold, emotionless, solitary existence, never experiencing the joys that others experienced at that deepest of human emotions.

Against all logic, all wisdom, everything that he was, he had fallen deeply and passionately in love. Because of that love, he was blinded to the destiny that awaited her with another man. When he finally learned of it, in that most common and disgusting of mortal ways—common gossip and rumor—he realized there was only one thing he could do: He must leave her. And so he had all those months ago, when he had returned to Camelot and to his duty to Arthur.

He had sent her but one missive in all that time—*I will always love you. But our paths lie in different directions and though my heart will follow your path, I must take another.*

Duty. He was singularly bound to that very mortal, for he would not betray Arthur. And so he left her. But in the months since he had left Lyonesse, he had discovered that neither could he remain at Camelot.

Perhaps his time was finished here now that Arthur was king

over all of England. The future no longer unfolded itself to him as it had once so clearly. Perhaps this was as it was meant to be.

But there was still one small matter, in the form of a very lovely young woman who possessed extraordinary powers; that was still unfinished.

By the Ancient Ones! Where was she?

It was unwise in the least, sheer folly in the extreme, and absolutely irresistible temptation. She couldn't help herself, or didn't care too. With an impish smile curving her lips, Rianne came up behind Merlin and tapped him on the shoulder.

"Were you looking for me?"

He whirled around, and she immediately sensed this went far beyond foolishness or folly. He was angry. He was more than angry; he was furious.

She had never seen him so upset. Not even when she'd replaced the water in the scrying bowl with an oozing, slimy concoction she'd mixed from ingredients pilfered from the kitchen—a harmless mixture of fruit pulp and honey that in the dimly lit chamber more closely resembled something vile and disgusting usually left behind by trolls.

He had been upset with her and lectured at great length that she must be more serious about the education of her abilities. He had been somewhat mollified later when she had exhibited unusual skill at summoning a vision from the crystal bowl.

But this was different. She sensed she had perhaps gone too far. He was beyond anger, beyond any other emotion she had ever experienced, and she sensed no amount of skill, promises, or charm would appease him now.

Her eyes widened as she sensed the spellcast he summoned. So, that was to be her punishment. With equal skill, she met challenge for challenge, warding off his spellcasts with ones of her own.

A shroud of isolation was shattered into a thousand tiny flashes of light that faded into nothingness. The silken restraints with which he attempted to bind her were flicked away like a bothersome fly. His attempt to transform her into a docile, complacent sheep was easily deflected. His reaction was a roar of frustration that echoed along the walls of the hallway.

She had perhaps acted unwisely in stubbornly defying each one. But the choices of isolation, being trussed like guinea fowl or transformed into a sheep, were not particularly appealing. She sensed, however, that her cautious countermoves had only infuriated him all the more. And that could be very dangerous.

There was only one thing left to do, Merlin decided. And that was to teach her a lesson she would not forget. She must learn discipline and self-control. He focused his thoughts and concentrated his powers and was about to . . .

"What is amiss, dear brother?" Meg asked as she stepped from the shadows and between her embattled brother and daughter.

His concentration broken, all he could do was swear again in frustration. "This child, your daughter, must be taught a lesson."

"Usually I would agree with you, brother. But it seems your intentions are mixed with anger. Something you have always counseled me against. What is it that has angered you so?"

"What is it?" he asked on a faintly strangled sound, and then repeated, "What is it? 'Tis her lack of responsibility, her flightiness. She will not take anything seriously. 'Tis all a game to her."

"What is a game?" Meg asked with a maddening innocence that had him grinding his teeth.

"She fled her lessons again. She uses her powers not with discretion and prudence but with recklessness and at her latest whim. She refuses to accept the importance of her abilities."

"You are wrong, brother," Meg informed him, with such matter-of-factness that his tirade ceased in midsentence. "She has not fled at all. She was merely using what she had learned.

How can she learn the way of something if you do not allow her to test her abilities?''

Then she turned everything around on him very skillfully. "You should be ashamed, brother, for trying to teach her so much in so little time. It would be overwhelming for anyone, mortal or immortal. There are things that come only with time. You more than anyone know that. And I seem to recall stories the Learned Ones told about a certain young creature who gave them particular difficulty at his lessons.''

Merlin silently glared at her. He couldn't deny it; they were creatures of truth. And while truth was often as effective a weapon against many things, it was also a sword one often found pointed at oneself.

"At any rate,'' Meg continued, "Rianne was with me the entire time. So you see, she was not neglectful of her responsibilities at all.''

They both stared at her. Merlin sensed it was not quite the truth. Rianne knew it was about as far from the truth as one could get.

Merlin's gaze narrowed. Was it possible his sister had lied to him? No, it was not. She was bound by the truth as much as he was. But still he had the nagging suspicion that he'd just been duped.

"Very well,'' he accepted her story. "Then we will continue her lessons at once.''

" 'Tis enough for one day,'' Meg informed him, thrusting a hand behind her in silent warning to Rianne when she would have voiced her own objections to more lessons.

"Rianne is expected in the village today and preparations must be made. We were just on our way to the herbal to prepare the medicants she must take with her.''

Then she seized her daughter by the wrist and propelled her ahead of her toward the stone steps at the end of the hall, strategically positioning herself between her brother and Rianne so that she could easily thwart any last-minute punishment he sought to inflict.

He did not, and she could only smile at his perplexed state of mind.

"Be at ease, brother," she consoled him through the connection of their thoughts as she and Rianne reached the steps. *"She is young. In time she will be all that you hope for. I know it in my heart."*

"Bah!" Merlin replied. *"She is too much like her mother!"*

"And her uncle, I think."

"You lied," Rianne accused her mother with a sideways glance as they worked side by side in the herbal.

"I did not," Meg insisted, savoring the congenial mood between them. With each passing day, she sensed the estrangement easing between them. With her guard down, she was discovering more and more what a delightful creature her daughter had become in spite of the difficulties she had experienced.

Meg smiled with that hint of mischief they seemed to share. "I merely expanded on the truth just a wee bit."

"A wee bit? It was about as far from the truth as you could get. You know very well that I was not with you."

"In a sense you were," Meg replied, and at Rianne's look of confusion, she explained, "You are always with me, daughter. As you have been from the day I first felt you moving inside me. 'Tis not a bond that can be broken either by time or distance." Then the mischief returned.

"And I just happened to sense that you might have need of me. I feared the outcome if the two of you came to blows. So, you see, I was indeed *with* you."

"I will remember that," Rianne replied with a smile at the secret they now shared. "I find telling the truth at times brings terrible consequences."

"And also great joy, most particularly when you can open your feelings to someone and share them with that same truthfulness and honesty. The reward is greater than any treasure."

"Not, I think, where Merlin is concerned," Rianne speculated. "That could be dangerous."

"I was not thinking of Merlin," her mother replied, and her smile softened with the look that Rianne knew was for her father alone.

She did not feel excluded or neglected, for both her mother and father had gone out of their way to show her their love even when she had convinced herself she neither wanted nor needed it. It was something far different, a longing to experience that same connection to someone, that completion that her parents felt with one another, as if one was not quite whole without the other.

"You will find that one day," Meg assured her as she sensed her daughter's thoughts. "I have seen the way Tristan looks at you."

"I am not so certain," Rianne replied more than a little wistfully. "He thinks me too stubborn and pigheaded. He thinks only of his duty."

Meg smiled with understanding. "Of course, my dear. After all, he is a man."

A most perplexing man, Rianne thought. More than once through the long afternoon, as she worked in the village with one of the women from the keep who had often assisted her mother.

At the last cottage they visited, a young girl labored with her first child. The labor had been long and difficult. Her husband, apprentice to the carpenter at Monmouth, nervously paced back and forth.

"Are you certain Mistress Meg could not come?" he anxiously asked.

Rianne sensed his fear and anxiety. Though she knew little of such things, still she sensed that the labor was a normal one, and with the midwife from Monmouth she had no doubt that they would see the matter done.

"She is with Lord Connor," Rianne explained, easing his fears with silent thoughts. "Your wife is strong. All will be fine. You will see."

But as the afternoon progressed and the child still had not been born, Rianne began to have grave concerns. The girl was growing weaker and a fever had set in.

She slowly poured a tisane that would ease the fever between the girl's dry lips. The midwife, Minna, who had accompanied her drew her aside.

" 'Tis her first child and therein lies the difficulty. Her body is small and the child is large. It cannot be born without tearing her apart. But if it is not born soon, it will die inside her."

"What must be done?" Rianne demanded.

"If only there was an herbal concoction that could ease the child from her. Mistress Meg would know what to do."

"Nay," Rianne replied. "There is no time. I will do it. Bring me more clean linen and send her husband on an errand."

"What errand?"

"More firewood."

"We have plenty of firewood."

"Do it!" Rianne exclaimed and sent the poor woman scurrying to tell the girl's husband that they needed more wood.

"He thinks we are both mad," Minna informed her as she returned.

"He will forget it soon enough when he holds his child," Rianne replied as she eased the gown up over the girl's hips and gently laid her hands over her distended belly.

She felt the child within. Its movements had ceased, but she sensed the feathery heartbeat that gradually slowed with each passing moment. She also sensed the difficulty. What little she understood about childbirth, she knew that the child must be born head first. The child was turned in the wrong direction.

With great care and gentleness she focused her power, surrounding the child with warmth and light, slowly turning it within its mother's womb.

"Soon, little one," she crooned through the connection of thought that the babe had no understanding of but sensed through that warmth and energy that surrounded it like a protective cocoon.

"Your mother and father await. The world awaits. And it is quite a wondrous place that you must explore and see for yourself. Come little one. See what is waiting for you."

Slowly and with great care, she guided the child, like taking a small hand in her own and leading the way. She held that vision in her thoughts as she eased the pain from the girl's body and the tension from her straining muscles, and then eased her child into the world.

The cool air in contrast to the warmth of moments before startled the child from its lethargy. He emerged kicking and crying, his face immediately turning bright red in an expression that made Rianne reconsider what she'd just done. On a fleeting thought she contemplated putting him back. But then saw the expression on the girl's face as she reached for her newborn child. It was an expression Rianne had never seen before, reflected in the face of her husband as he suddenly burst into the cottage, an armful of wood scattering across the floor as he realized that his child had been born.

The look on their faces was a combination of joy, wonder, and incredible love. And in that moment, Rianne sensed another such moment not far from this humble cottage, separated by the span of time, when another young woman had cradled her newborn child still covered with her blood. And the fierce warrior who had sired the child knelt at her side in awed silence, humbled as no enemy had ever accomplished.

With the certainty that this child was loved, she realized that she too had been loved. And for the first time accepted that it was that same love that had sent her from Monmouth.

"Why didn't you tell me?" she cried out in her thoughts.

"I did try to tell you," the answer whispered softly through the connection and she knew that Meg had heard her.

"But you did not want to hear it, daughter. Now you understand the bond of love between a mother and a child, love that is willing to sacrifice all, even life itself."

They stayed until they were certain the girl rested comfortably and there was no bleeding. Mother and father could not pry their eyes from their newborn son, who now slept blissfully unaware of the great commotion he had caused. But as Rianne prepared to leave, the young carpenter stopped her.

"I don't have coins to pay you, but I have this." He laid a carved wooden box in her arms. "I made it, and I would like for you to have it."

It was finely made with figures of a man and a woman etched into the surface with such lifelike exactness that it seemed they might step from the wood and come to life at any moment. Even the shadings of the wood caught the exact shadings of expression and emotion. She was inclined to think that the young man's talents were wasted as a carpenter when he possessed such artistic skills. But he had a family to feed and there was not much need of such fine artistic things in the village.

" 'Tis most beautiful," she said. "Thank you."

He nodded sheepishly, then returned to his sleeping child and wife, who had also nodded off.

As Rianne stepped out of the cottage, the sun sunk low over the western wall. She lifted the lid of the box, thinking that it would make a fine thing for storing her herbs, and discovered the true gift.

Inside were small carved wood figures. She immediately recognized her mother and father, his knights and warriors, Merlin and several others including the king, in a duplicate of the game board she and her father played at.

A smile curved her mouth as she thought how pleased Connor would be when he saw it. Perhaps they could play the game when she returned if he was feeling up to it. She tucked the box under her arm, eager to show him the fine gift.

It had grown quite cold by the time she and Minna returned to the main hall. The smell of sweet grass blended with the aroma of cooking food, and an inviting warmth wrapped around her as never before. This place that she had once refused to return to felt like home to her. But she knew it was those who lived within the walls that had made her feel as if she had truly returned home, with their love and patience.

The door to the small anteroom was ajar. Light from the fire that constantly burned at the hearth reflected softly off the rough-grained wood.

At this time of day, she knew her mother would be with the seneschal, going over the myriad details of the responsibilities she had assumed when Rianne's father became ill. The servants were in the kitchens, Merlin was nowhere about, and Tristan had undoubtedly not yet returned from the practice yard.

All was quiet and peaceful as she parted with Minna and made her way to the anteroom, where she knew she would find her father, reading over some missive he'd received, or perhaps dozing before the fire, waiting for her return, as had become their habit.

He was there in the high-backed chair, turned toward the warmth of the fire. His head angled slightly forward, no doubt in concentration of some weighty matter of importance concerning Monmouth and Camelot.

She crossed the chamber and rounded the side of the chair, eager to show him the beautiful gift. "Look what young Jarrod gave me in gratitude at the birth of his son," she exclaimed.

" 'Tis most beautiful. I thought we might play a game. . . . Her voice went still as she looked down at her father.

His chin rested on his chest and his eyes were closed. Pain, that familiar companion of the wasting sickness that had plagued him for months, no longer etched his face. His features were relaxed in gentle repose; his hand rested upon his thigh, as if he had but waited for her so that they could play another game.

"Father?" the word trembled at her lips, even as she sensed there would be no reply.

She knelt on the soft fleece carpet at his feet, then rested her cheek against that large, gentle hand that had welcomed her with unconditional love. Pain, regret, and unbearable sadness closed around her heart.

It was done, thought the creature, as it stepped from the shadows of forest that lay just beyond Monmouth. Torches blazed across the battlements and at every window opening as word spread.

He had found her and the next step had been taken, the creature thought, as the light of the setting sun glinted on the crystal rune that dangled from clawlike hands. Only that final step remained, and then he would destroy the one called the Chosen. And she would help him do it.

CHAPTER EIGHTEEN

Finally, her mother slept.

Rianne watched from the window opening in the chamber her mother had once shared with her father. Candles glowed softly. A fire burned at the brazier. Rianne felt his presence everywhere. In the chair where he often sat. In the wood trunk that held his things. In the battle sword propped against the wall beside the bed, as if it but waited for his hand. Yet she knew so little about him. And now that was gone forever.

He had been buried that morn in the stone crypt beneath the floor of the chapel at Monmouth, where other generations of his family had been buried. But not his father, brother, mother, or sister, for they had been brutally slain, their ashes scattered to the winds with no one to mourn them when he was only a child.

That much Tristan had told her, things she had not known but which made her feel somehow closer to him.

Meg had borne her grief with unusual calm. There was a peacefulness about her that at first had worried Rianne, for it seemed unnatural. But Merlin had explained that part of her torment came from knowing that her father suffered from the wasting sickness that slowly killed him. Now he suffered no more. Mortals believed that once the body was gone, the soul was at peace. Now her mother was at peace, even though the lonely days stretched ahead.

Meg had calmly watched as Connor was buried, the large stone rolled into place with its simple carving of his name. Then she had laid a hand upon the stone, as though reaching out to him, and had said words that no one, not even Rianne or Merlin sensed, so private had she kept them. Afterward, Rianne had given her an herbal draught that helped her sleep.

"You must rest," Rianne had told her, fearing that she might lose her as well, for she had heard of such things. She could not bear the thought that she would lose both her mother and her father after finding them again so recently.

"But I want to remember," Meg protested softly. "I want to remember each moment, each word, every thought." And with eyes that had glistened with tears said with heartbreaking sadness, "It will have to last an eternity. And I could not bear it if I did not have those memories."

Then she had at last given into the herbal tisane, nodding off, her mouth curving into a smile, as if she found something in those dreams that she had lost in this life.

"You must get your rest, child," Merlin said as he joined her at the window. "I will watch over her. We are kindred spirits and I will see that her sleep is peaceful."

"Will she be all right?"

"Aye," he assured her, laying his hand over hers. "Because she has something to live for. You have given her that and he is part of you."

Tristan had not returned to the main hall after Connor was buried, but had sought out the stables and perhaps the camaraderie of his men, as he had so often during the past weeks.

She did not seek her own bed but went down the stone steps

to the main hall below. The keep was unusually quiet, except for the sound of soft weeping. There had been too much weeping the past few days; she thought she would go mad if she had to listen to it any longer.

She went into the anteroom, where she had shared so many hours with her father. Too few hours stacked against all the hours, days, and years that had been lost. The fire had gone out at the hearth, but his chair still sat before the hearth, as if he would return at any moment.

The box with the carved game pieces sat on the floor beside it. She carried it to the table and set out the pieces one by one, as if preparing for their next game. Then she made the first move.

"What move will you make, Father?" she asked, as if he sat across from her contemplating that move. And then, "Ah, yes, I see." And she moved the piece for him, setting up a familiar challenge.

"You may just win this one."

She made several more moves, and then her hand went still on the board. She felt somehow closer to him with those pieces spread before her in just the same way as when they contemplated each other's move for hours.

"We'll continue later," she said as she rose from her chair and headed for the door, and then paused with a smile. "And do not attempt to cheat. I will know if you move any of the pieces."

Torches had been lit in the main hall as the afternoon light faded. Her mother would sleep the night through with the draught she had given her. Tomorrow and whatever it brought would wait. But she could not stand the silence of the hall, which reminded her all too vividly of her father's absence.

She left the main hall, mindless of the sharp bite of the wind that had come up and the clouds that darkened the fading sky as she ran down the stone steps, uncertain where she was headed or if it even mattered.

Tristan was waiting for her there astride the black stallion. Without a word he reached down. Without a word she took his hand. He settled her in the saddle before him as he had all those countless times before and swung the stallion toward the main gates.

The guards' shouted protests were whipped away on the wind as he sent the stallion at a full run away from Monmouth.

They rode down the lowland valley, past the village, past the fields and cottages of those she had visited often over the past weeks. Now those places had names. The faces had names that connected her to them in ways her life had never been connected before.

As the sun sank lower, they crossed the river, then rode through the rolling hills. Through all the places her father had ridden as a boy, then as a young man. The places he had loved and called home, fought for and been willing to die for. In seeing them again, she felt closer to him.

They rode on, each lost in their own thoughts, oblivious to the darkness that fell around them, oblivious even to the rain that fell in icy spears and soaked their clothes.

She curled against Tristan, holding on to his strength and warmth, feeling the fierce beat of his heart beneath her cheek, hearing its echoing cry in the beat of her own heart, filled with the pain of loss that had become too familiar to her over the years. But this was a double loss, having lost her father before, all those years ago, and again now.

As the rain pelted down on them she was vaguely aware of those same cottages and the village, then the gates of Monmouth closing around them as they returned, driven back by the storm, still driven by an emotional storm.

A boy from the stables appeared as Tristan lifted her from the saddle. Her clothes were sodden and heavy and she was certain she would have fallen if he'd set her on the ground. Instead, he carried her into the main hall.

All was quiet inside the keep. No one was aware they had

left, therefore no one awaited their return. Nor did he set her down when they reached the stairs but instead carried her, taking them two at a time. For quite possibly the first time since they met she made no protest.

He carried her down the hallway and nudged open the door of her chamber with the toe of his boot. One of the servants, Minna perhaps, had lit the fire at the brazier and several candles. Soft golden light played across the walls of the chamber.

Tristan carried her across the chamber to the hearth, then released her. Her legs, encased in the wet gown, molded his.

Pain, far different from the pain of their shared grief, knifed through him. Need, stronger than the need to assuage that grief, coiled inside him. Yet he clung to that sense of duty and honor that had shaped and defined his life and the life of the man he loved as a father.

When he would have stepped away from her, clear in that sense of duty and honor, she stopped him with a hand at his arm. She couldn't bear that he would leave her now.

"Stay with me."

His features were rigid, control etched in every hardened muscle and the set of his jaw. But the look in his eyes when he turned was filled with myriad emotions—anger, need, and pain. She understood all of them. They mirrored her own; anger at the loss they shared, need discovered in a kiss that was once intended to punish and exposed far more, and the pain of that need that connected them with that memory.

His voice was like rough velvet, tenderness and wanting sheathed in denial. "You do not know what you are saying."

She lifted his hand, turning it over in hers, then pressing her mouth against the callused palm in a tender kiss that spoke all the words he would have denied.

She looked up then, her flame-blue gaze meeting his, heat burning between them, and whispered, "I know exactly what I am saying."

He came to her then as he had refused to allow himself to

before, this time cradling her face between his hands with both certainty and regret, knowing that he had perhaps failed in his duty and that he was destined to fail from the moment he first laid eyes on her. He slowly lowered his mouth to hers.

His kiss was different from the last time he'd kissed her in the herbal. Gone was the anger. Gone was the barely controlled passion that was meant to punish but had instead aroused. His kiss now was achingly tender, complete surrender to what awaited them both and made her want to weep.

He traced her features with his fingers, gliding back through her wet hair, angling her head back so that the kiss was unbroken and went on endlessly, so that it seemed she would never draw a breath again. Or want to.

He slipped inside her with that kiss as he breathed her name, then moved deeper still with the caress of his tongue against hers, then unleashed the hunger with the heat of his hand at her breast.

The air shivered out of her lungs in quivering, needy words, ancient words that rose and fell with each breath she took, then surrendered to him again. Shivering words, longing words, words that had waited too long to be spoken, that now began with one and ended with the other in that long endless kiss.

Her gaze remained fastened on his as that kiss ended, and she slowly reached to untie the laces at the bodice of her gown. While he watched, she tugged them loose, the gown slipping from her shoulders to pool at her feet.

He dragged air into his starving lungs, certain even that would not be enough as she reached for him. He stood motionless as she slowly unlaced the front of his tunic, then pushed it back from his shoulders.

Her mouth followed, tasting him as she'd once tasted him, sinking her teeth in tender, hot, rousing bites that had the air trapped in his lungs and a curse spilling from his lips. He swept her into his arms and carried her to the bed. Going down on bent knee, he laid her across the thick pallet.

She was like golden sunlight amid a cloud of white fleece, her hair fanning the pallet, molten everywhere the light from the candles touched her. As if each found its light in her.

His gaze never left hers as he finished what she had begun. Untying the laces at his breeches, giving her these last moments to change her mind. She did not. Instead, she reached for him when he finally stood naked before her, her fingers lacing with his, pulling him down to her, those magnificent eyes assuring him there was no going back.

She kissed him as his legs moved between hers. Gone was the anger. Gone was the barely controlled passion that was meant to punish but instead aroused. Her kiss was achingly tender, complete surrender to what awaited them.

She traced his features with her fingers, gliding back through his wet hair, angling his head so that the kiss was unbroken and went on endlessly, so that it seemed he would never breathe again. Or want to.

Then she slipped inside him with her kiss as she breathed his name, moved deeper still with the caress of her slender tongue against his, then unleashed the hunger when she clasped his hand to her breast.

The air shivered out of his lungs in quivering, needy words that rose and fell with each breath he took as he surrendered to her; shivering words, longing words. Words that had waited too long to be spoken, and now began in one and ended with the other in that long, endless kiss.

Her fingers laced with his, her hands clasped his hands. Her slender legs wrapped around his, her hips rose to meet his hips. Then her body opened to his, and he was deep inside her.

CHAPTER NINETEEN

The fire was a living, breathing thing, the roar of the beast terrifying as it consumed everything in its path, scaling the walls, licking at the thatched roof of the cottage, devouring everything in its path.

Darkness wrapped around her. Cold cut like a knife at her back, while the flames seared through her memory. Nothing escaped the ravaging hunger of the beast. The child watched as she had watched countless times before, and felt the blood warm at her hand.

It ran through her fingers, spilled from her clenched fist, then merged to that single point, transformed into the gleaming stone at her hand as she reached out.

Then everything was gone. She was alone as she had always been alone. Except for the lone figure who stood at the edge of the darkness, features shrouded by the hood of his mantle.

She could feel those eyes watching her. Cold eyes that looked into her soul and called to her.

He was death and she knew him.

She awoke, cold, trembling, with the sound of the beast roaring in her blood.

Gradually the roar receded, until all she heard was the fierce beating of her heart.

The chamber was still and quiet. Nothing stared back at her from the shadows. There was only warmth at her back, strong and protective as Tristan's body cradled hers.

They had fallen asleep, but it was as if she could still feel him deep inside her, her body molding to his, the memory vivid of the pleasure he took in slow and tender ways, then gave back in equally slow and tender ways until she lay hot, needy, and wanting beneath him and finally could bear it no longer and demanded that he end her torment.

He had ended it in slow and tender ways, his fingers lacing with hers as his hands closed around hers and pinned them over her head into the soft fleece, his kisses teasing tiny protests from her lips even as his body teased tiny shivers from her body.

She had hated him just a little then, hated what he did to her, hated the feelings he roused so easily with the stroke of his hand or the stroke of his tongue, tasting her as she'd tasted him in slow and tender ways that drove her mad with wanting. Like crumbs fed to a starving beggar he had teased and tormented as she writhed beneath him, proudly refusing to beg, even as the words whispered through her thoughts.

Slow torture, with every thrust of his body deep inside hers. Sweet torture, with every kiss that fell across her heated skin. Savage torture, that she never wanted to end.

"Look at me," he'd demanded on a fierce sound that forced her to obey.

His handsome features were drawn in tight, hard angles. The tendons corded at his neck and arms.

Her gaze met his, dark like molten gold. The look in his eyes was intense, ravaged, filled with shadows and glimpses of the boy who had lost everything and everyone he had loved in a single moment. And she knew then that he had never loved anyone after that moment or before this one, never allowed himself to love anyone. It was too painful, too dangerous, and so he had shattered hearts as easily as he shattered the helms of the knights he met in battle.

It was as if he now battled her and the feelings she roused in him, dared her to defy him even as she gave herself so completely to him. It was not enough. He wanted more. He wanted all. Only that was enough.

"You are mine," he had whispered, a harsh, savage sound that spoke of all that pain and loss. "And I will not share what is mine." Not a promise but a solemn vow that demanded no less from her.

He had loved her fiercely then, thrusting deep inside her, ending the pain quickly, replacing it with a deep, hungering ache with each powerful stroke of his body within hers.

He marked her body and her soul as he took what no man had ever taken. He shattered her with all the things she saw and felt in the chaos of his thoughts, which lay bare and naked the need deep inside him. The need to feel himself reborn in her, to give all that he was and take all that she was in a joining that was hope, prayer, and solemn promise.

She joined him in that fierce exorcism of the past, meeting him equally, accepting all that he was at that final moment as her body clung to his, waves of pleasure spiraling through her, his seed spilling hot inside her.

Gone now were the lines that created those sharp, fascinating angles in his handsome features. In sleep there was a boyish innocence about him. Only the scar at his chin marked both the boy and the man, innocence in one, pure wickedness in the other.

Not so very innocent, she thought with a smile as she recalled the hours past and all the things they had shared. The memory of it heated her blood and made her restless.

She moved first one leg then the other, extricating herself

from the weight of his long legs, which pinned her. Then she carefully removed his arm from about her waist.

The stone floor was icy cold beneath her feet. She seized a thick fleece from the bed and wrapped it about her shoulders as she went to the brazier and put more wood on the fire.

It had gone out during the night; only cold ash remained. She opened her hand and extended it toward the pieces of pungent wood. On a single thought a ribbon of flame appeared at her fingertips. She gently blew at it, the single flame bursting into several flames that ignited the wood and quickly spread.

Soon light played across the walls and the air in the chamber lost some of its chill. She hugged the thick fleece tightly about her as she left the chamber.

Her mother still slept, but it was a restless sleep. She had kicked off the warm fleece blankets. Her pale golden hair was tangled beneath her, and her arm was thrown across the pallet she had once shared with Rianne's father, as if reaching out for him.

Rianne had once found it difficult to believe that this beautiful young woman was her mother. When she had first seen her again after all the years apart there were no traces of age in her face. Her skin was smooth and unlined, her hair still that rich gold color that she and Rianne shared.

Only now, in sleep, did she see the faint lines at her eyes and mouth, as if this unbearable loss had stolen her youth as well as her heart.

Now, as if their roles had suddenly been reversed, Rianne pulled the fleece blanket over Meg's shoulders and tucked the edges in to keep her warm. She gently stroked the soft cheek, as she knew Meg had once stroked hers as a babe.

"I am here, Mother," she tenderly sent Meg her thoughts.

Merlin watched her from the shadows; slender, beautiful, the power of the Light strong within her. Much stronger than he had ever guessed. She was different now from the defiant, angry girl who had returned to them.

There was a softness about her as she stood over her mother, a tenderness in her touch that spoke of passions awakened and passions spent, and he knew.

"You have lain with him." His thoughts connected with hers through the steeped shadows with an inevitability of sadness.

She had sensed him the moment she entered the chamber, knew that he kept his silent vigil, knew as well that he would immediately know the truth. There was no need for her to answer him.

"He is mortal; you are not."

Along with the concern she sensed deep regret, not for her lost virtue but, for something more, something that lay deep within him. He sighed heavily, a sound of pain and loss.

"Loving him will only bring you pain, as it has brought her pain."

There was a poignancy of sadness that went beyond his grief at the loss of a friend. It was much deeper than that, the pain felt through the connection they shared. And she knew the secret that lay there as surely as he had known that she had given herself to Tristan.

"You loved her." There was no need to seek out her name among his thoughts. It did not matter.

His gaze glowed at her from the shadows, an expression of such unbearable pain that she felt it through the connection of their shared thoughts.

"Far too much."

"And you love her still." Not a question but a certainty that whispered through the connection they shared, the truth kept safely hidden away in his heart, now exposed at her heart.

"As I love him," she replied, surprised at how easily the thought formed, instinctive as breathing, as natural as the beat of her heart. She sensed his next thought and flung it away with a fierce strength that stunned him. She saw it in his eyes.

"I will not live without him!"

"You will have to. He will grow old and die. You will not.

'Tis the way of things for us who are not mortal. 'Tis best that you learn that now."

"As you learned it."

She knew the thought wounded, exposing the truth that lay in his heart.

"Would you rather have not loved her?"

The expression in his eyes was wounded, filled with everything he had shared with the woman he had loved, including the pain of their parting.

"For too long there was no love, no tenderness, no gentleness. I no longer knew what love was." Her thoughts whispered through his. *"I would gladly feel the pain than nothing at all."*

He did not reply. There was no need. She knew that very same answer lay in his heart, even now after all the pain. He would choose the same again. Just as she had chosen.

She did not return to her chamber but instead climbed the steps to the battlements.

The wind whipped at her hair and cleared her thoughts as she gathered the fleece about her and stepped to the battlement wall. Wood, stone, and mortar sloped away into the darkness below, while a ribbon of gray appeared at the distant horizon.

The sound of the wind changed. No longer lonely and mournful, it carried the sound of voices; ancient voices that whispered to her from the past, before her mother had entered the mortal world, before Merlin had taken his place at Arthur's side.

They whispered to her of blood and death, darkness and light, incalculable loss and feeble hope.

And in the looming darkness, with only the light of nearby torches and those lost voices whispering to her, images flashed through her thoughts from out of her dreams.

Instead of the sun, flames burned at the horizon. They destroyed everything in their path—villages, cottages, and farms—until nothing was left. Then another image flashed through her thoughts and blood ran through her fingers. It slowly receded, merging to a single point that transformed in a gleaming stone at her hand. And she knew.

The creature was out there. She could feel him, cold as death, watching, waiting for her, no longer content to haunt her dreams. What she saw was not the past, but a vision of the future.

Tristan found her there, like a beautiful apparition of the night that haunted his dreams. The wind whipped at her hair, currents of gold turned to luminous silver in the quivering light of the torches. Her skin was pale, almost translucent over high cheekbones, the pulse visible at her slender throat.

She stared out into the darkness beyond the keep, slender brows drawn together, her gaze fixed, as if she saw something out there. Something that made her tremble and gather the fleece more tightly about her.

She turned then, as if she finally sensed his presence, or perhaps his thoughts.

He had feared this moment when he first discovered her gone; feared the pain he would see in her eyes, the regret he would hear in her voice. He saw neither in the gaze looking back at him.

Her vivid blue eyes were ablaze with color. Fierce color that burned through him, searing away all doubt, all fear, any uncertainty of the last hours they'd shared. As if she touched him, he felt her burning through his blood, setting him afire with needs and longings that whispered through his thoughts as if they had not recently lain together but had been apart for days, months, years, the hunger gnawing at him even as he saw it in her eyes.

A guard appeared. He glanced from one to the other.

"Is anything amiss, milord?"

Nothing but the wild beating of her heart. Nothing but the need that tightened deep inside her. Nothing but the hunger even now when her body still ached from the sweet torture of his body.

"Leave us," Tristan ordered, his voice harsh, thick in his throat, his gaze never leaving hers.

The guard retreated to the adjacent wall and they were alone atop the eastern battlement.

The torches quivered on the wind that brought with it the sharp smell of snow, but she was not cold, not even where her shoulders were naked above the edge of the fleece. Heat poured through her; slow heat that left a fiery trail in her blood; sweet heat at her lips as she remembered the taste of him; wild heat that burned along every nerve ending.

When he held out his hand, she went to him, slipping between the folds of the heavy mantle he wore. His gaze met hers and shimmered with the explosion of heat as her naked body moved against his, then closed on an agony of sound as her mouth sought his.

She was like fire in his hands, burning everywhere he touched. Soft heat at her breasts, silken heat across the curve of her bottom, wet heat as he stroked between folds of tender, swollen flesh.

She cried out as he thrust his fingers inside her, her hips arching against his, the need pouring out of her as her flesh molded his through the barrier of his breeches.

He was thick and hard, his erect flesh pressed high against his belly, straining against the taut fabric of his breeches.

"Rianne . . ." The sound of her name was part pleasure, part desire, all agony as one kiss ended and another began.

"If you do not stop, I will take you here on the battlements!"

Her answer was the sweet heat of her mouth pressed against his throat. His hands tangled in her hair as he tried to make her listen.

Her eyes gleamed with hidden fires and wild desires. Her mouth was softly swollen as her thoughts whispered through his, needs whispered to his needs, and her fingers stroked him through the cloth barrier that separated them.

The laces fell away before the seeking heat of her fingers until his flesh filled her hands, hot, swollen, and heavily veined. A tightness grew deep inside her at the remembered feel of that flesh inside her, the burgeoning feeling as he first pressed inside, sweet pain as flesh and muscles gave way to his tender onslaught, the certainty that she could not take all of him, then the aching need to take him deeper still until he lay full, heavy, and hot within her.

It was that which now burned inside her and strained her body against his. It was that which now whispered fierce and wild to him through the connection of her thoughts with his.

"Take me. Here. Now."

The wildness in her burned through him with those softly whispered words that moved through his blood.

He watched her eyes as he lifted her and guided her slender legs about his waist. First he saw curiosity, then surprise as his hands cupped her bottom, then stunned pleasure as he snugged her wet heat against him.

She clung to him, arms wrapped about his neck, as he gently kneaded the flesh at her bottom, torturing her with slow, rocking motions as he slowly guided her body up and down the ridge of his flesh.

The look in her eyes was wild, barely controlled. Her breathing hitched in her throat as he teased with that blunt tip, then eased her past it.

Frustration and heat collided. She nipped at his shoulder. No longer tender, but hungry, demanding, needy. Still he teased, until she thought she would go mad with the wanting. Finally, she could bear it no longer, and when next he teased, rocked her hips forward, taking him inside her.

The startled sound was his, part surprise, all agony as she closed her legs around his waist and took him high inside her.

The rules of the game fled, scattered to the four winds.

Whatever lesson he had sought to teach her slipped through his fingers as her tight flesh gloved his.

He lifted her in powerful hands and then impaled her with powerful strokes. Now her body knew him, welcomed him, loved him, and wept for him. They were both slick with her tears.

He felt the tiny shivers of pleasure that built deep inside her, the powerful spasms as her body shuddered against his, then his own release as his mouth closed over hers.

For long moments afterward, he held her against him. Rianne lay spent against him, her body deliciously full and tired, his flesh still snugged deep inside her.

"Are you all right?"

Her only response was the movement of her head against his shoulder.

" 'Tis growing light," he said, brushing his lips against her hair as he held her close. "We should return to the keep."

Again a faint stirring that might have been acknowledgment or nothing at all.

"Can you walk?"

Laughter bubbled up inside her, threatening to dislodge him. She tightened her legs about him.

"Aye," he said gruffly, feeling himself grow hard once more. "I suppose that means I will have to carry you." Again that faint nod.

"What will you do when you grow too fat for me to carry?"

That brought a reaction as her head came up and she looked at him with eyes still dark with passion.

She flexed her hips against his. "Do you think me too fat?"

He groaned, part pleasure, all curse as he tried to hold on to her. It was rapidly growing lighter and he had no intention of having their encounter talked about in the armory or stables, which was most unusual for him, since he'd never particularly cared who knew about his affairs, not even lazy, indolent husbands.

"Not at the moment. Cease! Or the entire guard will see what we have been doing." He turned, and still holding her folded within his mantle, turned toward the steps that led from the battlements.

"How about now?" she asked, her mood slipping from passionate to playful as she moved against him again. He pinched her bottom.

"Nay, not at this moment. But perhaps some months hence."

"I will not allow it," she said with simple logic. She saw absolutely no reason to let herself become large and disgustingly fat.

He made a sound that seemed very much like another curse as he descended the stairs, almost lost his balance, and did lose that precarious hold on her. Then he did swear. Shifting his arm beneath her legs, he swept her up into both arms and carried her as he had the night before. *Almost* as he had carried her the night before.

Then he had been gentle and caring, both of them battered from the storm and the feelings of loss that had sent them out into that storm.

She sensed something far different in him now, an edge of anger that wanted to fling her away from him at the same time his arms tightened about her.

He carried her down the hallway, shoved open the door of her chamber, and then dropped her, none too gently, onto the pallet. She scrambled to pull the fleece about her, for some reason unnerved by his anger and the sudden loss of intimacy.

He tore the heavy mantle from his shoulder as if it was no more than a flimsy bit of linen and flung it across the chair. She couldn't resist the temptation to look as he made the necessary adjustments to his breeches.

He'd pulled on boots before going after her on the battlements but wore nothing else other than the breeches. The wound had healed nicely at his shoulder—she congratulated herself on her recently learned skills—since he'd offered none, and then appreciated the hard lines and contours of the muscles at his chest and shoulders. Muscles that she hadn't had time to notice before, or on the one previous occasion in the herbal, and that alone was enough to make her mouth water.

He stalked to the fire and threw more wood on it. It seemed to her that she'd taken well enough care of that, but she said nothing. She somehow sensed that it was better that she not say anything at the moment.

He rose from the brazier at the hearth and splashed wine into a goblet from the flask at the table. Concentration lined his brow and his eyes were that dark golden color that she'd already encountered on too many occasions.

She grew fidgety and restless, much preferring the pleasure they'd found up on the battlements. It conjured up thoughts of other places where they might make love.

"Has it occurred to you that you might not have any choice in the matter?" he demanded, throwing himself into the chair by the table.

Had he heard her thoughts? She wasn't aware that she'd opened that connection; however after what they'd just shared . . . She shrugged.

"Well, if I have only two choices in the matter, then I suppose it will have to do," she replied. "The bed is quite nice. It allows for some interesting positions. But there is something exciting about the battlements. I suppose we could alternate the two."

He choked, the wine backing up through his nose and sending him into spasms of coughing.

Rianne was immediately out of the bed, mindless of the fleece that fell to her feet, as she crossed the chamber and commenced to whack him between the shoulder blades.

As his coughing eventually subsided, she knelt before him, wiping wine from his chest and stomach.

Father in heaven! She was going to be the death of him, Tristan thought, when he was finally able to draw air into his lungs once again. With bent elbows propped on his knees, he was on a level with her. Vivid blue eyes looked back at him with concern, her mouth knotted into a frown.

She was completely oblivious of the very arousing sight she created, naked as the day she was born, pale gold hair shimmering about her shoulders, one dusky nipple peeking through the gold satin, the other hidden.

He slipped a finger beneath her chin and tilted it up so that her gaze met his. "Has it occurred to you that I might have gotten you with child last night, or just now up on the battlements?"

Her eyes widened. So, that was what he meant about her getting fat. Then widened even further at the possibility. She shrugged.

" 'Tis always a possibility." And with that matter-of-factness and practicality that was so inherent, having looked after herself for so long, "I will take care of the child as I have always taken care of myself."

He held on, his fingers gently bruising as he tried to make his point. "That is precisely what I mean, Rianne. I would not expect you to take care of the child alone. I would accept the responsibility as well."

A delicate golden brow arched. He had seen that look before and had the distinct impression they did not exactly see eye-to-eye on the matter.

Duty. The word froze around her heart. So that was what he considered her to be. Now that he'd tumbled her into his bed—her bed—he would do his duty.

"Thank you, milord, for your most generous offer, no doubt befitting a knight of the king," she replied, her voice like arctic winter.

"But there are remedies that may be taken. Surely Meg knows of them. If not, then I will consult the midwife. She is learned in such ways." She rocked back on her heels and would have escaped had he not clamped a hand around her arm.

"You would deliberately rid yourself of our child?"

"I did not say that." Anger simmered just below the surface. "I said that I would care for it if there is a child, as I have always taken care of myself. I have no need of your help. And," she added for clarification so that there was no mistaking it, "it would be my child."

"You speak as if it crawled into your belly on its own," he snapped, losing patience with her and not quite certain the reason.

"Have you so quickly forgotten who fathered it?"

"How could I possibly forget, when you insist upon reminding me of it?" On a single burst of angry thought, she freed herself and stalked to the bed, retrieving her gown along the way.

He sprang out of the chair and caught up with her, whirling her around. Angry color stained her cheeks, and her eyes were the color of brilliant gemstones. A tiny warning voice cautioned what she was capable of; anger ignored it.

"Perhaps you wish to forget it. Perhaps there is another you would prefer warmed your bed." He could not say for the life of him what made him say it. But he hated every word the moment they were spoken, and couldn't call them back.

"Perhaps . . ." she drew the word out on an angry hiss, "perhaps, I prefer someone whose sole concern is not wherein lies his duty!"

She spun away from him, fighting the hopeless folds and voluminous skirt of the gown, cursing it to shreds, and wishing she still had her breeches.

It didn't matter that he was the first to mention it. Just the thought of anyone else in her bed was enough to make him want to kill whoever that person might have been. And the enormous irony of it all was that he'd never been the jealous sort.

He took his lovers casually, with the knowledge that they did the same. Even Alyce, with whom he had lingered the longest, made no secret that he was not the first or the last. He had simply caught her between lovers and it had proven to be mutually satisfying. Until now.

The thought that he might be jealous was intriguing. But jealousy, he knew all too well from friends who had made absolute fools of themselves, didn't suddenly manifest itself of its own accord. Jealousy came from another emotion . . . love.

He neither denied nor resisted the undeniable truth that he had fallen in love with her. It seemed as natural as breathing. He simply wondered when the devil it had happened.

Perhaps only a short while ago up on the battlements, when she had looked at him with blatant desire smoldering in those magnificent eyes; perhaps it was the previous night, when she had given herself without reservation, without tears over her lost virginity, but with needs that equaled his.

Possibly it happened in that darkened passage in Bath when she'd kissed him experimentally, a game that was no game at all. Or it might have been when she held that sword on him at the inn, facing him down with unflinching courage and defiance, and only a hint of surprise that was quickly hidden when he stood before her as naked as she was now.

He watched as she wrestled with the gown, muttering dire imprecations, the length of her hair brushing the curve of her bottom, wicked thoughts teasing him.

She was angry with him. No doubt she would be angry with him again over something that would be of little consequence. Was this what Connor had felt for Meg? The certainty that he could not live without her, along with the doubt of how they would possibly live together with their differences, with her independent notions and his sense of duty? Not to mention the fact that she was Meg's daughter and possessed unusual abilities?

He would simply have to find a way around all of it; some means of circumventing the anger and defiance, a means of making certain she didn't get the notion into her head to turn him into a troll. Or worse.

He would simply have to appeal to her more passionate nature.

On a sound of frustration, Rianne tossed the gown across the room. She was about to reach for the tunic she'd worn the day before when light from the oil lamp glinted off a steel blade only inches from her face.

She slowly straightened, the blade of the broadsword moving with her, shifting away only marginally as she turned around to face him, then returning to an angle on a level with her heart.

Those magnificent eyes narrowed only slightly as her gaze met his.

"Milord?" Composure mixed with cool defiance as her eyes turned the color of winter ice.

"Move," he ordered, indicating the bed of fleece hides with the tip of the sword. Those eyes narrowed fractionally. He felt the hair raise at his neck as it was wont to do before a battle and wondered if it was an instinctive warning of danger, or the first indications of transformation into a troll.

"Nay, milord," she said haughtily, her chin hitching up defiantly. "I am not tired. 'Tis daybreak and I wish to be about."

As she made a move toward the tunic, that blade sliced through the air so near that she felt the deadly whisper it made as a lock of golden hair drifted to the floor. Her head snapped up as several well-chosen curses filled the air.

Tristan shook his head, and waggled a finger at her, as if she was an unruly child. "Be careful," he warned, "you would not like to lose more of those golden locks," as he slowly lowered the blade well below her navel in the general region of those shorter golden curls much the same as she had once threatened him.

Her skin flushed gloriously pink, then drained to white, then flushed pink again. Slender fists curled at her sides.

"Damn you, Tristan . . ."

It seemed the boot did not fit particularly well on her slender foot. He nudged the blade closer, taking great care not to damage tender flesh. He had other intentions for that silken pink pleasure.

" 'Tis the last time I will ask it . . . move!"

Surely he jested . . . ! He wouldn't . . . !

Her gaze slid down the length of that blade, all too aware of the tip that nestled among the downy curls. It was maddening, perverse, and ironic, not to mention wildly erotic and more than a little symbolic.

She knew he would never hurt her. She sensed it with every part of her. If she challenged him, she was certain he would let her go. But there was that other part of her, that defiant, headstrong, unruly part of her that wished to see just what he intended.

One last time, he ordered her, "Get into that bed."

CHAPTER TWENTY

She kicked the fleece blankets aside as she sat down in the middle of the bed, legs tucked beneath her, arms folded under her breasts.

He angled the blade under that wonderfully stubborn chin. She stubbornly notched it higher, the look in her eyes enough to incinerate a man where he stood, if that was what she intended.

It was a game, with tantalizing stakes, and if he had his way about it—and that is precisely what he intended—there would be no losers. Only winners. Unless, of course, her stubbornness got the better of her.

He flicked that magnificent fall of hair back over one shoulder with the tip of the blade. Her gaze never wavered from his, only for a moment betraying some emotion other than anger as she inhaled slowly. As if to calm her fears. Or some other emotion. He sent ribbons of silken hair back over her other shoulder with a flick of his wrist, so that those beautiful pink-tipped breasts were revealed in all their magnificence.

She swallowed tightly as she saw the direction of his gaze

and struggled with the memory of his mouth at her breast, hungry, needing, tender.

He smiled as he saw those rosy peaks tighten. Either milady had been exposed to a sudden draft or a sudden delicious memory of the night before.

Next he aimed the tip of that lethal blade below a slender wrist, tapping it lightly. She obediently unfolded her arms.

"Lie back on the bed," he ordered her, the blade once more leveled at her heart, or more precisely at one delicate, well-rounded breast, which heaved with indignation.

He saw the protest that flared into those eyes and cut the words off with a sharp command.

"Do it!"

Intrigue won out over indignation as she lay back on the bed, slender legs snugged against her bottom. She immediately felt the cold caress of the blade along her thigh and straightened her legs. She glared at him for good measure. It wouldn't do for him to think she found this too fascinating by half.

The blade leveled at her eyes. "Close them." Then traced a cold path down her belly, paused, then continued down her left thigh to her knee, nudging them apart.

She obeyed out of sheer blind willfulness and obstinance. She would not let him think she was afraid. Nor would she plead with him to stop. With eyes closed, she let her other senses expand, feeling him, smelling him, and something else that smothered the warm air in the chamber. Passion. So sweet and hot that she could taste it, and feel it along each nerve ending as with blind expectation she wondered what he would do next.

She was a fetching sight. Like some primal goddess, or perhaps a sorceress, as many would have believed. With her hair spread across the pallet in golden disarray, her arms at her sides, her breasts rose-hued from the heat in the chamber and that other heat that stained her cheeks and slender neck, those magnificent, long legs that had clenched around him in passion delicately splayed, revealing just enough of that tender flesh between to harden him unmercifully.

Like those rose-tipped breasts, the slight tilt of her nose, and the defiant angle of her chin, that softly puckered flesh was all impudence and defiance, not to mention sweet temptation.

"Further," he ordered, his voice hardly recognizable to himself as his entire body tightened with desire.

She eventually obeyed, revealing the sweet dark center of her that had so recently welcomed him and, he vowed, would welcome him again. Even now the delicate folds of flesh glistened with the needs of her body.

"Keep your eyes closed." He lowered the tip of the sword.

She sensed it, envisioned it—that lethal tip lowering over her. He wouldn't! He couldn't! Surely not . . . !

Her thoughts closed out everything. And she exploded on a wave of pure sensual pleasure as he . . . slowly stroked the tip of the falcon feather across her breast.

The air convulsed out of her lungs. Perhaps a sigh of relief, or pleasure. There was no doubt as to the next one as he slowly drew that feather around the taut nipple of her other breast.

He repeated each movement, then watched with growing desire as her belly quivered beneath the tender assault of that feather, then slowly stroked lower.

He teased and tormented, brushing the feather across her skin in slow, tender strokes. Then stopping, hovering just above her skin, while her breathing quickened and her pulse raced in anticipation of the next touch.

Slowly he brushed the feather lower, circling one hip, then the other, then gliding down one thigh to her knee and back, to trace the same trail down to the other knee.

"Tristan . . . !" Her voice was different now, less defiant, more breathless, more needy.

"Keep your eyes closed." As he stroked the feather just to the top of those magnificent golden curls, lingered, then slipped down the inside of one thigh, then back, and down the inside of her other thigh.

He watched with darkening eyes as those curls between her legs glistened with wet heat. And slowly drew the feather back up the inside of her thigh, lingered, and then with agonizing tenderness drew the feather across that dark pink flesh.

She cried out, the muscles quivering at her belly, her skin suddenly damp in other places.

"Do not move," he ordered as he began another tender assault, retracing that final path, first up one thigh, then down the other.

"There is pleasure to be found without risk."

His low voice teased and tormented. Her slender hands were buried in the thick blanket. Her breasts rose and fell in deep, shuddering breaths of anticipation as he continued that slow, sensual torture.

Her muscles clenched, then shivered, with each lingering stroke, then clenched again as she waited breathlessly for the next silken touch. With eyes closed she imagined the path he traced even as she felt it, that gliding stroke up the inside of her thigh, then down the other, and back up again.

Then that torturous pause as her body throbbed for that silken touch between her legs, and then finally, when she thought she could bear it no more, with the air trapped in her lungs and her body arched for that wonderful sensation ... the tender, shattering stroke of his tongue.

His name rushed out of her starving lungs as she sought to push him away. Then the piercing, stroking heat as he parted those tender lips and slipped inside. And her hands clutched at him as her body convulsed in wave after wave of intense pleasure, drowning her in pure sensation.

She felt as if her skin was melting off her bones as heat consumed her. The air smothered at her lungs and dampened her skin. Then slow, gliding heat as he moved up the length of her body, his fingers lacing with hers. Aching, pulsing heat as he gently stroked her with his flesh.

Her eyes slowly drifted open. They were deep, darkest blue, gleaming with hidden fires.

"Pleasure without risk?" Her lips brushed his, tasting what he had tasted, and her body quickened with the need to experience the pleasure . . . and the risk.

The look in his eyes was dangerous, a sensual promise that gleamed back at her and made her breath spasm in tiny, wanting sounds.

"I lied."

Then sweet, piercing heat as he thrust deep inside her.

There were no words, no thoughts, neither fear nor regret. Only the sweet oblivion of passion.

She dreamed again. Of darkness, fire, blood, and death. But she no longer dreamed of the cottage in the forest. Instead she dreamed of towering sandstone walls and gleaming towers that reached into a darkening sky. And when she awakened Tristan was gone.

She vaguely remembered his parting kiss, the rough-tender brush of his lips, his hand at her cheek in a lingering caress, and then the coolness of the bed that sent her deeper into the fleece blankets, seeking a warmth that eluded her. As sleep finally cleared from her thoughts, her concern was for Meg.

She quickly rose and dressed, aware of her body in new and different ways in all the tender places that reminded her of the past hours. Her hand lingered over her belly as she smoothed the blue tunic into place.

She pushed aside her concerns as she poured water into the basin. It was surprisingly warm. When she stuck her hand into the water, it suddenly turned deep crimson. Rianne stared, horrified, as blood swirled around her hand.

It slipped down her fingers, across her hand, and then gradually receded to that point on her finger where it gleamed like a brilliant crimson stone. Instinctively she attempted to pull her hand back but found she could not. It was as if some invisible force held on to her, refusing to let her go.

Eventually the water ceased its frantic swirling and the surface was once more still and smooth as a looking glass. But the image that looked back at her from the surface was not her reflection.

The image that looked back at her from the shimmering depths of the basin was that of a young woman with long auburn hair, vivid blue eyes, and beautiful, strong features.

The young woman reached out to her, that slender hand seeming to touch hers, until it appeared that they became one, bound together by that gleaming bloodstone.

Then the surface of the water quivered and the image faded, swallowed into those dark depths that swirled about her fingers. The young woman was gone, and the reflection that once more gleamed at the surface of the water was her own.

This time when she instinctively tried to pull her hand back, there was no resistance. Nor was the ring on her hand. It was gone, along with that disconcerting image.

Rianne frowned as she tried to understand what had happened. She would have believed herself to still be dreaming, except that she was awake. That left only one explanation: what she had seen was not a dream. It was a vision. But of what?

Whatever its meaning, it would have to wait, as Rianne heard urgent shouts from the yard below her window.

She pushed open the shutters. From her window opening she could see the main gates. They were closed, as had become the standing order since Monmouth was attacked. But her attention was drawn to the smaller side gate.

A rider returned through that gate. He was greeted by one of Tristan's men, and quickly dismounted. There was an urgency in his manner, his expression grim as he turned and entered the main hall, and she immediately felt uneasiness at the news he brought. She finished dressing and quickly plaited her hair into a thick braid.

Meg was not in her chamber. Somehow that did not surprise her. It was not within Meg to mourn until she made herself ill with grieving, as had been known to happen. Nor, Rianne sensed, would her father have wanted it.

In the brief time since she had returned to Monmouth she had seen the bond between her parents. It was a bond of trust, deep abiding friendship, passion, but most of all, enduring love.

Love, she had learned from them, was not only passion and desire. Love also comforted, protected, sacrificed, and in the end provided the strength to let go. From that love they had shared, Meg would find the strength to go on.

It was midmorning, a time when the main hall was usually deserted after the morning meal. But this morning her father's servants laid out trenchers of food at two of the long tables. Instead of the usual coolness in the hall a fire burned at the massive hearth and torches were lit all around.

Her father's seneschal had set aside his morning duties of recordkeeping and instead issued instructions for food that was to be prepared for a long journey.

A greater number of guards filled the main hall, and as she reached the bottom landing the newly appointed captain of the guards entered the hall and quickly strode to the anteroom.

The past several weeks, the smaller anteroom had been a place where her father could find some ease before the fire and yet still be part of the daily activities at Monmouth. It had been softly lit by candles, and they often sat across from each other at the game board, contemplating their next moves. By contrast, it had now become a hive of activity.

Several knights who had once served Connor were present. They had gathered about the game table, which was now covered with the map she had seen in Tristan's chamber.

The rider she had seen in the yard pointed out locations on

the map, while Tristan listened attentively to the message he delivered.

The captain of the guards stood opposite, while nobles from regions beyond the borders of Monmouth listened in grave silence. Only days earlier they had come to pay their respects to Meg and swear their continued loyalty to Monmouth. It had been a solemn occasion, during which her mother had named Tristan protector of Monmouth.

Rianne had not felt slighted at Meg's decision. Tristan had been like a son to them these many years. There had been a fondness between him and her father as deep as any blood kinship, and she knew that Tristan felt the loss as deeply as that of any true son.

Monmouth would always be her home. Whatever the future held, her mother's other decisions made certain of it.

Meg sat before the hearth in the chair Connor had sat in these many weeks past, listening attentively to the conversation at the table while Merlin offered his counsel to those gathered about.

Tristan did not look up, nor acknowledge Rianne's presence by either glance or gesture. Nor had she expected it. His sense of duty was too strong to allow him to be distracted from matters of importance to placate a lovesick maiden.

Still, her gaze lingered on him with growing warmth—the taut fit of his tunic across wide shoulders, the snug fit of breeches at his lean hips and muscular thighs, the concentration that drew his brows together over the long, lean nose as he focused on the matters before him. And that curve of scar at his chin that she had traced with her lips and tongue, that was merely the beginning of the places she'd tasted.

She moved to her mother's side, reaching for her hand as easily as if it was a habit of years and not just these past few weeks. Yet she was the one who was comforted as that slender, warm hand closed around hers, laying to rest any remaining fears for her mother's health.

"All is well, daughter?" Meg asked.

"Aye," Rianne assured her. "All is well." And sensed that her mother knew far more than she revealed. Perhaps even sensed what had passed between her and Tristan. Though she did not speak of it, but merely squeezed Rianne's hand with gentle strength and love.

"Three border towns were attacked in the last two days," Meg quietly informed her as they listened to the conversations at the table.

"All lie just beyond Monmouth."

Rianne recognized the names of the villages. Only weeks earlier she had visited them, caring for the sick. It had been a long journey. Tristan had accompanied her and they had stayed the night with one of the villagers.

She easily recalled the names of those whom she had met and ministered to—men, women, and children—all now dead. A cold, hollow place opened up beneath her heart. Once such things held no meaning for her. Distant places, names without faces. They did not concern her because their world was far removed from her meager existence.

How shallow that all seemed now. How very much she had changed. As plans were made and strategies decided, she gently squeezed her mother's hand and then left the anteroom.

"What are you doing?"

Tristan had been aware when she left, just as he knew when she had first entered the chamber below. He had felt it in that way that was so naturally a part of her, and made him wonder again if they were really so very different.

She was flesh and blood, of that he was certain. There could be no doubting it after the night they had shared. But there was that other part of her, that essence that was part of him from the moment he first saw her—whether it was anger or frustration or all the emotions they had shared the night before, she was part of him.

Perhaps that was that other part of her, that illusive connection of thought and emotion that bordered on obsession; had been an obsession, he realized, from the first moment. But at the moment what he experienced was suspicion as she rolled a thick fleece blanket and tied it.

"I'm preparing the things that I will need on the ride to the eastern border."

"No."

No greeting, no lover's words that teased, just that one terse word. *No.*

"You will have need of a healer. I will not delay you."

"No."

She whirled around, with the growing suspicion that he meant it. He cut off any protest or discussion.

"There is nothing to discuss. You are not going."

Decision made, decision handed down. End of conversation. Except for one small point. There had been no conversation, no discussion, only *his* decision, which she had no part in.

He saw the warning in that delicate arched brow and again cut off any protest or discussion. "There is danger, Rianne. Would you put yourself at risk so soon after your father's death? Meg has already suffered one loss. Think what it would do to her if anything happened to you."

She knew exactly what he was doing and hated him for it. There was no argument she could offer, no protest, no persuasion. He was right. And she knew it.

In high temper she muttered several dark, horrible profanities learned in her misspent youth, at the thought that he would stoop so low to prevent her going with him.

The variety and texture of her vocabulary raised his brows. "Would you send me into battle with curses for our parting words?" he asked as he slipped an arm about her waist and, in spite of her protests, pulled her against him.

She arched her back stiff as a cat and planted her hands against his chest to prevent him from pulling her any closer.

"Aye, and more," she replied, eyes glistening with blue fire. "I can think of several more that are most appropriate."

"No doubt you can, but there are other things I prefer from those soft lips."

The fire smoldered as her gaze narrowed. "Pig!"

Amusement glinted in those golden eyes while darker intentions moved through his thoughts as he stroked the pad of his thumb across her bottom lip. The rough-tender texture of that caress jolted through her, making her restless and edgy.

"Cur."

As she gradually made her way through the different species found in most yards or sties, he continued his assault on her senses, lightly stroking his mouth against hers.

He felt the slow transformation in her body, from icy coolness to searing heat. Then he tasted it at her mouth—sweet, wet, hot, and conjuring up images of other places he longed to feel that growing hunger.

For the first time his first thoughts were not of wars or battles. For the first time he wanted only to stay here with her, to lose himself in the sweet oblivion of her passion, her soft sighs, and the searing heat of her body.

A kiss that had begun with such soul-stirring heat ended all too soon with aching tenderness as her slender hands clutched at the front of his tunic, no longer trying to push him away, but trying to pull him closer.

It wasn't in her to be shy or modest, nor deceptive or even to play games. She knew only the honesty and truth of the need that burned within her.

"I will be waiting for you."

He did not reply, but instead kissed her fiercely, and then he was gone.

* * *

She did not care much for waiting. She discovered that time weighed heavily, and the hours measured by the sundial in the garden crept by with amazing slowness.

Three days became five, then eight. Merlin had gone with them. She sought to join her thoughts with his but found she could not. She had to content herself with the certainty that they were safe. She would have sensed it if they were not.

Meg showed no outward sign of concern or uneasiness, but remained busy with the tasks of running a household the size of the one at Monmouth. She met daily with the seneschal as Connor had, returning to the familiar patterns of her life before he had been wounded. She seemed to find solace in the dullness of routine that made Rianne want to pull out her hair.

Only in the herbal was she able to set aside her worries and concerns for the worries and concerns of those who were ill and injured. She spent many long hours there. Often Meg joined her, passing along bits of this and bits of that, the things she had learned through the years. This too seemed to give her solace and comfort.

After evening meal they retreated to the anteroom. The fire was built high and her mother took up her needlework, a skill that Rianne still had not accomplished with any great success. She worked painstakingly on the breeches she was determined to finish, until she became so frustrated with all those blessed tiny stitches that she threw them across the room.

"Patience is a virtue," Meg commented, deftly applying several more small stitches with amazing accuracy and neatness, especially for one who was blind.

"Then I am sorely lacking yet another one," Rianne grumbled as she threw herself back in the chair, feelings of complete and utter hopelessness washing over her.

"You are young. Patience will come."

"It may be too late," Rianne replied. "What need will I have of clothes when my bones are old and rotting?"

"You have a while to work on it," Meg reminded her, looking up as her daughter restlessly paced the chamber, stopping to move one of the pieces on the game board. There was far more than stitchery that occupied her daughter's thoughts and emotions.

"Many times I waited for your father to return," she said in a quiet voice. "The sound of the door, his boots on the steps, the sound of his voice."

"How did you bear it?"

"Far easier than I bear the silence."

Rianne looked up at the poignancy in her mother's voice as the memory of all those times connected with her thoughts now in an odd, comforting way. Lifetimes apart, so much the same.

"Does the waiting ever get any easier?" she asked, and in the softness of her voice confirmed what Meg had suspected these many weeks. There was a peacefulness within her heart, a rightness that this was what Connor would have wanted as well.

" 'Tis not the waiting that you live for, daughter. But the coming home. That moment when you hear his footsteps." And Meg smiled softly at what she had sensed but her lovely, emotional daughter had not, as the doors of the main hall suddenly opened and the sound of boot steps echoed in the main hall.

Rianne's head came up at the sound that she first thought to be nothing more than vivid imagination. Voices filled the hall. The seneschal was heard shouting orders to the servants as Connor's hounds set up a wild commotion. Meg set her stitching aside.

"I'll go find Cook. Fires must be stoked. There will be many hungry warriors to feed tonight."

But none so hungry as the warrior who stormed the anteroom moments later.

He was covered with mud and grime. It caked his boots, streaked his tunic, and splattered his helm. His eyes were hard, dark, and bleak, filled with the shadows of the things he'd seen the past days, and the anger at the enemy who still eluded him. Several days growth of beard shadowed his face, making him seem fierce, deadly, and dangerous in ways she had never seen before.

Before he was the cynical captor sent on what he considered to be a foolish errand, more recently the knight who served her father and King Arthur, and then the dangerous lover who had loved her in ways she had not imagined even with her ability. But she did not know this man.

The eyes that looked at her now were haunted and cold. They were the eyes of a man who had killed and in the killing perhaps lost part of himself. That was what she saw now, and it made her heart ache.

She went to him with tenderness and soft words. There was no patience in him for either as he pulled her to him with that same fierce strength with which she was certain he wielded a sword in battle.

His hands were strong, urgent, bruising as he buried his hand in her hair and angled her head back for his kiss. His kiss was urgent and bruising, filled with all the pain and anguish of the last days, and other things that he would never tell her.

His mouth ravaged hers, as his hands ravaged her body. It was not enough. He tore away gloves, helm, and scabbard, needing to feel her softness without the restriction of battle gear or clothes. Then his hands clutched at the skirt of her gown, bunching the fabric, pushing it up over her thighs.

"Tristan, wait," she whispered breathlessly against the heat of his mouth.

She wanted to tell him that they must take care. After his leaving, her monthly courses had come, assuring there was no child.

But there was no reaching him, no words she could say that he heard. Or wanted to hear. There was only the need that came from the things he had seen and done and now needed to be exorcised from his soul with the sweet, searing heat of her body.

She felt the wildness and the urgency, and then the need as he pressed her against the wall of the chamber, his rough hands burning at her skin as he dragged up the skirt of her gown, needy words swallowed in the heat of her kiss. Then the low, dangerous sound as he discovered she wore nothing beneath the gown. And then he was inside her, in fierce, stabbing thrusts that she welcomed with all the passion of the past nights alone when she had lain awake, her body throbbing for his. Now her body throbbed around his, her wet heat taking him deeper with each thrust, her release crying softly against his neck as he poured himself deep inside her.

His hands trembled as he held her. Sometime later, when he discovered he could breathe again, he tilted her head back and tenderly brushed a damp tendril of hair from her forehead.

"Forgive me. I didn't mean to hurt you," he whispered against her cheek.

She smiled, turning so that their cheeks brushed, and then their lips. "I will forgive you later," and to make certain he knew exactly the meaning she intended, she tightened her muscles, seeking to punish him just a little. But she was the one who was punished in the slowly building heat that began again as she felt him grow hard within her once more.

"Oh, no," he warned, gently dislodging her, setting her back to her feet while he adjusted his clothing.

"I have no strength left. I need food, a bath, and . . ."

"And then you will have more strength?" she asked with a thick, sated tone that indicated it might not last.

"Then I will have more strength," he assured her as he pulled her with him to the chair where he immediately collapsed, taking her with him. Rianne curled up against him. She sensed the weariness within him, along with the grief and frustration. It was deeply personal. It had been since that long-ago time when a young boy was the only one left alive amid the death and destruction of his family.

He stroked her hair, finding in those thick golden waves that shimmered like yellow flame a healing warmth like light in the darkness, like golden flames that burned away the pain of what he had seen, and made hope possible.

There were questions she wanted to ask but did not, for she sensed he could not speak of it.

"Do not ask," he said, his lips brushing her forehead. "Do not ever ask about what happened."

CHAPTER
TWENTY-ONE

Rianne didn't ask. She didn't have to. Merlin told her what they had found in the villages and hamlets in the eastern land; of the death and destruction; men and women slaughtered, children murdered in their beds, whole farms, villages, and towns razed so that nothing remained.

Of those they found—what was left that could be buried—he had told of the way they had died. Something experienced only once before in his life and that he had hoped never to see again.

It was then Merlin told her of the time when her mother had been blinded, and he had been seriously wounded not unlike her father, with a sickness that was a darkness of evil, surviving only because he was not mortal.

For all the reasons they found in those distant villages and hamlets, Tristan made the decision that they must go to Camelot. They would be safe there. Camelot was defensible, with it's perimeter of outposts that guarded against surprise attack, while Monmouth in that secluded valley rimmed by mountains was not as easily defended.

It was not an easy decision, but one made not only because of the recent attack but because of the one months earlier in which Connor had been so gravely wounded. He was not there to protect his home and Tristan feared for the safety of those at Monmouth, with her warriors needed far afield in service to Arthur.

Meg understood all his reasons, but still she was hesitant to leave. Monmouth was her home, and while she had often visited Camelot she had no great love for the grandeur of its numerous courtyards, pavilions, and wide porticoes that overlooked lush gardens. But Rianne sensed there was a deeper reason she was reluctant to go. It was as if in leaving Monmouth, Meg was leaving Connor.

"Before that last time we had never been parted except for a few days at most," she explained one evening in her chamber, while Rianne brushed her hair. "And we always knew we would be coming back here. I feel his presence all around me here. If I was to leave . . ." Her voice trailed off on a thought they both shared.

"What lies beyond death?" Rianne asked, and Meg's pale blue gaze met hers as though she were sighted. She smiled.

" 'Tis a weighty matter for one so young."

"You are almost as young," Rianne pointed out. "In truth, there are many who would say we seem more as sisters than mother and daughter. And 'tis rumored that Merlin is several hundred years old."

Meg laughed at the incredulous tone in her daughter's voice. "And since I am his sister, I must therefore be as old."

"I did not say that. I meant only that you are not ruled by the passage of time and death as mortals are. Perhaps there is more than what mortals envision of life. Perhaps there is something that goes on beyond death."

Meg reached over her shoulder and found Rianne's hand. "I hope with all my heart 'tis so. I will live for it every day of my life for as long as I live, that perhaps your father and I will be together again in this world, or the world beyond.

"But it shall be a very long time, I think, and being parted from him is hard to bear. I was warned it would be so."

She sighed. "But I chose not to listen. And even now, with this unbearable loss, I can say that I would choose no different, for in doing so I would never have experienced the love we shared."

"Will it be the same for me?" Rianne asked, thinking of what she shared with Tristan, impossible to even think of not having that passion in her life.

"I do not know," Meg answered truthfully, for she could give no other answer.

"In making my choice I also made a choice for you. You possess many powers and abilities of the immortals, but you are also mortal." She turned Rianne's hand over in hers.

"Both are within you. Miracle and curse, I think." Then thoughtfully, remembering back over the years, "When I carried you it was my one hope that I had not doomed you to a life of loneliness as mine has now become. One day you may have to make the same choice."

"I fear it has already been made," Rianne replied. "And I was not even aware of it."

Meg smiled softly. "Aye, that is often the way of it. Such is the risk we take, living in the mortal world, that we become very mortal in our ways and our emotions, even though we are still part of the immortal world."

"Then there is no help for it?"

"Only by making a different choice, and that I could not do."

Nor I, Rianne thought.

* * *

Arthur extended his invitation and Meg finally agreed to go to Camelot. Preparations were made. Finally the day arrived and word was sent ahead.

Her mother did not look back as they left Monmouth. "Looking back is for good-byes," she said as she rode beside Rianne in the enclosed wagon. "I am not saying good-bye."

Camelot was only a day's ride from Monmouth, but with the slower carts and wagons necessary for moving an entire household, an extra day was required for the journey that was made over open road rather than the faster mountain passes, and much to Tristan's uneasiness.

His men constantly patrolled the hills and roadside, guarding against attack. They made their camp under a clear sky with a break in the weather, and continued at first light the following day.

Rianne had never seen Camelot, but she had heard various stories in her wanderings, including the rumor that the streets were paved with gold. It was not gold that gleamed at them when they first saw Arthur's city on that distant hillside, but pale sandstone walls and gleaming towers, the same as if they'd been plucked from her dream.

Camelot was much larger than Monmouth, a small city perched on the hillside and protected with fifty-foot walls that were connected by those towers that seemed to gleam at a distance. Arthur's royal blue standards flew at all the towers. His personal flag, resplendent with gold lions on a field of blue, flew at the innermost tower, visible even at a great distance.

Tristan explained that according to court protocol, the flag denoted that the king was in residence.

"What are we supposed to do if they aren't flying the flag? Go back?" Rianne asked Meg in a whispered aside, with absolutely no notion or concern for court protocol.

Meg laughed out loud, amazed at the wonderful sensation of laughter.

"Perhaps wait until they find the right one."

"We might find ourselves in considerable trouble, especially if the person in charge of flags is color blind like Grendel."

"I heard that," Grendel protested as he rode beside the wagon. He had been most displeased to find himself astride the palfrey again and had been complaining about it for most of the ride from Monmouth.

"And I am not color blind. I simply cannot distinguish between blue and green."

Rianne and Meg's thoughts connected on one single thought and both burst out laughing.

The messengers who had ridden ahead had delivered word of their arrival. As they drew nearer to Camelot a royal escort awaited them led by Sir Longinus, who extended the king's formal welcome.

The sun gleamed off his helm, his lean aquiline features obscured by shadows, but she easily recognized him in spite of the helm and the long mantle that draped his horse. Perhaps simply because they had met before at Monmouth, or perhaps because of his encounter with Tristan on that distant battlefield.

An accident, Tristan had called it, yet she knew from what Merlin had told her that Longinus's claim to knighthood lay not in his obscure lineage, which traced his ancestors to a royal Roman family, but in his skill on the battlefield. Yet Tristan had spoken of their encounter as a mistake. She wondered, not for the first time, how often such mistakes were made.

Longinus had not returned to Monmouth after his encounter with Tristan in that remote battle, but had returned to Camelot with his men. He was one of Arthur's most trusted knights. He was also said to be favored among the ladies at court.

They rode through the main gates and were then escorted through the streets to the royal residence. There they were greeted by Arthur, who crossed the yard on horseback as their wagon came to a stop before the royal courtyard. He dismounted and with that same ease of familiarity he had displayed at

Monmouth opened the door of the wagon and assisted Meg as she stepped down.

Formal greetings were exchanged, and then Arthur escorted her mother into the main residence, their heads bent together in conversation as they no doubt spoke of the man they had both loved. Her father.

"Mistress?" Sir Longinus extended his arm to her. On impulse she was seized with the sudden notion to repay him in kind for the blow Tristan had taken in their last encounter.

"I understand your reluctance, milady, but I assure you my encounter with Sir Tristan was an accident."

Startled that he had guessed her thoughts, Rianne quickly recovered.

"He was injured while you escaped unharmed," she pointed out.

"Not entirely," he confessed. "A minor wound that could have been much worse. It was my good fortune that my encounter was not with a less skilled knight or I might have lost my head."

"It seemed to me the other way around. That it was Sir Tristan who very nearly lost his head."

He smiled, and those solemn eyes glinted with admiration. "I should have remembered that you give no quarter either in games or with words."

"Aye," she agreed. "You should have."

The smile did not waver, and she could easily see the reason he was favored by the ladies at court.

"It seems your escort has abandoned you," he observed, and again she was drawn to that dark gaze.

"Will you allow me to escort you?"

She had hoped to see Tristan when they arrived. The entire journey from Monmouth, duty had taken him elsewhere. The previous evening, when they made camp, she had seen him only briefly. He took his meal with his men and rode out with them, staying far afield long after darkness had fallen. He had not returned, and the next time she had seen him was that morning, riding ahead of the long column that guarded their wagons.

Now he was gone once more and she had no hope of seeing him before evening meal, which, if Sir Longinus was correct, would provide hardly more opportunity, as Arthur had planned an elaborate feast in their honor. Merlin was gone as well, to meet privately with the king, who was pleased to have his counselor returned. Although it seemed to her that Merlin was not quite so pleased; she wondered the cause.

She accepted Longinus's arm, which she considered an amusing gesture. It seemed far more reasonable to simply walk up the steps and across the courtyard. But, she reminded herself, they were no longer at Monmouth. They were at the royal court now.

The day before, as they rode in the wagon through the long hours of the afternoon, her mother had instructed her in appropriate protocol, such as bowing one's head when the king passed by, waiting for the king to be seated first before taking one's seat, and—most difficult of all—not speaking until spoken to.

Longinus seemed most congenial, and she wondered which lady at court currently held his favor. As they reached the main entrance of the royal hall, he bent near, as though they were friends of long-standing and shared an intimate conversation.

"Lord Standford arrived several days ago," he informed her. "He has suffered great humiliation after his loss to you at the games."

"The games were by his choice," Rianne pointed out.

"Aye," he agreed. "And a fool and his money are soon parted, but he is most eager to recover those losses."

"I would be pleased to offer him the opportunity," she replied. "As long as the king provides the stones."

He smiled. "It will keep everyone honest." Then, still as if they were old friends, "Perhaps you would enlighten me as to your strategy."

"Of course," she replied, unaware of the one who watched them as they entered the hall together.

"My strategy is to win."

He threw back his head and laughed, dark eyes gleaming. "Methinks this evening shall prove most pleasurable."

Arthur had provided for all their needs. Meg was given the chamber she had occupied on previous visits with Connor. Rianne's chamber was in the same wing, separated by a garden at the inner courtyard. Those of their household who had traveled with them were given lodging in an adjacent wing that housed the servants' quarters.

She was informed by one of the servants that Tristan was normally given lodging in the military compound occupied by Arthur's knights in residence, although, she had added with a sly grin, he rarely slept there.

Rianne was aware of the intrigues of court. Her mother had spoken of them at great length, almost as a warning. And among the intrigues she spoke of was Lady Alyce, Lord Standford's wife.

" 'Tis no secret that she shares her favors with many," Meg had gently told her, and in the connection of shared thought, Rianne had sensed the name of one with whom she'd had a lengthy affair: Tristan.

"Does he love her?"

"For men there are different kinds of love, daughter," Meg had replied, and in the essence of their shared thoughts Rianne had sensed the sarcasm in her mother's response.

Perplexed and not a little displeased, Rianne had asked, *"What kind do you speak of?"*

"The sort that is paid for with coins."

* * *

Rianne was fascinated by the grand city within walls that Arthur had built. Before she'd returned to Monmouth she had heard preposterous stories of Arthur's magical city. One tale she had already discovered to be false—the streets were not paved with gold.

So intrigued was she by the sounds of the city beyond the walls of the courtyard that she was unaware that someone had entered her chamber as she leaned out the window.

She gasped as an arm snaked around her waist, cutting off her air as she was hauled back from the window opening. Then she gasped again as she was dragged back against a hard male body, and a voice whispered low at her ear, her assailant's warm breath tickling her neck.

"Do you know what happens to fair young maids who lean out of castle windows?"

"They get attacked by knaves who have nothing better to do than go about attacking fair young maids in windows?" she breathlessly replied, then was turned in strong arms and held prisoner by impatient hands.

"They get snatched away by a terrifying dragon."

She laughed breathlessly up into that warm golden gaze. "Then what happens?"

"The dragon carries the beautiful young maids away to his lair in the clouds."

Her gaze slowly fastened on his mouth. "Then what happens?"

"Then he devours them."

The laughter was gone. In its place was a low, breathless sound, filled with need, and hunger, and wonderful thoughts of dragons devouring young maids.

"I can think of no other place I'd rather be, Sir Dragon," she whispered huskily as his mouth closed over hers.

Her hands slid up over his shoulders, then back through the

thick, rich, dark mane of his hair. Then she gave all of herself in that soul-stirring kiss that whispered of the lonely days and the lonelier nights since they'd last been together.

"No," Tristan groaned into the softness of her mouth. And then against the silken heat of her throat. "I promised myself I would not ravage you like some love-crazed fool."

" 'Tis all right." She pressed kisses against his throat. "You have my permission to ravage me."

He laughed then, because she was so improbably logical and pragmatic, and honest. Wonderfully honest. He slipped his hand back through the heavy satin of the hair that had somehow escaped that perfect plaited braid while he kissed her.

"Later."

"Now," she insisted as negotiations continued through several slow kisses.

"Soon," he promised.

"When?"

"Very soon." He was already rethinking his promise to Meg about taking Rianne to see the city.

"Tonight."

"The king is giving a feast in your honor."

"I would rather share your feast."

He swore on a deep, throaty, thoroughly sensual sound. "You will be the ruination of me."

"That is what I intend, milord Dragon."

"I promised Lady Meg."

"To ruin me?" She leaned back with mischief dancing in her vivid blue eyes.

Father in heaven, she was wonderful. He pulled her against him once more, content just to feel her soft heat burning through him.

"I promised that I would show you Camelot."

"I have seen Camelot."

"You have seen the royal court. There is far more that lies beyond the courtyard walls. You have not yet seen the city."

"When?" she asked with the excitement of a little girl.

Contentment warmed through him. It was so easy to please her. It was such a pleasure to please her.

"Now."

The streets of Camelot were not paved with gold, but there were many wonders to see.

Rianne's experience with towns, villages, and hamlets had been limited to the dingy taverns, inns, and shops of remote outposts in the eastern frontier. She had only heard stories of places like London, Bath, and Camelot, with their shops, apothecaries, merchants, and craftsmen who plied their trade from storefronts, wagons, and at open markets.

Delicious aromas filled the air as roast fowl and pig were turned at a spit, while sweetmeats, candied fruits, and pastries were sold from carts beside wagons of fine silks, satins, spices, and flowers brought from seaports that had once been filled with Roman ships.

Tristan bought crisp red apples and a handful of gleaming silk ribbons from a vendor's basket. While Rianne admired the ribbons, he teased her with a piece of sweet apple clenched between his teeth, nipping at her lips with tender playfulness when she attempted to steal it away. And a feast of fruit became a feast of the senses while silk ribbons slipped from her trembling fingers in the crisp afternoon air.

As they wandered the streets of Camelot, they discovered jugglers who tossed wooden balls, fruit, and fragile eggs, then caught them with amazing skill. There were also jesters, acrobats, and mummers in brightly decorated costumes who acted out skits.

The character of the king was dressed in familiar gold and blue robes, the mummer's face concealed by a mask. The troupe acted out a scene that had become legendary in the years since—

the battle at Glastonbury in which Arthur had finally defeated Maelgwyn.

It was amazing the liberty that had been taken with the actual events, but those who gathered about didn't seem to mind. By turns they cheered the king and hissed at Maelgwyn, who wore antlers at his headpiece.

Tristan was recognized by a fellow knight who persuaded him to participate. Wooden swords were offered by two of the mummers, and the two knights joined the mock battle.

The fighting was "fierce," and Rianne burst into laughter as Tristan's playful attack was hampered by a small man the size of Grendel who attacked from the rear, poking him in the backside.

The crowd roared with laughter as Arthur's brave knights were then forced to fight back to back against their attackers. The battle was won in the end, just as everyone knew it would be, but with much hilarity and humor at the cost of Arthur's real knights, who gallantly bowed to the crowd while accepting ribbons and flowers from young women and girls.

Rianne wiped tears of laughter from her eyes. Tristan's mock battle with the much shorter warrior had reminded her of his verbal encounters with Grendel, and as in those encounters it was difficult to determine who had won.

As she waited at the edge of the crowd for his return, a voice called out nearby.

"Fortunes told for a coin, milady. Learn what awaits in the future."

A woman beckoned to her from among the vendors' stalls that lined the street.

"Come, mistress. Have your fortune told. Only one small coin."

Rianne gestured with empty hands. "As you see, I have no coins."

The woman shrugged. "A pretty ribbon, then," she suggested.

Intrigued, Rianne unwound one of the ribbons that Tristan had purchased for her earlier from her hair and handed it to the woman.

"Sit by my fire," the woman invited. "And we will discover what the future holds."

The woman was a gypsy, one of the nomadic peoples who wandered from town to town, plying their wares and trades. They called no place home. Instead, home was an open field, a mountain valley, or whatever direction their carts took them.

They paid fealty to no man, not even the king. Yet it was said that many gypsies had fought for Arthur during the wars. They were natural-born thieves, but thievery became difficult if not impossible with the entire kingdom thrown into chaos and desperate poverty. But with prosperity under Arthur's rule came prosperity for the gypsies. There were now ample pockets to pick and pouches to lift from the belts of the unwary. As long as they were not caught at it.

The gypsy woman had flawless golden skin and eyes as dark as the night sky. It was impossible to determine her age. She might have been as young as Meg or far older.

"Give me your hand," the woman invited. "And I will tell you the future."

Rianne knelt beside the fire and watched with great interest as the gypsy took her hand. The woman's dark hair was bound beneath the brightly colored silk scarf tied about her head. But it was her hands that startled Rianne. They were wrinkled and badly gnarled, as if she was much older than she appeared.

There were those who believed gypsies were capable of seeing visions in patterns of leaves found at the bottom of a bowl, in the mysterious shifting shadows and lights found in a crystal ball, or in the pattern of lines found in a person's hand.

She had seen gypsies before in her wanderings, but the things they revealed were no more than what a person might learn simply by observing people, or so vague in meaning that the gypsy was long gone before the person realized he'd been robbed because of his own foolishness.

She'd learned from Merlin that very few were capable of summoning visions that revealed future events. Such a thing carried with it a grave responsibility, and he warned that great care must always be taken in revealing the future.

Merlin and her mother both possessed that ability. It was a vision of the future that had compelled Meg to send her from Monmouth when she was a babe.

Rianne sensed nothing about the gypsy that led her to believe she might be a kindred spirit. Yet she watched with great interest as the woman gently spread her fingers apart, exposing the palm of her hand.

"You have traveled far," she began, and Rianne smiled as she leaned over and looked down at the palm of her hand and attempted to see what it was that revealed that amazing fact to the gypsy.

"Ah, but you have farther to go," the gypsy continued.

Rianne was highly amused as she thought of the great distance she and Tristan had ridden from the king's court. No doubt the woman had observed the cut of their clothes and assumed the same.

" 'Tis a dangerous journey to a distant land."

"Then I shall have to be certain to take someone with me," Rianne replied.

The gypsy's gaze held hers. " 'Tis a journey only you can make."

Bemused and intrigued because of the long journey she'd already made when she returned to Monmouth, Rianne then asked, "Where is this place? How will I know it?"

"You have already seen it," the gypsy's dark eyes gleamed with secrets, "in your dreams."

Rianne's startled gaze met hers. Had the woman made a lucky guess? Or was this merely part of her game? Journeys? Dreams? Most certainly the sort of thing that would frighten most people who were skeptical and superstitious. Or was it something more?

"Where is this place?"

"It lies beyond the known world, through clouds of mist, smoke, and fire."

She did not know whether the woman merely guessed or if it was some game she played with everyone who sought their fortune, but suddenly it was no longer entertaining. Rianne tried to retrieve her hand but found it locked in a surprisingly strong grasp.

Then the gypsy looked up, and her gaze met Rianne's. The woman's eyes were dark as night sky. There was no reflection there of nearby torches or the fire that burned beside them. They were completely void of all light, all emotion, except one—that coldness that seemed to reach out for her.

Rianne suddenly felt cold in spite of the warmth of the fire. It was as if some invisible wall of ice had descended around them.

The noise of the crowd seemed to fade, until it was no more than a soft buzzing sound. There was only the gypsy, the fire that suddenly seemed to burn higher, and the connection at the woman's grasp that held her imprisoned as surely as if chains bound her hand and foot.

" 'Tis a journey you have already begun. . . ." The gypsy's thoughts moved through hers, as her fingers closed around her wrist.

Pain burned all the way up her arm with a coldness that seared through her blood and burned deep into her soul, the pain and loss of that long-ago night burning through her thoughts with the gypsy's words.

She was paralyzed, as if a drug moved through her blood, slowly robbing her of strength and the will to resist.

"You cannot escape it. It waits for you. For you are the Chosen."

The words whispered through her thoughts as that coldness

seeped through her blood. And just as in her dreams, she felt the blood warm at her hand. It slipped down her fingers and dripped onto her gown.

She stared down at the nightmare come to life, the blood gradually receding, transforming into the gleaming red stone at her hand. A strange weakness swept over her, robbing her of her ability to resist, to fight back, even to breathe.

"Who are you?"

And the thought whispered back to her, *"You know who I am."*

Her gaze met the gypsy's across the glow of the fire . . . then across the span of years to that long ago night when she had stood at the edge of another fire and helplessly watched as those she loved died. And beyond the fire, in the shadows of swirling smoke and death stood the dark stranger with the same eyes that looked back at her now.

The gypsy smiled. Her fingers loosened at Rianne's wrist, releasing her.

Warmth flooded back through her frozen veins, strength returned, and that gleaming stone the color of blood slowly faded. When she looked up the gypsy was gone.

The noise of the crowd once more surrounded her. Jugglers tossed brightly colored balls into the air while children laughed and clapped with excitement. It was as if nothing had happened.

But it had. She could still feel the coldness deep in her soul. The same as it was that night long ago when those she loved had been brutally murdered and a stranger had stood at the edge of the clearing, his dark mantle whipping in the wind and smoke, those cold dark eyes looking back at her.

The sound of her name gradually slipped through the horror of those memories. Strong hands closed over her shoulders. Familiar warmth drove the cold from her skin and stirred at her blood.

She was deathly pale, her skin almost bloodless in the light from the torches that had been lit all along the square, and her eyes were dark, deepest blue, haunted by something he had never seen.

"What is it?"

"I wish to leave this place. Now!" Her thoughts frantically sought out Meg's, desperate to reassure herself that her mother was safe.

There was an urgency in her voice that he'd not heard before. And fear. He had never known her to be afraid. He glanced about at the crowd that moved about them.

"Has something happened?"

"Please! I wish to return now."

Tristan frowned. Something had happened. Something that had replaced her smile with a look of fear. But she refused to speak of it and he knew that nothing he could say would force her to do so until she was ready.

"Very well, then we will return."

He felt the tension in her slender body as she rode before him in the saddle, and saw the wariness in her eyes as she constantly watched those they passed, as if she looked for someone among the people on the streets.

When they reached the inner gate at the king's courtyard, she almost leapt from the saddle in her eagerness to reach the main hall. Tristan handed over the reins as a stable boy appeared and went after her.

Guided by that bond that connected her to her mother and the urgency of the encounter with the gypsy, Rianne didn't see the warrior who stepped into her path as she entered the main hall. Gloved hands reached out to steady her.

"Are you all right, milady?"

Her gaze came up and locked with that of Sir Longinus. He was tall, dressed in the dark tunic and breeches he preferred, his dark hair hanging to his shoulders, the dark gray mantle hanging from his shoulders. Moisture gleamed from the heavy wool, as if he had just returned as night fell across the city.

She instinctively took a step back, remembering that it was

Longinus who had had the encounter with Tristan when he'd been injured.

He did not immediately release her, but gently steadied her with a warmth of intimacy that slipped beneath her defenses and tingled along each nerve ending.

"Thank you." She took another step back and he was forced to release her. " 'Tis only that it is late and I wish to see my mother."

"Ah, the lady Meg. She eagerly awaits your return."

"You spoke with her?"

"Earlier, in the garden at the inner courtyard. She was walking and we spoke. I knew Lord Connor and wished to express my sympathy at his death."

"That is kind of you." When she would have turned to leave, he took her hand in his. Again there was that warmth of intimacy that moved through her blood and slipped past the will to resist.

"I also wish to express my sympathy to you. Lord Connor was a brave warrior. He fought well. You must feel his loss deeply."

She finally extricated her hand. "In the short time we were together, I learned many things from him. I am grateful for what little time we had." And then she bid him farewell.

"I will see you at evening meal?" he inquired as she turned to leave.

"Aye, milord," she replied, thinking the question ridiculous, since everyone who resided within the royal hall was expected to attend the evening meal.

Tristan had seen just enough, her voice edged with humor. Then she crossed the hall and quickly fled up the stairs. His gaze fastened on Longinus, and he wondered what had passed between them that had caused her to laugh when only moments before she had been silent and aloof.

Longinus turned as if only just aware of his presence. "Good eventide. You seem well recovered."

"Well enough," Tristan assured him.

"I am pleased to hear that. Arthur has need of all his knights."

"And you?" Tristan inquired, anger returning at the memory of that afternoon, and the foolishness of a skilled warrior who was never known to make foolish mistakes.

Longinus's gaze sharpened. "A minor thing. 'Tis already healed." He flexed the gloved hand that had taken a bruising blow in their encounter.

" 'Tis not a mistake I shall make again."

"Mother!" Rianne pushed open the chamber door.

It was cold and dimly lit. No fire burned at the brazier or glowed at the oil lamps. The only light came from the courtyard beyond the shutters that stood open at the window opening.

She quickly closed them. Then, guided by that gift of inner sight, easily found the oil lamp at the table. On a single thought flame burst to life at the oil lamp. It caught and burned brightly, a pool of light spreading across the walls of the chamber.

"Mother?"

The word connected their thoughts in the old way, pushing back the heavy fog that lay over Meg's senses. A word she had longed to hear through all the empty years that had separated them, and now reached out to her.

"Daughter?"

"I'm here."

"I was dreaming again. You were lost and I couldn't find you. I looked everywhere, but I couldn't find you."

"It's all right," Rianne's thoughts gently soothed as she put her arms around her mother's shoulders. *"I'm here now. And I won't ever go away again."*

* * *

They were asked to join Arthur at his table that night as his honored guests.

Rianne remained close to her mother, separated only once as they entered the main hall and she encountered Longinus. He wore a dark velvet tunic over leather breeches and boots. His dark eyes gleamed when he saw her, taking her hand with that sensual warmth that had surprised her earlier.

His smile was intimate, even bold, as he complimented her on her gown and her hair, woven through with the ribbons Tristan had purchased for her. She had worn them for him, but when they arrived at the main hall he barely acknowledged her, and she felt a stab of disappointment that he did not seek her out. It was Longinus who escorted her to the king's table, then took a place nearby.

She recognized many of the nobles who were guests at Monmouth when her father was alive, and the memory of that particular evening brought a certain comfort amid the imposing grandeur of Arthur's court.

Throughout the meal she conversed with Lords Hereford and Tregaron, nodded politely when Arthur spoke to her, remembered to wait until he was seated before she sat down along with others at the table, and tried to remember not to speak out of turn.

Almost as soon as the meal had ended the games began, a variety of board games including the now infamous cup and stones at which she'd relieved Lord Standford of a substantial amount of gold and silver.

All were familiar with the story, even those who were not at Monmouth that long-ago day, and she received several invitations to join the game. She was about to accept when Tristan spoke up from the opposite end of the table where he sat among Arthur's knights.

"Another time," he replied with quiet authority, his gaze meeting hers briefly over the rim of his goblet from the length of the table as he took a long drink of wine.

"She does not feel up to it this evening."

Did not feel up to it? How the bloody blue blazes would he know how she felt when he hadn't spoken to her all evening? She glared at Tristan, daring him to stop her as she turned to Sir Bedford, who had extended the invitation.

"I feel quite up to it. I accept." Her gaze met Tristan's in open challenge.

Tristan saw that silken brow arch. Color rose across her cheeks and sparkled at those vivid eyes. If a single look could slay a man, he would be run through, drawn, and quartered with just one look. As preparations were made for the game, he rose from his chair, rounded the table, and seized her by the arm.

Drawing her aside, he explained, "This is not Monmouth. There are those here, Standford included, who would like nothing better than to humiliate you as you humiliated them."

"I won fairly," she protested.

Tristan tried to keep his voice low. " 'Tis not a matter of fairness. 'Tis a matter of honor."

"Honor? Where is the honor in cheating?"

"There is none, and when you throw it in a man's face you humiliate him. Everyone knows that Standford cheats. It is accepted because he is a boorish clod, but a necessary boorish clod because his cooperation guarantees an alliance with Arthur."

"Politics," she summed it up in just one word.

"Aye, politics."

"The very same sort of politics that destroyed the Roman Empire, I believe," she flung back at him.

She was beautiful when she was angry. And at the moment she was furious. "If that is the way you wish to see it."

" 'Tis the way you see it, milord. Is that also the reason you bed Standford's wife? More politics?"

"That is enough!" he threatened.

"Aye," she fumed. "Far more than enough." Then she turned and joined Bedford and the others.

Standford had not yet joined them. She seized the stones. Wagers were immediately placed. She made one throw of the stones. They rolled across the table and came to rest against the backboard. She threw twice more, winning all three rounds, then handed the stones over to Bedford.

"Make certain Standford does not switch them when he joins the game." She returned to the table.

"You are to be commended, milady," Longinus congratulated her. "You should have waited until Standford joined the game. He has had much to drink and would no doubt like the opportunity to regain his losses."

Rianne's gaze met Tristan's across the length of the table. She smiled as she replied, "I prefer a challenge."

"What think you on the matter of thieves, mistress?" Sir Gawain asked of the current trouble with thieves in the city, and she almost burst out laughing for it seemed the conversation was much the same as before.

At his other side Lady Alyce leaned forward with sudden interest in the conversation.

"I would be most interested to hear your feelings on this," she joined in. "I have heard you lived among thieves for a time before you returned to Monmouth."

Rianne sensed the surprise and curiosity of Arthur's other guests seated about them as they overheard the conversation.

She could have denied it, but she sensed that was precisely what Lady Alyce wished.

" 'Tis true," she replied, and saw the gleam of satisfaction that leaped into the other woman's eyes.

"How did you come by such knowledge?"

She answered simply, "Because I *was* a thief."

Tristan was furious with her, but he couldn't prevent a smile at Alyce's stunned reaction, which almost matched the expression on Lady Meg's face. The last thing she expected was for

Rianne to admit it. Now that she had, it took her a moment to recover.

He thought of intervening and decided against it. She might not have a sword in her hand, but Connor's daughter still held everyone at sword's point.

He watched, certain that she had exposed a point of vulnerability. Alyce warmed to her game.

"Mayhaps you stole jewels?"

"I stole food," Rianne bluntly replied.

By the expressions on the faces of those who sat nearby, it appeared everyone thought she must surely be jesting. They were amused by the entertaining conversation.

"Did you steal other things?" Alyce asked.

Rianne shrugged. "A tart, a piece of fruit, a piece of candy."

"Gold coins, perhaps?" Alyce suggested.

"I had no use for gold coins," Rianne replied. "One cannot eat them."

"How fascinating. Pray tell, how did you steal these things without being caught?"

" 'Tis all in knowing where to hide something once you've stolen it," Rianne explained.

"A pocket perhaps?" Alyce suggested.

"Perhaps," Rianne replied. "Although many thieves prefer the sleeve of their shirt or tunic. 'Tis possible to hide something up one's sleeve quite easily."

Alyce laughed. "Only a fool would hide something in his sleeve. 'Tis the first place anyone would look."

She pushed her empty goblet toward Hereford to be refilled. As she did so, an odd expression suddenly crossed her face.

"Is something amiss?" Rianne inquired, for the woman looked as if she had just sat in something. Or, to be more precise, just put her arm in something as she raised her left arm and discovered the damp stain that slowly appeared midway down the sleeve.

She stood suddenly, practically knocking the wine pitcher

from Hereford's hand as she frantically shook the sleeve of her tunic.

Broken egg shells plopped down onto the table amid a slimy ooze of broken egg yolks. Hereford and the other nobles looked on with dismay as several more broken eggs slid down her arm and onto the table.

"Stealing eggs, milady?" Arthur commented. "I was not aware there was a shortage of eggs."

"You might try cooking them first," Gawain suggested, struggling to keep a straight face.

Lady Alyce was furious. Her tunic was ruined and she'd been humiliated, and worst of all she had no idea how. She glared at Rianne and then left the hall in a rage of humiliation, broken eggs dripping in her wake.

"Most intriguing."

Rianne turned. Arthur had heard most of the conversation and smiled at her with amusement.

"I do not now how you did it, but knowing Merlin and the things he is capable of, I have my suspicions."

"Most unfortunate," Rianne commented. "I would never have thought Lady Alyce the sort to steal eggs?"

He laughed. "Someday, mistress, you must tell me how you did it. Until then I am in your debt. Lady Alyce can be most . . ." He searched for the right word.

"Tedious?" she suggested.

"Aye, and more. She is much like a cat. She leaves her mark wherever she goes and claims all as her territory."

"Rather like a hedgehog," Rianne replied. "Prickly and foul-natured."

He threw back his head and laughed all the more. "You are indeed your father's daughter. He always said exactly what he thought, even when he was telling his king to go to blazes. The stories I could tell you."

Her gaze met his. "I would like that very much."

They spoke at great length while his knights and the other

nobles gathered about the hall in small groups and spent their time at wagering over the games or telling stories among themselves.

Through those hours, Rianne glimpsed the man her father had once been—the boyhood friend and companion to the young king, the fierce warrior, and finally the defiant rebel who had faced Arthur down and denounced him, only to take up the sword at his side once again.

She discovered that her father had been a man of honor, duty, unshakable loyalty, and undying friendship. A friendship that Arthur valued above all else, and now mourned as deeply as she mourned the loss of her father.

Hours later Arthur's personal guard escorted her to her chamber. As she stepped inside a man stepped from the shadows.

He smelled of mulled wine, the pungence of pine fragrance that clung to his skin, and soft leather.

She hated him for the way her heart leapt and the way her blood heated and thickened in her veins.

"Nay," she whispered, determined to punish him for the way he'd treated her that evening. But there was no stopping him.

His mouth burned at her throat, the sensitive place at her neck, then at her mouth. Her hands twisted in the thick fabric of his tunic.

Nay! Milord Dragon.

She was certain she spoke it. Or perhaps she only thought it, and that too was silenced by the assault of his thoughts burning through hers with all the ways he intended to love her.

This was not the tender lover who had come to her before. He was different, his hands were different, urgent as he removed her tunic and gown, his mouth urgent against her mouth.

No words were spoken of the anger that lay between them. It was in his touch, in the fierce heat of her body answered by the fierce heat in his until there was only one thought, one need, one fire that consumed them both.

CHAPTER TWENTY-TWO

The gates opened and the mud-splattered horse trotted through, the rider falling from the saddle at the feet of the guards.

He was carried to the servant's wing, bleeding from a half-dozen wounds, more dead than alive.

Rianne was summoned from her chamber. There was no time to dress, nor to think on the fact that she had awakened alone.

She hastily donned a heavy mantle over her night shift and ran to keep up with Merlin's longer stride.

The wounded rider had been taken to the servant's quarters and laid on a pallet near the brazier. The fire was built up, and Merlin quickly gave instructions for more light, water, and fresh bandages.

"I know this man," he said, his voice suddenly tight as he bent over the bloodied rider. "He is from Lyonesse."

His gaze met hers. Already blood soaked the pallet beneath the wounded messenger. Merlin's gaze met hers.

"This will not be easy to see. If you wish to leave, I will send for my sister. . . ."

She shook her head. "Tell me what you wish me to do."

He ordered everyone from the chamber, then set about cutting away the man's torn and bloodied garments. It seemed impossible that he was still alive, so much blood had been lost and so many bones were broken.

He faded in and out of consciousness, the pain rousing him until it became unbearable and he passed out once more. His breathing was labored and rattled badly.

"He is bleeding inside," Merlin said on a sound of frustration as he closed one wound only to find another that bled more badly. The man roused again, clutching at the front of his tunic.

"Lyonesse has been attacked," his voice rasped from between bloodied lips. "My mistress . . . you must help her." On a last rattling sound, his head fell back and the hand at Merlin's tunic went limp.

She had seen death before, along the byways when some hapless traveler was set upon by outlaws or a man made the mistake of fighting back when robbed of his purse. But still it stunned her, the finality of it. And then afterward, nothing was changed. Everything remained the same from one moment to the next, as if the importance of a human life had been reduced to nothingness.

"Is there nothing that can be done?" Rianne whispered.

Merlin shook his head, tossing down a bloodied cloth in frustration. "I can bind wounds and mend bones. I can drive out the poison and fever. But the one thing I cannot do is hold back death." He looked at her sadly across the pallet.

" 'Tis the thing that separates us from those who are mortal, our salvation and our damnation that while we live others die." His gaze met hers.

" 'Tis the price we pay for living as mortals that the day eventually comes when everything mortal passes away but we go on."

He pulled a linen bed cloth over the man's body and summoned one of the servants.

"Have word sent that I must speak with the king right away."

Within only a few hours preparations were made. A legion of Arthur's army encamped nearest to Camelot was ordered to Lyonesse. Arthur was to ride with them, along with eight of his knights and Merlin. Four of his knights and their men were to wait at Camelot until another legion of warriors returned from the eastern frontier. If Lyonesse had been attacked, then it was assumed Camelot might also be attacked.

Her mother said nothing as they worked side by side in the herbal, preparing the herbal remedies Merlin was to take with him, for it was assumed there were many injured.

Countless times Meg had done this preparing for war. Countless times she had held her tongue and kept her thoughts to herself. But not this time, as Merlin supervised the packing of the herbal remedies into the pouches to be carried across his saddle on the journey to Lyonesse.

"Why must Arthur go? Does he not see that 'tis not safe to leave Camelot undefended?"

"Camelot will not be undefended. Sir Roderick and three of Arthur's knights are to remain with their men, as well as the men from Monmouth. You will be safe, dear sister."

" 'Tis not myself I think of. I think of you, brother. Arthur is foolish in this. What importance is Lyonesse?"

"Arthur made a promise to the old duke upon his deathbed that he would protect Lyonesse," Merlin explained, forcing his thoughts to the task at hand. But Rianne sensed the conflict within him.

A jar slipped from his fingers and would have shattered if she had not caught it. Their fingers brushed and in that contact and the briefer contact of their thoughts, she sensed the image that he held there. An image of a beautiful young woman.

Their gazes met briefly, and in that connection, she realized the reason for the conflict.

"Lady Guinevere is in danger," he went on to explain, packing more of the pouches filled with herbs into the leather saddlebag.

"Arthur is bound to that promise."

Just as she sensed Merlin struggled with promises that he had made. Promises that could never be kept.

The day had dawned cold and gray. Rianne huddled deep within the folds of the heavy mantle, hugging its warmth about her as she stood on the steps of Camelot with her mother.

Tristan was among those leaving. The black stallion was saddled. It snorted with excitement, tossing that massive head against the restraint of the tether.

Half the guard from Monmouth was to ride with him, the other half remaining behind at Camelot. Tristan had informed Meg of his decision, meeting privately with her earlier.

Rianne watched for him among the knights and warriors who prepared to leave, frowning when she did not see him. Her frown deepened as Longinus strode toward them.

"Sir Longinus," Lady Alyce called out. She had joined them, along with several of the other ladies at court. While her husband prepared to return to Standford keep, it seemed that Lady Alyce had only just risen.

Beneath her mantle, she still wore her night shift and her hair was disheveled. Rianne had heard the rumors at court. It was impossible not to hear them. She knew Tristan and Lady Alyce had been lovers.

Tristan had not spoken of it, and in spite of the fact that he had been with her most of the night, she still felt a stab of jealousy and wondered whose bed Lady Alyce had just risen from. Surely not her husband's, for he had been up and about since first light, his retainers preparing for the journey to Standford keep. His wife had chosen to remain at Camelot where it was safe. But Rianne wondered if there were other reasons that kept her there.

Longinus's greeting was for her mother as he approached, but Rianne was aware of his gaze upon her, the way it lingered, dark and intense, intimate, as though they shared secrets.

"A token perhaps, mistress?" Longinus asked as he turned to her. "Something that I might carry into battle?"

Irritation rose as she glanced past him, hoping she might see Tristan.

"As you can see I have nothing, sir."

He smiled as he reached a gloved hand very near her cheek and slowly unwound one of the ribbons woven through her hair.

"A pretty ribbon from a pretty lady," he said as he slowly wound the ribbon about his hand, gently tugging it from the thick plait of her hair. He pressed it against his lips.

"I will treasure it, mistress. And pray I live to return it to you." He tucked the ribbon inside the front of his tunic, then suggested, "Perhaps you also have a ribbon for Sir Tristan."

She watched as Tristan approached. His expression was taut, the lean angles of his face somehow sharper, more fierce in the cold, frozen dawn. He had heard just enough of Longinus's conversation, and it occurred to her that that was exactly what Longinus had intended.

Anger had driven Tristan to her the night before. It was still there in too many things said, and too many other things left unsaid. His farewell was not for her, but for her mother.

"Farewell, milady. With good fortune we will return in a few days' time."

She gently kissed him on the cheek. "Come back safely to us."

Lady Alyce waited expectantly, but Tristan only nodded a brief acknowledgment. Then his gaze met Rianne's. He did not ask for a ribbon. Nor would she have expected it.

Pride. Duty. Honor. It was not in him to beg for anything. He bowed stiffly.

"Good day, milady."

Then he was gone, striding across the yard, joining his men as he swung astride the black stallion. Orders were given. Columns of mounted riders formed.

Arthur rode before them, his banners snapping in the bitter cold wind. Merlin rode with him.

Only a short while earlier he had met with her mother. Things were spoken of. She knew that Meg attempted to persuade him to remain at Camelot. In the end there was nothing she could say that would change his decision. Now he rode with Arthur ahead of that long column.

They rode toward an unknown enemy. They had only the messenger's words of the trouble at Lyonesse and could not know what lay ahead.

Meg's hand closed over hers as they stood together on the steps of Camelot. *"Do not let your last words to him be spoken in anger, daughter."*

Her startled gaze met Meg's. She had not spoken to her of her feelings for Tristan. She thought she had kept them well hidden. Yet her mother knew.

She gathered up the heavy folds of her mantle, ran down the steps, and across the courtyard as Arthur and his knights began the ride through the streets that would take them to the main gates of Camelot.

She angled her way through stableboys, servants, warriors, and nervous horses until she reached him near the head of the column of men from Monmouth. The black stallion tossed his head as she approached. Tristan reined him in hard. Then his gaze met hers.

"Perhaps you are looking for Longinus."

"I am looking for neither a fool nor a coward," she flung back at him.

She saw the anger and something else that burned in that

golden gaze—something that almost looked like amusement. He reached down, his arm going around her waist as he pulled her up against him. She felt the anger then in his hands and the arms that closed around her. But there was passion too, and the need to say words that had not been said the night before or even when he had left her.

Longinus had humiliated him. She understood that. She also understood that it was not finished between them. But this was not about Longinus.

She didn't argue or try to convince him that he was wrong. She was not even certain he would have listened. Instead, she gave him the one thing she possessed of value that had been with her always, given long ago to protect her. She pressed the crystal rune with those ancient carved markings into his hand so that it would now protect him.

Even in the cold wintry morn it gleamed with inner fire as it dangled from his gloved fingers—the fire of the one who had given it, and the one who had worn it all the years since. Then she turned from him without a word and would have dropped to the ground if he had not held on to her.

His arm tightened about her. The anger was still there. She felt it in the hand that fisted at her hair as he pulled her against him. And then felt it in his kiss as his mouth closed over hers.

It was a bruising kiss. She didn't fight him. Instead she gave into it, taking all the anger, all the questions and uncertainty, so that there was only one thing that remained between them.

When the kiss ended, he held her for long moments afterward, his hand still fisted in her hair. His breath was warm against her cheek. His heart beat fiercely beneath her hand.

The column of riders slowly moved past them. Eventually, Tristan released her and lowered her to the ground beside the stallion. Their gazes met briefly, their fingers touched, and he was gone.

She stood there long after the last man rode through the courtyard gate, with the cold December wind whipping at the folds of the heavy mantle and a deeper cold closing around her heart.

"Where are you going?" Grendel demanded, looking at her suspiciously.

No thoughts opened to his. No words reached out. She had deliberately closed her thoughts to him. He sensed it just as he sensed that she was up to something.

"I'm going to the marketplace," she replied casually. "Many of the herbal remedies I use have been depleted. Perhaps I can find what I need there."

" 'Tis the middle of winter," Grendel pointed out, his eyes narrowing with suspicion. "Nothing grows in the middle of winter."

"Precisely the reason I must go. There are far more complaints in winter. Perhaps I can find some powders or dried medicants among the merchants there."

"The cook can obtain what you need. She sends her people into the marketplace daily."

Rianne smiled congenially. Inwardly she entertained private, closed thoughts of what punishment might be suitable for pesky gnomes.

"Perhaps she will allow me to go along," she suggested. "Then I may find what I need."

What she needed, Rianne decided some time later, as she walked through the marketplace accompanied by four of the cook's helpers, four guards, and a gnome, was to disappear in a particularly crowded area of the marketplace.

At this slow pace and encumbered with the cook's helpers, she would never find the gypsy woman. Perhaps, she thought, gathering the folds of the heavy mantle about her, she might slip away when their attention was distracted. Perhaps in the open square where the acrobats performed.

As Grendel and the others watched their performance with

avid attention, she wrapped the mantle more tightly about herself, turned her thoughts inward, and as easily as stepping through a doorway, stepped through a small cloud of mist.

"Did you see?" Grendel exclaimed. "That is nothing! I can do that!" When there was no answer, he turned around.

"Mistress? Mistress?"

As smoke rose from cookfires near the vendor wagons, Rianne stepped through a cloud of mist. She was hundreds of yards away from where Grendel had last seen her.

The richly made mantle was laid aside, and those who saw the slender boy pass by in breeches, boots, and heavily padded tunic were unaware that he was not a boy at all.

"I'm looking for a gypsy who tells fortunes," she explained to one person after another, working her way from one end of the marketplace to the other.

Then she heard a rumor that gypsies were encamped on the other side of the peddler's fair under the watchful guard of Arthur's soldiers, only allowed to remain within the city because of the new danger. But when she finally found their camp, no one had seen the woman she described.

They were liars, cutthroats, and thieves. She was a stranger in their world and they were naturally suspicious. When three young men followed and cornered her, she merely turned on them.

"I am looking for a gypsy woman. She tells fortunes for a coin. She was in the square four days ago."

"What do you want with the woman?"

"I want to speak with her. It is important."

"Perhaps important enough to pay for, eh? What have you there, boy? Gold?"

She had sensed their mood and their thoughts, her gaze following them as they moved about her. It had been dangerous to come here; she knew that. But it was important that she find the gypsy, and find out exactly who she was.

The three men split up, each advancing from a different

direction. When the first came at her, she lunged with the blade, slashing open the front of his tunic. He yelped with pain and leapt back, wiping the blood from the front of his tunic, where it gaped open, exposing the cut at his belly.

Then a second one attacked. She easily sidestepped him, whirled around, and, planting her foot firmly at his backside, gave a hard shove. He landed face down in the dirt. That was when the third gypsy attacked her with knife drawn.

He came at her wildly, slashing with the knife. Tired of their games, she diverted the blade with a bare hand and then used the power within her to throw the man backwards. Her hood had fallen back during the encounter, her hair tumbling about her shoulders.

The three gypsies looked at her with a mixture of disbelief and rage. When they came at her this time, she sent pots from nearby cookfires flying at them. One was doused with a foul-smelling stew. Another yelped as hot porridge burned its way down his tunic. The third was hit by a flying cauldron of simmering pig's feet.

When the stew and porridge was cleared away they were a pathetic sight, groaning and nursing one painful lump or another. They were completely bewildered and she sensed no knowledge of the woman among them. Whoever she was, she was not part of their family or their encampment. Nor was she in the city. If she had been, Rianne would have found her. The woman had disappeared as easily as Rianne had learned to move through shadows and mist.

She returned to Arthur's court, slipping past the guards and through the stone wall and into the shadows just outside the great hall.

It was early evening. She heard the servants in the main hall, putting wood on the fire. Only a portion of the tables were set for Arthur's knights and those who had chosen to remain at Camelot. Rianne knew she would find her mother in her chamber, preferring the privacy found there, away from the gossip of the royal court.

Others had already gathered in the main hall. The inviting warmth of the fire and the smell of food made her think of Tristan and Merlin and those who rode with them.

Lyonesse lay a full day's ride to the west in fair weather. In the depth of winter, hampered by snow and freezing cold, the journey would take much longer.

They would not have made Lyonesse by nightfall, and memories of weeks past, when she and Tristan had made cold camps on the journey to Monmouth, were vivid in her mind.

Those thoughts distracted her. She did not sense the presence of the one who suddenly stepped from the shadows directly in her path. Surprise gleamed in Lady Alyce's eyes, followed by amusement.

"Why, 'tis not a boy at all!" She laughed.

She was not alone. Rianne recognized Sir Sagremore, one of the knights who had remained behind, and fleetingly wondered if Camelot was truly well protected. He nodded an acknowledgment, but did not share Alyce's amusement.

"Come along, milady."

"I shall be along momentarily," Alyce told him, and the heated look she gave him left no doubt that whoever it was who'd occupied her bed the night before, his place had not grown cold since.

Sagremore nodded stiffly and then joined two of his fellow knights as they entered the hall. Rianne seized the opportunity to leave also, but Alyce had other intentions as she seized Rianne by the arm.

"Is this one of your games?" Alyce asked with an amused glance that traveled from Rianne's tunic down to the toes of her boots.

"Or perhaps 'tis easier to steal when no one suspects your true identity."

Rianne shrugged. "I have no need to steal. There is nothing I want."

"Perhaps you think to steal Sir Tristan away," Alyce suggested as she warmed to the attack, her eyes gleaming with the memory of their first encounter and her humiliation before Arthur's entire court.

Rianne shrugged. "I cannot steal something you do not have."

She turned to leave. Alyce seized her by the arm once more. "There is more I wish to say."

Rianne glanced down at the hand clamped over her arm and slowly looked up, the blue of her eyes shimmering like the color of flame. She had grown weary of the conversation.

"There is nothing more I wish to hear." She extricated her arm from the other woman's grasp and started to walk away. She sensed when Alyce came after her.

"Do not walk away from me!"

Before Alyce could grab her, Rianne turned and brought the slender knife up. It was aimed straight at her heart, the tip pressed into the soft velvet of her tunic.

"Be very careful, milady," Rianne warned. "After all, as you well know, I have lived among thieves and cutthroats. My manners are crude and undisciplined. And at this moment I am far more inclined to slit your throat than argue with you."

Lady Alyce's eyes were the size of goose eggs and looked as if they might pop out of her head at any moment.

"All I have to do is scream and the guards will be upon you in a moment."

"And all I have to do is thrust this blade into your heart." Rianne pressed the blade of the knife deeper into the velvet-padded cleft between Lady Alyce's ample breasts. Alyce glared at her with undisguised hatred.

"Excellent choice," Rianne commended her. She turned to leave, then thinking further on it, turned back.

"I changed my mind." And with a flick of her wrist thrust

the tip of the blade into soft velvet, then sliced downward, severing the entire row of laces at the front of Lady Alyce's bodice. Her bodice popped open, exposing pale gleaming breasts. But that was not all that popped out. Several layers of padding also popped out and landed on the flagstones at their feet.

"What have we here?" Rianne remarked with amusement and skewered one of the pads with the tip of the blade.

"Hiding things in the front of your gown, milady? What will Sir Sagremore think?"

Lady Alyce did scream then. But it was more of a blood-curdling scream of rage than fear as she sank to her knees and frantically retrieved the pieces of padding.

Her screams brought guards from all directions, just as she'd threatened but not as she'd hoped.

"Get out of here, you oafs!" she screeched. "What are you looking at? If you tell anyone about this ... !"

Rianne left Lady Alyce to her tirade as she disappeared up the stairs. Inside her own chamber, she quickly changed and folded away the tunic, boots, and leggings.

She had not found what she sought at the market. But there was one who might be able to answer some of her questions. She heard distant laughter as she left her chamber and sought her mother's across the court garden.

"Come in, daughter," her mother greeted her before she'd even stepped through the doorway. "Come join me. There is more than enough food for the two of us."

Lady Meg had taken her supper in her chamber, preferring the privacy and solitude to the great hall with so many gone. Even at Monmouth, her mother had preferred the smaller, more private anteroom off the great hall to the larger, more formal occasions, such as a visit from the king and the other nobles.

She had no love for the royal court with its gossip, intrigues, and the political agendas of those who sought power. Just as

Rianne's father had no love for it. It was one of many things they shared.

Rianne found her mother sitting by the hearth. A warm fire burned, casting its light upon the walls and the thick fleece carpet on the stone floor. The meal had been laid out on the table.

It was simple fare—a portion of partridge, sliced meat, some sliced cheese, steaming apples, and the mulled wine that her mother preferred. Beside her was a frame set with a linen tapestry that she had been working on before Connor's death. She had returned to it, deftly weaving the threads through in a pattern guided by her fingers and a vision that she saw within her thoughts and dreams.

It always startled her how youthful her mother seemed. Yet Merlin had once jokingly commented that her father had obviously preferred much older women, for Lady Megwin was over three hundred years old!

It seemed impossible to her as she looked at the beautiful, graceful woman who sat there, weaving different threads with greater dexterity than one who was sighted.

In the world of the immortals there was no concept of time as people knew it in the mortal world. The score of years her mother had lived among the mortals had passed as little more than a heartbeat in the world to which she was born. And the young woman who had stepped through a portal in time into the mortal world that long-ago day looked hardly older than her daughter.

"What are you staring at?" Meg inquired. "Have I suddenly sprouted another head?"

"No, milady. I was just thinking that you seem barely older than me."

"*Milady?*" Meg inquired, her hands suddenly still at their weaving. "Why so formal, daughter?"

"Because there is something I wish to know. And I fear my mother might not tell me."

Meg set aside her weaving and rose from her chair. Her footsteps were sure and confident as she moved from chair to table and poured mulled wine from the decanter into two flagons. It was then Rianne realized that her mother had been expecting her.

"The wine is a favorite of mine," Meg explained as she handed her one of the flagons. "Your father and I shared it often."

Then Meg returned to the table and began slicing off portions of roast fowl.

"The wine is Arthur's, of course, but the mixture is a specialty of the Romans. It comes from the middle empires. They had a great love of spices, which I am told they traded for. The spices are rare, but your father always managed to acquire them from a merchant plying his trade at Monmouth."

She continued on, and Rianne knew she spoke of this and that, anything she could think of to avoid what she no doubt already sensed Rianne had come to ask her.

"Mother, who is the *Chosen?* And what does it mean?"

Meg suddenly ceased carving the roast fowl. "Where did you hear of it?"

"From a gypsy woman who read fortunes in the market."

"A gypsy?" Somehow amused by it, Meg began laying portions of meat, cheese, and bread on two trenchers. She laughed, but Rianne wasn't deceived. She sensed the undercurrent of desperation to hide emotions.

"Merlin would be amused. I must remember to tell him about it when he returns."

"The gypsy said that I was the *Chosen.* I saw a vision of blood and death, just like in my dreams. And when the blood disappeared . . ."

"It transformed into a bloodstone," she said, in a voice that had suddenly gone very quiet.

"You've seen it?"

"Aye," she replied sadly. "I have seen it."

"What does it mean?"

Meg's hand trembled as she laid down the knife. The food went untouched as she sat down in the chair once more, her hands clasped together in her lap. She stared at the fire in the hearth as if she could truly see the flames.

"Few have ever seen the bloodstone. So few that it was once thought to be no more than a myth, something the Ancient Ones spoke of but which none had ever seen."

And then she told the legend of the bloodstone—the sign of the *Chosen*, those born as mortals but with the power of the Light.

" 'Tis said the *Chosen* are the astral children, born of the Light in a time of coming Darkness. Their destiny is to protect the kingdom against the Darkness. 'Tis said the last *Chosen* was born over a thousand years ago in the mortal world. Since then there have been confrontations between the powers of the Light and the powers of Darkness."

She paused, touching her fingers to the side of her head where the vivid scar still remained after all these years, from the wounding that had taken her sight.

"I was blinded by a creature who had been seduced by the Darkness. 'Tis the way of the Darkness, to lure those who are greedy, ambitious, and who care for nothing more in this life than their own gain. They become the embodiment of the dark powers, and it is their purpose to seek out those of the Light and destroy them."

"But you and Merlin were born with the powers of the Light," Rianne pointed out. "I can see no difference. How could anything be more powerful than Merlin?"

Meg nodded. "Aye, 'tis strong within our family, for we are descended from the first *Chosen*. We possess abilities beyond that of mortal man—the power to heal, to transform ourselves, to cast visions, to sense what others cannot sense of the world around them. But the *Chosen* are the power of the Light. Within them are the total sum of the powers of the Light, and they have but one destiny—to confront the powers of Darkness.''

"You do not believe it is only a myth," Rianne concluded.

"I wanted to believe it was only a myth, because then there could never be any danger to those I loved." Her voice trembled, and Rianne knew she thought of her father.

"But I knew that long ago day when you were only a babe that the Darkness was there, waiting to claim the *Chosen* child. I foolishly thought that I could protect you.

"I sent you away to live in obscurity under a protective spell with no knowledge of the legacy you had been born to. I believed it was possible to keep you safely hidden. If the Darkness could not find you, then there was no danger. It was mortal foolishness that had forgotten nothing escapes the powers of Darkness.''

"You saw the bloodstone." Rianne sensed it within her mother's thoughts, the same image she had seen in her dreams and then in her encounter with the gypsy.

Meg nodded. "You were only a few weeks old when I returned to tend you and found your bed linens soaked in blood. There wasn't a mark on you, no injury, no sickness of any kind. But the image of the bloodstone was there. I have never seen anything more beautiful or more terrifying. I knew then that I must send you away. It was our only hope of keeping you safe.''

Then Rianne told her mother of her dreams, the images of fire and death at the forest cottage, and the stranger shrouded in a dark mantle, his features hidden by shadows.

"It was the Darkness that was responsible for the deaths of John and Dannelore. It had come for you, but my spellcast protected you. Your powers were so well hidden, even from yourself, that the Darkness could not find you.''

"What about Father? What has this to do with him? Why couldn't Merlin save him?"

"That was the trap even I could not see," Meg concluded sadly.

"The Darkness used my own weakness against me. I could not bear that your father might die and never see you again. I sent for you never realizing that I was putting you in grave danger."

Rianne thought of her father's slow, painful death that no one, not even Merlin, could prevent.

"It's still out there."

She sensed it with the fear of the child who had watched from the edge of a forest clearing as everything she loved was destroyed, and then stared into the eyes of Darkness.

"I do not like it," Gawain murmured, his voice low in the unearthly silence that surrounded them. "We can see nothing for this damnable mist!"

Tristan felt that same uneasiness. It tingled at every nerve ending, that instinctive warning felt before a battle.

Since before dawn they'd been astride their horses, shields and battle swords held in readiness after receiving word that Loedigan and his raiders were encamped in the Selden forest less than a half day's ride from the old duke's fiefdom at Lyonesse. From the safety of the forest they had struck three days earlier, burning and looting defenseless farms, crofters' huts, three outlying villages, and the small abbey at Listenaise.

When they arrived at Lyonesse they found Lady Guinevere, her household staff, her retainers, and a few farmers and their families armed with staffs and picks holed up in the chapel room of the keep. With no means of escape, they had decided to make a last stand there. Lady Guinevere did not hide among them, but fearlessly met Arthur, his personal guard, and Merlin at the chapel door with small sword in hand, as if ready to do battle to the death.

Merlin had communicated with those inside through the barricaded doors. The barricades were lifted and the survivors emerged to the sight of Arthur's armed knights and warriors filling the courtyard of Lyonesse.

During the initial attack, Lady Guinevere had sent her servant, Malcolm, to Camelot with a desperate plea for help. They had been without food and water for three days since, and each passing day they held less hope that help would arrive in time.

Tristan had heard of Lady Guinevere's youthful beauty. Merlin had spoken of it upon his return to Monmouth. But his words had been tinged with sadness, and Tristan sensed that more lay behind those words. He guessed at the truth when the doors were first opened and Lady Guinevere emerged unharmed.

The look on Merlin's face was like that of a man who'd been pardoned the worst death. And at that moment, Tristan was certain far more had passed between the counselor and the daughter of the old Duke of Lyonesse all those months past than merely the conversations of king's adviser and loyal subject.

Guinevere was much changed from the young girl Tristan remembered. There was a maturity about her of one who had endured the death of her father, accepting the responsibility of the title of Lady of Lyonesse, and something more in the somber sadness to her eyes that went beyond the hardship of the days past.

No words passed between her and Merlin. In fact, it seemed as if the counselor held himself apart. But there was something in his eyes that reached out to the lady beyond his official status, as if they had shared much.

Arthur had been taken with Lady Guinevere from the moment she emerged from the church, as brave as any of his knights, willing to lay down her life for her people. There was honor in her, as well as passion. Arthur sensed both and so had remained at Listenaise with Longinus and his personal guard, while his knights and soldiers encamped beyond.

Tristan had sent his men out through the night, moving afoot in pairs about the perimeter of the forest and the neighboring countryside. A chain link of listening posts was formed, with word passed along at regular intervals of anything that was heard or seen.

Just after midnight, the enemy encampment was sighted in the forest that bordered Listenaise. Then word was passed back to him that Loedigan led the raiders, who had come from the sea beyond the western pass. They planned to strike at Listenaise at dawn.

Loedigan was Norse by birth. He'd raided the coastal headlands off the Irish Sea with his father since before Arthur was king. Now the old Viking raider was dead and the son, Loedigan, was not deterred by the caution that had tempered his father's ambitions in old age.

But Tristan knew the Vikings well. He'd received his first lesson in battle from a Norse warrior who'd been friends with Connor. They were lessons learned by trial of blood even at the age of ten and had never been forgotten.

"Spread out your men," he ordered Gawain. "They will strike like Thor's hammer, hoping to gain the advantage with the first savage blow. But the hammer will find the target difficult to find if it is widely spread."

Gawain nodded and sent word along to his fellow knights. Behind the line of sparsely positioned knight were archers, and then foot soldiers with spears and shields. Next came the mounted warriors who, plunged into the midst of the Norsemen astride their war horses, would scatter the enemy's attack.

The blood-curdling cry pierced through the thick wall of fog. It unnerved the stoutest of heart and sent horses nervously sidestepping.

"Hold!" Tristan ordered, when the natural instinct of every last man was to strike even when it was impossible to see what they were striking at.

He glanced at the sky overhead and the thinning clouds of mist. Patches of pale blue were briefly visible. Then the pennons lifted at the poles carried by Arthur's signalmen as a breeze finally stirred.

"Now!"

The mist swirled above them, then thinned, exposing the sky overhead and the wall of charging raiders who bore down on them with fierce war cries as they charged.

The two armies came together in an explosion of battle cries, crashing bodies, and the sound of metal against metal. But to their surprise, the raiders discovered only a small portion of the army they'd anticipated.

Too late, they saw the king's knights who bore down on their flanks, surrounding them, cutting off any hope of escape, much less of the victory they'd been so certain of only moments before.

They fought to the edge of the forest, then drove the raiders into the forest, following after, cutting off retreat. Loedigan and his men had no choice but to fight.

Fighting in the forest was dangerous. Here a man could hide, then spring out at his enemy and cut the legs of his horse from under him. Tristan knew the dangers even as he sent the black stallion crashing through the scrub and brush at the edge of the forest, and then plunging into heavy tree cover.

Several of his men were already afoot, fighting through heavy cover. He'd lost sight of the man he was after, as if he'd disappeared into thin air. As he sent the black stallion charging down an almost invisible path between large trees, it occurred to him that he should have been more cautious.

The sword was already in his hand. He saw the glint of metal as the other man struck, not at him but at the black stallion.

He felt the black shudder beneath him, then that shrill sound of pain as the stallion went down under him. He was rolled from the saddle, the broad sword stunned from his hand in the fall. As he rolled across a small clearing, he got his feet under him.

Tristan rolled to his feet, the shorter sword immediately

drawn from the scabbard at his back. When he swung around to meet the attack, the blow immediately stunned his sword hand. He sidestepped, blocked another blow with his shield, and then struck back.

His attacker's face was hidden by the shadows of his hood. But he fought with the strength of ten men, recovering, striking, then beating Tristan back. A quick glance through the shifting clouds of mist that hung over the forest revealed that he'd become separated from the rest of his men.

He sensed that it was deliberate as the warrior drove him farther back from the edge of the forest. He dodged a blow, struck back, then found himself once more on the defensive.

He was weakening. He could feel the strength failing in his wounded shoulder with each blow. His attacker seemed to sense it as well, redoubling his efforts.

He didn't see the downed tree limb as he scrambled for better footing in the soft soil. It snaked about his ankle like a live thing, tripping him up. He went down on one knee, struggled to free his foot, then saw the blow that fell and stunned the shield from his weakened arm.

Trapped, his shield gone, Tristan made a fierce last strike that stunned his attacker. The raider was staggered back by the blow that caught him at the midsection, Tristan's blade sinking deep.

When he pulled it back, blood immediately appeared at the wound and through layers of heavy clothes. Stunned, the raider stared down at the gaping wound. Then he slowly looked up from the shadows of the hood he wore and a vague memory stirred.

The raider threw back his head. Instead of a wild Nordic death scream, he laughed, the hood falling to his shoulders. Tristan stared with disbelief at Longinus!

He continued to laugh, a sound that filled the forest, wrapped around the trees, and pierced the deepest hollows. Not a death cry, but the cry of Death itself.

Immediately Tristan thought of weeks earlier when Longinus had *mistakenly* attacked him in the heat of battle. Only the intervention of his men had saved him. An accident it was called at the time, and the knight had begged his indulgence. Now, Tristan realized it was far more than an accident.

"You are a worthy opponent," Longinus complimented him. "But now it is time for you to die."

The blood at the front of his tunic disappeared as the wound seemed to close itself. Once before, Tristan had seen such a thing, in Meg's battle with Morgana, and he knew that what he confronted was not of the mortal world.

It was then Longinus struck. Weakened by the battle and that old injury, Tristan was powerless to stop him.

"You may kill me, Longinus, but I vow I will hunt you down into the very depths of hell!"

Longinus couldn't help but admire such an unfailing sense of honor, futile as it was. With a final blow, he plunged the sword deep. It was a glancing blow. He felt it deflected at the last moment, then the gratifying sight of blood.

Sounds came from all around him as knights and warriors searched through the forest for their fallen and wounded comrades. Tristan made a horrible dying sound as he pulled the sword free.

He watched Longinus leave through the growing darkness as he felt the blood pool beneath him. Longinus paused at the edge of the small clearing and looked back, but the figure that gazed at Tristan was not the warrior he'd met in battle. Instead it was the figure of an old woman, bent and deformed with age. The same woman he'd seen that long-ago day in the ruins of the cottage in the forest, when he'd gone in search of Rianne.

And as she smiled, she transformed once more. Where the old woman had been, another woman now stood. She was young and slender. Her dark hair streamed to her waist. But there was a coldness in her eyes, a coldness of death that he recognized with the memory of a ten-year-old boy.

Morgana.

Rianne awoke, crying out with pain. It burned through her, seared deep inside, as if it had touched her soul. She felt the steel blade as if it had plunged deep inside her, then felt as it was slowly withdrawn, then the warm flow of blood that spilled through her fingers as if it was her own.

CHAPTER
TWENTY-THREE

Rianne moved through the marketplace with grim determination. She'd said nothing to her mother before she left, driven there by the horrible dream and the certainty that Tristan was dead.

Her heart refused to believe it, but her thoughts had not deceived her. In that moment when the blade struck him down they were connected as though they were one. She felt his pain, the shock and disbelief, then the blood. She felt his heart beating with her own. Then felt it as it slowed, felt the death that waited until she could bear it no more.

She sensed even as she moved through the streets, alleys, and passages of the city that even then she was fulfilling her destiny as the *Chosen*. That it had all been set in motion long before she and Tristan ever met.

It was her destiny. A destiny that her mother had tried to protect her from and had failed. Even as Meg told her of it, her mother had no sense of when that destiny would find her.

But Rianne knew. The gypsy was part of it. The gypsy knew. She had to find her.

She questioned vendors, innkeepers, and those who bartered or traded along the market square. She questioned everyone she saw, unable to believe that the woman had completely disappeared. The gypsies were still encamped within the city walls. But as she transformed and moved silent as mist among them, searching their thoughts, listening to their conversation, she realized they knew nothing of the woman.

Impossible. The woman couldn't have disappeared. The gates had been closed ever since Arthur left with his men for Lyonesse—where Tristan had been betrayed.

She could not find the gypsy because the gypsy was not at Camelot, had not been there since they left. She had gone with them, transformed as one of them, and with none—not even Merlin—the wiser.

It was late when she returned to Arthur's court, sunlight fading below the western wall. The main hall was dark. Torches had already been lit. The guards did not acknowledge her as she passed them by. They were not even aware of her presence. As if . . .

She ran across the inner courtyard and up the stairs to the wing of private chambers, past her own chamber to her mother's. The passage was dark. No torches had been lit. And there was a smell of cold and dampness. Her shoulder brushed the stone wall near the door of the chamber. She immediately felt the coldness at the contact.

It seemed to move through her blood with a cold whisper of warning, and her heart quickened as she seized the heavy iron latch. It would not move but seemed to have rusted tightly in place. She threw her weight against it, but it was not enough to move the bolt. Focusing her power, she concentrated all thought on the metal bolt. It grated loudly when she was finally able to move it. She pushed open the door.

The wind caught at her mantle, whipping it about her in a

powerful vortex. It caught at her hair, tearing it loose from the heavy plait. She scooped it back, squinting against the sting of the wind and the biting cold that filled the chamber.

It was dark. No light would have survived in the maelstrom that had invaded the chamber. She fought her way to the window opening and discovered it was tightly shuttered. Then she saw a faint shimmer of light at the chair beside the hearth, and followed the trail along the wall to the outside wall of the chamber.

Her hand passed through air as the wall disappeared and opened onto a great dark void, like a passage that suddenly gaped open before her. And along the wall of the passage was the glimmer of light that gradually disappeared into the void of darkness.

Then, as she felt along the opening of the passage, it began to disappear, the stones at the wall moving back into place, sealing up the passage as if it had never been there.

The wind ceased blowing. It no longer whistled through the shutters or whipped at her mantle and hair. The chamber was completely dark and silent as Rianne used the gift of inner sight to guide her across the room.

Everything was in chaos. Tapestries had been torn from their moorings and hung at crooked angles on the walls. Heavy fleece blankets were scattered across the floor. Furnishings had been knocked over and tossed about like pieces of fire wood. Oil lamps had spilled, the flames snuffed out by the whirlwind. And a layer of soot and ash from the fire covered everything.

She found several small pieces of wood and with a single touch ignited the fire at the hearth. It cast a feeble glow across the wreckage in the chamber as she went in search of candles. She found them in a niche near the door. She lit them all, light spreading across the floor and walls, including the wall where that opening had gaped open only moments before.

There was no need to search the debris. Her mother was gone. She sensed it immediately. Only her essence remained, through the bond that connected them to the immortal world, and that faint glimmer at the wall that reflected in the light from the candles.

She sensed another presence, faint at first, then stronger as she reached out with her powers. She righted a chair and pushed it aside, then lifted a heavy tapestry and cleared away the shattered remains of an earthenware urn.

She found the gnome beneath several more layers of debris. He'd been badly injured, his large round eyes slowly opening as she connected her thoughts to his and reached out with the power of the Light in the touch of her hand on his hand. Small stubby fingers weakly curled around her hand.

"What happened?"

"Too long," he whispered. "Too long have I stayed, stayed have I in this wretched world. No more, mistress. No more."

"Grendel, you must tell me what happened." She forced him to remain awake, taking away the pain of his broken body.

"Where is my mother?"

"Taken her, he has. He's taken her."

He was rambling, speaking in that strange little singsong way of his, the words barely audible above the struggle to breathe.

"Grendel, please! Who has taken her? You must tell me."

She didn't wish to connect her thoughts to his, for she knew it might very well kill him, and as ill-tempered and peevish as he'd been to her, she'd grown fond of the little man.

"Do it," he whispered. "I haven't the strength for more."

"No," she replied. "You must try to remember what happened."

"Cannot," he whispered, touching her cheek as the light slowly faded from his eyes.

"Stay with me, Grendel! I need your help. I cannot do this alone. Grendel?"

As his essence slowly faded, she joined her thoughts with his, and in that tentative, brief bond glimpsed what had happened: her mother's surprise as the door was thrown open, the sudden cold that invaded the chamber, the wind that extinguished the fire at the hearth and the oil lamps, Grendel's futile struggle to stop the forces of Darkness that had come for her, her fear that reached back across the years to another time and place when she had confronted the Darkness and nearly paid with her life, then the stones of the wall as they fell away and that dark passage gaped open.

She saw what the gnome had seen; the dark figure shrouded in the mantle that whipped about him, the hood that concealed his features, except for those cold, dark eyes, as if the creature had stepped from her dreams. And then the hood was thrown back and the creature of her dreams had a name.

Longinus!

The small hand was lifeless in hers. She sensed when the inner light no longer burned and his heart no longer beat. She had seen that moment when Grendel tried to save her mother, throwing himself at Longinus, transforming into a wild creature that went for the creature's throat. But he was no match for the powers of Darkness.

In the end, Longinus kicked him aside like a bothersome pest. The force of the blow had shattered his skull and broken his neck.

"Thank you, little friend," she whispered. "My mother could ask for no more valiant a champion."

Her tears slowly dried as she knelt in the debris that had been her mother's chamber. She ached inside. She had been searching for a gypsy with dark eyes. Now she realized that the gypsy had been there all along.

"A pretty ribbon then . . ." The words the gypsy had spoken upon their first encounter. The very same words Longinus had spoken in the yard the morning Arthur and his men rode out. . . .

"Your father was a brave warrior. He fought well." How could Longinus possibly know how her father had fought when Monmouth was attacked? Unless he was there . . .

Tristan attacked in the heat of battle. An accident . . .

The dream that had awakened her that morning, so vivid that she had felt the sword as it was thrust deep, and she knew that Tristan had been mortally wounded . . .

Her dreams of the dark stranger standing at the edge of clearing with those cold, dead eyes . . .

It had been Longinus all along. He had been there the night Dannelore and John died. It was he who arranged for the attack on Monmouth, knowing Meg would send for her. Now he had struck again at those she loved.

She knelt in the middle of the floor and wept until she could weep no more. Then she dried her tears. She knew where he had taken her mother, glimpsed in the gnome's dying thoughts.

He had taken her to the ring of standing stones where Meg had confronted the forces of Darkness all those years ago and was blinded. And she knew why he'd taken her. Because he knew Rianne would follow.

She was the *Chosen*. It was her destiny, as it had been from the beginning. Her mother had tried to protect her from it, but in the end she could not. Now the forces of Darkness had taken what mattered most to her. She would follow, not because Longinus wanted it, but because it was what she wanted.

She had seen the ring of standing stones in the distance as they neared the abbey at Glastonbury. Merlin had told her of her mother's encounter with Morgana when she was blinded. Now Longinus had taken Meg back to the standing stones.

Rianne went to the uppermost tower of Camelot. The city lay quiet and sleeping below her, oblivious to the forces of Darkness that surrounded it, moved through its streets, and cast a pall over the towers, turrets, and walls.

There at the tower wall, she summoned the power she'd been born with, the power of the *Chosen*. And as night mist slipped over the walls and through the streets, she transformed into a sleek hunting bird.

She swept down from the tower, over the wall and into the

darkness of night, following that glimmer of light that was like a beacon in the night, guiding her to the distant ring of standing stones.

It was nearly dawn when she reached the stones, transforming once more into currents of morning mist that slowly swept over them, seeking that familiar essence that bound her and her mother together.

Longinus waited for her. He expected her to follow. He knew that she was the *Chosen*. His own powers were great. He'd already proven that, living among them and all of them, even Merlin, unaware of it.

The sun caught the faint glimmer at the arch stone. She sensed her mother's presence strongest there and cast about for some connection, some response that her mother was near. But even as she did, she knew that Meg would give nothing away, would reveal nothing, would keep everything to herself, just as she had kept the knowledge of Rianne's whereabouts secret all these years protecting her. Nothing would force her to reveal herself, not even death itself.

She sensed something else with that faint familiar essence. She sensed that same coldness she had felt in her mother's chamber at the wall where it opened onto the dark passage that was void of all shape, all form, all light, and she knew that Longinus was near. She could feel him waiting for her. Perhaps just beyond that stone arch.

Had Merlin not taught her about the powers she possessed? But her father had taught her to think during those quiet board games in the anteroom at Monmouth. His words came back to her now, as if he stood beside her.

"You must be wiser than your opponent. Meet him on his own terms and beat him. Learn to use this," he had told her, gently touching her forehead, "then use the powers you were born with."

So much loss. Dannelore. John. Her father. Tristan. Now her

mother might well be lost to her as well. Longinus had played his game well.

He expected her to pass through the portal into the world that lay beyond, where he had taken Meg. But she had no idea what waited beyond that stone arch. She knew only of the evil that had taken her mother.

Snow surrounded the stone circle. But inside no snow stayed upon the ground. It melted, puddling around the stones and seeping between them. She transformed fluid as water, passing through the portal into the world beyond like the droplets of water that seeped the stones.

It was a world of stone walls and dark caverns and equally dark waters. A ribbon of water glimmered faintly at the end of the path. She slipped down the pathway, shrouding herself with a spellcast.

The air was oppressive, making it impossible to breathe. It pressed on her lungs, squeezed at her heart, and moved slowly through her blood.

The path wound through the stones into a distant cavern. She sensed the way of it, but reminded herself that this was Longinus's world. She could trust nothing. She must assume that everything was a trick and look for the deception. She must use what Connor had taught her and then apply what she had learned from Merlin.

Instead of following the path as Longinus no doubt intended, she swept along the ceiling of the cavern, transformed into a current of air among other currents of air, until the pathway opened onto a large cavern.

"You have learned well," the thought connected with hers. *"A worthy adversary. But I do not wish for us to be enemies, Rianne. We are much alike, you and I. We share many of the same abilities. The cosmos could be our kingdom, if you were to join with me."*

In those thoughts she sensed the same intimacy, the same seductive persuasion that she'd first experienced at Monmouth.

It was powerful. It moved through her senses, slipping beneath the protective shield she cloaked herself in.

"Do not be so quick to refuse," those thoughts persuaded. *"Not when I have something you want."*

She followed the passage, felt herself being pulled along on a more powerful current of cold air that wrapped around her, and realized that she'd been lulled into a trap. The current was strong as she was swept along with it toward that next opening, deeper into the dark caverns.

She was cast into a violent inferno, a maelstrom of intense heat and fire fueled by the powerful current of air, and realized that she was part of the cause. Then she saw her mother. Longinus had imprisoned her in a ring of fire. As the air fueled the fire, it burned hotter and brighter, feeding the ring of fire. He was using her transformation to endanger Meg.

She summoned the power once more and transformed again into a shower of flame that burned back on the fire that surrounded her mother, consuming it, extinguishing it, until all that remained was a slender ribbon of flame that expanded. Rianne stepped through, transformed once more into mortal form.

She went to Meg then, going down on her knees beside her.

"Mother?"

Meg slowly lifted her head, but the eyes that looked back at her were not pale blue. They were dark and cold.

"You cannot trust what you see." The thought connected with hers. And as the creature transformed, it took the form of another woman with long dark hair. But the eyes were the same, dark and cold, and Rianne recalled the stories she had heard of Morgana.

"Ah, you have learned well. But perhaps not well enough. Do you really believe you are any match for the powers of Darkness? Your mother believed that she was, but in the end she was not."

"Where is she?"

"She is safe."

Stunned, Rianne turned at the sound of that voice, spoken in the mortal way and as familiar to her as breathing. Tristan stepped from the path and came toward her.

He was dressed in the black tunic and breeches he had worn the day he left Camelot, the sword gleaming in his hand. His dark hair hung in silken waves to his shoulders, the light from those dying fires gleaming off the angles of high cheekbones, strong jaw, and sensual mouth.

She ran to him, then suddenly stopped. The hand that reached out to her was the same, the voice that reached out was the same. The handsome features, the curve of his smile, were all the same. But it wasn't Tristan. She saw it in his eyes.

"You have only to take my hand."

She backed away from him. "You are not Tristan."

"Are you so certain?" He touched her cheek exactly the way he'd touched her a hundred times. It was his touch, but it wasn't Tristan. She refused to look at him, closing her thoughts and her heart.

It wasn't Tristan!

"What of that last night at Camelot?" he asked. "How can you be certain who it was that came to you that night? And all the other nights before? Can you be certain who is the father of your unborn child?"

She whirled back around, stunned.

"You carry a child, Rianne. A child conceived of the powers of the Light, and perhaps the powers of Darkness. And even you cannot be certain who is the sire."

This was the cruelest trick of all.

"You are wrong," she defiantly told him. "If I carry a child, 'tis Tristan's and no other's."

Merlin found him in the forest, the sounds of the dying horse guiding him. He found Tristan only a few yards away. The battle had been here, the glade soaked with blood. A bloody trail marked where he had crawled, then dragged himself by plunging the long knife into the ground at arm's length and pulling himself that distance, and then again in a futile effort to follow his attacker.

"Be at ease, my young friend." Merlin gently pried the knife from Tristan's fingers, then turned him over. The wound was deep. There had been much loss of blood, but it might have been worse if not for the crystal rune. It had deflected the blow; the mark of it was evident on the crystal.

"Longinus," Tristan whispered.

And in that name, Merlin sensed the thoughts that went with it—the discovery of Longinus's treachery, the battle that had followed, and the certainty that it was also Longinus who attacked Monmouth, and Longinus all those years ago who had slain both Dannelore and John.

It was as Meg had feared when she first saw the bloodstone when Rianne was just a babe. Longinus had come for her. He had come for the *Chosen*.

Using the healing power within, Merlin closed the wound, sealing severed muscle, tissue, and flesh. Unlike Connor's wound, meant to slowly poison and kill, this was a clean wound. Foolishly, Longinus had felt no threat beyond the point of his sword.

Tristan's body convulsed at the pain that burned through him, more intense than the sword Longinus had thrust into his side. Sweat beaded across his forehead and soaked through his tunic. It was like being burned with a red-hot poker.

He felt his heart beat slowly until it seemed it had stopped. Then it beat steadily once more. Blood flowed through his body, driving back the coldness of death. It was like dying and being reborn again. With eyes closed he saw only one thing. Rianne.

She was all golden light and radiant, shimmering eyes, the way she'd looked that last night when she'd been so angry with him. And then there were other images of her—proud, defiant, courageous. Then he was certain he heard her, equally proud, equally defiant.

"If I carry a child, it is Tristan's. . . ."

The words reached out to him, a bond that connected him to the mortal world, to life itself. When he opened his eyes, he stared up into the canopy of trees overhead. It was snowing. Tiny flakes drifted down over him, but he wasn't cold. He didn't question, he simply accepted. He was alive. And he had to find her.

They followed the trail Rianne had taken to the standing stones. Meg was there, cold and weak but alive, just inside the ring of stones where Longinus had left her concealed by a spellcast.

"I tried to fight him," she whispered as her brother held her. "But I was no match for him. It was not me he wanted. It was Rianne. He used me to lure her here." Her skin was ashen and blood seeped from the wound at her head.

"You must find her."

Tristan was already on his feet and moving toward those two upright sentinel stones with the lintel across. Merlin went after him.

"You cannot go alone. You are not strong enough, and you have no idea what you are dealing with."

"You forget," Tristan reminded him, "Longinus and I have met before. I will not make the same mistakes again." He adjusted the sword at the scabbard at his back, wincing against the pain of the newly mended wound.

"There is a score to settle. For Connor, for Meg, and for Rianne. And," he smiled, a dangerous smile, "he thinks me dead. That will be my advantage."

In the end there was no argument Merlin could offer that would change his mind.

"Take care of her," Tristan said with a glance at Meg. "And if I should not return . . ."

Merlin held up a hand, refusing to hear it, "I would not care to deal with my sister if you do not return." He opened the portal beneath the lintel arch between the two standing stones.

"Remember, all is not what it seems to be in the underworld. 'Tis a world of lies and deceptions. They are Longinus's weapons, and he will use them against you. He has waited a long time for her. If she can be persuaded to join her powers with his, it will be the end of our world. But if you should prevail, there is only one way you can destroy Longinus. It must be at the moment of transformation, when he is neither one form nor another. It is his weakest moment."

The passage beyond the portal was long and dark, descending through darkness, then emerging in a wide cavern that linked to another, and another. All around was the smell of things dark and foul. Something brushed against his boot, then slithered away. The movement of air was not an opening to the sky in the mortal world, but the brush of wings as something flew near in the darkness.

His instincts warned of dangerous things in the darkness. The wall of the cavern fell away at one side of the path, but when he ran his hand along the opposite wall he discovered there was nothing there either. The walls of the cavern were an illusion. The path beneath his feet was a causeway that dropped into a dark void at either side. One misstep and he would be cast into the darkness that fell away at each side.

He reached the end of the path, guided by instinct and the glow of light across the cavern. As he came closer, he heard a voice not heard in a long time as Morgana's cold, dead laughter echoed along the cavern walls.

It was not real. Rianne told herself that, and yet even as she did, she saw the stairway at Monmouth, then the wide passage outside her chamber, and heard the sound of the door opening, as if she stood inside that room once more.

As in a dream she saw herself step into the chamber as she had that last night with Tristan. A man stepped from the shadows. And even as she watched apart from the dream, she became part of it. . . .

He smelled of mulled wine, the pungence of pine fragrance that clung to his skin, and soft leather.

She hated him for the way her heart leapt and the way her blood heated and thickened in her veins.

"Nay," she whispered, determined to push him away. But there was no stopping him.

She felt his mouth burn at her throat, the sensitive place at her neck, then at her mouth. She watched as her hands twisted in the thick fabric of his tunic.

"Nay, Milord Dragon." She heard the words whispered from that dream.

She was certain she spoke it. Or perhaps she only thought it, and that too was silenced by the assault of his thoughts burning through hers with all the ways he intended to love her.

This was not the tender lover who had come to her before. He was different, his hands were different, urgent as he removed her tunic and gown, his mouth urgent against her mouth.

No words were spoken of the anger that lay between them. It was in his touch. . . .

The vision slipped away from her. The eyes that looked into hers were dark and cold, and the hand that touched hers was equally cold. She whirled away from him, focusing her power. When he came after her, she flung him away from her.

"For God's sake, Rianne! Stop!"

Something in the sound of his voice did stop her. Something in those words. Then she saw a movement in the shadows among the rocks at the edge of the cavern, and Tristan stepped from the path she'd followed into that cavern.

Impossible! She stared at the two men, identical in every

way—in that lean stance, the restrained power of the warrior's body, the thick mane of dark hair that fell to their shoulders, the sensual curve of each man's mouth, and the heat in those golden eyes. One was evil incarnate, while the other . . .

'' 'Tis not possible!'' she whispered, staring at the one who had moved closer now. "You are dead. I saw it.''

"I assure you I am very much alive.'' He held out his hand to her even as he glanced at the man who stood several feet away. It was like looking at himself.

"Take my hand!'' he implored her. "You know me! Do not trust what you see! Touch me. Trust what you feel!''

She glanced from one to the other. A moment earlier she was certain the man who stood before her was Longinus. Now both claimed to be Tristan. Another illusion? Some trick of the senses that Longinus played on her?

As she backed away from both, she heard the sound of steel being drawn.

"There is only one way to find out,'' the one nearest her challenged as he carved the air with the sword.

"We will fight to the death.''

They thrust and jabbed at one another, lunging and striking in a blur of steel, straining limbs, and grunts of pain. They fought the same, each lunging, thrusting, then dropping back, changing position, then lunging again.

The tip of a blade caught the sleeve of a tunic; the fabric sliced like melted butter. Another blade sliced dangerously close to one man's throat. His opponent lunged to the side, narrowly escaping death. Or would it have meant his death?

Which was which? There was no way to discern. Longinus was far too clever for that. Both men showed signs of fatigue. Both refused to give any quarter.

Lies. Deceptions. A world where nothing was what it seemed. Then she saw drops of blood on the cavern floor. One of them was injured, one with mortal blood flowing through his veins, who had been wounded in the forest.

But which one?

It was impossible to tell as they lunged at one another, striking blow after blow, wearing each other down, in a battle to the death. And when it was ended, even then she would not know, could not be certain.

Can you be certain who is the father of your unborn child?

The words whispered through her thoughts and burned at her soul, a legacy of darkness that stretched into the future if Longinus was not stopped. But how could she be certain?

Blood covered both warriors. Steel rang out against steel. The sound was like the crash of thunder that echoed off the cavern walls. She had to stop them. But how? And then how would she possibly know which one was Tristan and which was Longinus?

Longinus concealed his evil soul. There was only one thing he wanted, and he would do anything to have her. She saw no way around it. Whatever spell she devised, he would counter it. Whatever trick she conjured, he would see through it.

"You must be wiser than your opponent. Meet him on his own terms, then use them against him." Her father's words turned over and over in her thoughts. If Longinus had created an illusion, then she would create one as well.

She turned her thoughts inward, drawing on the power she'd been born with as the sounds of battle rang out in the cavern, transforming, changing, becoming that which surrounded her—air, water, fire, and earth.

Then she created the illusion of a young woman with golden hair and eyes the color of blue flames. And as the embattled warriors redoubled their strength and lunged at one another, the young woman ran between them, determined to stop their deadly battle even at the cost of her own life.

The sword plunged deep into her side. Blood appeared at the blade. She stared with stunned eyes at the warrior who had struck the blow.

"No!"

Longinus transformed, the bloodied sword dropping from his stunned fingers. And at the moment of transformation, Tristan struck the death blow, plunging his sword deep into Longinus's dark soul.

Tristan went to her, but even as he reached for her she disappeared, an illusion of mist and air that slipped through his fingers.

Rianne reached out and gently touched his shoulder.

EPILOGUE

The labor had been long and difficult, perhaps the most difficult thing she had ever done. But her mother had been there, encouraging her, speaking to her gently, giving her strength when she needed it.

Several times she heard Tristan's voice as he returned to the chamber door, by turns anxious, angry, then overwrought.

"It is taking too long. Something must be wrong. If anything happens to her or the child . . ."

Through the pain that gripped her body as if in a vise, she heard and felt his thoughts, the fear he had not felt even at that moment of his own certain death under Longinus's sword. Nor in the dark caverns of the underworld when he had come after her. Not even when he had found her, bloodied and wounded from her own battle with Longinus.

But with birthing drawn out so long and memories of the loss of so many whom he'd loved, she had felt the fear in his heart and in his soul that matched her own for reasons she could never tell him.

Whose child was it inside her? A child with Tristan's golden eyes and dark sable hair, or perhaps her own fair features and the eyes of legacy passed down through her family? Or would she find those dark haunted eyes, cold as death gleaming back at her from the face of a child, her child, and the spawn of the Darkness?

Was that to be Longinus's final legacy, as he'd promised her, so that even with her powers she was not certain that he lied, could not be certain until the final moment that it was Tristan's child that had grown inside her all the months since?

What would she do then?

In her heart she believed what her thoughts doubted—that it *was* Tristan's child inside her. She could not believe otherwise, so deep was her love for him, so completely was he a part of her thoughts, every breath she took, each beat of her heart.

In the end, hours after it had begun, she focused all of her strength and the power that was so inherently a part of her, forcing that strength into her straining muscles until she thought she would be torn apart. Then she felt the sudden, intense surge of pain, followed immediately by another, and felt the child slip from her body.

Intense fatigue followed. She was only vaguely aware of her mother's smiling face wet with tears, an infant's sudden lusty cry, and then the flurry of activity as the midwife finished her task.

Through the haze of that fatigue, she felt and heard Tristan's sudden presence beside her; the tender stroke of his fingers against her cheek that she instinctively turned toward, the quiet strength of his hand closing around hers, then the rasp of his beard against her forehead as he kissed her.

She held on to his hand, floating as the pain left her, drifting in a soft, warm cocoon of sleep that wrapped around her as voices murmured.

She wanted to know about the child. Why didn't someone tell her? Then there was only sleep. Dreamless sleep.

She awoke slowly, feeling the dull ache of bruised muscles as the memory of the last hours returned.

How long had she been asleep? she wondered. It had been late evening when the pains began, and they had continued through the night. She remembered that Tristan held her, refusing to leave, afraid of what lay ahead, for many women did not survive childbirth.

He had left her later that next evening only when her mother insisted. She remembered they called for more candles as the night wore on, and she had asked Meg if it was taking too long.

Two days she had labored to bring the child into the world—Tristan's child.

But now hours later, rested from her ordeal, those fears returned with a vengeance. The child lay on a thick fleece pallet beside the bed she shared with Tristan, wrapped in warm linen.

Drawing back the fleece coverlet, she discovered a small tightly fisted hand, then the curve of a round pink cheek. She hesitated, fear twisting deep inside. Slowly she pushed back the linen that cradled the child's head. Dark hair swirled a glossy cap on that small head.

The eyes. She had to see the child's eyes. Her fingers trembled against the warm, soft skin. The child wakened, the tiny fist thrusting into the air, quickly followed by another.

For so long she had felt the child move inside her, no more than a flutter at first, then a wave of sensation that moved across her belly, and finally the thrust of an elbow or a small foot that Tristan had felt as they lay together.

What if . . . ? she thought, those thoughts that had tormented her every waking moment since she discovered that Longinus had seen true when he told her in the caverns that she already carried a child.

He had tormented her that it was he who had come to her that last night before Tristan left with Arthur for Lyonesse. That it was he who had made love to her, giving her a child. And then to seal her agony he had transformed, so that she thought that he *was* Tristan. Except for his eyes.

That he could never disguise. For the eyes that had looked back at her then were the eyes of her worst dreams. Eyes as cold as death—the eyes of Darkness.

She reached for the child, slipping one hand beneath the small head, the other beneath the small body, those fists waving in protest as the blanket fell back and the child felt the cool air. Then that lusty cry, a hungry cry, as the small face turned bright pink and turned toward her.

Only Meg knew of her fears. Only her mother sensed her thoughts and had tried to ease them. All children have dark eyes when they are born, she cautioned. Even the midwife had said it was so. But she would know if the eyes that looked back at her were Longinus's eyes. She would know, for she had seen them in her dreams every night since she was a child.

The child squirmed, fists knotted, tiny mouth like that of a bird. Then the babe's eyes opened, dark lashes framing eyes that were a brilliant, radiant blue. As blue as the heart of a flame.

Tristan heard those lusty cries as he approached the chamber. Then the sudden silence quickened his steps. When he pushed open the door he suddenly stopped.

Rianne lay on the pallet, soft furs wrapped about her and pulled high over one shoulder. Then the fleece gaped away and he saw the curve of a round breast and her hand as she guided the babe to her.

That tiny mouth opened and closed, small fists waving; then came a faint suckling sound as the babe latched onto her. Small eyes closed as Rianne turned toward the babe and tenderly kissed the small forehead. She looked up then, having sensed his presence. Tears glistened at her cheeks.

He went to her then, slipping an arm about her, cradling both her and the babe in his arms.

"Why are you crying?" he asked, brushing his lips against her forehead just as she had kissed the babe.

"Because I am so happy," she confessed, all doubt laid to

rest in her heart. "And because I suppose you will want to teach your son to wield a sword and train as a knight like his father."

"He has a rich legacy awaiting him," Tristan replied, thinking of the man who had been like a father to him, and the immortal blood that flowed through the child's veins. He would have to learn to live in both worlds, whatever that might bring him. Perhaps the one would help him to live wisely and long in the other.

"And I will teach him to use his wits as well as his hands," Rianne added, cradling one of her son's tiny hands in her fingers.

"You will not teach him to steal," Tristan informed her emphatically. " 'Tis bad enough his mother is a thief," he said as he slipped his fingers beneath her chin and angled her head back for his kiss.

It was a long, slow, deep kiss—a kiss of thankfulness that they were together and safe, a kiss of hope for all the days that lay ahead, and a kiss of promise of all the other kisses that awaited.

That was the one thing the Darkness had never conquered—not when Longinus had struck Tristan down and she had believed him dead; not when he had disguised himself and come to her as Tristan. She knew as she had known then that of the powers that defined her world—earth, wind, fire, and water—and from which she drew her strength, that the greatest strength and power of all was love.

Light from the hearth glowed across the walls, the floor, and the three who lay there wrapped in love. And shimmered at the image of the bloodstone that suddenly appeared and gleamed at the child's tiny hand.